X-7

H-O

(50)

My Year in the No-Man's-Bay

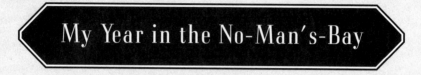

My Year in the No-Man's-Bay

PETER HANDKE

Translated by Krishna Winston

Farrar, Straus and Giroux / New York

Farrar, Straus and Giroux
19 Union Square West, New York 10003

Copyright © 1994 by Suhrkamp Verlag Frankfurt am Main
Translation copyright © 1998 by Farrar, Straus and Giroux, Inc.

Distributed in Canada by Douglas & McIntyre Ltd.
Printed in the United States of America
Designed by Abby Kagan
Title page photograph by Greg Goebel
First published in 1994 by Suhrkamp Verlag, Germany, as
Mein Jahr in der Niemandsbucht
First American edition, 1998

Library of Congress Cataloging-in-Publication Data
Handke, Peter.
    {Mein Jahr in der Niemandsbucht.   English}
    My year in the no-man's-bay / Peter Handke ; translated by Krishna
Winston. — 1st ed.
        p.   cm.
    ISBN 0-374-21755-6 (alk. paper)
    I. Winston, Krishna.   II. Title.
PT2668.A5M4513   1998
833'.914—dc21   97-48948

Contents

PART 1

There was one time in my life when I experienced metamorphosis. Up to that point it had been only a word to me, and when it began, not gradually, but abruptly, I thought at first it meant the end of me. It seemed to be a death sentence. Suddenly the place where I had been was occupied not by a human being but by some kind of scum, for which, unlike in the well-known grotesque tale from old Prague, not even an escape into images, however terrifying, was possible. This metamorphosis came over me without a single image, in the form of sheer gagging. Part of me was numb. The other part carried on with the day as though nothing were amiss. It was like the time I saw a pedestrian, who had been hurled into the air by a car, land on both feet on the other side of the radiator and continue on his way, as cool as you please, at least for a few steps. It was like the time my son, when his mother collapsed during dinner, stopped eating only for the moment and then, after the body had been taken away, went on chewing, alone at the table, until his plate was empty. And likewise I, when I fell off a ladder last summer, immediately scrambled up it again, or tried to. And likewise I myself again, just the day before yesterday, after the knife blade snapped back and almost severed my index finger, revealing all the layers of flesh down to the bone, while I held the hand under the stream of water, waiting for blood, methodically brushed my teeth with the other hand.

That era of my life was marked by a daily back-and-forth between feeling trapped and serenely carrying on. Neither before nor since have I had hours of such complete peace. And as the days went by, and I, whether panic-stricken or serene, remained focused on what I was doing, in time the "end" that still gagged me now and then was more and more firmly replaced by this metamorphosis thing. Metamorphosis of whom? What kind of metamorphosis? For now I know only this much: at that time I experienced metamorphosis. It proved fruitful for me as nothing else has. For years I have been drawing nourishment from that period, with ever-renewed appetite. For me, nothing can sweep that fruitfulness from the world. From it I know what it is to exist.

But for some time now I have been waiting for a new metamorphosis. I am not dissatisfied with the shape of my days, am even pleased with it. By and large, what I do or leave undone suits me, likewise my surroundings, the house, the yard, this remote suburb, the woods, the neighboring valleys, the railroad lines, the hardly visible and all the more palpable proximity of the great city of Paris down there in the Seine basin beyond the wooded hills to the east. I would like to stay as long as possible in the exquisite stillness here.

With my work, too, my writing, I should like to continue as long as I can, but with a different point of departure. Never again will I return to the law, to which I remain grateful, for the problems it poses have often stimulated my mind, and its thought patterns have in many respects paved the way for the profession of my dreams. I shall go back neither to that water tower in New York, the United Nations, nor to my partner's office, with its view of the vineyards along Austria's Southern Railway.

I would be more likely to put a sudden end to everything here, my living, my writing, my walking. As always, I am tempted not to go on, to break off the game from one moment to the next, and let myself tumble, or run head-on into a wall, or hit the next person I see in the face, or not lift a finger ever again and never speak another word.

My life has a direction that I find good, lovely, and ideal, yet at the same time my ability to get through a single day can no longer be taken for granted. Failing, myself and others, even seems to be the rule. My friends used to comment that I took small things too much to heart and was too stern with myself. I, on the other hand, am convinced that if I had not found, time and again, a new way of covering up my lifelong pattern of failure, but had admitted to it even once, I would no longer exist.

I was already failing long ago, as a young man, whenever I slipped away early from all those social gatherings to which I had looked forward more than anyone far and wide, and my ultimate failure grew out of the notion that my work and my life with others—why do I shrink from using the word "family"?—not only could be integrated with each other but actually belonged together in the best interest of my undertaking. Meanwhile, my house is empty once more, probably for good. I accepted everyone's leaving me, and at the same time I wanted to punish myself. I failed yet again because I did not know, or had forgotten, who I am. Almost fifty-six now, I still do not know myself. And at the same time the wind off the Atlantic has just sliced into the damp winter grass outside my study, which looks out on the yard.

This new transformation should come without the misery. That gagging, two decades ago, which went on for a year, with moments now and then of blinding brightness, should not be repeated. It also seems to me that something like that occurs only once in a lifetime, and the person involved either perishes, body and soul, or shrivels into a living corpse, one of those not uncommon desperadoes—I recognize them by the language they use, and they are near and dear to me—or, of course, he is transformed by it.

At times back then I thought all three had happened to me. After that year I could taste the light as never before, yet I also no longer felt my body, at least not as mine, and I still terrified the world with my old rages, which now, unlike earlier, were ruthless, and at the same time unfounded.

I was afraid the added light had made me lose my diffuse love. On my own I could certainly still be swept with enthusiasm, again and again, helped along by stillness, nature, pictures, books, gusting wind, as well as the roaring highway, and most powerfully by nothing at all, but I no longer took much interest in anything except certain thousand-year-old stone sculptures, two-thousand-year-old inscriptions, the tossing of branches, the gurgling of water, the arch of the sky, or at least I felt it was far too little interest, and far too infrequent.

I hardly lived in my own time anymore, or was not in step with it, and since nothing disgusted me as much as smugness, I became increasingly irked with myself. How much in step I had been earlier, what a fundamentally different sort of enthusiasm I had felt, in stadiums, at the movies, on a bus trip, among complete strangers. Was this a law of existence: childlike being in step, grown-up being out of step?

I enjoyed this being out of step yet longed to be in step; and when the former pleasure actually fulfilled me for a change, I found myself aglow with passion for those who were absent: to validate the fulfillment, I had to share it with them at once and widen it. The joyfulness in me could find an outlet only in society, but in which?

In keeping to myself, I risked withering up. The next metamorphosis was becoming urgent. And unlike that first one, which had sneaked up on me, I would set this one in motion myself. The second metamorphosis was under my control. It would begin not with a narrowing but with my purposeful and at the same time prudent effort to open myself wider and wider. I wanted nothing dramatic, simply a steadiness of resolve that would dictate one step after the other.

Wasn't what I had in mind a simple opening-up? Didn't I see in my imagination a series of doors, which, though closed, would be child's play to open? But easy for me, with all my years?

A scientist has described the state of certain living beings on the verge of their metamorphosis more or less as follows: they stop eating; attempt to hide; rid themselves of all wastes; feel restless.

All that has been true of me, more or less, for quite some time. Disorder and dirt in the house literally bombard me; I hardly get hungry anymore; I no longer merely play at living in hiding; for the time to come, it seems absolutely appropriate. But above all I am restless. In anticipation of that effortless opening of doors in the offing I am strangely restless.

Thus I become aware that my planned undertaking is dangerous. If I fail at widening myself, I will be finished, once and for all. That would mean the end of my homey seclusion; I would have no choice but to get out of here. I would have freedom of movement, of course, but I would no longer have a place of my own.

On the other hand, I have always felt drawn to failures and the down-and-out—as if they were in the right. I see them, from a distance, as positively ennobled; or as if today they alone among us were figures with a destiny. And thus I travel in my dreams to the harbor farthest from the world, dissolved into thin air as far as the others are concerned, a mere breeze brushing their temples.

This morning there was a constant whirring up in the cedar, as if it were already early spring, and yet winter still lies ahead, with its rigid cold, with the pinging of small stones skidding over the frozen woodland ponds, with flashes from the belt of Orion, sweeping all night across the hills of the Seine; though snow would be eventful for this area—the occasional overly thin icicles, with not a trace of snow far and wide, usually congeal from frost on the roofs.

I am determined to pursue this new metamorphosis here, in this land-scape, as a permanent resident. I do not know what I need specifically for this enterprise, but certainly not a journey, at least not a long one. That would merely be a form of escape now. I do not want to forget how close beauty is, at least here. This time the departure will be ini-tiated by something other than a change of place. It has already occurred, with the first sentence of this story.

As I turn from the cedar back to my desk, I have before my eyes the empty, creased outline of my rucksack in the corner of the room, almost close enough to touch. But for as far into the future as possible I want it to remain empty; at the very most I may sniff the inside now and then, trying to pick up, for instance, the scent of that trail that led from the Julian Alps all the way across Yugoslavia to the bay of Kotor. And the sturdy shoes left outside around the house on the stone, wood, and concrete thresholds must weather there, unused, getting stiffer and more brittle with every downpour and drying wind. The laces have long since disappeared, or when I pull on one of the remaining ones, it breaks off. The dead leaves that the wind still stirs up in the middle of January tend to accumulate around the shoes left out there. Their insides are also filled with leaves, and sometimes, when I reach into them or step into them for a short walk through the yard, I expect to find a hibernating hedgehog. Occasionally I go around the house and rub polish into my worn-out mountain, valley, and highland shoes, deep into the cracks, and then make a second round to polish them.

But this story is supposed to focus on me only as one subject among several. I feel compelled to affect my times by means of it. As a traveler today, unlike earlier, I could no longer affect anything. Just as one can exhaust the possibilities of places, regions, entire countries, I have exhausted the possibilities of being on the road, of traveling. Even the idea of roaming, no matter where, without an agreed-upon destination, which in a transitional period offered me something tangible, has closed itself off to me with the passing years. A kind of openness beckons, and not only of late, in the form of staying here in this region.

That does not mean that no reference to travel will be found in my notes. To a great extent this is intended to be a tale of travel. It will even deal with several journeys, future ones, present ones, and, it is to be hoped, still journeys of discovery. True, I am not the hero of these travels. It is several of my friends who will endure them, one way or another. They have already been on the road since the beginning of the year, each of them in a different part of the world, one often separated from the other, as also from me here, by entire continents. Each knows nothing of his comrades, making their way through the world at the same time. Only I know about all of them, and my spot, downstairs in the study, with the grass almost at eye level—a moment ago, in the mild air, a January bee buzzed over it—is where the news from them comes together and is collected.

Nor do my friends know that I have plans for them; they do not even guess that the fragments from them that find their way to me from time to time, and in the course of the year are supposed to keep flying in this direction, will create news, connections, transcendences, yes, for moments at a time, actual vicarious participation. My friends do not guess that they are on the road for me—one of them does not even know that in my eyes he is on a journey at this very moment—and that I am traveling along with all of them, from afar.

Such vicarious traveling forms part of the widening that I, while remaining a permanent resident here, have planned for myself and for this region. A conventional rally brings people from all directions to a central point at a specific time. This will not be that sort of rally. And yet I have in mind for my undertaking a kind of rally that will reveal itself as such in the end. This is to be a story about my region here and my distant friends. Yet I am not even certain whether this is my region, or whether those travelers are my friends.

As a rule, in the past I was able to accompany in my thoughts only those distant friends who were off on a journey, preferably a crucial one. Seriously intending to reach a destination was what I considered a journey, and only that. The person in question could not simply take off; he had to set out. Being on the road this way could be replaced only by work or activity. Engaged in any other way, at home, in their accustomed routines, my people could easily cease to exist; I lived pretty much without them. If I was still their friend under such circumstances, it was an unfaithful friend. And I hardly ever saw the other person surrounded by the aura of adventure if, instead of staying behind and watching from afar, I actually set out with him, even if to the islands at the end of the world. So doesn't my gift for sympathetic vibration at a distance actually result from an incapacity for presence?

What a pleasure it is at any rate: while I sit here at my desk on yet another new morning, watching the droplets of rain from the night before on the needles of the spruce outside my window, at the same time I am on the road in northern Japan with my friend the architect, who calls himself a carpenter, after the trade he learned first.

He got up very early and, the only foreigner in the hotel, like the other guests ate dark soup and a piece of greasy eel down in the labyrinthine basement. Out on the streets of Morioka, which stretched across the broad valley ringed by hills, there were large hummocks of glare ice, old and black with dirt. The snowy massif, visible in a gap between the hills, rising in one fell swoop from its base to its peak, looked in spite of the distance somewhat like a city on a hill.

The architect walks along without a plan; one will take shape in the course of the day and with the still-unexplored environs. He is merely flirting with getting lost, as he did yesterday farther south in Sendai and a week ago on the mountainous paths of the national park south of Nara, and the sight of this urban area, in which even here in the desolate north every corner is built up (passages of only a hand's breadth, hiding places for cats, have been left between the houses as earthquake protection), gives him the first impetus for this day's excursion or for the rest of his journey: to find a no-man's-land, however tiny, in this Japanese plain, linked together into an unbroken surface for habitation or cultivation. A no-man's-land could comfort him as the rising of the moon might comfort another.

It is easy to get lost in a Japanese city, even in Morioka, which is not exactly old, and with this in mind the architect moves with increasing zest through this regional metropolis in which suburban street follows suburban street, and I accompany him. I can feel him better from afar. If I were eye to eye with him, his appearance and his manner would perhaps distract me from him. In his absence I forgot every time what he was like; only his essence counted, free of characteristics and idiosyncrasies.

If he then appeared in flesh and blood, I was distracted as always—in the meantime I had merely forgotten it—by his skimpy mustache, which drooped over his lips; I was shaken out of my equanimity by the way he walked a few steps ahead of me; it even took my breath away that he was next to me, around me, present.

Was I better off altogether at a distance? Was this the only way I could save my breath for the others?

Alone with a friend, unlike with a woman, I often felt out of place, even if I had been full of pleasure when I set out to join him. At the sight of him, I looked in another direction. Something jolted me out of my enthusiasm for the other person and turned my head. (According to one of her friends, the poet Marina Tsvetayeva, whose home in exile during the thirties I recently passed on a side street in this area, is supposed to have shown him only her profile when he was around.)

In the other person's company it seemed to me time and again that our friendship had no basis. Maybe love was also a swindle, but a tangible one, whereas friendship was an illusion? After talk of friendship didn't one often hear, from a mouth that spoke the truth, the observation that he had no friend: "My only friend is dead," or "My best friend was my father," to which the others had nothing more to say?

I, too, was so overwhelmed at some moments by the thought that twosomeness among friends rested on complicity and was sheer illusion that I had to pull myself together so as not to see grounds for a squabble or even a schism in every comment made by the person I happened to be with. One time I let something of the sort slip out, and a friendship ended on the spot. If it had been love, the end would at least have been drawn out. Here there was not the slightest hesitation. We immediately burned all bridges. It was as if we had both been waiting for a sign before putting an end to our game of lies. Enmity broke out between us like that between two leviathans, even more powerfully from his side than from mine.

But wasn't it more than simply our loneliness that had previously attracted us to each other? And why did this kind of falling-out never threaten us when we were in a group? Why, when it detoured through other people, did our friendship cease to be something flimsy, proving instead heartwarming, cheering, for instance in a glance exchanged over the shoulder of a third party, in our simultaneous noticing of the same detail, in a common determination to overlook or overhear something unpleasant? Also, when in the midst of hustle and bustle one merely sensed the presence of the other person, an exchange would take place between us friends, by roundabout ways, past the heads and bodies of the others, of events, sights, sounds. Such experiences helped me grasp Epicurus' epigram, "Friendship dances rings around the human world."

In this connection a little parable (which does not quite fit, and is not meant to): In the forest that extends westward from Paris over the hills of the Seine to Versailles, there used to stand, in the clearing of the Fontaine Ste.-Marie, an old dance hall from the turn of the century, where, in cages stacked one on top of the other, the proprietor of the inn next door raised birds for participation in international competitions. While their singing and their colors were of great importance, it was primarily the bearing of these altogether tiny creatures, particularly that of neck, head, and beak, that counted. The most showy color, the finest voice was not enough; what made the difference was the way the bird turned its head. A bird could be considered for a prize only if its body, neck, and beak did not form a straight line, and also only if it did not suddenly break into song. Singing to another bird could not be done directly; a crook, a bend, a curve, was required, and one that aimed slightly past the other, out into space. Deviation, along with this slight oblique turn, was right, and also beautiful. As he showed me through the shed and explained the rules of competition, the breeder pointed out to me the many incorrigible birds who burst out in song, and their directness actually did strike me as crude and inappropriate. It was unacceptable. Then my *patron* removed the cloth from his champion's cage. The bird was no larger, more colorful, or more elegant than his fellows. But when his master positioned himself in front of him, he stood up straighter, and his neck and head formed a bent arrow, with the beak as its point. The arrow was aimed a few degrees away from the man, and at the same time slightly upward. Although the bird, unlike those around him, remained silent, he seemed to be singing. Or is it only my imagination that now makes it so?

The older I became and the farther I moved from my native region, the more it meant to me to be among friends now and then. The clan from which I come has almost completely died out, and my own small family, which the dreams of my youth conceived or conjured up for me, has fallen apart; at the same time I cannot even muster the certainty that I have failed.

To be united with my friends, not merely with one of them, but with several at the same time, preferably with all those who have been scattered to the winds, has meanwhile become my highest goal, aside from reading and writing. But I must not be the focal point; none of us should be that, and this also entails meeting in a place equally familiar or strange to each.

In poem after poem, Friedrich Hölderlin, in an era that was probably not much rosier than mine, could as a rule call as many as three things "holy." In my story that adjective would have a place at least once: for our rare celebrations of friendship. Each time—and often years intervene—I feel more moved by such gatherings, most of which have a prosaic purpose. Earlier, when I still felt attention directed at me, I would acknowledge it with an abnegating gesture, breaking the existing harmony by employing a counterspell. Now, when none of us any longer is at the center of attention, I gaze into the circle and would like to lift up my voice when the moment comes.

I would probably have less to say explicitly than any of the others. I would begin humming, would fall silent in the middle, and, like one of the singers from that flamenco family on a street corner in the mountains of Andalusia, gaze about wordlessly. And like that time in Baeza, someone else would take up the arabesque and carry on the sound, narrating more thoroughly than I, and more sonorously, for the continuation would issue from the throat and thorax of my friend who is a real singer (at the moment on his way through the wintry darkness of Scotland, by the bay of Inverness, where the buoys bobbing up and down are the heads of a herd of seals, he is trying out the lyrics of what he calls his "last song").

Yet as of today the proper moment for me to lift up my voice has not come; or I have missed it every time. And later the sense of being deeply moved left me. Things between us could even become dangerous again?

The earth has long since been discovered. But I still keep sensing what I call in my own mind the New World. It is the most splendid experience I can imagine. Usually it comes only for the flash of a second and then perhaps continues to glow dimly for a while. I never see visions or phenomena with it. (Inside me is distrust toward all those vouchsafed illumination without its being a necessity.) What I see as the New World is everyday reality. It remains what it was, merely radiating calmness, a runway or launchpad from the old world, marking a fresh beginning.

"The swamps of mysticism must be drained!" someone said in a dream. "And what will we do without the swamps?" someone else replied. That new world may have appeared to me earlier as a revelation, as a second world, the other world. Meanwhile, now that I am waiting for that moment, it brushes me almost daily, as a particle of my perception, and its space flight, followed by stocktaking and reflection, merely indicates that for the moment I am in a good frame of mind. Birds flying in a triangular formation can thus become two airy balls in my armpits.

Often the New World reveals itself in an optical illusion, which makes me perceive this mast not as an object but rather as the space formed by it and the other mast. And the New World wafts toward me less from nature than from a place with human traces. No-man's-land, yes: yet as I pass by, a brush fire is burning there, the branches freshly shoved together. A plank on a garbage heap. A ladder leaning against an embankment. A spanking new house number on a shanty. A stack of abandoned beehives on the edge of a forest in winter.

The special thing about such a New World is that it presents itself as completely, unmistakably there, and at the same time as not yet entered by anyone. But it can and will be entered! The New World has simply not been penetrated yet, made known, has not become general property. And one person alone with it does not count. And at all events access to it must be created, and is sorely needed. The New World can be discovered. Why else did I see those who would bring it to light neither as dreamers nor as fantasts but as craftsmen and engineers? What was keeping them?

Sometimes I am on the verge of saying that this pioneer world that reveals itself to me, more and more as I get older, glimpsed in passing and even more often in a glance over my shoulder, ready for my, and our, breakthrough, is not new, but rather the eternal world.

If indeed eternity, however, it would not be something that is always the same. It would have changed over the course of history, would have become more inconspicuous, would no longer form a consistent whole, would instead be taking place somewhere off to one side, more distinct in its remoteness—though not too much so—than in the middle of things. It seems to me as if the New or the Eternal World has its history as well.

I do want to stick with "new" after all. I had my New World experiences in the last few years not only with pieces of equipment and no-man's-landscapes but also with people. But there they occurred less often and also took a different course. They began splendidly like the other kind, yes, even more splendidly, and in the end they made me miserable. I learned that it was both natural and right to be with certain other people. I had already had this thought earlier: with my wife, with my son. (The former has disappeared, the latter has become a distant friend, just now on the road between Yugoslavia and Greece.)

In every case it had been a single person, or a twosome. It was true that mankind had always counted for me, yet never as a belief, rather as a source of powerful emotion that could not be eliminated by any rational measures. In the meantime it has ceased to be a question of any sort of belief in mankind. It is that rational New World of which I become aware in glancing over my shoulder.

From an exchange of glances a couple of weeks ago with a cashier at the shopping center up on the plateau I learned how extraordinary it was to be fond of someone else, an unknown person—and how natural it seemed at the same time. In harmony with oneself, with a thing, with a space, with an absent person: that's fine with me. But nothing could surpass the harmony I was feeling now with the person across from me. The difference was that, in contrast to perceiving the New World in a landscape, I now went on without air in my armpits. To be sure, I viewed permanence with one person and another as the ne plus ultra, and that no longer merely moved me. It was overwhelming. But the experience tore me apart. For one side of me felt excluded from something at which quite a few apparently succeeded. I shied away from happiness in a communal setting, out of a sort of fear of annihilation. Hence also the rareness of such New World moments with my contemporaries and the lack of consequences, because they occurred not with my friends but almost exclusively with unknown passersby? I began to wonder whether this meant that my end was near.

Didn't I decide to be a marginal figure in this story? The heroes were supposed to be the others, the architect, who, searching in Morioka in northern Japan for an unbuilt-up piece of land, slithers over the hummocks of ice; the singer, just now caught in a winter storm that keeps flipping over the map in his hands as he makes his way to the prehistoric stone monument in a meadow behind a farm up in the hills to the south of Inverness; my son, who just came of age, and, after his year as a volunteer with the Austrian mountain troops and after soon-interrupted university studies in history and geography, is working at odd jobs, the day before yesterday as a builder's helper, yesterday morning as a language instructor, last night as a tile layer in a Viennese café, this morning, on his first journey undertaken alone, sitting on one of the limestone blocks that line the harbor basin in Piran, Slovenia; the woman I consider my special friend, who set out a week ago, unaccompanied as usual, on an excursion that will take her on foot and by boat from bay to bay along the southern coast of Turkey; the priest from the far-off village where I was born, who still makes his rounds in that same area, a traveler only in my eyes; my friend the painter, about to shoot his first film on the *meseta*, in Spain; and that is not quite all of them.

In the books I have written since giving up the legal profession, the hero is more or less me myself. If I reached people that way, I was successful only because I was a character in a book.

Whenever I have wanted to be a protagonist in life as well, I have not managed to sustain the role. Time and again I have thought I could pull it off and made the attempt: as captain of my school team, as a speaker in the student senate, as a defense attorney in criminal court, then as the only diplomat who publicly spoke out, abroad, against his highest superior, the federal president; and likewise as a lover, at times even as a womanizer, then husband, father, builder, gardener, vineyard owner. In every case, after a more or less promising beginning, I fairly soon fell out of character. As a hero or man of action, after the first surge of activity I became a charlatan. I stopped the play, which I had initiated with the best intentions of living life completely. I am too impulsive to be a protagonist in society. As a hero in everyday life I am a public menace. When I confront my past as an activist I see over here a house in ruins, over there a neglected plot of land, perhaps also a betrayed soul, maybe even a dead victim. In my writing, where I could shut myself off from the others, and as the hero of my books, I could act differently, above all more reliably, and there I was primarily and ultimately a danger only to myself. Interestingly enough, I often received the most positive reaction for my equanimity.

Yet I now think I am finished with myself, at least as far as stories are concerned. I have hardly anything left to tell about myself, and that I consider progress. So I note the following: if you are looking for a person to assume a major role in the community, I am out of the question, and I am out of the running for the time being as the central character in my narratives. In life, the proper place for me is that of an observer, and in my writing I want to posit myself less as an actor than before and function first and foremost as a chronicler, chronicling both the year in this region here and my friends far and wide beyond the hills, and I want to preserve the chronicler's distance and tone in regard to myself as well. My decades of working with legal texts, especially the most ancient ones, like those of Roman law, will guide me and trace the line I must follow.

But who knows? I really want to be decisive, yet already questions are cropping up. Wasn't it possible for observation to be a form of action as well? Something that affected what happened and even transformed it? Wasn't a certain observer also a possible hero? Hadn't I learned, either through directing my gaze at someone, or experiencing someone's gaze on me, that looking could avert an act of violence, could let the air out of a scream, bring a toy to life, turn a joke into something serious, blow away a delusion, eliminate a reason for depression? I once saw such a gaze captured in faces painted by Giotto: narrowed, very elongated eyes, as if they were merely glancing at what was happening and at the same time intimately participating in it. Such observation would impose shape, impart rhythm, cast light.

And hadn't it been known to happen that observation led to something's being created, an object, an other, a connection, even a natural law? And how far did I get recording such a thing in a reportorial style? How adequate was the language of the chronicler to capturing his own involvement or his possible initiating role? No matter how comprehensive the Latin network of codicils appeared to me, airtight and yet applicable with the lightness of air to all the vicissitudes of life: could the precepts of an imperial legal system also provide a model for my present plan of writing?

I have already touched on this: when I glance behind me, I see a thing differently than if I were looking at it head-on. For a long time in my life this looking behind me always occurred abruptly. I hardly ever took in more than a distorted image.

It was different when women turned their heads sometimes, on a street. Women glanced over their shoulder so naturally; it seemed to suit them. Their beauty became accessible as a result. What emanated from their glance was not so much a provocation as serenity, or a line traced in the air.

Twice a story resulted. The first one came about on the great drawbridge in Maribor, with the woman who in the meantime is my special friend from afar; the other during my time in America on a windy street in El Paso with the woman who then became my wife, whom our son calls "your woman from Catalonia," and whom I, wherever she may be at the moment, consider (under certain circumstances) my enemy. The woman from Catalonia continued to glance behind her long after we had ceased to be strangers—on many streets, bridges, landings, wood roads. And when her glance fell on me, I always swore anew to take it as the measure of all things, not to let myself be dissuaded from considering it the only one that counted in all our other moments. This woman's glance behind her seemed so joyful to me, so kind, so innocent, so original, so refreshing.

In the meantime I myself am the only one looking over his shoulder. Starting with the period when I renounced a life of action, I even cultivated this habit, and I now practice it purposefully. A glance to the side glides into a turn to the rear hemisphere. From a certain degree on, my head-turning is feigned, but so unobtrusively that if bystanders happen to be looking they miss it.

With moments like this I hope to achieve something, and when my excessive consciousness does not spoil the game for me, I do succeed. First of all, so long as it is peacetime, objects light up as they never would if viewed frontally. It is an inner light that provides shape and focus. In this way I impose a pattern on clutter, whether of underbrush or buildings. And the pattern is set in motion. Along with the pattern I derive a theatrical spectacle from this behind-the-back world.

Time and again I find myself surprised by the richness that exists in places where there is very little to see, or nothing but air. The spectacle fills me with amazement; "Oh!" is often my only thought about something seemingly not worth mentioning in the countryside behind me. Or I think, as I become aware of a group of trees, a cluster of roofs— these things seem to have gathered in as close as if they had crept up on me and were waiting to take me by surprise—like an athletic coach: "So: you're all here. Come on, guys, let's move it!"

Since I began to deny myself any social life, this has become a feature of my activity, a part of my day.

Yet not every world landscape lends itself to this kind of observation, adopted with the intention of setting something in motion, not by a long stretch. My landscape here, which I have known now for twenty years, nestled between the heights of the Seine, separated from Paris by a wooded chain of hills, is suitable, I would assert. Whenever I glance back at its features, what emanates from them I always see anew as the "glow of the reverse colors."

Despite my familiarity with this countryside, acquired in the course of daylong walks—dreaming and walking, my motto—from suburb to suburb, over hill and dale, across highways and railroad tracks, I still know hardly anyone, still have no friend in the *département*, which stretches in the form of a half-moon around the western half of Paris, from Bourg-la-Reine and Fontenay-aux-Roses in the south all the way up to Asnières and Clichy in the north—except perhaps for the so-called petty prophet of Versailles-Porchefontaine, who sometimes provides my rest stop behind the next chain of hills.

To give a sense of the effect of such a glance, no longer that of a participant but that of an observer, on people, on strangers, I must move from my Roman-law generalizations to narration. This has been waiting inside me, in my fingers, my knees, my shoulders, from the beginning, and has already begun tuning up now and then.

A few weeks ago, after just such a day of walking, I took the local bus home; it goes from Jouy-en-Josas in the Bièvre Valley across the plateau of Vélizy to the upper valley here.

In my younger days I was a friend to strangers, to passersby, to cross-country travelers. I felt I belonged among them; I was in love with them, with their faces, their bodies, their silhouettes. In the meantime I have to fight my inclination to find any and all strangers ugly and repulsive at first sight, even children. There is no longer any ideal that guides me, and yet I miss having one, as if without it my activity cast no light, and if my publisher had not talked me out of it, my last book would have had "loss of images" on the title page. Especially in late afternoon on my long days, an hour arrives when, dizzy from all the paths and places, I see the faces of others approaching like the masks of automatons, and my own face matches theirs. Even our outlines and shadows appear utterly shapeless. Only a dead, stillborn mankind appears to me, wretches who provide no sense of a path to follow.

On that evening bus trip when, on the plateau of Vélizy, in accordance with my daily observation practice, I almost unconsciously turned toward the people behind me, I finally managed to see people as distinct again.

In turning my head I got away from judging and condemning. My era, my enemy: this thought, which had been solidifying in my mind with the passing years, lost its content. At that moment no era mattered, or only all eras together: through the faces behind me I gazed into a primeval time, and simultaneously into a new time. Even though nothing connected the passengers to each other, my glancing back created unity among them. Although none of them seemed conscious of it, it was no fantasy. It would have faded into one if I had approached them now with these tidings of joy. (My friend the singer repeatedly did something of the sort during one period of his life: he would appear before a random gathering of people to sing them awake, and as a rule each one would stare all the more fixedly into his corner, and a certain Pentecostal spirit would arise only if he broke off his song and pelted them with curses.) I certainly felt a wave of feeling sweeping me toward those people, but at the same time some instinct kept me at a distance. "That's it!" I merely thought, and then: "That's how it is." And further: "You should not try to do anything with it, just go off to your corner now and tell about it, and—since oral narration has never worked for you—in writing." And further: "The faces of strangers, the most reliable source of pleasure."

What was there to tell specifically? It was already dark on the plateau. It was raining. The windows of the bus were steamed up. The passengers were of all ages and yet seemed of the same age. That had to do with their eyes, which my gaze took in all at once, in the shadowy light back to the very rear of the bus. My fellow passengers were outlines, with eyes in them, as if scratched by a blade into the otherwise indistinct faces, there in full, like a flock of birds jam-packed into a certain tree or a lone bush.

And then the bus came downhill from the plateau through the forest into the valley and stopped at the station with connecting trains to Paris and Versailles. We got out in the rain, and each disappeared, after thanking the driver—as they do in the country—into the various suburbs, barely lit, in contrast to the city of light behind the chain of hills.

Other than that I have nothing to tell about this event. And at the same time I feel an urge to start telling it again, to find a new rhythm, or even just a single new word.

That is how it has always been for me. I was sure of having something original on the tip of my tongue. And the only thing I could think of was: portraying it. And then all that would appear was a deserted street, a bus passing, a gust of wind. A flood of words, hesitation, nothing more to tell, the story at an end; I tried again, then again, and again.

Maybe that took a toll on me earlier. In the meantime I have come to accept it. My habit of winding up, grinding to a halt, starting from scratch, is all right by me. If I am a stutterer, at least I am a self-aware one.

And come to think of it, my friends who are to appear in this narrative are all stammerers: the singer, but also my son, the priest, the architect or carpenter, also my woman friend (less so the painter, who now joins this company for the first time, to narrate with his film, and even less the friend who right now is tracing the stations of my "writer's tour" through wintry Germany, the reader).

From the very first word, I believed in their way of telling stories. Perhaps that is also why I see them all gathered far away from here. Tell stories, my friends, but don't tell histories, at least nothing from world history, don't reproduce world history. Tell me prehistories, which then turned out to be all there was. Hesitate, or bungle, take wrong turnings over and over again; perhaps in this way I will develop an ear for the tensions in your stories that the prettied-up world histories do not have, at least no longer have nowadays, not since *War and Peace*. And thus I also notice that you, in this respect unlike most of my earlier friends, who long since stopped needing anything, still need something, and for that reason, too, are my friends.

I want to try again with the people on the suburban bus that evening. No, I did not see any universal law in effect. It even seemed that the darkness, not only around the passengers, but also in the faces themselves, grew deeper each time I glanced back. The common element that emanated from all of them was a desolation in which I could detect a still-unidentified tremulous patience. This story had to continue.

And in fact didn't it then continue? At the open-air stand in front of the railway station an adolescent was buying a few things for supper, and every time he asked for an item, he added, "For me and my mother!"

until the woman behind the counter corrected him: "For my mother and me!"

And before I went into the nearby Café des Voyageurs as always, I looked up into the plane tree that during the winter months served the sparrows on the square as a sleeping place, the same birds' sleeping tree for all these years; at night the sparrows roosted only in this one, although the square in front of the station is ringed with trees, and not far beyond the embankment crowned with lindens begin the wooded hills whose trees extend almost down to the houses, an upland forest of oaks and narrower edible chestnuts: the proprietor of the Voyageurs, whose upper stories are a hotel for itinerant workers and salesmen, called "sales representatives," says the plane tree became the sleeping tree because of the warmth escaping from his heated hotel rooms. In any case, at night I have never seen a single sparrow in the other trees on the square, or only briefly, for a moment, chased away by the large crowd nearby, because it was disturbing their peace.

And on this rainy evening there was a gleam of wetness through the entire tree, both on the stumpy sparrow beaks and on the black, shriveled round pods of the plane tree from the previous year, yet only the latter, hanging by threads, moved, swayed, swung: the sparrows, even on the thinnest twigs, kept completely still, and had I not known that they were assembled there, their pale gray bodies would have merged with the blotches on the tree's bark, which resembled them in form and coloration. And later at the bar I succumbed to the temptation to repeat my glance from the bus with the others standing there: nothing. And even later the *patron* behind the counter taped shut with adhesive tape the mouth of someone who was getting obstreperous. And in the brightly lit trains passing up above on the embankment silhouettes sped by, fewer and fewer. And on the way to my house a neighbor's wolfhound, locked in the garage, was hurling himself as usual against the steel door.

And then I ate in the kitchen and listened to the news on the radio. And toward midnight—it had stopped raining and a warm wind was blowing—I went out and sat in the yard, at a distance from the house, where I had turned on the lights, and let the music from Radio Beur, the station of the North Africans in Paris, drift out through the open kitchen window, as I had done the night I moved in here, even then at a distance from the house, in the farthest corner of the yard. From the other houses, long since dark and wrapped in wintry silence, came through the often very narrow gaps that separated them the rustling of the forest, or it was the wind in the cedar right next door, pretending to be the growling of a forest. And the business with the bus continued to stir me. This was not like we-experiences: I did not feel torn between my longing to merge with the others and my congenital inability to do so. Here I was the observer, and could say "we" only from the sidelines. Observing was my project. And it was a big project. Never again could I let myself get involved in action, or in any action but observing and elaborating upon it. Wasn't it also a fact that dreams in which I myself was the hero had become increasingly rare? Even as a dreamer I had been transformed from a figure in the plot to a witness. As such I was not helpful to anyone, true, but I knew that I was active. And that night in my backyard was not the first time this became clear to me—and why had I drifted away from this insight every time and aimed for a fatally wrong target, whether as a lawyer in court or as an author of articles who believed he could make history as Emile Zola once had? Would I betray my realization this time, too? Where would I go shooting off to in my next hotheadedness, deluded anew that this action was something that would last? And didn't I think at the same time that my very own life, in all its uneventfulness, was my only basis for pathos?

It had always been night in those hours when I participated purely as an observer, deep night.

Here in this remote suburb, where there is no theater, also no longer a movie house, the local weekly reports that an association has formed whose program calls for something known as "The Night of the Story-teller."

I do not know what form this takes, and plan to attend at least one such night in the course of the year. But the very expression brings back to me a whole succession of nights in my life. I am thinking less of evenings in late autumn in my grandparents' barn, where half the village would gather on benches and milking stools to husk corn and would go around the circle clockwise telling story after story until far into the night. The nights of the storyteller I am thinking of were by and large silent, although there, too, each time a more or less large company was sitting or standing around.

That was true a few years ago of an evening with two friends in Dubrovnik, Yugoslavia. On a trip, of which I was not yet certain where it would lead me, I had invited the painter and the reader there for my fiftieth birthday. The painter flew in via Belgrade from Perpignan, where he had one of his studios in the nearby Pyrenees. The reader had traveled parallel to me, through Italy, down the eastern coast as I was going down the western coast of Yugoslavia, like me by train and bus, and had then taken a boat in Rimini straight across the Adriatic to Split, hot on my trail by that time, but then, in his usual way, had done the last part on foot, so that I could be alone on the morning of my birthday, as I had requested.

I would have remained alone until evening if the reader and I had not been drawn to the same part of Dubrovnik at the same time, outside the city walls. Where we ran into each other by chance, there was nothing but an open stony field, high above the little fortified city on the sea in its shell-shaped hollow. I found myself driven there by thoughts of my mother, who had spent the last summer of her life in this area, sickened by the heat and yet out walking every day, leaving the shade of the town for the countryside, for the goat and chicken sheds in the middle of nowhere, for the stone walls, for the sparse grassy triangles where roads crossed. The ocean down below had merely blinded her, and the islands meant nothing to her, unlike me. The shrill sound of the cicadas tormented her ears. The light of the limestone karst raged. By a doorpost, all that remained of a house, autumnal sky-blue like the background of the Slovenian roadside shrines, she breathed a sigh of relief in passing. His eyes wide, a wooden cudgel over his shoulder, a native came toward me; at second glance I recognized the reader. At least I had been in Dubrovnik before and could then play the role of host in the courtyard of the most obscure tavern. At that very place the painter later hunted us down, coming straight from the airport. He stood between us, without a word, and him, too, I at first took for a local.

That evening each of us did open his mouth now and then, but for the most part we remained silent. And precisely that was the night of storytelling. One incident followed the other without need for words. From the darkness outside only a breath reached us; the deeper the night became, the richer in material. More than listening to such storytelling, we sat through it. We did look around again and again, get up, go outside, leaving the others alone for a while, but the most active element in that night was the blackness. I had never seen the black of night so full of color, and seldom a color so massive, and in the same breath so fragrant. It had often made me suspicious when the painter came out with his dictum about black's being the richest of the colors, interacting with light. Now, long after midnight, also long before the first birdcalls, no moon, no stars, I perceived the blackness as the color of a first-day fruit.

It was winter, rainy along the southern Adriatic coast, mild. The late night was windless. We had not stayed in Dubrovnik. I had invited my friends to Ston, a village on the tongue of land toward Korčula. There were the saltworks on one side, on the other, in a bay, man-made oyster beds, with a restaurant adjacent. The previous morning, having gone out there by bus, I had looked into the particulars, and now I guided the painter and the reader from place to place. The table by the bay was set, the white cloth a rarity for Yugoslavia. We had come by taxi; the driver sat at a table at some distance, he, too, having Dalmatian wine and oysters, a common and inexpensive meal in that area. The shells were hardly larger than a coin, and the oyster flesh was correspondingly tiny, yet firm.

Although it was my special day, I set out a present for the others, the same thing for both, a wooden box carved and painted by Albanian craftsmen in Kosovo, purchased the week before in the Croatian town of Zadar, filled with the coarse gray crystals of unrefined sea salt, mixed with sand and autumn leaves, gathered from a pile in the middle of the saltworks, shut down for the winter. The painter stood up and handed me a collection of dull black pencils, all of them already started by him, with dabs of paint on them, for the rest of my journey, so that I could draw in my notebook, for he said he found it unfortunate that I had stopped. And the reader, too, stood up and gave me a book he had printed himself: the notes he had recently discovered, made by a stonemason on a trip between Souillac, Cahors, and Moissac in France around the middle of the twelfth century, in that transitional period between the Romanesque and the Gothic style. The notes were in Latin, true, but having to decipher something, reading a text that did not flow smoothly, always had an animating effect on me; and this commentary dealt with something that might apply to me. It was this remark in particular that caused me to carry the little book around with me without reading it: it scares me off when I am told something seems made for me, and only now do I sense that the time may have come for the stonemason's story.

It was much later when the night outside, silent as it was, became so overpowering around the village of Ston, about twenty kilometers from Dubrovnik in the big country of Yugoslavia. Here a verb suggests itself, a somewhat odd concept, yet it imposes itself on me. What did the night do? It surged, it surged over us: the surging night. The hill by the bay was girdled by medieval ramparts, which because of their length and breadth, up and down around the mountainous fortress, was called the Chinese Wall (of Ston). This wall now seemed close to where we were. It was the same with the row of spruce on the saltworks dam farther away, on the other side of the hill. The trees' needles rustled, and the heaps of salt at their feet glistened; a tipped-over wheelbarrow was covered with salt, except for the rusty wheel.

And meanwhile on the gleaming cobblestones of the Stradun, the main street of Dubrovnik, the local residents were still promenading, with the place to themselves now in winter. For the participants in this regular evening corso there was an invisible demarcation line toward both ends of the broad street—or square?—at which every stroller who had not yet done so would pivot. In the course of this parading back and forth by the population, not at all casual but downright energetic, no one continued on to the ends of the Stradun, unless he disappeared completely from the mass, heading home, or elsewhere. But anyone who kept parading made an abrupt turn at that demarcation line, swerving his entire body, leading with the shoulder. The majority swerved long before, those who were arm in arm swerving all at once, as if on an inaudible command, heading back in the opposite direction; even groups taking up the whole width of the street turned this way, magically. The few who continued on to the end seemed for those few steps like sleep-

walkers. But at the last moment, within a hair's-breadth of the imaginary
boundary, even the solitary stroller or scuffer would wheel around like a
swimmer at the end of a lane. The city elders joined the procession,
calmly and deliberately, and the most relaxed and dancerlike ones were
the children; they had the pirouette at the turn in their blood. In these
hours leading up to midnight no one made a false step, none of those
strolling up and down missed the turning point. Several people in uniform mingled with the crowd, also a Catholic priest, sailors, an idiot,
whose siblings held him by the hand; and not even he lagged behind
in the loop. Down by the harbor the cars came rolling out of the belly
of the last ferry from the islands. On the night plane to Zagreb
sat a Croatian basketball team, almost the only passengers, after their
training camp in Dubrovnik. The tallest of the players, also the team
captain, sat next to his Serbian wife, who years before had been Miss
Yugoslavia.

The waitress and cook of the Ston restaurant had gone home and had
left the back door open for us; it would lock by itself. What distances
could be opened up simply by such a going to a door in this Yugoslavia.
The night light was sufficient for us. The taxi driver was asleep outside
in his Mercedes, bought with his factory earnings when he was in Germany. When we finally climbed in, someone roused himself way in the
back of the car. It was one of the workers from a construction company
with branches all over Yugoslavia that was building a hotel on the bay.
He had just been informed that his father had died, far down in the
south, in a village in the mountains of Montenegro, and he asked to be
allowed to go with us to catch the first bus from Dubrovnik to Titograd.
Along the way he told us his father had died suddenly, of a heart attack,
a construction worker like him, forty years old. Since the son did not
seem that much younger, he was asked his age. He was twenty-five;
when he was born, his father had barely started his apprenticeship, and
his mother had still been in school. We said nothing all the way to the
dark, locked-up bus station outside the city walls. The buses parked
around the barracklike station would stand there empty and inaccessible
for hours. Their marker plates, with two letters for the place they came
from, bordered by the little five-pointed star of the partisans, ranged
from MO for Mostar, SA for Sarajevo, BL for Banja Luka to ZG for
Zagreb, TG for Titograd, BG for Belgrade, and there was even an LJ for

Ljubljana, very far away, and a VŽ for Varaždin, probably even farther away.

O f that night of storytelling I also thought at the time: Actually this should continue now. So although each of us was already supposed to go his separate way, I urged the others to spend one more hour sitting with me the next day on Dubrovnik's Stradun. And my friends did indeed come, laconic and full of anticipation. I was the one who did not know what to do next. I wanted a continuation and could not pull it off, at least not in their presence.

And therein lies one of my fatal mistakes in life. Just a few days ago I wrote a note to myself: "Always, even in moments of fulfillment, your tendency to think: It's not here yet! You always experience even the most perfect present moment as a mere advent. You always expect something more afterward, something bigger, the ultimate. Look! It has been here and is here. And why force something unique into repetition, into a series, into permanence? Consider your monosyllabic friends, for whom once was everything."

Even this morning, for instance, here, behind the house: when I was using a crowbar to loosen the gravel surface compacted by wintry downpours, sparks flew repeatedly; the chain of hills along the Seine contains a good deal of flint. And once I hit a flintstone hidden so deep in the ground that for a moment I saw a spark that shot not into the daylight but down into the dark, and lit it up with a lightninglike reflection off the soil, whereupon the momentary cave disappeared again. And again the unique occurrence was not enough for me, and I wanted a continuation, hoped with every further blow to see an even more splendid hollow illuminated, until I finally went inside and jotted down: "Your greed for continuations, your mania for completeness."

But didn't I long ago establish a principle to guide me in such matters, which went something like this: your experience may be fragmentary, but your narration must be complete!? And apparently this maxim, too, like all those that ever lit my path, dissolved gradually, or, as they said where I came from, a wee bit at a time. Goethe, it seems to me, became increasingly sure of himself as he grew older, despite all the childlike qualities he preserved; the child became an imperious child (and at the same time wrote "gently" and "transitorily"), while I am becoming less and less sure with every passing year, and at the same time would like to write as penetratingly and pointedly as ever. Perhaps I still need a master, and doesn't the itinerant stonemason from the twelfth European century seem closer to me now, his travel notes beginning with an exclamation and a plea: "Oh, where will this drab highway, along which I now stumble for the third winter, among legions of others, finally become my own green path?"

I have experienced nights of storytelling more often with strangers than with my friends. In such hours, the former come together with my friends, as in the fragment of Heraclitus in which the sleeper taps the one who is awake. And I have experienced this most frequently among strangers since I settled beyond the hills, in the hinterland of the great metropolis. The light here probably also has a little to do with it, but mainly it is particular places, the eating places in the region, the bars that close early in the evening. Whenever I can, I want to be among the last. For the most part nothing happens then; the rule is prompt locking-up and the disappearance of all the regulars into the tongue-shaped settlement surrounded by wooded hills. But from time to time the bar —of which there are only two in this particular district—stays open even after the lights have been turned off once, for no particular occasion, in a general, gradual winding-down.

In this transitional moment, a brief, much too brief, night of story-telling takes place among us strangers here. Unexpectedly, the excitement wakes me up, and at the same time I find peace: peace, the great eye. Now the majority of guests leave the café, at the latest at the next hint, the switching-off of the fan or, in winter, of the ceiling-mounted heater. The few who stay behind stand around the room, except perhaps for the one older woman, who sits on the only chair not yet put up on the tables. The iron shutters have been let down almost all the way, the door locked, the key on the inside, and anyone who wants to leave turns it, whereupon someone inside locks up again.

Somewhere a crack is always left open for a glance out into the night. Hardly anything is going on out there; all the roads in the settlement are access roads and end at the base of the chain of hills, or, if they

continue into the woods, then only as wood roads, with white-painted
barriers where the forest begins. As a rule they merge with a route that
makes a loop around the remotest corner of the suburb. This ring road
somewhat resembles a breakwater, and the section enclosed by it a harbor, for instance the harbor of Piran on the Istrian Peninsula, where
thirty-five years ago I first sat by the sea, as a student, after a major
examination, and, there among the limestone blocks, for hours on end,
knew nothing at all of myself and my origins, of jurisprudence, of limestone; I was refreshingly oblivious, and appearances were quite enough;
I did not want to know what lay behind anything, a state to which I
sometimes long from the bottom of my heart to return.

Part of this civilized surface carved out of the woods actually is water,
the water of a pond that has been here for centuries. When you glance
out of one of the bars at night through the remaining crack, the black
water gleams, now and then ruffled by a gust of wind, and the headlights
of the infrequently passing cars dart across the water like those of speed-
boats. But in the second bar, too, outside of which only the empty
pavement gleams, when you look out at night you can sense the presence
of water right around the corner, not only of this pond but also of the
couple of others in this corner of the world, most of them already in the
forest.

Those standing in the bar at night appear at first stranded, and in my
imagination they have already been there a long time. Not a few of them,
as I gather from scraps of conversation, without specifically listening for
the information, have lived in their region here since childhood. Although the bars are not dives but rather the only public places in these
outlying towns, serving also as tobacco shops, where you can buy newspapers and postage stamps, and in the summer, when the bakery is
closed, as bread depots, I have never met a single one of my neighbors
there. The citizenry is not included among the guests at the local cafés,
at least not in the evening.

But it was premature to describe the last holdouts in the bar as
stranded. For among them I recognize one tradesman or another who
has done work on my house. Or the older ones, in the minority, seem
in the way they silently follow the smallest happenings anything but
failures: calm retirees, solemn anglers, dignified widowers (as the older
woman sitting by herself always has the air of a not so dignified widow).

And nevertheless it was there at night that the whole area appeared to me for the first time as a bay, with us as driftwood. At the same time that was one of the rare occasions when I saw this isolated suburb as a part of the large city of Paris beyond the chain of hills, to be precise as the most remote, hidden, least accessible bay of the metropolitan ocean, separated from it by the barrier formed all along the horizon by the hills of the Seine, with the road between Versailles and Paris that cut across them forming the only link with the open spaces. And we, too, came from the turbulent sea, swept in, washed in, rocked in the tides that rolled in and out for years or decades on end, now calm, now more hectic, past thousands of capes and cliffs, through the straits of Meudon, through the narrows of Sèvres, through the first inlet, called the "Puits sans Vin," fountain without wine, and a second inlet, called the "Carrefour de la Fausse Porte," crossroads of the false portal, into the narrowest, most twisting and turning, remotest metropolitan bay, all the more fathomable for me in its namelessness, we, the driftwood that had come the greatest distance, and thus also rarer than in the mouths of the bay, yet for that very reason amazingly distinct.

At the same time, those in the bar, since they all stand alone, somewhat resemble an ancient tribe on the only remaining reservation, and in reality I encounter them, when they are going about among the local passersby out on the street, as the remnant that hardly counts anymore, the remnant of the remnant of the original inhabitants of this region. They seem fundamentally misshapen, as if smashed out of their child's and youth's forms by a single blow from a fist, a moment's impact, which I sometimes, in a different sense, wish on the other passersby, who have apparently remained unharmed, and likewise on myself.

No such sense of expulsion in the few minutes of the night of storytelling. There are simply some standing—I do not know who they are—there—I do not know how. If any outside lights were still on previously, they have gone off in the meantime, for instance the barbershop's, in front of which could be a sign: "Last Chance for a Haircut Before the Big Woods," and by eight at the latest that of the bakery, which in fact already has the woods in its name, and whose reversed Ν in BOULAИGERIE suggests Cyrillic script to me, as if I were looking out the window of a bar on Lake Ohrid. Only the outskirtishly pale light of the streetlights, leading to the wooded ridge and breaking off just before it, remains. The pinball machine and the video game inside have been turned off, their flashing lights extinguished, the seductive mechanical melodies and voices silenced. The cards or dice on the tables way in the back stay as they are. No one is doing anything more. At the very most the tradesman among us is casually repairing something for the proprietor, moving back and forth between the counter and the kitchen, as if he were at home. Otherwise there are no distinctions among those present, no barriers anymore. Even when the *patron* is not standing among the others, he could be just anyone behind the bar. No one is smoking now. The day's debris on the floor has already been swept up. No one is loud or especially quiet. Everyone who speaks has the same intonation, and it matches the peaceful atmosphere in the dim café.

In the sense in which people use the term "intake personnel," during such nights of storytelling I experienced those who were standing around as a sort of "uptake personnel," whether one of them happened to be talking, listening, or listening to something else. Now a sort of game was in progress, one without rival players and sides, the opposite of all the games that I, at least, had witnessed over the years, which were accompanied by both hotheadedness and coldness, of which in the end only the coldness remained, most rigidly in the so-called game of kings, chess.

What we are playing here comes closest to a team's warm-up before a match—except that the match itself is already there. In the brief interval, a transformation has occurred in those remaining behind together, stranded or not, even if the next day on the street one will look right through the other.

It may be that I will never see humanity this way again. Yet it existed in those nights there. It exists. I do not need any image as a continuation; it has been told to me.

Or was that just my imagination? Did I fail to consider that one of the people standing there no sooner got back to his room over the garage than he beat up the woman he lived with, perhaps that very woman sitting over to one side, his mother, who was just waiting for him to come home; that the second took a detour through the woods, where, on one of the banks of the pond, he injected himself with dope, that the third, I myself, with each such night was drifting farther from those who were his real kin?

Yes. And nevertheless it is not something imagined, but rather a fantasy. Fantasy is not something imagined. And when it came, I realized how much I had needed it, all this time, all day. Observation, absorption, abstraction: my daily bread. So didn't we need a continuation after all, recapitulation?

It would have destroyed my equanimity if one of my acquaintances had joined this obscure company. Yet he would see me there as I would wish to impress myself on him, as a pure participant, far from hubs of activity of any sort, beyond immediate relevance, having stepped out of all my roles, no longer a lawyer, or a writer, also no longer a father, but also no shade of the dead, and also not isolated but accessible and present. Which, if an old familiar face unexpectedly showed up there, I would have to become conscious of, and that would put an end to it.

Yet it would not be this way if, on such a night, in such a bar, my wife appeared before me, the woman from Catalonia, who vanished long ago.

Did she really vanish? Two days ago, in my study, on the second of February, Candlemas, the festival of the threshold of light, didn't I see out of the corner of my eye something black flit by outside the window, whereupon I dreamed that night about the steps of the woman from Catalonia on the bridge over the Rio Grande between El Paso and Ciudad Juárez?

Of the people I know, only she would have eyes for this kind of a nobody—although in fact it was she, during our years together, who propelled me from one role to another, from one undertaking to another. And if she showed up here, I would continue to play the person I am, all the more believably, just for her. I would have presented myself to her as a person different from the one with whom she was familiar, if only she had let me. "Let me!" was my constant refrain with her. But she did not let me. If she had let me, she would have been my benefactor.

Now the woman from Catalonia, full of amazement, would let me. She would see me with open eyes: the abruptness gone, and in its place my original equanimity, familiar to her otherwise only from my books, and in which she had soon lost confidence because my life belied it. And at the same time she would see something even worse lifted from me, which likewise had not been part of me from the beginning but only after my years in boarding school: my tendency to drift away from the person I was with, often precisely in brilliant company, and to disappear into myself to the point of no longer being present. I let myself wander into nowhereland, and especially with those closest to me. And yet that vanishing caused me great suffering. How often I had struck myself on the brow and wanted to scratch blood from my scalp, saw my breastplate in two with a two-handed saw.

Yet now I would be standing there without armor. For a certain period of time the night of storytelling would have burst open the dungeon. If the woman from Catalonia approached me now, I would see her immediately as a whole. With a flourish I would give her my hand, and although this gesture always repelled her, especially between a man and a woman, she would not object. I would have matches ready for her cigarette; she always grubbed around endlessly in her deep cloth bag for them. And then I would begin spontaneously to speak of the forest of plane trees in her hometown of Girona, of the winter day long ago when, on the way to the forest, on her command I had closed my eyes and then—"You can look now!"—the shimmering filling my entire field of vision had blinded me, from the gray of the plane trees' trunks standing there shoulder to shoulder, almost without gaps and air in between, and the crowns, likewise gray, intertwined up above. Never had I seen a forest like that. Since all around me there was nothing but the bone-gray glimmering, it seemed as if the plane forest had swallowed up the entire place. It was like when you are carried in your sleep out of your room without realizing it—from childhood, especially from the time my family was fleeing, I remember this happening more than once—and you wake up in a nowhereland, for instance facing a terror-gray surface, which only today in retrospect do I recognize as the dawn sky above one of the borders we had to cross, while the shifting gray below is a load of gravel in the back of the truck in which we are fleeing.

"How dizzy I was that time in your forest!" I would tell the woman from Catalonia in such a night of storytelling. And likewise I would then explain to her calmly that at times she was not the right person for me, either because during our time together, whenever I needed something to remain empty, she would fill it up: the house, an evening, a day off, the summer, the yard, our trips, our son, even my room, my table, whose leaves she pulled out to make it bigger, my window, on which, when I wanted to look out at the grass, day after day new notes greeted me, me myself.

"It was not only for me that you weren't good," I would be able to tell her to her face again. "You aren't good for anyone." Or: "The right man for you doesn't exist; there will never be someone who suits you, not even death, at most a god. But which one? Just as you not only filled the house with objects but also kept shoving them around, you have constantly been on the move from place to place yourself. Never will you find your place anywhere, with anyone, certainly not alone with yourself. And even with your god you will feel hemmed in sooner or later."

On such a night the woman from Catalonia would actually listen to me, unlike earlier. At the very most she would say, in a quiet tone like mine, "You sound like your pal, the petty prophet of Porchefontaine." And all the while the men next to us in the bar would have been trying not to hear us, making occasional remarks like "Smells like snow," "When I was in the service in Indochina," "Red gets you riled up; that's why butchers are so riled up," or "Before the war there were still charcoal kilns up there in the woods."

But at a time like that, when I appeared as I am, and with patience to boot, the woman from Catalonia would never ever show up unexpectedly. She is not capable of taking anyone by surprise. Surprises were something she expected exclusively of the other person, if possible daily. If I managed to pull one off now and then, she was quite overwhelmed. I can recall a sideways glance of unusual gentleness, such as you sometimes receive from a child who has been given a present. But she herself never took me by surprise, as if that were beneath her dignity and were also not appropriate for her.

And besides, nothing would bring her back to this region, and certainly not at night. The very word "suburb" was repugnant to her. She equated it with *banlieue*, and had the conventional adjectives at her fingertips—"dreary," "characterless," "gray"—like a travel writer who goads his readers to seek out exotic places, as far away as possible, with a title like "Forget the Banlieue!"

She, who came from a town in the provinces, had always dreamed of getting away, and in the end found herself in a similar region, with the same poky houses and streets that were deserted at night, while the proximity of the metropolis just over the hills, its glow lighting up the eastern sky, tore at her heart rather than soothing it. With time she came to see some virtues in this particular suburb, made fun of the teeny-tiny middle- and working-class houses as amiably as she made fun of Gaudí's edifices in Barcelona. She got to know merchants and tradespeople with whom I hardly ever exchanged more than a hello; in the special silence of the wooded hills she had her own spots, which she alone visited and which were off-limits to me. Yet life on a grand scale could take place only in the hub, on the other side of the mountains, as she called the barely hundred-thirty-meter-high ridge. The suburban world here remained for her—to use the expression of the singer's, who, a child of this area, composed one of his angry songs about it— "rotten."

No one would come. I would remain alone with a couple of strangers at a bar in the most remote recess of the bay. And stories are told, for instance: it snows; or: something is going on. I am receptive, and the others, I sense, likewise. And up there in the woods sparks would fly from a nocturnal horseback rider, and that mythical beast, which I expect to turn up any day now in the forest, almost devoid of wild animals and yet so overgrown, has pricked up its ears at least once already for its first appearance.

But every time this nocturnal storytelling has no effect. Because it takes place so remotely, among marginal people, and only there, only there now? "But that can't be," I think, "it has to have some effect."

———

A year ago, when the priest from my native village visited me in this obscure corner while on his way to Chartres—about which he did not want anything said—"I'm here with you, not on my way to somewhere else!"—he spoke of how solitaries belonged together in the diaspora, which nowadays was the place where, for people like us, things were most likely to go on, one person here, another there, which I denied: I expected nothing from a community of the scattered people, the chosen, from secret circles with secret writings and initiation rites, but rather . . . and here, as so often before, I had no idea what I wanted to say next.

The priest, standing there, legs apart as at home, winked at me as if he did not believe me, and as though we both knew better. I now felt even more left to my own devices than before. He had come unannounced, as though my house, three countries away, belonged to his parish, and in the back of his car, which was splattered with mud from top to bottom as only the forest ranger's was here, he had a plaster cast of the Romanesque kings from our village church, which the two of us then hauled to the farthest corner of the yard, where the three knee-high torsos now present their thick-lipped smiles.

A community of the scattered was something I believed in only during a period of transition.

And just as little am I guided by an earlier idea, the product not only of a lack but also of something visible: that of a people. I have never believed in a national people, equally little in a religious people, a linguistic people, and never in The People with the definite article. But neither can I believe anymore in a people of minorities, of people waiting, of readers, of sufferers and victims.

There was only one period in my life when I had the notion of preserving all the changing, indefinable peoples in whom I believed in some more durable form, and even then that could be only something written—not legal files—only a book.

That was at the time when I was a lawyer, barely thirty, and was not yet writing. I was renting a room in a house up in the hills of Sievering, in the north end of Vienna, and I was working with an older colleague in his firm out past Baden, outside the capital, along the Southern Railway. For several years my existence alternated almost daily between completely anonymous travel by bus, trolley car, and train, and contact, which grew more and more intimate from appointment to appointment, with society, the highest levels as well as the lowest, not only that of the city of Vienna but that of all of Austria. In both realms, as an anonymous observer and as an actor in the plot, I became completely engrossed. Yet I was not leading a double life, but rather a twofold one, each part in harmony with the other.

That finally amazed me so greatly that for a time I visualized a human comedy, loosely modeled on Balzac, a narrative of society moving constantly back and forth between names and the nameless, but even freer than Balzac, I imagined, more open, less obsessed with death, since I, like him, believed not so much in a specific people as in this one or that one, even if only in walking or driving by. In my head the book already had a title. It was called "The Apothecary of Erdberg."

My contemporary novel of society—through which wafted the ever-present epic of the undefined people encountered on the street and in public transportation—came to naught. I did not even begin it (although the real apothecary of Erdberg, who in those days sat next to me at table for an evening, still sends me material year after year from far away and hints that if we were together he would have a lot to tell me for my book). The more closely I scrutinized my plan, the less the people with whom I had daily dealings seemed suitable as heroes or even as characters in a book. And if they did fit into a book, then only one that had long since been written, for instance Doderer's *Strudlhofstiege*.

But even in this saga, in those days already situated far back in the past, I did not find my Viennese and Austrian acquaintances anywhere as participants. When I sat in my room out in Sievering at the end of the 1960s and closed my eyes to the beautiful view and thought about them one at a time, they all, even the oldest among them, lacked that "depth of the years," even in their fragmentariness, that would have qualified them to be developed by Doderer.

Whether as a thirty-year-old then or now, a quarter of a century later,

I was not really interested in finding a past that would lend depth to the people in question for my book. But some sort of background, even if it were lit up just for a second as if by lightning, was what I needed for them, for each of them, to let me get launched on telling stories around them, and finally even about all of them at once, if possible.

Nowhere did I see such a background, no matter how often I went over my acquaintances, one after the other. Although most of them, except for my outsider and criminal acquaintances, constituted members of one and the same society, in my mind they did not fit together anywhere. That had nothing to do with my assessment of them or society. They were simply out of the question, no matter how I respected or hated them, for inclusion in a book. Not even the solitaries, the outlaws and strangers, with whom I often had a more intimate association than with the others, appeared to me against the background of a book, or the background remained dull and lifeless. For my imagination, for the book, it had to be alive, bright or dark, short, incomplete—as short and incomplete as possible.

I knew too much about my people in those days. Since I was someone to whom people confessed things, I knew the most secret lives of many. Of course, the heroes of my book were supposed to have a second, secret life. My image of it was completely different, however. So why not attribute it to those unknowns who, as fellow passengers, as people in line with me, as passersby, were supposed to populate the book from beginning to end? No; for then the passersby would lose their fantastic contours in my eyes, too. In those days I was coming to know so many in my country's society from close up that eventually all sorts of people hurrying through the streets appeared to me, when they spoke their first word, if not before, as those I had known by heart for a long time. There, wearing a Tyrolese hunting cap, went the police commissioner, or someone just like him. There, crowded together on the back seat, were all those I had defended that year. There, leaving the perfume shop, was a woman who could be the secret mistress of the professor of Roman law. On the outskirts, in Rodaun, in Mauer, in Weidling, in Hütteldorf, in Heiligenstadt, in Schwechat, I encountered in strangers the waiters, teachers, judges, pimps, and women with whom I had been on first-name terms for what seemed like forever, and to whom I had just said goodbye in the inner districts. That silhouette over there on the commuter train was my landlord. When the exotic-looking person on the bus opened his mouth, he turned out to be my neighbor, the one with a boat in his backyard, with the wife who took a fatal tumble on the stairs, with the child whose heart stopped beating during a tonsillectomy.

Only once during that time did a stranger pierce me through and through and yet remain unfamiliar, without dissolving into the double of a type I knew from society. It happened on a streetcar, not an ordinary one but one that went out into the country, the so-called local to Baden. One day, for almost an hour, a woman I did not know sat diagonally across from me, all the way from the Opera House to a central market somewhere outside the city. Beauty is something I have very seldom seen in people, and then always this way: a person was initially not beautiful but became so, over time or all of a sudden. The woman in the local was beautiful immediately, and remained so until she got off; nothing could touch her. When I say, "The beautiful woman was warm and friendly," it sounds to me like "The grass was green" or "The snow was white," and yet it is the only thing I can say about her (although I recall various features). She made me see what mattered, in my life, in the book.

It was summertime, many empty seats on the streetcar, a lot of light, especially out there in the meadows, beyond the city limits. A child, not a small one, was sitting beside the beautiful woman, then on her lap. I did not manage, and this was fortunate for me, to see the woman as a mother, as the wife of some man, of a doctor, an architect, a soccer star. She defied all categorization. She could not be a hairdresser, a businesswoman, a television anchor, a speleologist, a poet, a model, a motorcyclist, a second Marilyn Monroe or a second Cleopatra, a queen or a singer.

And during all this time I played soccer on Saturday afternoons with, among others, a cabinet minister of about my age, who once confided in me, in the cafeteria of our suburban stadium, that since childhood he had been waiting for his father, who had disappeared in the mountains, to come home. And a surgeon, with whom I went hiking in the Vienna Woods on quite a few weekends, half circling the city, once described to me how during operations he often felt the urge to plunge both hands into the patient's liver, for example (he had very large hands).

And frequently I also sat in a certain outdoor café alone, the last one there, and the proprietor, after the waiters and kitchen help had long since left, would come and join me, expounding on the variations in Austrian dialect, intoning the nuances in pronunciation from valley to valley, with barely perceptible sound shifts, like a series of magic incantations; or he would trot out hunting adventures he had as a specialist in sick animals, none of which he had ever left alive, and when he had followed their sweat trail for days, clambering over cirques and dodging avalanches: "There you are, finally!" and "Always a clean shot!" Often almost the whole night would pass while we talked under the linden tree, which kept the rain off the two of us, except for occasional drizzle. Or I stood in half-darkness in the closed ward by the rails of the bed to which the notary's wife was strapped, while she implored me to report her situation to her husband (who had committed her to the mental hospital).

And the man who sat down next to me in all my regular bars, dressed in the light-colored suit of a man-about-town, was a monk, and every time he was coming from giving religious instruction to pupils each of whose ears he would have liked to box. And the man in a too small gray smock who waved to me from a distance while loading packages in the yard of a local post office on the outskirts of town—I realized it only out on the street—had been the headwaiter at the Bristol Hotel just the week before. And when I rang the bell of the artist couple's apartment because I had left something behind, I heard from behind the door cries of passion, which the most insistent ringing could not interrupt—and just a moment ago, in my presence, and all evening in fact, they had been spitting their mutual hatred in each other's faces. And the traveler to India told me that in the place where he went every year, to get away from society here, he rubbed shoulders with the world's elite, whereupon his equally gentle girlfriend told me he went away only because he had his brother's death on his conscience, and as she spoke these words she slipped her bare foot between my legs under the table.

I knew the place where the former Olympic bronze medalist in the slalom, long since homeless, slept in an underground parking garage, knew that the deputy mayor went fishing only because of his depression, spent several nights with my construction-worker brother in the barracks in Simmering where his crew of itinerant ironworkers from Carinthia was staying, was one of the few allowed to attend the funeral of the murdered gambling kingpin, a book publisher on the side, at which his SS friend, a presidential advisor at the time, delivered a graveside eulogy during which he repeatedly broke down, and his wife then had the St. Stephen's concert choir sing the Mozart Requiem, practiced specially for the occasion.

M y *comédie humaine* from the Austria of that period, modeled loosely on Balzac and Doderer and the Civil Code, remained a figment of my imagination.

Although at times I saw all the characters sharply delineated in my mind's eye, there were still several rather strange reasons why the story did not allow itself to be written, at least not by me. Perhaps the strangest: on the one hand I intended to capture all of society, including the terrorist (today a housewife once more) urging her cause on me in a staccato whisper as we huddled in a broom closet at the chancellery; including the Yugoslav guest worker, his skin reddened from his work in a laundry, in his free time painting signs for pubs on the eastern outskirts of Vienna, a man who despised the Albanians because they "didn't have any butts in their britches," father of a half-Albanian child, off in distant Priština with its mother.

On the other hand not a single person in this society seemed to fit with anyone else, no matter how I closed my eyes and racked my brains, not even within the established groups, academic and social classes, associations, clubs, and cliques.

Each of these people appeared to me in my imagination alone, without a link to a second or third party of whatever sort.

Not that I had in mind a connectedness, even the most fleeting unity, for this society; its members merely refused to let themselves to be pictured in one and the same story. And the others out there simply appeared as doubles.

Another problem was that on the one hand the individuals whom I was considering as preliminary sketches for my own inventions did not cease to baffle me the more they revealed themselves, and on the other hand not one of them seemed inspired by anything—a cause, a mission. (In my conception, "The Society of the Inspired" had been the book's subtitle, after "The Apothecary of Erdberg.") After they unveiled their secrets I actually found not a few of them good and decent, and could even admire and respect quite a number of them, and not only a doctor for being on call at night or a politician for switching his allegiance from one segment of society to another or a bus driver on snowy mountain roads. The only problem: not one of them revealed anything that sparked my imagination.

And similarly I was preoccupied with the evildoers, no less numerous; they assailed me, would not leave me in peace, even in my dreams. Yet they, too, did not galvanize or stimulate me, not even the public speaker during whose hate-filled tirades I could picture all the manhole covers blowing off around his followers gathered on the open square, and the skulls of the dead emerging.

Neither the former nor the latter were anything for my book. Among all these many people, none provided the appropriate starting point, or even the most delicately traced first initial; this only my ancestors offered, the dead and the disappeared.

At the time I came to believe that people in a story could not have anything to do with the living, no matter whom.

When I explained this one time to the petty prophet of Porchefontaine, he replied that I should have started nonetheless. A false start was often more productive than the right one. And besides, nowadays there were nothing but false starts for books. How could I be sure that with the first sentence of my present project I hadn't turned my key in a door that led nowhere? And wasn't it possible that I had been deterred from writing my novel of society merely by the prospect that it would have to be one of those obscenely fat books that both of us despised on sight?

———

Even when writing was not yet my profession, as in those days when I was still an attorney, it already guided my life, less the *how* than the *where*. As the years went by and I realized that the country and people of Austria were antithetical to the book of my dreams, I went away to be among the most distant foreigners.

I never attended the School of Foreign Service. When I was with the United Nations, whether first in New York or later as an observer in Israel and Mongolia, where I was working for UNESCO, even if I was called an attaché or a vice-consul or something else, I was either an office worker or the right-hand man to one and the same clever diplomat I knew from my days in Vienna.

Almost every day in New York I would bump into our future federal president, who confused me with someone else, and always with the comment that I spoke remarkably unaccented German for a Slav. The woman from Catalonia said later that I had written my article attacking him just to get revenge; she herself, who at the time knew him from the East River, sometimes held him up to me as an example, with his way of never revealing his thoughts, also his bearing, his dress, his refusal to touch anything for which others, inferiors, servants, could be called upon, his way of never showing any feelings, either joy or sorrow.

In Israel, when she visited me, I found just enough time to get away from the gun emplacements on the Golan Heights for a week on the Lake of Gennesaret, lying there with its locked-up villas and tied-up boats like the Austrian lakeside resorts in winter, except that it was not frozen over but rain-gloomy, then farther into the basin of the Jordan and the Dead Sea, where, far below normal sea level, in that region that had always attracted me, we begat our child, amid her cries of pain—from the salt—and then uphill through the desert to Jericho, with its sand-shimmering desolation, its rustling palms, interminable Arab music blaring from the terraces, among natives who seemed invisible, and then also up in Jerusalem, until that night outside the walls, on Mount Olive, where suddenly in the moonlight, crisscrossed by jet trails, stones came pelting down, if only against the wall, not on the two of us sitting there.

In Mongolia, where I then spent three summers and three winters with a group providing development aid from various UNESCO countries, I remained just as much on the outside, though in a different way.

Previously no opening had presented itself to me anywhere. In Ulan Bator, on the other hand, as in the whole empire, one opportunity for participation after another turned up. Except that I—did not want to? —resisted.

I shared an apartment, two rooms in one of the few multistory buildings in the nomads' capital city, with a German friend who belonged to our group and was my exact opposite as far as dealings with the Mongolians went. Although he had more trouble than I with Russian, the lingua franca, from his first evening on he immersed himself in the population, and that became his nickname, "Mr. Immersion." No sooner had he set down his luggage than he was outside again and in the midst of the natives, and since the surrounding area offered neither a teahouse nor a refreshment stand, he located the nearest gathering place, downstairs in the doorless entry to our building. As I leaned out of the window upstairs, he was standing on the nonexistent threshold among the much shorter native inhabitants, already one of them. He gesticulated, laughed with them, nodded, and when I looked down again was already squatting like a tailor or a Bedouin or a camel among them, rocking his head like an initiate, with the hand of the man who was toasting him resting on his shoulder.

In our team, my German friend was the most taciturn of all. In our shared apartment, too, he remained silent, only bursting out now and then with a snatch of an almost unbelievable story, and promptly falling back into his brooding, which got on my nerves so much that I, who as a rule also liked to keep still, became the one who did the talking. But the minute he saw natives, anywhere, he would join them so effortlessly that my eyes could not keep up, and would gab with them until late at night, fluently, yes, passionately, and at the same time casually, as if he had always known them, even if no one from his new tribe could understand a word he was saying. And later, from the Yukon River in Alaska, from the bar at the trading post, he sent me on his first evening there a postcard with the signatures and X's of all the Indians of Region Circle City, and then the Tuaregs in southern Algeria recited immediately after his arrival their most closely guarded poems for him, even into a tape recorder. Although he was German, never really at home and at the same time crowding the available space with his bearing, gestures, and language, he remained out of place only among whites, among Westerners. Among his Tuaregs, Athabaskans, and Kirghiz he seemed to be borne up by the others' gracefulness, swallowed up in the twinkling of an eye, their long-awaited faithful comrade.

I, on the contrary—who from my first day in Mongolia vibrated with the people there as previously, at all hallowed times, only with the Slovenians, my mother's people—I ducked every opportunity to immerse myself in their company.

I was timid about getting involved in situations where something resonated in me simply as a result of my standing by. The steppe and its peoples inspired me. It was as if I had already sat here as a child, over there next to the door, wide open in summertime, in the village of Rinkolach on the eastern edge of the Carinthian Jaunfeld Plain, or over there in the grassy triangle at the junction of two roads—except that the image was now animated by figures, more numerous than in those days, and the right ones. Yes, here I did not even make a judgment as to whether I was with the right ones or the wrong ones: it was obvious that on those dusty streets, under those wooden colonnades, and on the savanna, on runways or over the grass and far away, it was my people wobbling, stumbling along, waddling toward each other. Not only from the almost treeless wide-open spaces but also from the crowds of people such light streamed over me that I moved about day and night with my eyes half closed.

After several months, when I no longer stood out as a foreigner anywhere, even among the children, I thought I had taken on the appearance of a native and saw myself in the mirror as such. Not only that I no longer saw any eyelids; even my eyes seemed to have blackened. From beneath similarly black hair I gazed at myself inscrutably and amiably. And for those three years this carried me along out there among the people, without conflict or any other complication.

At intervals the woman from Catalonia came to visit me, the second time with our son, still blond at the time, and a complete stranger to me, and once I invited my sister to Ulan Bator for a few weeks.

How astonished I was, and disappointed, that members of my family recognized me, did not so much as raise their eyebrows.

Yet I was increasingly fearful of disappearing. I felt completely at ease among the Mongolians, included in whatever was going on, and at the same time I was afraid of never getting home. I would not have known where to go home to, yet I felt driven to go home—or a creature that came alive inside me did, like a dog abandoned on a highway median strip. Again and again I had flying dreams, which began blissfully and broke off not with my crashing but with my no longer existing.

Later I read in the works of anthropologists that they experienced something similar. Except that in the beginning they always set out planning to study the foreign people or tribe systematically, and only later recoiled in alarm from it, or from themselves, whereas I did not want to know anything in particular about the local people. Precisely because the things I had known about them beforehand hardly mattered anymore in their presence, I felt at home among them. My very enthusiasm about being among them was partly a function of my ignorance.

Of course I took notes and made sketches, and did both regularly, day after day, to keep both feet on the ground and avoid dissolving in ecstasy. But it was not a question of observing this particular country and its people. The sketches showed only things that might have been anywhere, like a pair of unlaced shoes, viewed from above, or a lightning rod that disappeared at the bottom into a block of concrete. But: were there ever lightning storms? And the Tatars who turned up in my notes were not referred to as "Tatars" or some such thing; they were just villagers or people I encountered.

As we know, on the heels of those anthropologists people journeyed to all the still halfway unspoiled landscapes in the world, arriving by plane, bus, all-terrain vehicle, sometimes covering the last stretch on foot, each of them proudly alone, and even before they got there from their American and European headquarters, they were on intimate terms with the most closely guarded traditional tales of the natives, no matter where. They called themselves "nomads," had the lightest and sturdiest footgear on earth, as luggage a little backpack with two books; they mingled with the original inhabitants as if they had known them from earliest childhood, and upon their return, in the period before their next departure, this time for Tibet instead of for Australia, they had hundreds of amusing stories, anecdotes, and hair-raising adventures to tell.

I knew a man like this who set out each time with his hands completely unencumbered; he had nothing but his passport and his pockets full of dollar bills. I became fond of him. From each adventure he survived—the coiled snake he encountered when coming down from the Andes and chopped in five pieces with one blow of his machete; the skeletons he stumbled upon in the water at the bottom of a gorge as he let himself down on a rope in the sacred Cenote of the Yucatán Peninsula, victims of the Mayas or recent?—he returned more lost and confused to his Central European wife and his meanwhile grown-up children: Where am I? And what now? And at the same time his stories were much too carefully constructed around a climax for my taste, not that he ever bragged—as though he himself were not really experiencing anything in telling them—and also too matter-of-fact and unamazed: a sweeping gesture, and he was the shaman himself, acted out the dervish. After an evening with him, chock full of perils he had miraculously survived and fluently rattled-off secrets of the bush, from Tierra del Fuego to Hokkaido, I took leave of my nomadic friend with a certain ennui, and found myself longing for a place where there was nothing, yearning for nothingness, nothingness upon nothingness, right around the corner (and half a year later was looking forward to his next visit).

More worrisome were the new nomads, who had no sooner tracked down what remained of the aboriginals anywhere in the world than they put them in a book. These books all shared the characteristic of presenting the most intimate portraits of a people-outside-of-civilization as something that existed in only one place, and then, in the same breath, exposing these portraits to the entire world, with the result that all the fuss about protecting and supporting these peoples ended up by wiping them out once and for all by means of facile stories in which the narrator from distant parts pushed his natives back and forth like pawns and mucked around in their dream as if it were his special property. And perhaps it actually did belong to him, and in the traditions of various obscure tribes he was seeing the cosmos of his childhood, spent in Friuli or in Glastonbury. Except that these journeyers to the ends of the earth never told us that. Their own half-vanished notions, of time, the cosmos, nonbeing, ancestors, doubles, were of no interest to them. To them only the dreams of the last more or less aboriginal human beings constituted a valid book.

But perhaps I was merely envious, as the woman from Catalonia expressed it one time when I was raging against the "plunderers." Their stories, she said, were more worldly than mine, and also more dialogic. I got in my own way, she said, with my endless brooding over form; I lacked narrative technique, while they deployed such technique effortlessly and wrote now like nineteenth-century Russian novelists, now like American novelists of the first half of the twentieth century. And when I continued to rant about these books that had no narrator any longer but instead a master of ceremonies, about those purveyors of reading fodder whose material was so thoroughly processed that nothing was left to read, she commented that I was also jealous because they had caught on. They had a following—and I? A year ago, that crazed woman standing at my garden gate every morning; and that man dying in the local hospital; and that travel-agency courier; and that farmer's son in Ontario, Canada.

One way or the other, I continued to be guided during those three Mongolian summers and winters by the idea of a book, and then I did write one, my first, the "Drowsy Story," which dealt not with the local population but with my village ancestors, long since dead, in Carinthia along the Yugoslav border.

I did that during my day job, which consisted of teaching German or English, or handling correspondence, or giving typing lessons. In the summer I put my table outside, by the edge of the road. Neither dust nor sun nor people bothered me. And from those days I still have a longing to be able, just once in my life, to write an entire book from beginning to end outdoors, and not just in a backyard, but far out on the steppe. Never have I breathed so freely, and moved along with the day so effortlessly. And the local people did not seem bothered in the slightest, and eventually not even the people's militia. A militiaman who stopped each time on his rounds and looked at the sheet of paper in front of me one day even predicted a glorious future for this beginner.

Writing the book became the one great experience of my years in Mongolia. Although the woman from Catalonia hardly visited me, I did not take up with any native woman. Only once did I walk with a girl down a dirt road, behind a herd of cattle, which, although we were too far back to overtake them between the stone walls, let loose with their constant farting and defecating one stench after the other on the half-infatuated couple. And when my sister came to visit, I did lie in her embrace, but only in a dream.

Back in Europe I went through that period in which I firmly believed in the possibility of connections among individuals separated by great distances, including people who did not even know each other personally.

With my first writing phase behind me, I saw myself as pretty much alone in my further undertakings and thus caught wind of a person here and a person there, particularly beyond the borders—a writer, a naturalist, a linguist—who had likewise struck out on his own to track something down, and thus, as he moved along his particular orbit, belonged to me as I to him. These few, all of whose works I studied, appeared to me in my imagination like the landscapes that filled me with greatest enthusiasm: in the midst of all that hemmed me in, they provided an inner source of light. That was a feeling of exaltation such as I never experienced with friends. These others like me caused something within me to glow, or saved me, like my two or three favorite parts of the world, from despair. It was not merely a way out, but rather a destination refreshing to my heart.

The two lights inside me have gone out. First the distant and the closer countries vanished from within me—the steppes of Mongolia, the highlands of the Cerdagne in the Pyrenees—then my imagined allies beyond the seven mountains. (My only remaining ally resides on the nearest opposite slope, and at the end of our visits to one another I see in this petty prophet of Porchefontaine more and more a caricature of my idea.)

Was this merely because I later met my absent figures of light face to face, or rather was brought together with them, through intermediaries?

Each of them seemed possibly even more reluctant than I, at any rate less generous with himself, or, on the contrary, proposed an alliance to me, thereafter plaguing me across the continents with dedications of his early-morning aphorisms, his minutest linguistic or legal glosses, his exhibition catalogues from Lübeck to Solothurn and Osaka.

None of these scattered folk casts light anymore. Nowadays the diaspora does not provide a community for me, and offers me nothing for my book.

Meanwhile it is almost March here in the bay, and finally snow has come, too. Last night the roofs of the cars coming down from the plateau had a thick layer of white on them, and the sparrows in the birds' sleeping tree in front of the Hôtel des Voyageurs crouched there in the cold, fluffed up to twice their size.

And in front of the unlit palace of Versailles, shining out of the darkness, after an hour's walk in a westerly direction along the Route Nationale 10, veils of snow crystals slithered and lapped over the huge, deserted open square, and a young stranger, his Walkman over his ears, the only person out and about, smiled at me out of the snowstorm, and I thought of several people who had once meant something to me, whose day I had accompanied in my thoughts for a time, and who nonetheless were now out of the question for this story of my distant friends.

In contrast to the singer as text seeker, the painter as filmmaker, the carpenter as architect, the reader, my son, the priest, my woman friend, I have lost those others. A whole series of people who for years were very close to me no longer exist, and not because they have died. They are all living, on the other side of the railroad tunnel, in Paris, farther away in Munich, Vienna, Rinkenberg, Jerusalem, Fairbanks, Ptuj. From time to time I still hear from these people with whom I was once on such good terms. But it no longer moves me, there are no sympathetic vibrations inside me now; when I hear them mentioned, I feel reluctance and revulsion. Unlike my rally participants, no matter how I would like to recall their image from before, I cannot bring them to mind. The trail of light left by these figures, who once seemed cut out to be companions for life, has been extinguished, and its place has been taken by something dark, without our having become enemies.

And that seems final. Never again, I have to assume, would we find our way back together, either through a heart-to-heart talk or through your or my masterpiece.

And then yesterday, continuing around the side of the palace of Versailles, between those pitch-black former edifices of power, on the street with its massive cobblestones, on which the tires made a deep, humming sound as the cars rounded the bend, I saw the snow dancing tier upon tier into the night sky, transected by a dove, and thought of the only politician who had ever been close to me, who now, after his fall from power, sat there in his retirement quarters, around the corner from his successor, in the heart of Vienna.

He had been a professor of jurisprudence, with an international reputation, summoned from everywhere to deal with urgent situations like a crack firefighter; then minister of justice, and it was no mere rumor that he secretly ran the government. Abroad, too, this little Austrian cabinet minister was received as a major statesman. And it was he who phoned me himself, long after I had left the diplomatic service, to say he had just finished my book about my youth in the rural boarding school; he had stayed up all night reading. He invited me to call on him as soon as possible, at the office or elsewhere, at any time of day.

So I met with him again and again, this man whom I had previously known only from a distance, at the university, where he had never been one of my examiners. We met either at his place in Vienna, on the rare occasions when I came to that city, or in Paris, where I was already living at the time, or later outside the city, in the Seine hills, though in a different suburb. The double doors in his ministry seemed to swing open by themselves, and not until I was leaving did I notice how high up the latches were. And likewise, whenever I stood with him at the window in his cavernous office, the squares and parks of the city seemed vertiginously far below, and I was in a hurry every time to get back on a level with the ground and out into the fresh air as soon as possible.

Perhaps he did not have that much power, but it was his power I sensed above all, specifically as a sort of remoteness from ordinary people, even when he recited to me his entire schedule of meetings for that day, with people from all levels of society, from a reception for the Boy Scouts to having a glass of wine with war veterans. I, who spoke with no one for days or weeks on end, saw myself in comparison, at least during those hours, as closer to life, perhaps even immersed in it.

Astonishing how formal his bearing was there, so entirely different from the way he came across on the telephone, although of all his visitors that day I was the only one who had no agenda and also as a rule came at noon, when in any case he merely slipped behind a screen for a snack, in half-darkness. Each of his gestures he acted out, repeated, as if to call attention to it. It was as though this hour with me had an agenda after all: to bear witness to him in office. To be sure, he never said so, but it became apparent that he was inviting me as a chronicler, or at least as one such. Even the delicately rolled slices of ham and dill pickles he shared with me in his niche were supposed to be recorded for later. He never asked about my work, only reported on himself, his next piece of legislation, his most recent trip abroad, not exactly in the form of dictation but certainly with a few repeated turns of phrase that I was supposed to note. He shared these stories with me—about his illnesses, his mistresses—in the tacit conviction that I was there to capture them for posterity.

This became the game that brought us together, operative particularly during his visits to Paris, where each time he appeared with such a large entourage that to me, the witness, at least during his period in office, the country we had in common seemed to possess worldwide importance. When he strode through a salon or a hall of mirrors, with his likewise dark-suited, though much younger, more athletic-looking gentlemen at his heels, always about to dash off to his next appointment, he left in his wake the aura of a historic moment; that was how matter-of-factly and majestically he embodied his power.

And in his presence that impression never faltered, even when he ducked away from his retinue and drove with me out to the little restaurant in Fontaine Ste.-Marie, in the first forest bay beyond Paris, sat there outdoors under the giant oaks and sniffed the cloth napkins, always still a bit damp, pointed out to me the button missing from his double-breasted suit, or the way his eyes were watering because they were no longer used to the country air, enjoying his anonymity with almost child-like pleasure, one among others on the terrace, yet with emphatic, constantly repeated references to the next gathering expecting him over yonder in the metropolis.

Since his fall from power he has been traveling almost more than before, but I have seen him only once, at his own place. Whereas previously I could call on him at the office whenever I liked, now I was given an appointment—"We'll squeeze you in." And when I came, I had to wait a long time—as I get older, I like waiting—in a windowless vestibule; the "minister" (they spoke as if he were still in office) was being interviewed over the telephone by Swedish Radio. There was a dizzying to-and-fro of secretaries, butlers, bodyguards, chauffeurs, masseurs, creating the impression of an entire court. In the room I was ushered into, there was also only artificial light; although it was daytime, heavy draperies covered the windows. And when the retiree descended the staircase and also later, when he talked at me, in the presence of a third party, a sort of recording secretary, it was as if he did not recognize me, and I, too, found this politician, whom I had respected as I did no one else, more and more unrecognizable the longer he talked.

What he said reminded me of visits to mental hospitals when I was a lawyer. Here, too, areas shielded from the outside world, and indoor air, hovering near the floor, closing in around your feet; here, too, delusions of omnipotence. Except that in this case the pale figure, shuffled off into nowhereland, had really been—and not that long ago—the major historical actor for whom he now took himself. And that made the situation far less funny than with an obviously insane person in an asylum, and at the same time far more uncanny. There was nothing to laugh or smile about, and no one could even muster any sympathy for this man (as had strangely happened to me once on a visit to the commandant of Vilna, responsible for the murder of many Jews, who took himself for the author of "He who never ate his bread with tears . . ." and recited the poem accordingly, sternly and proudly, as if even the meter were his own creation, not Goethe's). And while the former politician continued to play at power, I tried to catch the eye of the recording secretary, to exchange a conspiratorial glance, but in vain: she ignored me. In the past he had shown himself a statesman in the way he glossed the world situation with a casualness that breathed authority.

Now, too, he issued an uninterrupted stream of commentary, but his casual remarks to those around him had turned into a sort of prattle. If in power he had been laconic and pithy, he now repeated each hollow comment at least three times. If as a man of power he had been the epitome of presence of mind, impossible to dupe, at the same time displaying a charming roguishness, he now seemed absentminded and humorless. Previously, even when he was reviewing the troops, his independence of mind had manifested itself; now he was merely officious, like a wooden doll (and his handshake felt mechanical when I took leave of him). As a man in power he had appeared muscular, massive; now, although he spent time every day in his workout room, he looked pasty and shapeless. And if he still read books at night, it was only to find material for the ones he himself was dictating.

I stood for a long time on the street outside his darkened house, horrified at this phenomenon that had once again leaped out at me, a chimerical world.

Several writing days have passed since the snowfall. It was snowing well into March, although close to the ground it was not cold at all; the early stinging nettles were already sprouting, the most painful ones. The snow came in fitful gusts, out of the underbrush, as if from a tree blooming in secret or as if tossed, just a handful of grains at a time, tiny snowballs that dissolved in flight into single flakes, floated down, parachutelike, and immediately melted, leaving little dark spots on the asphalt.

But then with the waxing moon it turned bitter cold over the bay. The ponds, especially the wild nameless one deep in the woods, froze over, the dark ice patterned in the form of kinked reeds, and during my walk out there, before I settled down in my study off the garden, I skipped pebbles over the surface, which pinged, whirred, snapped, peeped through the forest as if from a plucked instrument, and sometimes one of the birds hidden in the water shrubbery felt spoken to and replied.

I did that also to invoke the image of another person who had once been close to me. It was maybe ten years ago that he and I had been out walking here on a winter's day and came upon a frozen forest pond where we made the pebbles sing.

As I threw them alone this time, I recalled having him next to me, and I was reminded of his windup, awkward, like that of a chubby child, and when we played soccer, he always missed the ball with his foot, and yet it was always he, the clumsy one, who found the more innocent pleasure in such things. How else to explain his crowing laughter, even when, after a huge windup, his stone, always too large, plopped through the ice without a sound.

This man had been a reader for years, so full of enthusiasm that when he talked about a book even people soured on writing or on distant terms with books got fired up or at least grew pensive or puzzled, and those who still did read, halfheartedly, remembered what it had been like when they first discovered books. He, like the politician, was some-what older than I, a teacher at a Jewish school on the western edge of Paris, without wife or children; in response to a book in which I de-scribed living with my son for the first time, he had written me the shortest, most trenchant letter, the kind I would have liked to bestow on someone else: "The story you have written is true. The child is your work."

This man loved being outdoors, "even though I'm a Jew," as he said, and thus as often as once a month the two of us would walk the two stretches of forest from Paris to Versailles, the southern stretch from Meudon and the northern one from St.-Cloud.

Along a firebreak, the piles of felled trees all pointed one time in the same direction, every treetop facing toward the mosque-white domes of Sacré-Coeur, many kilometers away, a vista I still look for today and do not find again, unlike the wild strawberries along the path that can be counted on to redden in the same ditches at the end of June.

No matter how citified he looked in his hat, tie, and oxfords, the teacher found no terrain too arduous. His clothes soaked by rain, his soles slipping and sliding in the clay, his glasses fogged up, he trudged along gamely. All through the war, while still a child, he had been in hiding in a cellar in the heart of Paris, and now he enjoyed life every day, especially the parts without deep significance. At certain moments while we walked, the tiered horizons of the Seine hills up ahead, even as he stumbled along—this seemed to be his rhythm—he, who was also often gripped by fear of death, preached of a sort of immortality there in the region beyond the hills; wasn't the fact that this area repeatedly promised immortality a kind of proof in itself?

Yet even at that time he was convinced that the end of the world was imminent, and it would come from Germany, all of whose landscapes he carried around with him—and here he would point to his chest. In response to the violent acts of the Baader-Meinhof gang, he commented, "This is the end!" and then the same when they committed suicide in prison. We were sitting that autumn evening on a quiet, well-lit square in Paris, and he stared into the darkness, which under his eyes grew denser among the trees and seemed to close in on us; he said it without a trace of smugness, filled with childlike or primitive horror.

Years later he began to mistrust me, although he continued to write interested letters about what I was doing. This change, I now thought, as I made the little stones ping over the ice of the nameless pond, had started with my asking him to do something for me. I had noticed much earlier how difficult he could become the moment you specifically requested something of him. Any schoolboy lie was good enough for him when it came to dodging others' expectations. And one time he was supposed to mail something to me in Germany, where I was spending a few weeks to be with my father (which yielded the "Writer's Tour"). I managed to persuade him, although he said he had dislocated his leg; the post office lay in the opposite direction from his school; and the air in post offices brought on asthma attacks.

He finally mailed the envelope, but because he had put it off so long, I was no longer at the address I had given him, and the item was sent back. And upon my return he suddenly burst out in a hate-filled tirade. In Germany they had looked at the return address and seen "a Jewish name," and that was why they had sent the envelope back. "A Jew! Return to sender!" And those were my countrymen!

He calmed down, and for a while things were all right, until he wrote that he had tried to read my first book, the story of my ancestors, but all these villagers disgusted him. In his eyes they were all anti-Semites, who, if he had grown up among them, would have driven him into exile. Yet my "Drowsy Story" dealt only with rural life after the war, and the

characters were Slavic peasants, many of whose sons had been killed for
a Germany that had never meant anything to them. And in our region
there was not a single Jew, and I recalled a chronicle from the turn of
the century according to which, since even at the village fair, the day
of greatest sociability, there was no Jew among the outside vendors, one
of these had to stand behind his booth dressed as a Jew, in wig and
costume, to make the festival complete—which, however, only confirmed
my acquaintance in his opinion. He continued to announce he was coming out for a walk, but when I was already expecting him he would call
to say he had been detained in town. The times he did come, he would
remark as he was leaving that I was probably glad to be rid of him.

He became most alienated from me when he stopped believing in the
possibility of writing new books, or in books altogether. He, who had
once been able to trumpet his opinion on a book, and books, with the
best of them, now did not even mention a book, no longer asked me
about any book, or refused to listen. It seems as though he has given up
books, and sometimes I can sympathize with him. Only he no longer
comes to see me, and so I cannot tell him that. In his old age he now
walks alone, with his immortality on the horizon, and I daresay he probably never needed me for that.

And I, did I need him? Whom have I ever needed? No one, as the
woman from Catalonia always reproached me.

There would be tales to tell of several others with whom I once considered myself connected and whom I have lost in the meantime, or
can no longer bring to mind. I know they exist, often hardly changed
since my time with them. But whenever I try to picture them and their
day from a distance as I used to, nothing comes to me. I have no associations with them; at their very names darkness closes in.

The same thing happens to me with my previous publisher, whom I
once pictured as showered with happiness when he was reading a manuscript; for entire summers I swam next to him in the icy waters of
mountain lakes, heading for the snow on the opposite bank; we were of
one mind about our books, past and future. He has long since sold all
his book rights to a magazine publishing conglomerate and commutes

between his faith healer in Scheveningen, the Institute for Thalasso-
therapy in San Sebastián, the Rheumatism Center on the Plattensee, the
sulfur baths of Saturnia, the Clinic for Zero Diet in the Caucasus, and
his guest cell in the monastery on Mount Athos. I know where he is at
any given moment; we are not estranged—it is simply that I no longer
see him anywhere. That the rights to everything I had done over the
years did not belong to me: that was wrong.

And it is the same with the woman whom I could view from a distance during one period in my life as my Muse. I knew her from her
letters, but at that time it was enough to think of her for a moment
across the continent and the ocean, and she would be there. Once, when
I was sitting at a loss for words at my writing table, waiting since
morning for a first sentence, which kept announcing its imminent arrival
yet had not come by nightfall, I felt her draw near and silently write
the sentence out for me, and then the next sentences, down the entire
page. And once, when I was flat on my back—and never again would I
be able to get around—she came to be with me and rolled, pulled,
rubbed, stroked, pushed, licked, seasoned, breathed, kneaded, and rendered me mobile for a long time, at least well past Easter, which was
then approaching.

For decades that woman, whose appearance I cannot even describe,
remained in charge of me. From a distance I would turn to her and try
out questions on her that were perhaps being asked for the first time
since the world began, and she would answer without delay. I included
in my books not a few of her letters, always written without corrections.
Yet I did not want to know what she was doing; pictured her as having
children, going to work, tending her house and garden.

In the meantime she no longer answers, has fallen silent for good.
Even before that she gave me to understand that she was disappointed
in me. Then she suddenly turned against me, in a letter of pure hatred.
She severed all connection. I was not the person she had taken me for.
This happened, I told myself, because I always went on as though nothing were wrong. To keep her respect, I would have had to perish. I
would have had to go to hell, and instead I took refuge in my writing.
I would have had to go smash at a certain moment. I would not have
been allowed to have a wife or child or an everyday life. I was supposed
to suffer, or at least not hide my suffering, experience martyrdom many

times over, and die a terrible and at the same time pitiful death. Only thus could I have remained true to myself and to her.

During the last days of winter I walked and walked in the cold wind through the woods, and pondered whether it was not I after all who had been forgotten by the others, who had been given up for lost by them. Perhaps I am the one who no longer counts for them, who holds no more surprises for them, who appears in neither their daydreams nor their night dreams?

What, for instance, about the one who of late has been most powerfully present for me in my thoughts as I walked, Filip Kobal from Rinkenberg, the next village over from Rinkolach, whom I once viewed as my successor in writing, more flexible than I, more generous, more warmhearted, more colorful? Yet at one time we often said to each other that it should actually be the other way around, since I came from the village on the sunny side, and he, a few years younger, from the village on the shady side, beyond the hill, which was much steeper there.

We first met as adults, he a lawyer as well; I already had a book to my name, and he at the time was nowhere near that. He did become my successor, at any rate in the legal affairs bureau of the Southern Railway, as a tenant of the house in Sievering, and in other respects, too. Although he was bigger and broader than I, had a more powerful voice, lighter skin and eyes, many mistook him for me. Then, at a distance, I read his first texts and talked him out of all the guilt and self-flagellation he had put into them: "From the shadow of Rinkenberg into the light of Rinkolach!" He, who had previously groaned at the thought of having to go down to the garden gate, learned from me to go walking. Likewise he, who at one time had to clear his throat before every sentence and even then remained almost impossible to understand, became a sought-after reader and panelist, from the heart of Switzerland to Schleswig-Holstein. When he told me, his confidant, that he secretly felt superior to all those around him, that he spent entire evenings sitting alone as if enthroned, with the lights out and the entire world at his feet, I encouraged him to go ahead and let people see that from time to time; it was appropriate for him and his writing, within limits, and since then, whenever he stands up and reads, out comes a mighty voice that drowns out any contradiction, a most remarkable contrast to the diffidence, mumbling, and word-swallowing he still displays in everyday situations. Perhaps he has become an authority even more with his voice than with his books, and at the same time a folksy figure; wherever he appears, he is immediately invited to sing along, to play cards, to go bowling, which is probably unique for our Austria and a homegrown writer, especially nowadays. Yet he still dreads the physical work I recommended to him, partly for waking and schooling his imagination; he recoils at the thought of it, as if this were asking too much of him; a quiver of revulsion runs through him if he has to so much as pick up a trash can. True, he has moved from the shade to the sun of Rinkolach, his house is open to all—natives, refugees, readers—but his elder sister does everything for him, from polishing his shoes to chopping wood and mowing the lawn; with her there, he hardly lifts a finger.

And this Filip Kobal, who could count on being understood by me in a way that a person probably experiences only once in a lifetime, has, I think, turned his back on me forever.

The last straw was his visit to me here in the bay over a year ago. Since then he has sent me not a single sign of life, not even a card from the places where he gives readings, whereas previously I would receive big fat letters from him in his enormous sign painter's handwriting, for which I once praised him, like so much else. A reason for his silence toward me may perhaps lie in the country once so dear to both our hearts, Yugoslavia, which he, as he puts it in an article, has unmasked as his "own personal illusion" and has "smoked out of himself," and which still shines on before me as a reality. But I know that one hour of double-voiced storytelling about that country would suffice, and Kobal and I would be reduced to completely unanimous weeping and cursing, weeping, laughing, and cursing.

No, Filip Kobal has written me off because I settled in a faraway country, rather than where he is convinced I belong. He disapproves, as he told me at the end, of my obstinate, and, according to him, arbitrary, abandonment of my place of origin for something that in no respect seemed necessary, certainly not essential as an "exile" (which, to be sure, I have never in my life asserted a need for). It did no good that on that last visit he roamed for days at my side through the hills and valleys of the Seine, dropped in with me on hundreds of bars, churches, hermitages, houseboats, transmitters, and local radio stations.

I took him to the wintry birds' sleeping tree by the railroad station, even had my opera glasses with me, so that my nearsighted friend could distinguish the massive branches in the plane tree's crown from the motionless sparrow-balls. I shared with him the minutes of the last session of the town council, filled him in on the proportional assignment of seats to the various parties, from community to community within the *département*, with its population in the millions, gave a scintillating account of the early history of the region, from the days of the Romans and the Middle Ages to the liberation in 1944 by the division commanded by General Leclerc. In the church in Sèvres he found himself standing with me by the tiny spiral staircase from the twelfth century that began high above our heads in the wall—there was no other staircase, not even a ladder—and ended who knows where; in Ville d'Avray, as the wind feathered the water, I showed him the ponds painted by Corot; on Mont St.-Valérien near Suresnes we breathed the air in the former Gestapo death cells; in La Défense we stood together, buffeted by the night wind, in the ghostly light of the Grande Arche.

In the forests we crouched side by side over the secret springs from which I had scraped away the leaves for him, whereupon they began to pulse before our eyes. I slipped with him into the underbrush to find the foxes' lair, climbed down with him into the ditch of the giant toad, pointed out to him in passing the rivulet flowing around a menhir, bought apples and milk with him on a farm on the plateau of Saclay, sniffed at his side the great mill of Versailles, passed with him four forest rangers' lodges in a single afternoon, approached with him, without saying a word, as we made our way uphill on the path taken by Jean Racine and Pascal through the meadows along Rhodon Brook, the barns of Port-Royal, of which I hoped to hear my Filip Kobal say that he had never, not even in our Jaunfeld region, seen such noble threshing-floor roofs, soaring so high toward the heavens, mirroring the centuries.

I introduced him to the waitress in the church-bar of Jouy-en-Josas, who unexpectedly addressed him in Slovenian and turned out to have been born in Kosovelje on the karst and to the tarot players in the back room along the Route Nationale 10, who were a group of itinerant

Serbian stonemasons; attended with him the Russian Orthodox Sunday service in the blue wood-frame church in the bay here, no larger than a garden shed, but how many people unexpectedly inside, what an enormous missal, and above us all, in a cloud of incense, the eagle of St. John the Evangelist. I showed him the smocks of the local craftsmen, just as blue as those of the cottagers back home, the shopping bags of the older women, dangling from the crook of their arms on long handles, the pocket knives with wooden grips, so similar to our penknives back home, the numerous blank windows in the houses along the bay, even a hillside with ancient cow paths.

Yet Filip Kobal, after all the days we had spent hiking together, after he had remarked briefly that the region here was exceptionally lively and varied, and that anyone could see I knew my way around like a taxi driver, geographer, and forester all in one—why else would the many people who got lost here instinctively turn to me and receive reliable directions—Filip Kobal said I had spent enough time away from home now. For a long while I had represented a standard for him. As long as I had stuck it out, as his fellow countryman, in writing and also in life, that had given him and a few others the strength to carry on, he would assert. But in the meantime my example was no longer valid. Of course, he himself repeatedly left our country and its people. I, however, had overstayed my time abroad, and it was henceforth inconceivable that he should read my admittedly very original and special writings as before. Of course, he saw the similarities between this place and the region from which we both came, precisely through the differences, but a spiral staircase in Sèvres could never be "my" or "the" spiral staircase, something characteristic, something for a book. With all due respect to the pear tree in my yard, likewise to the even older cherry tree, to the neighbors, to the bar acquaintances, to the cattails, bullfrogs, snakes, and otters in the forest ponds, to the air base, the atomic plant, the secret vineyards, the tangle of vines above the brook known only to me: when described, woven into a narrative by me, one who had come of his own volition, they amounted in his eyes to nothing but interference in others' business, the opposite of a well-founded book—something superfluous, and with all those plane trees, cedars, bamboo stalks, even fig trees and palms, to boot.

And abruptly, as Kobal was lecturing me, he seized me around the midsection, hoisted me in the air, and continued to speak, thus: "It's true, in the course of these days you've let me see, without pointing it out, always only in passing, the Easter fungus on the tree trunks just like that at home, the moss in the ravines, the almost identical rural railroad station, the woman with the washboard, the cassis or currant bushes deep in the woods, the bus station like Klagenfurt's, the wooden balcony with red geraniums like Kobarid's, the root cellar like the one behind my family's house in Rinkenberg. But it isn't here. This here is a substitute. The originals are somewhere else and have been waiting for you a long, long time. What do I care if you keep a journal on the landscape and the people here, even a chronicle? Even if you sit out and walk out another twenty years here, nothing will acquire mythic depth for you. And the mythic dimension, the earth-fissure world, was your specialty, from the beginning. Without the mythic dimension your books are certainly more manageable, less circumstantial. But they aren't really yours, don't really yield a proper book. And don't tell me you're on the trail of the mythic world of the Ile de France just because you know the appropriate story to tell when we get to the 'Crossroads of the Woman Without a Head' in the forest of Meudon, and likewise at the 'Crossroads of the Broken Man' on the other wooded hill, which is called the 'Forest of False Rest,' and likewise in the forest two hills farther on, called the 'Forest of the Hanged Wolf.' Though the original inhabitants here, of whom, I admit, there are quite a few, like to describe how things looked in their childhood, even they are far from having a unifying history, let alone a legend, a tale, a fairy tale, a tradition. This people is simply not your people, and I mean not only the people of the suburbs here, but the entire French people, so enlightened and linguistically so-phisticated that for every situation on earth it has, without even looking it up, a polished, definitive, if not always lucid formulation on hand. From what I know of you, the Mongolians were a more appropriate people for you, also the Indians, the Mexicans. Here in France not even all the stone graveyards with their exclusively elaborate plaques to which I've followed you have a mythic aura, certainly not those; these fields of sarcophagi look to me like nothing but sarcophagi, flesh-devouring containers. In this country you have to go back to the Middle Ages to encounter the fairy-tale colors and the gust of myth that at home brushes your forehead around every corner. You mustn't be without a people,

not you. You're not cut out for mere reporting, for the role of the uninvolved bystander. Consider the warmth, rare though it may have been,
that you've received from your people in the past. There's no warmth
like it. You've sidestepped your people, again and again, and now you're
in the process of losing it. Only yesterday when you came home you
were hailed as 'someone special.' Today from one end of the country to
the other no one greets you. You've spoiled your relationship with your
people by your absence, and even you stopped believing long ago in a
people of readers in the diaspora. By the Milky Way above the Jaunfeld
Plain, by the double onion towers of Heiligengrab, by the brewery of
Sorgendorf, by the fir forests of the Dobrava still full of chanterelles and
a Russian sense of vastness, by the train shooting by in the autumn mist
like several trains in one, by the freshly renovated clay bowling alley, by
the monument to the partisans, by the IHS carved on the barn gable in
Rinkolach, by the woman under the apple tree, by the windows of the
farmhouses so low that children don't need a door to go in and out, by
the wilted wildflowers in tin cans in the wayside shrines, by the manna
ash trees on the Liesnaberg, even without a pilgrimage up there, by the
owl in broad daylight on the chimney of the house next door: connect
again, if there's still time, with our shared Slavic litanies, which always
made you quake inside as otherwise only the Psalms, the *Odyssey*, and
the bells of the Resurrection could."

In my recollection, Filip Kobal dropped me as he spoke these words,
rather than setting me down. I struggled with him, half hoisted into the
air, half scraping the ground with one foot. But he was not my angel,
not then, and not since. For his next folk novel he has returned to the
valley we have in common.

For a time the region was poisoned for me by his presence, as had
never happened to me with anyone before, or at most with my publisher, the other one, who, when he still came to visit me in the bay,
left me each time, after his equally hectic arrival and departure, feeling
the kind of loneliness in my house, my region, and particularly my
writing such as a writer can probably experience only through dealings
with those who buy up the rights to his work: no sooner was his greed
for the manuscript satisfied, or the obligatory visit, like one to a ter-

minally ill patient, hastily taken care of, than he found my existence as incomprehensible as tedious; the silence around the house and grounds made him restless, the chair on which he perched seemed too small, the countryside in which I lived, with its forests, birds' flight paths, barracks, orchards, all of which he took in sullenly, was not part of the civilized world, anyone with whom I had dealings was not worth mentioning. In the meantime I dream of a third publisher, a new pioneer for my books, and by the light of day have no hope for any such thing.

Yet only my obstinacy has saved me from that damning judgment rendered by Filip Kobal, my old pal, that I and my place of residence are out of the question for a real book, for a "Gregor Keuschnig book." While Kobal was speaking in such terms, my obstinacy whisked me away to the titmice hopping about in the spruce outside the window, to a helicopter above the ridge of the hills, and to a ball of paper that kept rolling back and forth in the sun on the sidewalk as he hurled these charges at me; whenever something became threatening to me, I have always taken refuge in such sheltering images.

During the first period after this, when I walked the countryside, alone again and determined to remain unaccompanied in the future, I wanted my eyes to compel those mythic phenomena to appear that Kobal had declared absent from these parts, and, contrary to my usual practice, even questioned the bay's native residents about them, like a researcher doing fieldwork, which I regretted as I continued on my way, precisely when the answers betrayed secrets and yet more secrets.

But perhaps only now, however confusedly, would I be capable of responding to him, thus: "It may be that where we come from myths and fables are cultivated more than here. Yet that very fact renders them hollow. No, for now I am not going home. You see, when I come home, no one is there. It's actually more likely that I will move even farther away. In the meantime things are more lively here than at home, with the cliffs I've just discovered, something you missed most in the Seine hills, the blackberries, the yellow-headed dragonflies and hornets; and just a moment ago the first peacock butterfly of the spring crashed into the window, and yesterday the mythic woman from Catalonia brushed by it, and this evening in Porchefontaine I am meeting someone who collects ladders! And how do you know in any case that I'm still dreaming of archetypal images and stories? And that, if indeed I am still dreaming of them, I still have confidence in them? The following, for example, is the dream I've had repeatedly over the last few years: all the animal species in the world are running, galloping, flying, in all their variety and in harmony from all directions toward a watering hole in the desert, and each of the animals is equally large or small, the horses, the birds, the lions, the rabbits. But then when I reach the water after them, I see nothing but an infinite number of bees circling and about to drown. May it not be that the myths are still potent, but at the same time warped, corrupted, spoiled? Perhaps I would like to get rid of them once and for all, lest they, which only lead me astray now, become dangerous to me; perhaps I would like to cause them to vanish, and why not through the practice of making notes, lists, charts every day? Yes, it sometimes seems to me now as though the mythic may still be beckoning to me from a great distance, but it turns out to be a labyrinth with no way out. And by contrast I'd like to let the simple present have its say, the current day, the moment free of myth, and capture and accompany it in the language of the chronicler; smoke out my addiction to myth. And perhaps I left my country and yours because unlike you, Kobal, I'm not capable of maintaining a fraternal distance there, at least not in the long run, but get too close to people, know too much about them, and then become petty from all my knowledge. Yes, in my own country, no matter how happy I am to return each time, sooner or later I feel stifled, as much by its unique people as by my own pettiness. In a foreign country, away from the metropolis, surrounded by a language that is not my own and never will be, I can't help preserving a distance, and I also do my utmost to avoid learning anything about the local people (question them only out of weakness), thus preserving all the more my peculiar intuitions, and as a result can do something that was impossible for me back home, namely dream deeply of one or the other of the absent ones, even dreaming at times, for instance now during the long winter nights, in almost unmutilated forms of myth, fable, or primeval tale."

Since childhood I have had in me a readiness for fallings-out of the sort I had with Filip Kobal and my Jewish friend, and with others. When it came to a parting of the ways, each time I accepted it immediately. To have a falling-out at first gave me satisfaction, in some cases a sense of triumph. Finally I was alone, which agreed with me and suited me perfectly. Almost never did I later experience disappointment or regret. What had happened was right, and in moments of uncertainty I had only to recall my fallings-out to feel confirmed.

That is no longer the case. True, I still have quarrels with people. But by the next day my sense of satisfaction has gone sour. On the other hand, since my childhood I have also had in me a readiness for reconciliation. And in my memories I always made the first move toward restoring good relations. It came from a bright surge of feeling pushing or propelling me toward the other person. In its abruptness it could also give rise to misunderstandings, which drove others to run in the opposite direction. Alternatively, I was the one who misunderstood—I would throw my arms around the other person, thinking he was leaning toward me, when in fact he merely wanted to whisper the next obscenity into my ear. Mostly, however, my surge of feeling would sweep the other person along as much as it did me, and without wasting another word on our conflict, we would go back to doing things, talking, or playing, in new harmony.

In the end that is what happened to me with my sister. It was the summer before her death, and one afternoon I found myself driving through the Austrian town where she, with whom I had broken off relations over the dissolution of our parents' household, was in the meantime living. Suddenly I stopped. At first, on the way to her house, I almost hoped she would not be there. But when I was standing in front of it, she absolutely had to be there; if not, I would wait for her, would go looking for her. And of course she was home and leaned her head against my shoulder, and without hesitation brought out buttermilk, bread, and elderberry brandy for me. We sat outdoors side by side on the bench, at our backs the unevennesses in the whitewashed wall of the house; she told me about her operation—her hair was growing back over her bare scalp, which shone through the fuzz. I told her about my house in the foreign suburb, which, with its unstuccoed sandstone walls, she had once mistaken in a photograph for a castle, the occasion, in turn, for an angry letter from her about my forgetting my origins. I told her how the woman from Catalonia had fled, how my son was becoming alienated from me. Now nothing would ever come between us again, and as we sat there in summery relaxation, for the duration of that hour a song was playing around us, unpolished and free and easy, somehow suitable for my sister and me, like the sawing away of a country fiddler at a square dance or a Tyrolese country dance.

And thus I can also picture reconciliation with someone with whom I have seemingly broken for good. Yet if I spin this out in my imagination and examine the idea to see if it is serious and realistic, most of my former loved ones or kin become even more shadowy to me.

Restoring good relations with someone in my imagination, where images seize hold and hold true, has proven successful thus far only with the woman from Catalonia once, and once with Filip Kobal. In that daydream, while the woman from Catalonia was raging silently against me, her eyes dull black and her lips almost white, without hesitation I led her into the next room, where I sat down beside her and held her head, jerking as if bolts of electricity were darting through it, held it between my two hands, which did nothing but wait until the wild gallop inside her skull had subsided.

And in much the same way Filip Kobal came toward me on a sunny forest path in early spring here in the bay. The shadows of the trees' crowns, still without leaves, cast a pattern on the sand of the path, and when I reached his spot, with another movement of my two hands I casually conjured out of the earth and the light the mythical beast of this region. It was not a chimera, but rather a tiger of the steppes, peaceable, sunshine yellow, branch-shadow black, whereupon my companion and I continued on our way together as though nothing had ever come between us.

These are my fantasies of reconciliation, and I believe in them. But along with them there must also be at work within me a dream-deep distrust, even a revulsion against any form of coming together again.

How else to understand last night's dream, following right upon the day on which I wrote about the happy ending to the trouble between me and my sister? In the dream she was raging and enormous, hurled clumps of earth at me, then stones, heavier and heavier ones, and was finally intent, in a massive murderous impulse, on bashing in my head with a boulder.

And even the friends and family whom I now accompany from a distance have all been on the point of disappearing from my sight.

With whom shall I begin? With those who merely by virtue of their profession are so similar to me that trust was accompanied from the beginning by something like a natural distrust. Thus even before I knew the singer, I often felt a certain uneasiness when music began to play or so much as a single instrument, as if such sounds were false, indeed presumptuous, lacking harmony with the moment, especially when the music was an actual performance.

My inner conflict over music has meanwhile become insurmountable, my uneasiness as a rule more powerful than my emotional response, especially after the fact. It upsets me most when a voice or an instrument rings out above the rest or emerges all by itself. In this connection I recall from childhood in the Jaunfeld region a singer in our church who now and then performed the solos in the hymns, letting his tenor ring out, especially at night, during outdoor performances, where he stood apart from the choir and invisible, somewhere in the darkness high above the heads of the congregation, for instance up in the bell tower, and suddenly from that heavenly height sang out above the people below and over the entire quiet countryside, arousing general emotion, also in me, the child, who, however, even then felt the clammy touch of something revolting in those solo nights and recoiled from such song, as from the sense of community it created. When I think back now, of all the cultural events in that rural area, I found this the most unsettling, and when I mentioned it one time to the village priest, he revealed to me that before his days with the church choir this particular singer had been the most full-throated herald of Hitler's Greater Germany.

I could open myself up to singing or music making only if it took place incidentally, among other things—sounds, silence—and if I was not the audience, or if it did not address itself to an audience at all but turned away, toward the heavens, or inward, or into the void. Kobal knew what he was summoning me home with when he spoke of the litany and hymn singing. I can still be overwhelmed by a speaking voice that imperceptibly passes into chant and then goes back to speaking. All it takes is for the priest of the Russian Orthodox church here in the bay to raise his voice slightly during his sonorous Slavic recitation of Scripture, and I have to rein myself in to keep from weeping. Yes, as Kobal said, I quake. And it is enough for me if music is heard from afar, by chance, not intended for me. After an all-day hike across country, in the dusk, in an unfamiliar region, a few notes knock almost inaudibly at one's ear: the larger world opens up.

Sometimes all it takes is the sight of an instrument. It need not even make a sound. And thus the mere fact that my friend is a singer can fill me with elation, while as soon as he opens his mouth to sing, I am again overcome with exasperation, although his voice sounds like almost nothing, or not like one of those trained voices that put me off at the first note. When he plants his feet firmly on the ground and sings, I often feel at odds with my friend; but when I hear him speaking, and in my imagination his singing voice accompanies his speech, or simply in his silent presence, it makes me feel good to know that he is a singer. (In the meantime there are concerts in which he hardly sings and instead does almost nothing but speak, murmur, gesticulate, laugh out loud, as if talking to himself.)

I feel less exasperation with painters, at least with my own, who meanwhile has made his film in Spain, as well as the architect, here in the person of the carpenter, who I know is at the moment somewhere by the sea in northern Japan, in deep snow, sketching a telephone booth to which several steps lead up—thus it remains accessible even with this depth of snow.

When it comes to painters, I am sometimes repelled by their unrestrained or panic-stricken rush of images, which makes me able to sympathize with, if not understand, the various historical instances of iconoclasm (yet book burning remains incomprehensible to me). This happens with my friend in particular, so that, unlike with the singer, for whom I find it entirely justified, I cannot approve of his having all that money, and furthermore find it suspicious that he always appears so cheerful and extroverted. Nothing, it seems to me, gets under his skin anymore. He rejects anything resembling a new beginning or a metamorphosis. He has had his hard times, he says, and now he has a right to pleasure, in his work and otherwise, and also to wealth. And indeed, for a long time now every one of his pictures, in spite of their monotonality, has something uniformly supple about it, entirely consistent with the impression this sixty-year-old makes, which caused someone to write about the innate capacity for transformation that makes particular metamorphoses superfluous, and another wrote: "He speeds from victory to victory." Things were different only with this film, which he kept wanting to call off, and which, despite his intense seriousness and fresh excitement, made him feel for the entire two months, just as in his early days as a painter, as if he were dancing in a dream, constantly at risk of falling down.

But perhaps I am the one who is bad for my worldly friend? I once heard from a third party who had visited almost all the painters and writers of our times that the former seemed quite tranquil in old age, sociable, cheerful, whereas the older writers seemed dissatisfied, touchy, disgruntled, and even the successful ones apparently felt cheated.

A rchitects remained alien to me in a different way from painters. My friend in Japan is the only one to whom I have become somewhat close, and that certainly has to do with the fact that in recent years he has transformed himself back into a woodworker, a carpenter, and comes across as such; someone who once stopped by when I was here in the house with him at first failed to notice him and then said, when he finally saw him, that he had not realized I had workmen in the house.

In the region where I grew up I certainly knew painters, if only as painters of signs and wayside shrines, but never an architect; even the word was hardly known there. There was the master mason who was also a master builder. And the structures that captured my imagination were hardly ever built of masonry, but rather of wood, also on the small side, and their construction did not require master craftsmen: the barns, the rough board toolsheds, the shelters for harvested crops, and those racks for drying grass, with narrow shingled roofs, scattered at all angles across the mowings; even today I will squint past a monumental stone structure in search of something unobtrusive, of wood. It is simply a fact that to this day things I did not encounter early on can make me skittish; it is a reflex, one I cannot get rid of. I think it comes from the jolt I got at the sight of the boarding school, which at one blow cut me off from my familiar world, that fortress seen from far below that took up an entire hilltop. It did not help that the final and steepest part of the path leading up to the building passed a mausoleum as big as a house, windowless, with a half-open door from which, every time we returned from summer vacation, a cold breath of decay wafted, coming, I imagined, from the sarcophagus of the bishop who had retired in old age to what would later become this boarding school for future priests.

Although large cities were my element for a time, I have never been on friendly terms with city buildings, either castles or railway stations, either palaces, cathedrals, medieval squares, or high-rise buildings of any sort, bridges spanning rivers or inlets of wonder-of-the-world length, subterranean twin cities. They intoxicated me, dizzied me, but never sparked my imagination. To this extent, even if my siblings have accused me of the opposite, I can say that I have never become a city person. Structures that suggest "city," and perhaps also "power," "grandeur," "authority," were not on my scale, least of all in places where I was supposed to study: at the universities. These never became "mine," the one in Vienna as little as the one in Paris, except for a summery campus one time, far out of town near Santiago de Compostela. City people— in my eyes that is what architects are, and I often see them as antagonists.

Only with my distant friend is it different, and even so we are threatened, if not by a falling-out then certainly by wariness. He does not want to build anything more. For years now his work has consisted entirely of travel, and of searching for material for repairing and completing what is already there, which he never wants to see torn down anywhere, no matter what it is. My architect is not a city person, or one sees no signs of it in him. What could drive a wedge between us is the opposite of what so often aggravates me in my painter. Whereas the latter enjoys being celebrated as a winner, the architect presents himself as a loser, and for some time now has actually come across as just that, with the ironic style he adopts at the beginning of any conversation, as if he did not trust himself or the other person to be serious, his veering between impulsivity and rigidity, his interrupting of himself. And this makes me realize that an apparent loser disconcerts me as much as a declared winner.

Even the Japanese police, who otherwise look right past foreigners, as does the rest of the population, except children, have already stopped him several times on his trip—that is how derelict my friend looks, a white man stranded on the coasts of Japan, at least from a distance, where a pedestrian like him, with his broad-brimmed hat on his bowed head, can only be a mendicant friar, a stranger to the country; from close up, however, even with his worn soles and his threadbare shirt collar, he is elegance personified and humility in human form, which causes anyone spoiling for a fight to step out of his way and even salute him. And he, the most frugal and resourceful of us, who now sleeps in temple enclosures instead of hotels, lives almost exclusively on rice and fruit, and wears his clothing so gently that it veritably blooms, has enough money even in Japan to continue his travels for a good while longer, this entire year.

In the cavernlike fish market of Aomori, where everyone smiled at the carpenter, an older woman with a rubber apron has just given him a few fillets of raw salmon, which he is now eating, crouching in the dusk on top of a snowdrift, behind him poles, swaying boat masts, for the drift has formed right by the ocean, across which he is looking in a northerly direction, toward the island of Hokkaido.

Evening is coming on there, while here in the bay between the hills of the Seine beyond Paris it is the morning of the same day, already spring, with brimstone-butterfly yellow seen out of the corner of one's eye and thousands of frogs softly fluting, piping, or peeping as they mate in the nameless pond, overgrown with underbrush and trees, out in the forest glade. What kind of alienation is supposed to be hanging over me and him? Don't I see us as together across the continents?

And now it occurs to me that it was stone buildings that put me on the alert, for instance the house of the harbormaster of Piran, Istria, on my first day by the ocean, the way it stood there alone on the dock, the sky in its windows, without anything around it, without a yard or a portico, stone rising perpendicularly from the horizontal paving stones.

I move on among my friends to the reader. Mightn't he, too, disavow me and write me off? Metamorphose into someone who despises me?

There was a time when our relationship was in danger. It did not even go that well at the beginning. I met him for the first time in one of the two railway-station cafés in that other Parisian suburb where I lived before coming to the bay here; it was the Bar de l'Arrivée, while the other is called the Bar du Départ. I was sitting there waiting for my son's piano lesson to be over, and now, whenever I sit out on that terrace, I can still hear, through the roar of the traffic and the rumbling and screeching of the trains, from the top floor the obedient and defenseless groping of the six-year-old child on the huge instrument.

At first the gaze of the person who turned toward me from the next table struck me as that of a double, an evil one. Then he addressed me, without transition, without a greeting, without a question, without hesitation, as if I had been his acquaintance from time immemorial: "Gregor Keuschnig, I'm one of your readers," which, with my son's disconsolate scales in my ear, filled me with the uncomfortable feeling that I was this stranger's chosen victim.

That dissipated as he began to summarize, verbal image after verbal image, my books for me—there were only two or three of them. For in this way what I had created came back to me and seemed solid. As reproduced by the reader, in his tone of voice, my stuff sounded robust and at the same time surprising, and I felt in the mood to go and read it myself right away, thanks to the other man's roguish acting-out, his dastardly laughter at passages quoted verbatim—as if he were taking revenge on the state of the world.

But later on it was disconcerting again that the reader had eyes only for me. When I had picked up my son, he ignored him, as he did the people and places of the suburb, through which he then accompanied us on our errands. At my house, where I invited him to stay for supper, he did not even glance at the fire in the fireplace, and before that, while I was splitting wood in the yard, he stood around and continued to recite from my books, until I found myself wishing a piece of firewood would fly up and hit him in the head. And even the woman from Catalonia did not exist for him, she whom otherwise no one, not even an animal, ignored.

And then again, as we made our way in the gathering dusk across the backyard to the house, I with my arms loaded down with firewood, the reader holding forth with both hands free, he began to make delicate trilling and fluting noises, his lips pursed, whereupon little birds, sparrows and titmice, came whirring from the trees and bushes and perched on his elbows, which he held akimbo.

Things settled down with the reader only when he was gone, far away, back in his Germany (which at the time seemed more distant from France than it does now). At intervals he wrote me letters full of little stories about the seasons and reports on his country, and never expected an answer. I could say of him that he let me alone, and that did me good. Of course, my father lived in Germany, too, but I was completely indifferent toward him. Germany, a nonplace, despite my sense of finding myself and feeling at home in the smallest German word-hamlets: through the reader it became a country for me. I viewed him from afar as a poet. He was a court of appeal. And you could rely on the reader as on no one else. I took his letters along on my hikes and pored over every word, swore to be guided by them and never to disappoint him. I had confidence in him as otherwise only in the poets Goethe and Hölderlin, in Heraclitus and John the Evangelist. He was the epitome of constancy, never got worked up, and when he spoke, and not only about books, he gave a definite yes or no—my ideal, which I never attained. I, the writer, followed him on his expeditions in reading: just as I came to enjoy my own work through him, I read, after his telling me about them, the writings of others whom I had previously not known or even disliked. I went so far as to copy out sentences from his letters: "I exist in order to read." Or: "When I don't know what to do next: the light shed by reading." Or: "If I start a family someday, down to the last generation it will be a family of readers."

Then, with the passage of time I noticed something about the reader that made me angry at him again. He was not content to be alone with his reading; he was on the lookout for others of like mind. Like me, there were quite a few here and there in Europe and even overseas who followed his example and read the books he recommended. He encouraged that, too. Through his reading he wanted not only, as he expressed it, to "keep myself in top form," but also more and more to wield power. True, he felt no desire for public prominence. Nonetheless he presided over a circle whose head he was, the great reader. He presented himself as the authority in a most intimate circle, and thus it fell to him to dictate, without television appearances and newspapers, what was worth reading and what not. I saw the reader on his way to founding a sect, a sect of readers. And thus he claimed for himself and his followers exclusivity, infallibility, singularity vis-à-vis the mere crowd.

The moment came when, after he had again begun to talk in conspiratorial tones about an exceptional book, an exemplary contrast to the prevailing literary nonentities, I wanted nothing more to do with such a reader. And I told him so. Wanting to wield power through reading, and surreptitiously at that, in a whisper, made no sense, I said. He was a bogeyman, a corrupter of children, the antireader, the equivalent of the Antichrist. "Clear out, beat it, let books be books again, each one as best it can!" I blurted that out, unthinkingly, as always when I am in a rage, and when I finally looked at him, his lips were trembling terribly.

Thus we became friends. He continued to write his letters to me, but he never made mention of a particular book. For a time he tried to refrain from reading altogether, but then found that unnatural. Without reading, he said, he could not see the day in a day. The work that suited him was, and remained, reading and deciphering things. And wasn't writing an invention that to this day held a secret power?

To be sure, since then I have never seen him reading his book in public. He does it surreptitiously now, under the table, as it were, which reminds me of those carved medieval stone figures holding their book in their hand, and the hand as well as the book is shrouded in cloth. As a sideline he prints and binds books himself, one every couple of years, like those fragments of the twelfth-century itinerant mason.

At the moment he is walking along Jade Bay by the North Sea at Wilhelmshaven, where my father still lives. It is night, after the first day of spring. The lights far out on the ocean probably belong to the island of Helgoland, and when the reader turns around, he sees Orion disappearing in the haze on the horizon, "until next winter!"

It is not long until Easter now; hardly any sparrows are sleeping in the birds' sleeping tree here by the local railway station, and the few who are left perch there at night in their normal size, no longer puffed up against the cold. I go or roll along to the priest of Rinkolach on the Jaunfeld Plain, where I was born.

Today, Sunday, he is driving back and forth across the countryside because he has to say Mass in several scattered villages, one after the other. His rectory is elsewhere; Rinkolach is merely his branch church. It is a long time since there has been a priest in residence there.

Patches of snow can still be seen on the plain, especially on the edge of the woods; unlike here, the climate is not determined by the ocean.

Yet even where he is, in continental Europe, the air in late afternoon has a lingering mildness, and thus the priest is struck all the more by the contrast between the warmth outside in the open air and the massive cold inside the churches, particularly in the sacristies where he changes for Mass, always in haste, as now in the particularly chilly church of Rinkolach.

On the table the elderly woman who helps the priest with his robing has placed a jam jar with a bunch of wood anemones; far off at the railway station on the border one of the infrequent Sunday trains blows its whistle, and down in the gravelly soil of the cemetery are piled the bones of my kinfolk, all jumbled and intermingled, with spaces between where there is nothing but the absence of my grandparents' two sons who died in Russia for the Third Reich, most recently joined by the ashes of my sister.

Thus I could close my eyes as I just did and spend this Sunday with the distant priest, sit next to him as he eats his midday soup, breathe in the smell in his car, and, stronger than he, who is always in a hurry, be with him in the afternoon when he nods off at his desk, and perhaps myself let my head sink onto my desk here; I would know my friend's day inside out.

But even with him there has already been danger. How indignant he has made me at times. It had almost nothing to do with his way of speaking, even if some of his expressions left an unpleasant taste in my mouth, for instance when he said he gave the dying members of his congregations "the death escort." (Gratifying, on the other hand, that he never called a thing or a person "stupid," "evil," or "bad," but used the term "simple" for it all: a "simple man" was a stupid or limited person; a "simple book" meant something inconsequential, somewhat humorous, and had nothing to do with "admirable simplicity.")

What put our friendship to the test during one period: that during the one or two times a year when I returned to my old region he took it for granted that I had to be mainly with him, if with anyone, not with my brother, the only surviving member of my family; I was allowed as little as possible or not at all to go about by myself. As the overseer of the parish, he imposed on the visitor the requirement of registering his arrival, his presence, and his departure, and all in the name of friendship. If I came, he was in charge; nothing else would do.

He, who in his profession was always there at once for anyone who needed him, expected the same of his friend as a matter of course, as a duty. He could not imagine that the primary reason for my coming might be, for example, a certain path at a certain time of year, or a stone wall around a field, or the entire region with its milk pickup stands, new or rotting away, and not some living being, and certainly not him.

If previously I had usually informed him of my coming, in time I began to keep my arrival secret and then even tried to avoid this man, who otherwise would have lain in wait for me far outside the village, at the train's flag stop, standing there by his car, his arms crossed and his legs apart, destroying my monthlong looking forward to the footpath across the fields in the autumnal light, and, even worse, making it impossible for me to take a single step by myself even way out there, far from human habitation.

And besides, it irked me that if anyone it should be this particular person with his clerical collar picking me up upon my return home, and with the local railroad workers as witnesses: it was as if I were letting myself be co-opted by a particular party in front of the whole population.

From now on, no one, not even the priest, was to know in advance of my visits to my old home. At the right moment I would instead simply show up at his house, as I was accustomed to do with my brother. But he, although I changed the times of my visits, seemed to intuit my return to his territory, even if it was only for a matter of hours. On the deserted highway to Rinkolach, my footsteps making the only sound, the wind between my fingers, at sunset, when I pictured him at evening Mass in Moos or Šmihel, suddenly I would hear a honking behind me, followed by a curt wave from the village boss that brooked no contradiction, telling me to get into the car, whose door he was already holding open. And the next time I got off one station earlier and slunk by back roads to the village, which I reached long after dark. Heat lightning flashed ahead of me. In its glow, the familiar figure was suddenly there by the cemetery, spreading his arms wide and greeting me, as usual without first saying my name, with loud singing: "Salve in domino!" There, on the way to the graves of my kinsmen, I backed away from my friend, as one would only from a foe, and at the same time I felt like a person who had been caught in the act, as though by being here without his knowledge I was a sort of poacher. And while I was cross at his cutting me off and blindly assuming that we both felt the same way, my recoiling and my reluctance to speak wounded him.

Although we remained standing next to each other and talked, in the alternation between the darkness, which I have experienced so concretely only on the Jaunfeld Plain, and silent heat lightning, it felt as if we had just taken leave of each other for good. I said, when he reproached me for my unfriendliness, that he was a "despot," "clueless," a "cannibal" (etc.). He said only that I was "a very simple person."

I am describing this incident also because the nightmare of that particular nocturnal hour had already faded by the next day. Or had it? At any rate, on the way back from my brother's house, where I had slept as usual on the couch under the staircase in the hall, I was honked at from behind my back, louder and more imperiously than ever, and then in addition had the headlights flashed at me, in broad daylight—when I had been sure that at this hour he would be teaching his religion at the elementary school in Bleiburg. Without hesitation he gestured to me, just with his fingers, to get in on the passenger side. We then moved to the trunk the crate filled to the brim with early white-skinned apples, just picked by him in the rectory garden. The quarrel of the previous evening, which had seemed absolutely final, was not even mentioned. He did not alter in the slightest his behavior as lord of the village, omnipresent; displayed it even more insistently, exaggerated it. And he also robbed me of that hour alone by the train window, that hour of slow departure, in an arc, one station after another, from the place of my birth, which I need in order to experience the region fully; instead he drove me in his car to the regional capital to catch the express, turning a deaf ear to my protestations. "Leave me!" I said. "No, I'm not leaving you," he said. And then, after we had arrived much too early in Klagenfurt, a town that had never meant anything to me except for its movie houses, which were gone now, and after we had sat together somewhere, I was the one, as is not uncommon with me, who would not let the other go. "Stay a while, I'll take the next train, I have time," I said. "Don't you remember that they're waiting for me to do a baptism in Humtschach, and that after that I have to go into the rift valley and call on a parishioner who's dying? That I'm not the master of my time the way you are, but rather its servant?"

And this is how we worked things out between us. I always keep my arrival secret from him, and whenever I come home to Rinkolach I double back again and again, under cover of darkness, through the underbrush, and the district priest tracks me down, blocks my path, confiscates my open space, ruins my time at home, and after my initial resistance, I accept the unwelcome company, indeed even want to be with this other person for the time being.

But who knows? What I do know is that after that nocturnal quarrel, the new beginning we both made, despite the powers of reconciliation I ascribed to myself, must be credited exclusively to my local friend. Was it only during my childhood that I could make up so matter-of-factly, for instance with our neighbor's son? Didn't I cultivate not long thereafter in boarding school one or two insurmountable enmities? Have I in the meantime become one of the "irreconcilables"? At any rate, that word appealed to me for a long time. But even there I no longer know.

I see my woman friend under the Turkish sun, while here in the Seine hills the first blossoms are raining down from the trees, or rather, I sense her this way, in her environment there, the white-glistening delta of a river between the place where it flows out of the Taurus range and where it reaches the sea. She is turning a piece of wood in her hand that has lain in the water for a long time, in fresh water and in salt water, a narrow cylinder whose wooden parts, the fibers and splinters, have been almost completely replaced, into its very core, by finger-long, spiral-shaped bivalves that have grown into it. Only the outward form remains that of a cudgel, which lies heavy in her hand, heavier than one made of wood could ever be, heavy as stone.

Remarkable that I can think my way to this woman (although she also helps me, as do the others on the road, by writing to me now and then or sending me a sliver of wood, and although I carried with me just such a shell-encrusted piece of wood along the southern shores of Turkey until it began to stink, and the captain of the ship threw it overboard, as he did with everything that did not belong on the ship).

Remarkable, because we were once a couple, and our story ended in a way that makes a subsequent friendship appear miraculous. At the time I fled in horror from this woman who loved me.

And here I interrupt this passage. For it seems questionable to me, and not for the first time, by the way, when I refer to the person I was in the past as "I," not only the child, but also the person from as recently as last year. My "I"-uncertainty is equally great for all the years, and pertains to almost everything I did, everything that was done to me, and everything that happened to me. It is as though I constantly had to put quotation marks around myself in my memories. "I" looked after my three-month-old sister. "I" was mugged. "I" was resuscitated. "I" gave a speech. A moment in which I am not questionable to myself is a rarity, even reinforced with an exclamation point. Then I woke up next to my dead grandmother! Then I walked with my grandfather, facing into the raindrops, through the dust from the path across the fields! Then I sat all summer and fall, and wrote, looked out the window, yes I! Then I caught sight of my son, yes, I! Then I swam in the middle of the year in the middle of the river, yes, I! Yet with most of my experiences I find it difficult to say "I," would rather substitute some other word, except that none presents itself. I have no choice but to use an undifferentiated "I" as the subject of my active and passive experiences, no matter how false it rings to me.

Onward. Through. So at that time I was my present woman friend's lover. I was thrilled by the two of us. I wanted to tell everyone I knew about her and me, and did so, too, in my circle: about our first meeting on the main bridge in Maribor, where I knew at once that we would become a couple. I even told my son, at the time still a child, about her, and had to hold myself back from flaunting my rapture with the other woman in front of the woman from Catalonia.

Yet our story, as far as I am concerned, had begun beyond the body, as an idea, long before I knew my friend: it was that my woman should come from the country most closely related to me. Of course, this idea, which, by the bye, was as erotic and captivating as anything could be, had been forgotten instantly when the woman from Catalonia turned her head on that very different bridge in El Paso, and also remained forgotten for years; it came back to me only with the appearance of my friend on the great bridge in the southern Slavic town of Maribor, with people streaming by and the Drawa flowing underneath at an autumnally slow pace, as wide and bustling as a river in China.

I then avoided any touch for a long time. I did not even want to look her in the eye, as if that would have been too familiar. One night, when the moon was full, she led me to a snow-covered field high above the city, and I did nothing but stand there for an hour; the snow lying on the ground and rustling, its crystals on top forming tiny gables, made more noise than I, and when she reached for my hand I slapped hers away.

When we finally became a couple, more as a result of her prodding, almost pushing, it made me unhappy. As she undressed, with the agility of a teenager, I was thinking that it was all over.

And something was over, namely my idea about her and me and our people, and something new was beginning.

After we had been together, she promptly disappeared, without saying goodbye. Utterly downcast, I fell asleep and awoke the next summery morning as the entirely different person at whom "I" had already marveled as a child, usually also upon waking: unspeakably happy, shot through with sweetness, connected to everything outside of me, irrepressible.

And in the months that followed, this sort of immediacy prevailed between us as a particular elegance, without any danger of a false step or a misunderstanding. It was a grace that made us invisible. When I think back, I see neither a face nor a body, but in its place the roots of spruce trees growing across the wood road, the clothesline on the terrace, the succession of moraines rushing by on the horizon through the open train window. When I was with her I felt as if I had been swallowed up by an earthquake. That boy who looked right through us as he passed the place by the forest path where we were lying. The band of reed cutters who poled their boat past our sandbank, each looking in another direction, anywhere but at us. Once we lay together under a cherry tree, and again the two of us disappeared, and the only memory image that remains is of the cherries up in the tree, as if each time I looked up there were more of them, small, round, glowing red.

And every time, my memory reminds me, I found myself alone afterward. I see her dashing away from the circle, and already she is around the corner, out of sight, inaudible. Since she always presented herself as a sort of adventurer, disguised or shrouded and veiled, she did not leave behind the smallest image.

As a rule we arranged to meet in third locations, settings neither of us knew, usually even in third countries. In one such foreign city we were lying once in the summery darkness, and suddenly I heard her saying that I should live with her. It was less this statement than the voice echoing from the pitch-black emptiness that made me fall silent. And then she repeated what she had said, with the same ghostly echo.

I have never known what verb to use to describe physical love. The verb that came closest was from the *Odyssey*, where it is said of a man and a woman that they "rested" together, often "all the night through," "until rosy-fingered dawn." That is how I had rested with this woman, time and again.

Such rest was now at an end. The voice talked and talked, saying always the same thing, with variations. And then the invisible being next to me, a moment ago nothing but a giddy summery body, resorted to violence. At first there was just a kind of stomping in place. Then it began to flail around and grew to giant proportions, or as our lover of local legends, Filip Kobal, would say, became a "Berchta mummer," a worshipper of the pagan goddess. And the heavy, massive body of this spawn of darkness sat on her victim, just as in legend, threw herself over him, kneaded him, plucked at him, pressed down on him, stuffed him into herself. I have felt horror like this only in the one dream I had of sleeping with my mother.

It was also appropriate for a dream or a legend that I "freed myself with my last ounce of strength," "I do not know how." I fled the bed, the room, the dark house, and when I turned to look as I ran, the devouring woman was perched above the door, like in olden times in the village, as tall as the façade, her legs spread over the lintel and dangling to the ground on either side of the entrance, and as I ran I got hopelessly lost, took the bus going in the direction opposite from the railroad station, ended up in suburbs where, in the bright light of morning, I could not even decipher signs that were as clear as day. And I did not feel liberated in the least, but rather, in spite of the fresh air and the passersby who shielded me, still suffocated by that slimy placenta-darkness.

Since then I have never rested with my former chosen one. For a long time we also did not meet, and neither sent the other any sort of sign. Then I saw her again, in the harbor of Split. At the sight of her I at once felt summery all over. And suddenly I had no other memories of her, had forgotten everything else in her new presence. She was rolling with a stream of others down the gangplank of the car ferry just arriving from the Dalmatian islands, and what I had seen first was not her face but the bunch of flowers in her hand, which was also holding the steering wheel, flowers so small and richly colored and native that they could have been gathered only on an island, on island cliffs.

Then she approached me perfectly naturally. She had married in the meantime, but she still played the adventurer, the independent woman, or, as she had been called during our time together, the "loafer," taking off on her own once a year, though with her husband's money and also with her father's, and going far away. To be sure, I kept thinking as she talked, "How threadbare this woman is!" or "How worm-eaten!" But such thoughts did not count. And she acted as if nothing were wrong. And thus nothing was. And that is how it has remained between her and me ever since.

It is not she I see at the moment, not even her hand, but only the white pebbly seashell cudgel in the midday light at the foot of the Taurus range, still snow-covered on the peaks, while here outside my study a thrush leaps like a cat out of the bushes, and the shadow of a bomber from the air base passing high overhead darkens my writing paper for the twinkling of an eye.

The wooded hills around the bay are greening. The greening began on the ground, crept upward, and in these first days of April has reached the level of the underbrush. The trees themselves still look bare, except for some crowns rounded out by a veil of green, which yields tiers of parachutes floating down. Here, too, lizards leap and dart, a type different from those my woman friend sees in her Middle Eastern delta, more adapted to tree bark, and the other day, when I dug out the rotten stump of the poplar tree in the garden, then sawed it up and split it, along with still-motionless stag beetles, the pulpy interior was swarming with hornet larvae, from which, some of them already clearly formed, the heads with their hornlike protuberances stuck out and stirred, next to them their dead ancestors as mummies, surrounded by wood in which, when I dumped them out, their hollows remained.

Before I move on to the seventh and last of my distant travelers and also describe, describe in an interrogative mode, the temporary rift with my son, consummated only in my thoughts, already long past, yet still alarming to me today, I should like to try to clear up a problem of form, perhaps for the last time in the course of this undertaking. (My son, still retracing my footsteps, in Yugoslavia, far to the south in Montenegro, will have to hurry to reach by Easter Sunday that tiny church in Thessaloniki where Christ resurrected after the Crucifixion is portrayed in a way that I, so needful of images of resurrection, have otherwise never in my life seen.)

It sometimes seems to me that in my writing, and not only this present project, I am threatened by completeness: instead of leaving space, of filling up all available space, something of which I always accused the woman from Catalonia; of not creating a line for my story but cluttering it up with intricate variations. So: away with variations? Away with completeness, which threatens to reduce my freely streaming narrative to a kind of catalogue? I, the cataloguer, as the internal enemy of my other I, the narrator? To avoid a catalogue, should I now leave the episode of my alienation from my son out of the narrative? I do not know.

If this were the case, that internal enemy would have to be the one with my first profession. Might I, the lawyer, the doctor of jurisprudence, be obstructing me the narrator? Might the form of the laws I once studied be turning against the form, not amenable to study, of my story? And again there come to mind the catalogues belonging to that Roman law I so greatly admire, codified later in Byzantium under the emperor Justinian. Although they constitute a closed system, as a legal code should, reading them still opens and refreshes my mind. And long ago that legal language helped me find my way out of myself. That was true especially for my writing, to which I was drawn as never to a place and also never to a human being. (It did not become a substitute for a country and its people; rather it stood for them from the outset, had from the beginning no intention of doing anything but narrate—but what?)

The question was: what language was suitable for my writing? When I was a young man, each time I sat down to write, full of inchoate longing, I found myself hesitating at the very first letter and realized that I had no language—no writing language. Usually I would then slink away from the desk or wherever, my mission unaccomplished, and whenever I wrote something down after all, it was the same word covering the entire page, or the stammering of mere syllables. And that was supposed to be the story I had just seen before me in chiaroscuro?

Until I learned the language of the law, and in particular the Latin terminology, I did not succeed at getting a single sentence to capture properly the light that at times shone so far up ahead of me, within me? Only the language of the historians, of Thucydides among the Greeks and among the Romans especially the laconic language of Sallust, had something to offer me, so it seemed, yet then as now I could not think of a story to fit this language; I, the inlander, would have had to go to sea like Joseph Conrad.

There was no question of using the language of novels, no matter which, for my narratives: I soon learned that that would condemn my primal longing to lifeless imitation and singsong. How, then, could I hope to find revelation in the language of the law, which instead of narrative sentences consisted of paragraphs, usually conditional statements following the pattern of "If someone . . . then . . ."? First of all, this language sobered me up, without in the slightest impairing my attraction to writing. The light I had previously intuited, who knows where, cleared my head through this language. And then the language the law offered me was by no means its own, but an entirely different one, one I still had to find for myself, a narrative language parallel to the language of the law, like it given to circumlocution, at a remove from the thing described, with a limited stock of concepts, so that the myriads of words that previously had perhaps contributed most to my linguistic confusion were now out of the question. Such avoidance, such a limited choice, as a result of which, above all, descriptors for feelings were eliminated, actually strengthened the presence of feeling in the writing process, and with the help of the language of the law, and also mindful of the historians, I was able to complete my first story, even if I occasionally ran into snags, as I still do today.

But even then the wholesome influence seemed to be coupled with a threat. As the law did not omit any facts of a case, insisting on one variation of the premise after another, and was also not at liberty to omit any variation, for otherwise it would not be a law, anywhere near a just one, I was correspondingly tempted to add to each detail in my story a further one, and yet another, all those that in my eyes pertained to the matter at hand, as if I could do it justice only in this way.

In that compilation of old Roman law, for instance, a distinction was made, in the case of one person's striking another, on the basis of whether the blood "fell on the ground" or not. For if the blood dripped onto the ground, the penalty had to be more severe. And it also made a difference under the law whether the blood ran down to the ground from a blow on the head or from a blow lower down, and even whether blood flowed only after the third blow or sooner, and whether the blow was administered with a flat hand or with the fist or with a whip, and whether the act was committed by a freeman, a slave, a "Frank," or a barbarian, which also applied vice versa to the victim. And the provisos for women who were beaten this way were different from those for men, so that the paragraph or "title" on hitting and bleeding, in order to be halfway comprehensible, expanded into subparagraphs and sub-subparagraphs. Likewise the determination of the penalty for someone who had cut off a boy's hair without his parents' permission could not make do with a single sentence but, as a law, had to have variants, at least depending on whether the child was long-haired or not, and so on, and in the eyes of the law at that time it was also not all the same if a native (Roman) man "squeezed" a native (Roman) woman's arm or "grabbed" it, and whether he committed this offense against the arm below or above the elbow. (Then a completely contradictory form of justice in the paragraphs on setting fire to others' houses "with people sleeping inside," which differentiated according to whether the sleepers were natives or not, and in the last section extended likewise to setting fire to cattle barns, and in its final variant to pigsties, for which, I imagine, it imposed the same penalty as for arson involving non-Roman sleepers.)

Be that as it might: what attracted me so much, even on a first reading of the code, was, I now think, not any particular model of justice but rather a kind of ordering, a fanning-out, illuminating, an airing-out of chaos or of so-called reality, both in ancient Rome—which, at the time when these laws were codified, had already collapsed quite a while earlier and was probably supposed to be revived as an empire by this means—and in the present, my own reality, both internal and external; as I spelled out the pandects (digests), paragraph by paragraph, subparagraph by subparagraph, no matter how different the topics treated in them were from contemporary concerns, confusion and obscurity vanished from my world. Even distinctions that appeared at first to be hairsplitting organized this world more precisely and accurately, and at the same time widened the larger picture.

Was that a paradox? The more possible conflicts the law carved out of formlessness, the denser its net; the more chiseled and discrete the vicissitudes it illuminated, the more spacious the world appeared to me as I read on, and also the clearer and more open—linguistic form, whose deciphering, detail by detail, had the effect of unlocking, enlarging, completing, complementing me?

And another paradox connected with my reading of the laws, the most curious of all? That these laws, focused on everyday misdeeds and atrocities, of which they treated exclusively and on which they rang the changes exhaustively, gave me, the decipherer, more than a millennium after their compilation, fresh certainty under my feet, something like rootedness, simply on the basis of their language, generally applicable and binding, which first named stabbing, killing, ripping out limbs, raping, exhuming corpses, pillaging in all conceivable degrees—that in itself created order and tranquillity!—then organized them, and in such a way that even the most deviant and malicious act was, to put it briefly, "provided for."

Because the legal dicta provided for every possible turn of events, I was no longer threatened by chaos, and the unreal—than which there was nothing more catastrophic in my eyes—evaporated. A legal work that catalogues crimes and punishments comprehensively does not merely order them, but, as I still feel when reading this text, also welds the world together and validates it. What then emerges at times is indeed something like an empire; not a vanished Roman one, but rather one that again brings to mind the phrase "New World"; I experience in this case the very opposite of a trance.

I also became rooted in another sense through the language of these laws: even while I was a student in various capital cities, whether in Vienna or in Paris, the occurrences circumscribed by the Latin paragraphs were always transferred in my mind to the rural area from which I came. Although, as far as I knew, violations of the law had hardly ever occurred there, at least no criminal offenses—there was just one person in the village who was constantly in litigation with his neighbors, as probably happens everywhere—I thought I recalled, as I worked my way through even the smallest subparagraph, a corresponding situation in and around Rinkolach. Such a memory would shoot through me, brightly outlined, an oscillating, vibrating image, electric in quality. What flashed by me as I pored over my texts were fragments of narrative images such as I had never seen in any actual narrative from my native region. The village tales told by my grandfather, who everyone agreed was a "born story-teller," never aroused any memories, nor did the novels of Filip Kobal, he, too, as people said, made of "epic bedrock." Memory, marvelous in quality, did come to me, however, by way of the generalizations and ramifications of those long since inoperative prescriptions.

As recently as this morning, when I was trying, with my now fairly faded Latin, to decipher the paragraph in the digests about stealing flour from a mill—and it mattered for the penalty whether the flour belonged to the miller himself or to a customer—I found myself transported, with the force of a hallucination, to the Jaunfeld mill, deep down in the already dark rift valley, furthermore on a gloomy rainy day, sacks of grain under the tarpaulin outside on the ladder wagon on which I had been sitting only moments before, facing backward, while now I was standing inside the deserted mill, surrounded by the shrieking and roaring of the millrace, high above me the guttering light of a naked bulb.

And when I read on, another situation is evoked for me, from the same region: "When a person enters a stranger's garden for the purpose of stealing . . ." "When a person steals grain from a stranger's field and hauls it away with a cart or on a horse . . ." and "But if he hauls it away on his back . . ."

One section even reminds me of a specific person, my grandfather, who, after the death of his wife, when he was already quite an old man, fell in love with a neighbor's hired woman. In the law it is mentioned that anyone who consorted with the king's maid and openly entered into relations with her was sentenced thenceforth to serve the king likewise. And thus, when I read the Roman law I see my grandfather on a certain Sunday afternoon, when he had been left alone on purpose with his forbidden love, which was known to the entire village, being caught by his family when they returned unexpectedly—his own daughter, my mother, and also his second daughter are there. The almost seventy-year-old man stands there with his pants down, the hired woman, not much younger, in her slip. None of the witnesses laughs; that a man, and an old man at that, should enter into relations with another woman so soon after the death of his wife, and with this kind of woman, is serious, and the two daughters look most serious of all. The two elderly dissolutes have flushed cheeks, two times two small, bright red, perfectly round spots there, not from shame, but because they were just kissing, their mouths almost closed and their lips pursed like birds or children, and just as eagerly, at a frenetic pace, head against head, yet their bodies at a distance from each other. The hair of this purple-cheeked couple sticks out from their heads, the woman's gray, the man's still black. She looks at the bystanders while he gazes into her eyes as before. They do not pluck at their clothing, either one of them, and thousands of Sundays later, in his charity cubicle, with room only for his bed, this man, meanwhile almost ninety, pulls the blooming young woman from Catalonia, visiting with his grandson, onto his knee and breaks into dry sobs.

Where I come from, I was never considered a native, a villager. But I can say that deciphering the aforementioned legal code helped make a villager out of me in the cities, at a distance, and only there. I read: "When someone steals the bell from a stranger's pigsty . . ." and I recall the bell, although there was probably no such thing, in a pigsty back home, and see or visualize our village as located in an imperial province, isolated yet within easy reach of the capital.

And yet the law, even that of classical antiquity, does not provide sufficient reading for me. Give me a sentence that begins with "In the days when" instead of "Whenever," and I am electrified altogether differently.

I fear, though, that I have read all the "In the days when" books I am referring to. The last one was the Bible, and there I kept putting off the end, finally rationing myself to two sentences a day of the Apocalypse. After that I stopped my kind of reading for the time being. I do continue to read, but it is really more a reflex action, like watching television, no longer a way of life; it does not penetrate to a deeper layer, and just as I soon switch off the television, I soon hit a snag in my reading.

The "In the days when" books still rank highest, as far as I am concerned, although those written nowadays usually soon catapult me back into the outside world, the here and now, instead of keeping me in their "It was" and "It happened." And I feel just as comfortable there as earlier when reading stories, even if nothing happens but a cloud's passing overhead. I do not know why. The only strange thing is that I am back outside most quickly, have no desire to enter into a present-day book at all, when the story pretends to be one from olden times, like a classic tale. I also cannot manage to read the "In the days when" books that merely make a game of those earlier ones in which everything is possible. I need a kind of narration that is initially problematic, lifelike, urgent —"What is the question?" means to me "What comes next?"—and then, when it can finally answer all questions and take up where the earlier or eternal stories left off, comes across as something very rare, as a happening, suitable to the kind of narration I have in mind.

At the mere idea of such a thing achieved in this day and age, I, who have not taken leave of my reading, feel immeasurably relieved, a feeling that is conferred on me only in bits and pieces by the kind of hairsplitting over definitions that occurs in the texts of the various scholarly disciplines, no matter how animating and pleasurable that may be. An idea or merely a wish? A new book full of narration, that's what I wish for. And then I again see before me and in me something grand that calls for a form entirely different from that of conventional narrative. But what sort of form?

As recently as last night I had a dream in which I was doing nothing but reading. It involved a passage from the Gospel according to St. John with which I was unfamiliar, a pure narrative, with nothing but "And he departed . . . and he ate . . . and they said . . . and when it became evening . . . and they gathered together . . . and he sat down . . . and when the sun rose . . . and we washed ourselves . . . and he said," in large, clear print with large spaces, as if winged, and I could see simultaneously everything I had read, in the form of a constant succession of "he" and "they" and "we," set in motion by letters and blank spaces, concrete and at the same time dancelike in a way I have not once encountered outside this book.

And like my reading, so too my writing. I need . . . and I hope . . .
and I wish . . . and I have a dream.

For this narrative I have needed for a while all the open questions,
the working-out of possibilities, the greatest possible comprehensiveness,
as if it were a law. Now I hope to extricate myself from the dovetailing
of objects as well as of words and to shake off the heavy hand of compulsion. More than ever I wish I could be swept away in unquestion-
ing narrating, vibrating sympathetically just as with reading, the kind
of narrating to which, it seems to me, I have not once had a breakthrough
for more than a paragraph.

But I have dreamed the dream of it again and again, and that was the
most profound thing in me. And in my imagination for some time now,
precisely because of my taking so many detours with this present project,
my starting off down so many side roads, I can feel this dream shaking
free, ready to soar aloft and take wing, for the day, the desk, and the
deed. I sense that it is no longer a dream. The image has changed into
a tone, a voiceless one, to be detected only by my sense of taste, with
which, instinct tells me, something will begin and continue, and persist,
finally without more fuss or reservations or question marks, that will
give whoever reads it the ability to hear without sound and to see without images and to sample without taste.

I also find myself wondering whether this might not be my second
metamorphosis, which I have been waiting for and working toward since
the beginning of the year. Might this presumably last metamorphosis consist in my setting out to narrate, in sentences that would be absolutely
straightforward, in the sense of "Let your speech be yea, yea and nay, nay"?
And might I thus be at the moment no longer the one I was at the beginning, nor yet the person I will be, but also not the one I appear to be?

The more freely I sense what is coming, the more constricting my
present condition feels. This becoming aware has always been a problem
for me. Whenever it has manifested itself, it has cut me off in the midst
of life from living. Suddenly I become aware, and instantly my breath
falters and runs out, in the middle of a sentence, in the midst of life, in
the midst of an upswing. My awareness has nothing in common with
any form of reason, but rather meddles like a daimon, destructively. Like
my love, it has also destroyed my narrating every time.

But now, having advanced as never before to a stage on the verge of what appears to me as my destiny, I sense that I could rid myself of my daimon, my nemesis, the crocodile in my heart, the antithesis of the mythical beast. This metamorphosis—is it going to turn into a struggle again after all: between me, the monster of awareness, and me, the Tom Thumb of narration? I have gambled away my social being, my life with others, through my awareness. Grant that through my writing I may, at least in its main purpose and its main theme, find my way back to the realm of the dream, preserve the underlying tone and become as clear as day.

From the window at which I sit, I see my narrative every morning, see how it should continue in broad strokes. It is a place. I noticed it at the very onset of winter, for the first time in all my years here: a spot in the woods on the hillsides, which since then, as a result of daily observation, has become a place (as Filip Kobal, at home on his Jaunfeld, takes those apparently insignificant little spots to which he is drawn time and again and "declares them a place").

There are trees there, as everywhere, only these stand out more distinctly than usual, up hill and down dale. In part that has to do with my distance from them: they grow halfway up the hill, approximately midway between the forest's edge below, of which the other houses allow only little glimpses, and the line of the horizon higher up, where the plateau of Vélizy begins, of which only the sky above it is visible, arching over the farthest treetops. Thus the place strikes me as the heart of the forest, removed from the foreground with its smoke rising from chimneys, but also certainly not yet far off in the distance. And for another thing, the spot has something special about it, for the oaks, the birches, the edible chestnuts are lined up on the brow of a foothill, behind which the land apparently descends again into a hollow. Of this hollow, with the fuzzy gray background of the forest rising again on the next slope, nothing appears from my vantage point but its light, which, however, picks out individually each of the few trees in front and forms them into a group. Sometimes in fog the entire line of hills appears lower by about half and ends right there, with everything above it and behind it vanished. For me, the hilltop and the hollow mark the boundary to distant parts, no matter what the weather.

In this particular section of the forest I then saw a water meadow, which in fact is probably nothing of the sort—for that there would have to be water flowing through the depression—and named it after a painter, the "Poussin Meadow."

In the beginning I still visualized scenes from some of his paintings there: figures dancing off into the distance, two men carrying a basket of wine grapes as large as themselves on a pole between them, a man with a woman at the edge of a summery field of ripe grain, and all that at the bottom of the bright, broad hollow, which took on some of the qualities of a corridor. Yet I soon started looking up at the place on the hill, just to lift my head in the morning, for instance. But then, every day, against the background of more distant vistas, I perceived something in the silhouettes of the trees, illuminated by the light from the hollow below, or the sight set me to thinking. On the Poussin Meadow, even on dark, dim days, color predominated. Although nothing was happening, it was a lively scene. Although it was not far off, I saw far into the distance. Once I saw us there walking below the Acropolis.

Against the glow in the background, the trunks and branches of the promontory became struts, themselves already the finished structure. Or the one oak tree there, almost as large as the one named after Louis XIV in a neighboring forest, its form starting at a central point and rounding out toward the top, had the appearance of a wheel, with hub and spokes, driven only by the light in between and the upwind from down below in the meadow. Nicolas Poussin in his self-portraits was looking out, as I pictured it, into just such a slice of landscape. And early this morning—Easter week has begun, with storm and a haze of rain—I saw the branches of the royal oak, almost motionless, only slightly shaken amid the general swaying, and next to them and around them a wild tumult, a massive surge of green from the tops of the birches, the first trees in the forest to leaf out completely, and at the edge, the blooming torch of a single wild cherry, an isolated ghostly whiteness there in the depths of the forest, far from all the blossoming closer by in the suburban yards, while the predominant color of the meadow was still gray, a sporadic, all the more strongly glistening pre-vernal gray, whose light came straight across the forest from the east and gathered in the branches and in the multiple tall, thin trunks typical of the trees in the Seine hills. Not a person to be seen there, and yet the meadow appears as a window on the world.

Instead of "Who am I?" I have taken to asking myself "What is most unique to me?" I do not know. But I know its place, every morning, halfway up the hill, thataway.

But Poussin's meadow often disappears with the morning light, or at least appears at midday so shrunken that the hilltop as well as the hollow could belong to one of the thousands of craters left by the bombs dropped on Vélizy in 1944, whose victims are buried in the cemetery farther up on the flank, and at most I can still see Poussin's Eurydice in the bushes, just bitten by the deadly snake.

And I belong to the green and gray glow out there only as long as I sit indoors at my table and stay put. The meadow loses its picturesqueness if I go so far as to look at it not from downstairs in my study but from upstairs: either I cannot locate it at first or there is nothing remarkable about it. And whenever I went up to the forest looking for it, I was never quite sure if this was the place I had fixed my eye on that same morning from my window, had scrutinized, studied, observed— even the oak, unmistakable from my house, multiplied as one approached, and had no regal dimensions anymore. And similarly, from my table here, morning after morning the eastern rays of light will dissipate more, like the columns of smoke from the suburban roofs gradually disappearing in springtime. The place is being overgrown. Its image is being veiled. Is its image being veiled?

Well past his childhood I did not think or say "my son" but "the child," and was also more likely to address him that way than by his name.

Many were put off by that; my own father reproved me in a letter, in his own way, by reporting that one of his girlfriends was "puzzled" by it, and the woman from Catalonia felt that by my constant invoking of the "child" I wanted to immortalize this in my son and, on the other hand, keep him at arm's length, as an exceptional being.

But what about the moment when I no longer saw Valentin either as a child or as a son, and he did not even have a name, except perhaps

"him," or "that boy," or "the stranger in my house," "the ruffian," "the
good-for-nothing," and the only thing I could manage to say to him was
"I don't know you"? When for his part my son, whenever we still went
anywhere at all together, would rush on ahead, strike out in an unfore-
seen direction, and leave me panting along behind him? When the adolescent's notebooks, which I did not leaf through until last year when I
was cleaning out his old room here in this house, are full of hatred and
loathing for me, the man who, according to him, merely put on a show
of love, whose presence just got in the way, me, the false father, whose
solicitude was an act; who took nothing seriously; whom he wanted to
get rid of every single day, wanted to kill with his own hands, with the
ax, with a club, with a medieval morning star; about whom he prayed
night after night to the heavens above, when I happened to be away,
that I would never come home; and in comparison to whom even "my
so-called mother," "the modern woman," "the woman with the cold
shoulder," "the mournful wanderer," ceaselessly roaming the world, at
most leaving him a scrap of paper with a heart scribbled on it in the
empty house, already off to her next nondestination, represented a reference point?

   If I think back, it is touching that there were two different times
when my son and I were at loggerheads this way: there was the time he
secretly raged against me for about a year, while I, according to a memory
that does not register the past but feels it, and of which I can therefore
be as certain as of a fact, was intensely fond of him, as in the years before
that. And the time when I, on the contrary, the father, moved away from
him in my thoughts—this is putting it too innocuously—that was later,
and I feel, likewise in memory, several glances of my son's resting on
me, as if from the far corner of a dim hall, and I know they stemmed
from helplessness, a wondrously tender helplessness.

Unthinkable, back in his childhood, that there should be a question
of anything between the two of us but a lifelong story. I experienced
hours, even entire days with him that above and beyond that had to lay
the groundwork for something, something enduring, a bond that could
not be banished from the world.

   That did not come immediately with his birth, when, at the sight of that fuzz-covered, dark-skinned little creature, in the presence of his almost bloodless mother, I recoiled as if the woman from Catalonia had foisted a changeling on me. During the first years of his life, which I spent without my family, far beyond the Urals, I saw him so seldom that every time he failed to recognize me and at the word "father" was more likely to look at the Mongolian faces around us than at me, and I, too, felt as though the word did not refer to me. Although I had felt a powerful urge to have a child, and with this particular woman, who would clearly bear me someone extraordinary, whenever "my family" came to mind, it was never the three of us, but, as always before, my grandparents, my mother, her brothers, long since dead, my sister, my brother; and that most decisively where I find the measure for what I call "real": in my dreams. Deep in my dreams, the woman from Catalonia, my son, and I never appeared in the context of a family; the three of us did not even appear together. Even when we were finally living together in Paris, at first I felt so ill at ease with my son that I avoided being alone with him and often did not come home in the evening until he was sure to be in bed already.

Yet my memory also preserves a few very different moments from that period: the face of a child, behind a door in the dark, where he has hidden and is smiling, a smile in profile such as one sees only during hide-and-go-seek. And in a particular stretch of sidewalk, which I let him walk on the day they were paving it, his footprint, next to that of a large dog. And my searching for refuge and élan, and not only once, in his cowlick. And then, in our first suburb, initially so quiet after the roar of the metropolis, up there in the Seine hills, on the side streets the postman's regular morning whistling, and inside the house the two of us, intent each time on not missing a note of it, our moment of shared experience.

And in spite of that our life together continued to be determined by an expression in my son's eyes that has been gone for many years now, and even then appeared only occasionally. I understood that look as one of distrust, as a sign of a serious disturbance. The child's distrust focused on no one in particular. It was a matter of principle, or at least in the process of becoming a matter of principle. I knew that kind of look from earlier, from myself, in the only photo from my boarding school, a group picture, and I encounter it likewise in children today, more and more,

including smaller children. I see it every day in some here in the neighborhood.

For one in particular—he has not been walking that long, and speech
is still new to him—the word distrust does not seem strong enough: it
should be suspicion. This child looks around for suspicious sights, and
not only from time to time—he does so uninterruptedly, eyes darting,
somberly from below or over his shoulder. Paraphrasing a saying of the
petty prophet of Porchefontaine, I then think, "Two years old—and
already it's all over," and although it is clear to me that the blame rests
with his parents (or someone else), I cannot help condemning the little
fellow himself; that's how upset I am by his unremitting wariness.

My son had that look, but quite unexpectedly, between two looks
quite normal for a child. Yet even then I was repelled and felt a surge
of rage, directed against him, myself, something unknown. In the face
of this sudden darkening of his gaze it seemed to me that it would take
only a little for that look to become permanently fixed on his face. I felt
an urgent need to dispel that facial expression, by force. Something had
to be done about this distrust, unbearable to someone who was subjected
to it day in, day out from close up. But I did nothing.

The person who did something after all was my son. Valentin, in
defiance of the usual expression, did not "come" to me. He ran, galloped,
flitted, leaped, stumbled, dashed. That usually happened after periods of
separation, which had meanwhile become infrequent. Previously, even if
he had caught sight of me the moment I appeared, his first movement
had been a looking away, almost a violent swiveling of his head, as if
he had been waiting for anyone but me. But now, picking me out without any particular peering around, even from among a crowd of people
in a railroad station or airport, he would promptly break into a run,
looking straight at me from way across the building. I did not see the
need for help and the pleading quality that later replaced distrust in his
eyes and can still appear there, even now that he has come of age; rather,
it was an instance of uninhibited pleasure, never preceded by the slightest
surprise, even when he could not know I was going to turn up. For he
took it as a matter of course that when he had climbed the lighthouse
at the end of the earth with his grandparents, in La Coruña (or somewhere else), on the platform at the top I would appear around the corner.
And he did not even need to be separated from me to run toward me

that way. Once we had just spoken with each other and then met by chance on the street, on opposite sides—he surrounded by friends—and he immediately slipped away and came flying and leaping toward me, a glow on his face that embarrassed me and at the same time made my heart bleed.

For an entire decade the child and for a while also the adolescent and I lived together this way in harmony; or we were of one mind, without words, each of us, wherever he happened to be just then, equally preoccupied with nothing of moment, like two idiots.

Only when we walked together did this boy otherwise so silent—to his teachers "silent Val"—begin to speak, the first speaking in tongues I ever witnessed. As a rule, it occurs to me, this happened when we were going gradually downhill, after a longish ascent, and if I still feel drawn today to places from the past, it is to those nameless stretches where my son did nothing but enumerate the world for me.

One time, after we had gone up and down in the Seine hills, we descended to the Métro station in Issy-les-Moulineaux, located in one of those suburban streets for which the dictionary of commonplaces would offer the word "gray," and he began to speak about the colors of the houses, and by the end of the street each house had its own color, shading, and nuance; yet he was not inventing or adding anything, simply comparing what was there, making distinctions, emphasizing, and when a building remained gray, which was the exception, it became dove gray, beech-trunk gray, slate gray, so that when we looked back over our shoulders the row of houses stood there as a strip of colors, more varied than any human being could dream up, and even the asphalt of the sidewalks displayed that tinge of red that is a fact in this region on the outskirts of Paris and takes on the deep red of animal blood in the lightest showers.

I was always threatened by a kind of numbness: losing any sense of coherence, whereupon the world continued to move along without me; instead of conceptual bewilderment, which I welcomed, I was struck with something like a visual bewilderment, for which in the area where

I grew up they had an expression—"to stare into the idiot box"—comical only to those who watched someone actually doing it. In the meantime I have been trying to avoid this condition with the help of an aphorism from Goethe's later years: he says we have an obligation to keep ourselves alive and impressionable, following the example nature gives us. And accordingly, my decade of association with the child seems to have brought this notion of impressionability to my attention—a word I am now writing for the first time, although it has accompanied me since the beginning of this undertaking and actually showed me the direction in which it should be going, far in advance; a multisyllabic word, uncommon in this usage, that set me on the path for an entire book.

I learned that a child could make one impressionable, much as nature does, simply in its way of being there before one's eyes, to be perceived without Goethe's microscope or magnifying glass, for instance with that cowlick, from which the eye moved on to the bracken, the door, the pebbles, the rusty key.

Then my son and I had a falling-out. It was never put into words. Had that happened—and how close I was to blurting it out, and probably he as well—there would have been no going back. By holding back the final word, each of us made a fresh start possible.

And yet our falling-out was a fact, and no mere growing apart such as they say is usual for parents and children in a transitional era.

I see its origin in myself. Even when we were of one mind, I had an ulterior thought: to be alone and on my own again. Back in my family period I was already leading a double life. In hours of harmony I was still on the lookout for something else—the wind in the leaves over there, the quivering rain puddle far off in the light of night—and considered my being with the others a mere episode, though it might last for decades; afterward I would be able to go my way as never before. I lived with those who had been entrusted to me and recognized that inside me something was turning in a different direction, away from closeness, away from fulfillment, away from the present. That counter-direction within me often became so powerful, even during the day and when things were outwardly tranquil, that I could not stand being touched by a child, not even my own, although I was happy with him, in harmony.

And then came the time when he did not believe in my affection anymore. He did not expressly avoid me; I simply did not exist. At our morning encounters he took cognizance of me without really seeing me. I, who with the passing years had come to need a greeting at least once a day, greeted my son myself, often through a door behind which he had locked himself, usually greeted him two or three times, hardly ever receiving a response. Upon occasion he looked right past me, jostled me, and did not even notice. Although Valentin and I continued to live in the house, more and more rooms, corners, even stair treads, door handles, and dishes seemed to become orphaned.

In the evenings he came home later and later, and I never knew where he was. Although I asked him to, he never once telephoned; I had simply dropped out of his consciousness. When he did call one time, the people he was with had reminded him of me.

Finally, while still a child in age, he began staying out all night, and I could not help waiting up for him. I got dressed and went out. In the suburbs, shortly after midnight, neither trains nor buses are running, and the headlights, shining, of a car, moving, become an unusual sight, and someone there, waiting in the house or in front of it, on the street, as I did time and again in those days, until that hour of night when only a barely audible, but all the more penetrating, hissing comes through the air, as if from all the electrical and gas conduits in the area, and still waiting when the first birds begin to sing and the racket of the day begins again—this person will perceive such a place, and with it the isolation, the silence, the ponds, the forests, only as his enemy. And on just such a night, a bitter cold one, with the glory of the sparkling winter constellations in the sky above the hills of the Seine, fresh snow was on the ground, and every time I walked down the white street in the direction from which I expected my son to come, and each time saw only my own tracks ahead of me, not those of any other pedestrian or any vehicle, I cursed the bay, together with its bamboo, palms, stars, and snow.

After a series of nights like this, the moment came when my son strolled toward me in the early light with the dreamlike gait of a dancer, and it became a certainty to me that I would reject him. I wanted to disown my child. And I had that thought in these very words, fired up by my intention, as though, having made a breakthrough to a biblical story, I had attained a life goal. While he was asleep in his room, I paced up and down in the yard and repeated, "I don't know you anymore; go away from here." But I never spoke any such thing out loud, and not because on one of the following nights he had an accident but rather because the other story was still there between us, biblical or not.

Yet I know of one father or another who has expressly disowned his son. How irrevocable such ruptures are. How such fathers retroactively deny their sons any good qualities, even those things for which they once unhypocritically praised them to the skies. And besides I am preoccupied with the question: What happened to the prodigal son after his return? And: What if in reality God the Father had long since forsaken his human, crucified son—see God's disdainful expression in many of his oldest portraits. And: Is there also a prodigal father?

These are my background stories with my friends, who, while I sit here in my study off the yard, are on the road in different parts of the world on behalf of a new—what kind of?—story.

But what is it that makes precisely these people my heroes, and not my many other acquaintances, who lend themselves far more obviously to being exemplary figures and contemporaries: my young journalist friend, who just last summer was covering the Tour de France and in the meantime has become a war correspondent; the professor of ancient languages, who now and then comes by here on his Japanese motorcycle, dressed all in leather, each time with a different beautiful woman riding behind him? Besides, don't I know a great deal more about these acquaintances?

Yes. Yet precisely the fact that I know so little about my son, my woman friend, the singer, the architect and carpenter, the priest, the reader, the painter, and the filmmaker makes them interesting to me or draws them to me, more from afar.

That means: fundamentally I do not know any more about all the

others, but the little I do know about them already seems to be everything, as if there were nothing more to be learned beyond that. No
matter how I view them: they look complete to me, as Austrian society
used to; inside me there seems nowhere else to go with them, and not
merely because most of them have succumbed to what the petty prophet
of Porchefontaine calls, with reference to all of contemporary humanity,
"desperate self-deification."

The attractive quality of my heroes is precisely that I see them as
unfinished and cannot imagine that that would ever change. Unfinished?
Incomplete. Incomplete and needy. And they will be incomplete and
needy all their lives. Close to despair, none of them will seek salvation
in the worship of false idols.

Of all those whom I know somewhat, only these seven are this way:
eternally unfinished, incomplete, needy, cool, hot, always on the go. My
poor carpenter, my rich painter, my loafer woman friend, my empathizing reader, my high-handed singer, my somnambulistic son, my jubilant
pastor, the only ones with whom I can be together from afar, strike me,
in the morning perhaps more, in the evening perhaps less, as figures of
light—bold, fiercely decisive. Whenever I was in their presence, I had
only to touch them accidentally to feel to the very tips of my fingers
that they were in my head.

I expect something of us—what? Something from the New World.
That is unthinkable for me with a single hero, even with two: but from
three on it becomes exciting. And to make clear what I mean, I shall
offer a variation on an experience of the early Gregor Keuschnig: place
beside the pencil on the table a hairpin, for instance, and push a shard
of mirror next to them: how astonishing this threesome is. But how
much more so when you then roll a pebble toward them, and fifth, blow
a piece of string in their direction, and sixth, plop down a lump of resin,
and seventh—is this maybe too much already?—flick an eraser among
them: what a metamorphosis occurs in every one of the individual objects
with each addition, and likewise in all of them together. What an experience, and how it wakes one up, tension created out of nothing, nothing at all.

———

Yet as far as my heroes and I are concerned, there have been times when I thought in terms very different from "we." One of the incentives to my present undertaking was actually the question: "Who is the hero? All of you or I?" In the midst of accompanying these absent ones, at the same time as I was observing things around me, the thought repeatedly interposed itself that I was the only one of us doing the right thing with his life. Only a moment ago I might have been wafting away with the smoke from the house next door or traveling with the passengers in the train to Brittany up there on the embankment, at the same moment so wrapped up in a distant friend that what he was doing just then was a first-person experience for me, and already a voice inside me was severing me from such unity, insisting that my life was entirely unique. Particularly in the backyard, there and present in the procession of impressions offered by the seasons, from within the earth-spanning stillness I became indignant at all the absent ones because they did not know what was beautiful, and were leading such a false life.

Even now, separated from the yard by the closed window, at my table in the study, when I look out at the cedar, at the beech, at the three stone kings in the grass, and order my distant friends to file past in review, for a moment also seeing them together as a frieze, I can find myself wondering: Who is more where he belongs, the pastor in his forester's vehicle, by his deathbeds, or I at my table; which of us is on the right path: the singer with his rising and falling notes, the painter with his pictures, materials, tools, machines, or I with my pencil script?

Am I also a self-deifier? A self-crowned king? One of the millions of self-anointed emperors running around today? The new metamorphosis all the more unavoidable? Or should it be called: expulsion?

Several weeks ago, on a sunny day, at the very first greening, that of the moss, I traced a wide arc through the woods in the bay here. Beside a sandy path, along a newly reforested area, where it was light, I sat down on a tree stump. Although on one side of the path the trees stood far apart and on the other the recently planted ones had barely reached the height of shrubs, I felt as if I were deep in the forest—it was so quiet, hidden, and at the same time lively there. The occasional airplanes, high above, white, hardly visible in the blue sky, were part of it. The whirring of the highway on the plateau at my back receded behind that of not yet fallen tissue-thin leaves in the oaks, still there even now when spring was beginning.

As if it were a marker for the middle of the forest, at this place, unlike at everywhere else I had walked earlier, no more water glistened, not even the usual patches of standing water, and no rivulet. The sand, which had not been dumped on the path as elsewhere in the bay but had worked its way up from the subsoil, breaking through a thin layer of humus, fine as dust, was that of an extended dune, which emerged just as nakedly on the slope, although there it was firmer and more clayey, crisscrossed by roots, riddled in places by the mining bees, slipping into daylight en masse before my eyes, as if from ancient cave cities, reeling, flying upward.

The path ran straight ahead, though continually forming humps and hollows, and disappeared into a distant realm, where a far-off light beckoned, with the same pattern of crooked branch shadows as at the tips of my shoes. The sand changed color from one section of path to the next, going from a loessial yellow to an ash gray, from coal black to a beach white, brick red, desert brown. The colors appeared sharply separated, section after section, and for each one a corresponding animal turned up, as if growing out of that particular sand.

From the pale yellow a brimstone butterfly fluttered up. I saw the gray stretch enlivened by the similarly gray lizards, seemingly just born, a threesome, matching the coat of arms of the suburb, which extends into the woods here. And there, where the path suddenly blackened, to complement it a huge raven stalked along and sparkled, his bowing and scraping reminiscent of a duck, his sparkle reminding me of my runaway wife (a note from whom I had, just that morning, when I stepped into the study, found taped to the outside of the window). But the unpopulated places, too, were churned up by the tracks of animals, not only those of dogs, horses, and cats—which are led through the woods on leashes by their owners—but also those of mice, rabbits, birds, and then at my feet I searched for the print of the local mythical beast; but saw only clumps of rabbit droppings, as if expelled in mortal fear; mouse innards breaded with sand; feathers with tufts of animal fur stuck to them.

As I continued to sit on the tree stump at the edge of the dune path, my mind more and more vacant, I began to feel as though at any moment a horse-drawn carriage would drive by, garlanded, with my departed or defunct ancestors riding in it.

Meanwhile midday had come, balmy air, and the familiar yet always alarming joggers turned up, from the hundreds of office buildings up on the plateau, colorful like nothing else in the forest. One of them, as usual (and, as usual, a different one), called out a greeting. A little later, after the howl of a jet landing at the Villacoublay air base, squadrons of helicopters flew by carrying visitors of state, heading northeast over the hills toward Paris, whereupon it occurred to me that on that day a conference on a civil war was taking place.

I saw a man going straight ahead along the dune path, between sun and shade, up and down, dark stretches of sand and light ones. I caught sight of him while he was still far off, in the place where I could sense that other zone, veiled in distance. It was the medieval stonemason, tramping alone through France at the end of the Romanesque period, the man whose notes I had been reading just that morning. He strode along, although overtaken again and again by one of the joggers, maintaining the same even gait whether going uphill or down, and likewise in the deepest sand, the gait of a villager, shoulders back, arms and legs swinging wide, not of a contemporary villager, but rather of one from prewar days. He was dressed accordingly: a black suit with an open jacket and trousers fluttering around his knees, a white shirt without a necktie, a gray vest. With every change of color in the sand of the path, in a hollow, on a rise, the walker glowed in new splendor, one colorful panting figure after another circling around him. When he paused for a moment, I fantasized that he was hammering his stonemason's mark into a tree with a chisel. At my spot it was I who greeted him. A laconic greeting in reply, and already his back, shoulders rolling, as if there were balls of air in his armpits.

I followed him with my eyes, past all the bomb craters to left and right, obscured by the joggers as he was, until he disappeared into that so very different section of the path, no longer in the present but also no longer in his Middle Ages. And what had I just read in his notes? "I do not belong in the current era. I only wreak havoc there." And on the other hand: "Today I shall find something I thought lost forever; there are such days!" And what was written on the paper the woman from Catalonia had stuck to the outside of my window? "We must remain at odds for a while longer. And even longer. And even longer." But didn't that thought come from me?

PART 2

1

Where Not? Where?

The adventure stories that meant the most to me told of a person's search for the most suitable place for him to live. For example? And weren't those actually fairy tales? And which ones?

In my youth I wanted to be swallowed up by a metropolis. But none of the Austrian and German cities through which I passed fit that description. Not only the manner of the passersby but also the sounds, the smells, and the buildings made me feel like a stranger to those parts. And at home in the country I had perhaps been everything but that. Being a stranger to those parts also implied the opposite of what I desired: to be swallowed up. Even the springlike fragrance of lilacs in the villa sections of Graz, Vienna, Munich, Berlin could plunge me into misery. At the sight of the palaces of Schönbrunn, Nymphenburg, and Charlottenburg, of the magnificent hanging gardens along Hamburg's Elbchaussee, of the Cologne Cathedral, even of the great rivers, the Rhine, the Main, the Danube, running through great cities, I had the sensation of dust in my eyes.

———

The first time I felt I had become one with the wide world was in a
town: that time among the limestone blocks on the harbor of Piran
on the Istrian Peninsula. It was a mild evening between Easter and
Whitsun, the same as now, thirty-five years later; I had just taken that
examination on Roman law and wanted nothing in my mind but the
white-gray boulders rearing up before me, with the gentle harbor waves
breaking in the gaps between them. In Spanish towns, the largest and
the smallest, I then had a similar experience, for instance during my
summer semester in Santiago de Compostela, with the sensation, which
always took me by surprise, that these places expanded from day to day,
with more and more corners emerging from the shadows, even if today
it may be no more than a newspaper stand far back in the dark lobby
of an apartment building or tomorrow the wooden ladder leaning against
part of the church ruins on an overgrown island in the river.

Yet neither there in Spain nor in Piran in Yugoslavia was there any
question of staying. At the time, for my further training, the suitable
metropolis seemed to be Paris. That stemmed first of all from the fact
that beginning with the moment of my arrival nothing there repelled
me or excluded me; that not the slightest element interposed itself between this world-class city and me, who, and I felt I was this, was open
to the world. And then again it was a color that revealed the place to
me: the light, expansive gray of the asphalt on the boulevards that gave
me the impulse to set out, to walk and walk—something I had had no
desire to do everywhere else—and to cover the entire city, in all directions. Here was my future; here I would later on live as well as work.
And at the time I could picture doing both only in the center, where I
actually did have an apartment—at least it seemed central to me, which,
indeed, gradually became true of almost every part of Paris; I never had
to go through even the smallest lifeless stretch between my lodgings and
the lecture halls, the left bank of the Seine and the right, the laundromat
and the movie grottoes; and besides I had got away not only from the
lilacs and the jasmine but more importantly from the whole Western
European great outdoors and was quite content with the unchanging
gray trunks of the plane trees.

When I had to return to my country for my year in the Viennese courts, and after that a position in the legal department of the Austrian Southern Railway, it occasioned a pain similar to what I had experienced in childhood when I was dragged away from the village of Rinkolach to that horrible boarding school. I sat with my suitcase in an outdoor café by the Gare de l'Est, the asphalt at my feet showing the innumerable overlapping imprints of bottle caps from the hot times of year, and I felt as if I were experiencing all this for the last time. As if along with the gray of Paris I had to take leave of the world. A few drops of rain fell and were gone at once. At the thought of the coming years in Austria and my profession as a lawyer, I became aware for the first time of that black cloud, of which I could not tell whether it welled up inside me or on the horizon, which was poisoned by it, the cloud that meanwhile, I imagine, is merely resting, always ready to become active again. But a decade later I was living back in the metropolis where I belonged and working in the profession for which I am halfway suited, if for any. Working? Profession? I embarked on my project.

Not until I began to look for a place to live did I come to know the outskirts of Paris, along with the gates leading out of the city, arranged like the markings on a clock. There had been no real gates for a long time, merely streets, which as a rule widened into squares at the point where they crossed into the suburbs. The apartments I saw in the inner *quartiers* were usually more beautiful or more elegant, often even quieter. But I chose a place near one of those squares, which, as time passed, came to signify to me more departure than entry gates, unless I was away for weeks and somewhere else entirely, for instance in the mountains: thus I returned once from a hike in the Pyrenees, dozed off on the evening bus from the airport, was surprised in my sleep at the unexpectedly more powerful and at the same time more even noise of the engine, finally appropriate to the wheels and the enclosure of the bus, opened my eyes and saw myself turning onto one of those well-lit boulevards that lead straight from all the provinces of France into the center of this city, for which the word "metropolis" seemed fitting as for no other in the world—and behind us, as a broad outlet into the blackness of night, the square of the Porte d'Orléans.

And there I also lived for a couple of years with the woman from Catalonia and our son. All the rooms except Valentin's, which gave on a small walled garden, were dark and with no particular view; from one of the windows I could see the city bus depot at the gate. From her Iberian childhood Ana was used to darknesses of a very different order in houses, from the front doors far into the interiors. And I actually appreciated the lack of a view. From my years in the vineyards, with a view of Vienna, the hills of the Vienna Woods, and the Pannonian plain, stretching to infinity, I still felt ill at ease with any panorama or belvedere (the street in Sievering where I lived in a rented apartment was also called "Bellevue"). Sometimes, when I sat facing that view for a long time, I could feel the pain, agony, and death struggles in hospital rooms down below, all mixed up together, and I understood that neighbor who during the winter months saw the bare stakes up and down the hills of the vineyard outside his picture window as the crosses in a cemetery, and likewise that other neighbor who, to get away from the distant and even more distant horizon of the lowlands, including the magnificent sunsets, finally moved to the most confining hilly moraine country, from where he wrote me that the lines of the landscape crowding in on him had cured him of the fear of death that had haunted him on his "Bellevue" property.

So it was also a blessing to be shielded at my desk and elsewhere in the apartment from wide-open spaces and boundlessness. When I raised my head, there was water at eye level, close enough to touch, running in the gutter; or a truck, with a load of sand and a shovel stuck in it, drove by. I often worked there, and the hours with the family could be surprisingly festive.

By compensation, wide-open space entirely different from that of my bird's-eye view awaited me when I stepped out of the house with its dark nooks onto the square at Porte d'Orléans and began walking. In the beginning I still headed into the city, going from one center to the next: Alésia, Montparnasse, St.-Germain, whose fraternally broad tower I could always rely upon to give me a sense of arrival.

For a good year I did not get past the city limits, at most crossed to the middle of the bridge over the beltway and immediately turned back. All the harmony characteristic of the metropolis, not only in the buildings but also in the movements of the passersby, seemed abruptly to fall apart over there in the suburbs of Gentilly and Montrouge, the former to the left of the arterial road, the latter to the right, the two indistinguishable at first sight. Just as the houses lost their common features, so, too, the pedestrians, far scarcer than inside the gates, without so much as a by-your-leave lost their character. They seemed slower to me—an inelegant slowness like that of people who are lost—also more awkward. Although there were few of them, they avoided each other, as I saw from above from the vantage point of the bridge, on the much narrower suburban sidewalks, turning in the wrong direction and not infrequently colliding with each other, while on the other hand the people of the metropolis filed past each other in the heaviest crowd with the grace of dancers. And the slower the pedestrians moved, the faster the cars went there beyond the gate, where the avenue with a name turned into a national highway with a number, "Nationale 20." They no longer glided, but whizzed by, and the stretch of highway that followed was also infamous for its accidents. I understood those who translated the word *banlieue* as "place of banishment." Even the sky above, no matter how blue it may have been, lost its Parisian materiality (which of course came into view again when one glanced over one's shoulder). It became clear that the appearance of the sky took its cue from what was down below and happening on earth. At the time I felt the sky was not operative above the suburbs. It did not reach down to the ridgepoles and streets, and outside the city limits no longer extended into the splinters, pores, and bubbles of the asphalt. *Extra portas* its gray no longer had color value.

Nevertheless I felt drawn more and more powerfully out into this nothingness. Soon, long before my fortieth year, I had recognized that city life, even on the edge of town, was not for me anymore: for all the casualness it lent me, to the point of a redeeming self-forgetfulness, for all the verve (with which, to be true, I often no longer knew what to do), almost nothing from this environment gripped me, and without being gripped by something, something before my eyes, I was deprived and felt lifeless, or at least not at my best. Over the years, things in the metropolis had stopped having a lasting effect, cafés and movie houses, the boulevards, the Métro, even water flowing in the gutter, scraps of paper blowing across squares, cats dashing between the rows of graves in the great cemeteries, clouds passing overhead. As pleasant as things in the metropolis could continue to be, they had become meaningless. They no longer signified anything, no longer gave me intimations, no longer reminded me of anything (did not connect with anything in my childhood memories), had ceased to make me dreamy or inventive—and that was all necessary for feeling enthusiasm or even an everyday sensation of life. Although I was still young, big cities no longer held any charms for me. In my eyes they were dominated by inconsequentiality; and my days were not supposed to be inconsequential. And in the meantime I have realized: in the metropolises, just as in the sun, I easily lose my memory; in the shade, in the dark, it comes back to me, indefinite yet monumental. In the time of Gilgamesh the gods still belonged in the capital city of the land. And now?

B ut it was without ulterior motives that I then ventured beyond the Porte d'Orléans into the suburbs (I later read in a book by Emmanuel Bove that for one of his heroes, who moved, initially still in a cheerful mood, from the edge of Paris out to Montrouge, even the flies on the walls gradually lost their luster).

And with the very first step over the line my curiosity was transformed into a sense of peace and my uneasiness into amazement, and the two produced great alertness. All the houses in the suburbs continued to look either too large or too small to me, the noise on Nationale 20 had something hostile about it, and the few people who had crossed with me on the overpass promptly fell out of step and became isolated from each other (whereas those crossing toward the city were picked up by a common tailwind as soon as they set foot on the overpass). Even the splendid and luxurious articles available only in the metropolis, with which they were loaded down, like border crossers from an underdeveloped country, promptly began to dangle from them, and rubbed against them like ugly and useless trash.

And yet I felt I was in territory that was not merely different but also new. A special realm began there, as when one enters a forest, when the world through which I have just been moving—one step among the trees is sufficient—draws back and in its place an entirely different one opens up, surprising, infinitely more sensuous, its first effect being to make me listen more attentively. That is followed by looking, smelling, tasting, perceiving as a mode of discovery.

That was what I experienced, to my amazement, with my penetration into that region outside the city limits. A new realm only for me? No, I felt altogether as if I were in a realm of the new: like the people, things there on the outskirts presented themselves in isolation, which meant that although they might lack the grace and brilliance of their counterparts in the capital, they appeared fresh as the morning. That was not so clear to me at first; I merely sensed it—but how!

These things and this area had to be something solid, different from all the phantoms with which I had fooled myself every time, in my lifelong pursuit of the place that was right for me, a blind believer who over time had become almost an unbeliever. I had an intuition that in such suburbs there was something to explore. I glimpsed, scented, sniffed it out. Finally, in accordance with an early dream of mine, I could view myself as an explorer in my own way. And I scented and sniffed out, beyond the roar and rumble of the Route Nationale, an as yet unheard silence, which was there as soon as you turned off the road, tangible, to be fingered, licked, and savored, silence as an as yet undiscovered and undescribed wind.

After that I made my way every day to the suburbs—without this excursion my day felt incomplete—and not only the ones to the south. But my main route remained the zigzag back and forth between Montrouge and Gentilly, crisscrossing Nationale 20, into the silence and back again into the racket, as far as Arcueil and Cachan, where, as I had learned in the meantime, Eric Satie had spent the last decade of his life all by himself (the cemetery on the slope above the Bièvre, with the stone aqueduct higher up, was sometimes my destination).

Satie was one of the few composers who did not strike me as alien beings, inwardly warped and inaccessible. His pieces came across to me as a quiet, clear conversing, in which a particular voice never rose above the others, and that was musical enough for me. After all, I wanted to be stimulated by something other than music; stimulation by music was not good for me. Or: music that is supposed to open me up must already be inside me.

And I learned furthermore that Satie had also had the habit of walking through these suburbs. Except that he went in the opposite direction, to Montparnasse in Paris, where he might meet his friends at an outdoor café during the years between the wars. I imagined us passing each other now and then, on a side street or by the railroad line that crossed the valley of the Bièvre. Apparently he always dressed properly for his excursions into the metropolis, in a dark suit with hat and bow tie, and I, too, was in a period then when I wanted to look more everymanlike than everyman: in custom-made things, including my shirts and even my shoes—which proved excellent for walking—necktie and a broad-brimmed hat, which took the place of an umbrella, and hair as short as I had been advised on every occasion to wear it during my earlier days in society. Sometimes the hallucination of encountering the composer was so powerful that I saw each of us on his side of the street tipping his hat to the other. If I was enamored of an image, a series of notes, a series of sentences, it always meant something to me to be in the native region of the person responsible for it, and even more if this person was long since gone from there, and most of all when he had not been part of an entire group or horde of like-minded others, as happens almost everywhere in metropolises, but had been the only one in his region.

There in the suburbs I also became friends with the painter, whom I had known for some time from the center of town without our growing closer.

Again it was the particular place that altered our relationship. I did not know that he had a studio in Bagneux, still farther to the south, already up in the hills overlooking the Seine. One day I saw him there, coming out of a bistro in the palpably different light and wind. At first sight he immediately seemed different from my Paris acquaintance, who, if not worldly, his glasses propped on his head, at least appeared official (perhaps because he was also a professor at the Ecole des Beaux-Arts). Here he hardly stood out from the tradesmen and local white-collar workers, who, like him, were on their way back to work after a quick lunch. He appeared as inconspicuous as they, and just as formless, or rather unassuming, and yet on closer inspection he had an added air of vulnerability and melancholy that revealed itself to me in the almost humble way in which he held the door for the others, who took it quite for granted. I sensed in him the shoulders, neck, back of the head, and eyes of a child lost to the world, who—I followed him secretly as he went on his way—was visibly becoming high-spirited.

And then he was also delighted to see me. We hugged each other, as happens only with two people from the same village who hardly had anything to say to each other and suddenly, each of them alone on a long journey, really become aware of each other for the first time on a dock in New Zealand or at a trading post in the Yukon in Alaska.

I experienced the painter outside the city, far from our usual meeting places, in a moment that had to bond me to him. And it was mutual. He urged me to go with him, wanted to have me along that afternoon when he went on with his work (though invisible behind a screen), and accompanied me, since I had to pick up my son at his school in Paris, many kilometers back to the Périphérique, where we took leave of each other only after a great deal of back-and-forth, as later became our custom when saying goodbye.

Many streets in these suburbs bore the names of resistance fighters or opposition figures killed by the Nazis. Along one of them, rue Victor-Basch in Arcueil, I was acquainted with a particular tree. It was a cherry tree that stood not in an enclosed garden but in a turnout on a street in front of an apartment building, right by the rail line. First came the blossoms, without a single leaf greening, and the trunk was dressed in a swirl of white, dense and lightly flared, piled sky-high and glowing up above more brightly than any spring cloud. Then the blossoms floated away, one day with the April snows or hail, another day with the suburban butterflies. At the beginning of June the fruit was ripe, not tiny like that of a wild cherry but of biblical proportions, and where earlier everything had been white, now everything was a rich red. And on each new day of that week, when I got to the tree, the fruit was unharmed. No blackbirds fell upon it (did the trains streaking incessantly past the tree frighten them off, as elsewhere strips of foil might?). And the occasional passersby there did not help themselves either, although the lowest of the cherries almost caressed their heads; no one even stooped to pick up the plump balls, some of which had split as the wind knocked them to the asphalt, which became dark and darker from the squashed fruit. Only I ate and ate, first the cherries from the ground, since I had no way of knowing whether an owner might not appear from somewhere, and later those within reach of my toes and fingertips.

Then it was clear that the tree was common property, and once, when I saw a painter's ladder in the wide-open lobby of the apartment house, I promptly borrowed it and climbed up to the crown, where the cherries are said to be tasty as nowhere else (and that turned out to be true).

In the village of Rinkolach there had been just such a generally accessible cherry tree, in the middle of the village, or, conversely, was the middle established by the tree? Not only the taste from those days but also that special feeling at the top—more powerful than being high in the air on a mountain peak, along with the swaying that is probably unique to a cherry tree—this I rediscovered in the foreign suburb; rediscovered? no, for the very first time this becoming aware of the past occurred: a becoming reflective, a recognizing of something from before, taking its dimensions, a sort of precision—memory! It was the semi-shade in which I saw the world so much more clearly and astonishingly (and that remained true from suburb to suburb, out into the forest bay here).

At home we had picked the cherries with our lips, also because with the violent swaying of the branches we had no hand free. And even outside of the fruiting season that tree meant something to us, an unspoken place of asylum: anyone who fled to it could not be harmed in its precinct, and as soon as the pursuers entered, too, it meant that a reconciliation had to take place. And the public cherry tree of Rinkolach still exists; I pass and walk around it at least once a year. It is alive, despite several lightning strikes, it bears fruit, now somewhat sour and watery; except that each time it seems more orphaned (or who is the orphaned one?); no more children, either around it or in it, and if in the meantime another spot has become the middle of the village, I do not find it; but perhaps I do not stay around long enough.

And now I sat, who?, in the tree in Arcueil, hidden, in my custom-made suit and necktie, felt my thirst for cherries diminish at the mere thought of the Bièvre down there in the valley, though it had long since gone underground, scraped my fingertips on the fissured, especially sharp bark of the old cherry wood and sniffed them, to make myself more receptive, receptive just as I still do today on my very own cherry tree, dead except for one branch, here in the bay between the hills of the Seine, in fear of becoming numb and number, starting with my extremities.

I thought at the time, no differently from now, that everyone's eyes and ears had to be opened by these things as mine were, and so at the beginning I occasionally invited one person or another from the metropolis, who I thought would have a sense of place, to join me on my pilgrimage beyond the city limits.

Either this was never taken seriously, or while we were out there together hardly anything emerged having to do with the particular region. The region lost its value; did not even begin to reveal it. First of all, as soon as the other person was at my side, I had to fight off a bad mood, as if by his mere presence he were displacing our surroundings, and then most people, and not only the dyed-in-the-wool city dwellers, after at most a brief period of alertness, stopped paying attention, were somewhere else entirely in their thoughts, and what they said neither had anything to do with the landscape we were passing through together—which was almost all right with me—nor was affected, guided, or inspired by it in the slightest (which then enraged me against my companions).

In my imagination they should have stood up straighter, moved their whole bodies, looked around them, spoken in a calmer, deeper, solid voice, and instead they fell in on themselves, stumbled repeatedly, kept their eyes on the ground, and now and then one of them lost his urban-sophisticate tone, which turned out to have been an affectation, and spoke in a labored way, without emphasis and resonance, precisely as one imagines a lifelong resident of the suburbs.

And I was infected by it: I mumbled, hobbled, and stumbled along just like the man next to me, and we two formed a pair that was not merely ludicrous like Bouvard and Pécuchet but also out of place.

Walking with others, I usually experienced something similar to what I had earlier experienced when I read aloud, to a person to whom I felt close, something I had just written: although I had been glowing with pleasure as I set out with my manuscript to see him, and he, too, had been eager, it was as if each of us scuttled away into a corner, farther and more apart than ever before, and I still have those stranger's eyes before me whenever, after reading aloud, stumbling more and more, I with effort raise my head.

Thus, with rare exceptions, I stopped taking others with me to places where for me, and, as I realized, for me alone, a new territory opened up—where my personal field of exploration lay.

I even kept my forays, pushed farther every day, a secret from my family, as if they were a vice, something pointless, at the very least selfish, unworthy of an adult responsible for himself and his kin. If at home I was asked where I had been so long, I would lie, saying, for instance, that I had gone to a movie on the Right Bank, an unusually long one; had played billiards at the Place de Clichy, had crashed a reception at the Austrian embassy and drunk an entire bottle of wine, had got into an argument with a policeman in front of Les Invalides; with the woman from Catalonia I even used the lie that for professional reasons I had spent hours following an unknown beauty, a "worldly woman," from the Pont Neuf to God knows where; I went so far as to lie to my son, unnecessarily and inexplicably, as I have often lied in my life, groundlessly, without enjoyment, simply because of being asked and having to open my mouth.

But for me that disappearing day in, day out into the suburbs was the first good habit I had acquired up to then. Here was finally a habit I could be happy about; never would I want to be rid of it.

The morning after a trip the first thing I did, under the pretext of going to the doctor's, was to plunge into the bushes on the far side of the Périphérique overpass and head for the wide-open spaces in the no-man's-land between Malakoff, Laplace, and Fontenay-aux-Roses. The first tree beyond the city limits, no matter how scrawny, rustled at me more tangibly than the more luxuriant exemplars of its species on the other side. Drinking coffee, more bitter than anywhere in the city, in one of the cavelike bars, I tasted a more penetrating reality, and the sight of the old aqueduct stretching high above the Bièvre Valley, not just one monument among many like the monumental structures of Paris, gave me a sense of monumentality different from that in the city, as did the similarly scattered churches in the region, often lower than their surroundings, also sunk deeper into the ground, as if forming part of the ruins behind them, where I regained possession of the past and of history, which in the course of my life had made me skittish, regained it for instance in the stone figures around the arched portal of the church in Bagneux, made easier to overlook by the fact that the devotees of progress who participated in various revolutions had thoroughly smashed their faces and limbs, leaving only a few curves of shoulders, heads, and toes: never again, was the message that came across to me from that scratching-out of eyes and smashing of skulls, would the perpetrators go back to the saints, whose stories had been told to the end. They had stood there as the idols of a power that had become illegitimate; this had to be hammered into the world with each blow.

I was increasingly suffering in my metropolis—and it seemed to me it would have been even worse in New York, let alone in Rome—from something that had already menaced me in childhood, since my time in boarding school: from loss of place, or space deprivation. (The prophet of Porchefontaine, who originally, before he became an innkeeper, going from one bankruptcy to the next, in suburb after suburb, had been trained as a philosopher, uses the word "dereification.") And my suffering was not improved by stays in the country, even in the most remote villages, which, after all, should have been familiar to me from childhood.

Those suburbs, on the other hand, no matter how ailing they might be themselves, became something like my healer. I needed them, urgently, imperatively. "Dull in the head" is for me the same as "ill." And then there were times, in Paris, and even close to the edge of town, when I became so dull and ill that I wanted nothing but to get out. I felt at once locked in and locked out. The sounds, which my son, whom I otherwise believed unquestioningly, found quieter and more uniform than in small towns, hemmed me in, just as I experienced the absence of sound in the middle of the night as a sort of trap. Sometimes, on my way out to the suburbs, I suddenly broke into a run, as if I were fleeing, all the while scolding myself angrily for not setting out much sooner, and spreading my arms wide, in all seriousness, once I got out there into the empty spaces. More than once tears even came to my eyes, as when a pain is cured all at once, or rather is transformed into something bearable, something sweet.

Thus I welcomed the widening circle of the suburbs: to the east, windy Ivry-sur-Seine, where more crimes occurred than just those that were always solved in the books of Simenon, which were often set there; to the west, Vanves, furrowed and difficult to take in; spreading up the mountainside, Châtillon with its scattering of buildings, from whose highest point in 1871 Prussian cannon had fired down on Paris, and occasionally even those towns with which nothing could be done and which, along with those responsible, deserved to be blown up. My greeting was silent, and at the same time somewhat resembled an exclamation, and it was directed at the three-dimensionality I had so greatly missed and had now found once more outside the gates, in the form of an apple crate, a dwarf palm, but also for instance the Eiffel Tower, which, discovered outside the city, suddenly appeared as astonishing as it probably is. And day after day, as I was walking through the suburbs, although I myself did not always know exactly where I was, I was trustingly asked by the many people lost there, especially in cars, for directions.

I made up my mind to live somewhere out there, for a time. I felt a powerful urge to experience the nights out there, and to expose myself to the nights. I thought it would not be forever, just as I pictured myself as married only temporarily, sort of playing at being a father, and also not writing forever.

So from people who wanted to go to Africa for a couple of years I rented a house in an area still unfamiliar to me. (Even today, when I consider myself knowledgeable about every corner of the *département*, almost daily I find myself standing, to my surprise, in a completely foreign world, often simply because I have approached from a slightly different direction.) The house was still occupied by the owners, but how impatient I was for them to get out and disappear to Senegal or wherever. Was that possible, for a person to be crazy about or infatuated with a place to live, and, what is more, with one that tended to reduce every one of my friends to monosyllabic responses when I rushed to show it to them, proudly, the minute the lease was signed?

One could also see the house, as one of my companions described it, as an "oversized stone grain bin, empty and gutted," in a row with very similar lumps, roofed in tile, slate, or tin, with a sidewalk in front that barely had room for one person, yet snaked toward an infinitely distant misty vanishing point, of a color that another of my companions, barging along with me in the rain, called "oxblood red"—even my child was alarmed by it, as I could feel through his hand—on a street of the same color where every second car belonged to a driving school, no store and no bar to left or right, and all that in a suburb which, if anyone knew of its existence, stood for monotony and gloom, as witness the newspaper headline intended to spur people to take long trips to palm-lined beaches: "Oublier Clamart [forget Clamart]."

I remained infatuated with my future home; was burning to move in. The woman from Catalonia thought at first that I liked the place only because, as usual, I wanted the opposite of everyone else; I felt comfortable only in the role of the loner, the solitary understood by no one, wronged time and again even by those closest to him, with the whole world against him; for otherwise why, when I had it out with her, my wife, would I regularly berate her with the reproach "You all!"—even more significant in Spanish: *"Vosotros,"* "You others": "You others are . . . ," "You others have . . ."?!

But I had no desire to position myself in contradiction to anyone else, to my surroundings, to my times; I was simply filled with enthusiasm, and then I managed to find the words to win over the woman from Catalonia (my son, on the other hand, merely seemed to obey, which for moments at a time undermined my certainty about the direction in which we were going). "Look how transparent the house is!" I said. "Through the front door and the windows overlooking the street the lawn behind the house shines through, with the apple tree there, under which I shall dig up the ground next spring to make a little vegetable garden, so the blossoms will fall white on black."

And in her presence I patted, tapped, and circled the plane trees of this suburb, which, standing there pretty much on their own, seemed like the advance guard of the plane forest in her native Gerona; I called her attention to the sounds from the nearby railroad station, which changed according to the type of wind, also to the vibrations of the trains shooting by, already at full speed, toward Brittany, toward the Atlantic; I pointed out the tip of the Eiffel Tower, which she would see from her room or study, through the chimney pots of the houses next door; I reminded her that our street was named after the philosopher of law Condorcet, perhaps the first proponent of equal rights for women, on whom she had written a paper; he had been arrested here while fleeing the radicals of the French Revolution; in my exhilaration I even lied to her that Joan Miró had painted in this very place for an entire summer and fall, up there where the forest began, in a hut belonging to the pea plantations that used to be typical of this place, the spot marked now by a footpath overgrown with blackberry brambles, and then I convinced myself, along with her, that Miró had actually been hard at work once behind the thorns and was still there today, a figure floating in the air.

Yet on those first evenings in the house out in the suburb, outside the city walls, I was overcome by uneasiness, of the sort familiar to me from childhood when someone in the household was even a little late getting home.

So here I had similar fits, though everyone was there. I put away the owners' things or pushed them all into a corner, the African masks, for instance, turned on the lights in all the rooms as soon as dusk began to fall, was afraid to go down to the labyrinthine cellar (sent the woman from Catalonia and our five-year-old son on ahead; neither of them feared anything in the world), frenetically sawed up firewood, far more than we needed, in the farthest corner of the backyard, and on those mild September evenings built a fire in the fireplace; while my wife sat by the fire for hours, gazing into it in silence, her eyes glowing, I grew weary and irritable at the flames I myself had lit and could not bear her and

my hypnotized idleness. This sense of desolation accompanying new beginnings is part of me and is also necessary.

And one morning, after another night of being utterly petrified, I
pushed open a window and found myself, and us, as in a fairy tale, in
precisely the place I had wished for. The hostile zone had dissolved in
the early-morning air. Now I lived there, and the living was mysterious,
as it was supposed to be. And that was to remain the case for a time.
What does "for a time" mean? For a continuation, for a moving forward,
for a staying in place.

How comforting and strengthening these fairy-tale-life moments were.
From them I learned what freedom was, as on that first day after the
eight years of boarding school, except that this time it was immensely
more powerful, under the shoulders (a word that in French seems to be
derived from the word for wings), in the nostrils, in the fingers, under
the soles of the feet. I had time. Go. Up. Out. Do it.

Every step in that house in the suburb seemed to be that sort of doing
or shaping. Whether I was going shopping, taking Valentin to the
local school, or hanging around the house: I was doing something, simply
by being present in the region day and night. I kept seeking out different
ways of getting places, observed, differentiated, compared: the bread in
the various bakeries, the gardens, at that time, two decades ago, more
vegetable than flower gardens, the cafés, supermarkets, and shoe-repair
shops in the upper and lower suburb.

I read histories of the place and acquired a geological survey map of
the region—I had to go to the national institute in Paris for it—so as
to have firmly in mind the base, layer upon layer, on which I was moving
around.

I found particularly appealing the houses, almost without exception
unstuccoed, especially in the lower town, built of the local sandstone,
most of it obtained at the beginning of the century from underground
quarries, which, long since abandoned, invisibly pock the landscape; half
a century later, a new high-rise building collapsed into such a cavern,
which the builders had not wanted to think about; the collapse caused
as many deaths as an earthquake, and since that time anyone who buys
a house in the affected area receives a certificate: no mine shaft below;

the ground at this location is solid. I concentrated on the façades, which were laid course upon course out of these unequally sized stones, so obviously extracted from the local soil, each in its apparently accidental form and yet all of them fitting together so perfectly; in this way I honed my ability to perceive color, sometimes calling on my son for help with characterizing the shadings.

The blocks, and also blocklets as small as a child's fist, were a light gray, in which you could see on closer inspection a tinge of yellow, as if from clay, shot through with darker veins, which with time could go slate blue or moss green, also glassy bulges, unexpectedly sparkling in all colors, ranging to coal black, also pure white grains, such as you find in the sand of a brook, the size of ant eggs, and like them oval.

As a result of the prominent yellow, all these façades could give an appearance of sunshine, even on a rainy morning, a very odd sunshine, coming up from below, which is otherwise a peculiarity of clay landscapes, deserts, badlands. (The woman from Catalonia, on the other hand, felt mocked by this phenomenon: for what stretched before one out in nature in the similarly colored familiar Spanish *meseta* here flickered before her as a structure.) The closer I came to the stones in the suburban house, often bumping them with my nose, and examined them, the more I had an entire planet within my grasp, embodied in this one thing, as once before, very long ago in childhood, the sight of a drop of rain in a yellow-brown-gray-white bit of dust on the path had made the world open up to me for the first time. And it was not some strange planet but here, the earth, and one that was peaceful through and through.

In similar fashion a crater now opened up in the building stone, fresh for the touching with the tip of a finger; ridges formed, and the observer, moving above this scene at barely an eyelash's distance, was showered with a sense of shelteredness brought on by the barely perceptible crumbling of the tiny weathered bits, which recalled the strangely meaningful glow along the eroded edges of the sunken roads back home.

Another feature of this world in miniature was that when you looked closely it turned out to be inhabited, if only by a tiny creature, the size of a pinhead, dangling here on a thread from a cliff, and a shimmering something like a one-celled animal on the opposite slope, beyond the seven mountain ranges, the two of them reminiscent of Robinson and Friday.

All my life the unapproachability of the world, its incomprehensibil-
ity and its inaccessibility, my exclusion from it, has been terribly
painful to me. That has been my fundamental problem. Belonging, participating, being involved was so rare that each time it became a great
occasion for me, worthy of being recorded. Every time the world, the
peaceable one, became a world, nature's and civilization's bending, extending, taking on color, was not only an event but a moment of recognition: with this recognition there would be no war.

There, during my first stay in the suburban region, at the midpoint
of my life, for a good two years, such events fell into my lap almost
constantly, on some days there for the plucking every other moment like
the cherries in the treetop in Arcueil. The planet took on shape and
became good to the touch. During that period it seemed erotic.

That applied also to eating, which began, along with the walk, drawn
out as much as possible, to the restaurant, together with its spaces and
vistas, to awaken a barely discovered pleasure (though immediately at-
tenuated when the dinner table was not located in my new region). And
of course I had drunk previously, primarily to be a part of things—see
above—but it was here that I first realized what it meant for wine to
be delicious. I often withdrew to the most remote corner of the house
with a glass, after midnight, turned out the light, took a sip in the pitch
darkness, and then, when I could feel the first sip actually rising to the
tips of my hair, another.

And in their first years the woman from Catalonian Gerona and the
man from the Jaunfeld Plain in southern Carinthia had certainly found
their way to each other quite often, in passing, in brushing by each
other, like sleepwalkers, as if the exciting element were more the air
between them, each other's presence, their mutual strangeness. But not
until we were here did we have each other personally in mind, and this
marriage, although it may have lasted only through one late summer
and a fall, appears to my memory more complete and eventful than all
that had gone before—of epic proportions; with a horizon.

Always in the same spot, always in the same corner, with the same
gestures, in a never varied tempo, a sort of spaciousness emerged, different from that of all the countries and continents from earlier: we

created this space and were its center (and likewise felt stronger there than ever before, two who were lost for all eternity, as if we were coupling far off on the moon). "I think this region is good for love," she said one time, her words as usual spoken more to herself than directed at me.

Only a third party could do justice to our history as a couple, and, since no such person is at hand, I must play the role myself, or at least take a stab at it.

So this was the only era in which a person and a place became identical for me, or in which a person meant a place, took me in. Even the most intimate connectedness with another person—this or that ancestor, my son—did no good when the place we inhabited together was fundamentally unhomelike to me. All the love in the world could not achieve anything if I did not have the place.

This existed independently of my family. At home I felt like myself the minute I set foot in my region, but not, however, with my mother or my grandparents. And later, when Valentin and I were living alone together, if I returned with him after a long absence to a place that was not my own, even on the approach I could try to persuade myself as much as I liked that the person at my side meant more to me than anything else in the world, and, and—still, all the blood would drain from my heart. And even now, when I have the urge to visit him, my repulsion at having to go to Vienna to do so is even greater.

The place always gained the upper hand. My near and dear and my places always failed to coincide except, in particular moments and in a nowhereland, with a friend, and that time with the woman from Catalonia—when she, to be sure, did not substitute for the place but rather potentiated the existing place and gave it élan. For the first time in my life I came home to a person, to my wife. For this period the house and wife belonged together. In her I came home to my house-within-the-house.

As far apart as we were in years, we became the same age. For the first time ever I saw myself as young, as I had not for a moment seen myself in my youth. And being faithful became a source of pleasure, and at the same time was nothing special.

Didn't our spontaneity and complete absorption in one another also result from the setting of the house and grounds in that gentle hollow, as if at the bottom of an abandoned quarry, or in the so-called depression of the Dead Sea, where we had begotten the child? Now the two of us lay together like two long before a child; and as if we still did not have one. Would anything similar have happened between us on raised ground? Has anyone heard of a couple who were flooded with desire in a storm on a mountaintop? And as we lay there, one floor above us our child talked in his sleep, the pedestrian cycle switched on and off at the night-shrouded railroad station across the way, the chains of hills huddled behind us, and there was a rustling of leaves outside our window.

That was the time when I could touch another person, when I felt a powerful urge to do so, and simply for the sake of touching her. For hours I wanted nothing else but to feel every part of this woman. I wanted to grab her from the top of her head to her heels and take her between my fingertips. In bending her, tapping her, plucking at her I convinced myself of the two of us. And on the other hand it was as if I were supposed to measure her for something, an additional, very special, amazing dress. And even in my dreams, as I slept at her side, this fingering, tying, hooking, cutting out, continued. I felt fulfilled by it: that was it. And I saw myself smiling secretly and silently to myself, turned away, in profile, like my son in his hiding place when he was very small. And rested against her rib like a mountain climber in a trackless waste.

For the continuation of the story a flesh-and-blood third party would be appropriate here, a person who would not merely make a pretense of distance, a chronicler: "In the first days of winter the woman left the house in the suburb."

I have my own opinions on the matter, as on more and more subjects (O harbor of Piran, and me at twenty, with no opinions on anything), yet what I think resists taking written form, or, for me, being written excludes the former. And I have the same problem with all rational explanations, deductions, and parallel examples, however clever, even if for a moment they made sense to me orally, and occasionally even do me good. Faced with being written down—with authority—even the most profound understandings have gone up in a puff of smoke every time, leaving me temporarily at a loss for words. I could then make a fresh start only if I had no idea how the few remaining fragments fit together, if at all. From the moment I set out to write, the path I took was different from the previous one, fundamentally so, a stumbling path.

And so I feel the urge here, too, to have no context, and to remain that way to the end of the following paragraph.

The woman from Catalonia was divinely carefree, in the sense I once found in an epistle of Horace, seemingly directed at me, where he says I should shake off the cold compress of cares in order to achieve divine wisdom. And when she was delighted she delighted an entire circle; a sort of cordiality communicated itself then to almost all the others, whereas I remained alone with my delight, shut it up inside me and brooded over it. And likewise her happiness shone forth and disarmed others; put to shame my occasional incredulity, healed my disintegration; beautified along with her also the person near her. I, on the other hand, did not know what to do with my happiness, or, overcome with awkwardness, at least did nothing good with it; seemed to lack an instinct for happiness, came across as abrupt and unloving.

And then things would change drastically again. She trusted no one, distrusted every moment. Even in her radiance there was a constant checking to see whether the person on whom it shone was actually receptive to it and was in agreement with her; if she observed the slightest contradiction or even a momentary distractedness, her face became an evil mask, without any change except the loss of its characteristic soulfulness, perhaps in a single quick glance over her shoulder, with which she thought to trap the other in not being in agreement with her. Nothing about her startled me more; with the passing years I feared nothing more, and in the end nothing sent me into more of a rage than this everready suspicion in the midst of her glowing, followed by sudden mood swings, when a huge tongue would be stuck out at me, while her lips remained tightly closed. Often all I had to do was leave her alone when I went to do an errand, and on my return she, who had just been rejoicing in our closeness, would be staring hostilely at a spot on the wall, feeling let down, indeed betrayed. And every time I had a sense that she was right. Although I came to her without ulterior motives, captivated by her cheeriness and also her cordiality, at such moments of sudden reversal our relationship appeared as unfounded and meaningless to me as to her. I was the wrong person. I was not the one she had been waiting for; I was a surrogate husband. To be sure, I was not yet unfaithful to her, and nevertheless I understood why I was suspect to her, just as I have always understood why, wherever I go, a patrolman eyes me and then detains me as a possible thief, terrorist, child murderer: I have never done or planned anything truly evil, and yet from the time I was very small I have felt worthy of suspicion—for what? For whatever the case of the moment might be, the current outrage. Even when things were this way between the woman and me, I still considered every other man wrong for her. Strangely enough, the hours, and, in that period, days and weeks, of harmony merely heightened her expectations and at the same time her fear: just as she trusted no one, she also did not believe anything could last. A dream could separate her from her lover; our merely sleeping side by side, without any particular incident, after an evening of fulfillment, could spark dissension overnight.

And then, when, like the previous times, something not worth mentioning had happened and she again lost her "belief" (her last word to me) in me, but this time as if in a gush, and from then on just went in circles, alternating between staring at me contemptuously and making imploring gestures to some unknown being, it came to me that the right person for this woman could only be a god. But what kind of god, and where was he? Certainly he would not come from heaven, or in the shape of a cloud or a rainstorm, but rather in human form, like you or me, only more radiant, and he would blow away her primeval distrust by finding it amusing.

But as it was, both of us, one as stubborn as the other, allowed our relationship to go to pieces, and without consideration for our child, who at the beginning silently stepped between us as a mediator and then just as silently retreated from the field of battle. Without her belief in us two, I also lost mine. Just a moment ago I had been carrying around her image within me for life, and now: the image was gone.

———

And as was almost the rule whenever I broke up with someone: the separation seemed to me, in contrast to our being together, the higher reality, likewise the struggle, fierce, body against body, that preceded it.

The harmony had seemed like someone else's experience, a fairy tale, and it has not been that long since I came to think of the fairy tale as embodying the highest of all realities. I saw the real me only in the person affected by the loss. I was at home in sorrow and dissension, in absurdity. Catastrophe involving those close to me was the place where I belonged. If, in the midst of happiness, I seemed gloomy, inaccessible, and frightening to others, it was in pain and helplessness, in despair that I began to glow and inspired general confidence.

And in actual fact I never felt so close to the world as when there was no one and nothing left for me. "Serves me right!" was a thought that warmed me through and through. "You have a drive toward nothingness," the woman from Catalonia told me, and not only during that period. But who was saying what to whom? Did what with whom? Of the two of us: who was who? It seems to me as though, in order to get close to the truth, I would have to tell the story of someone else, of others, which I suppose I have been doing in any case for a very long time.

There was something great between us, and she went, and I let her go. Finally she went. Her last glance, over her shoulder, was hatred, so pure that everything round about seemed dipped in white, a white that was intent on destruction and also had the strength for it. I had to turn away immediately, feeling my skull on the point of exploding in its rays. (Fratricidal wars, it is claimed, especially those in which the participants have no emotional stake and are also not convinced of the necessity of the struggle, are the most cruel, and in this sense a fratricidal war broke out between Ana and me.) And at the same time, in my turning away as she was going, I got caught up in observing, found myself absorbed in the television antenna on a nearby roof, which in the evening sun appeared to me as a gleaming arrow, and likewise I felt the presence of a distant friend as he sat quietly at his daily work somewhere, while here the drama of my fate was playing itself out. My head was buzzing, felt as heavy as a boulder, and that was all right. There was a raging storm between the woman and me, and I was in good spirits. Things were not all that bad. I could study them.

Afterward, alone as never before, I lived without any conviction that man and woman belonged together. In my eyes there was nothing that connected anyone with anyone else. Later on I experienced with one woman or another days of ecstasy or merely of exaltation, which both of us mistook for adventure, even happiness. Each time, observers, friends as well as strangers, saw the relationship as beautiful and found our pleasure contagious. Especially older people, no matter how grumpy they normally were, became cheerful at the sight and gave us their blessing. Only children eyed us without comprehension, or disapprovingly, and I myself felt almost constantly queasy.

But such episodes actually entailed a freedom that I experienced at the time as progress. However discreetly this casual, blessedly superficial flowing into one another occurred: we thought we were on the cutting edge of our era, its avant-garde and secret protagonists, and with our physicality—which was a sort of soulfulness, wasn't it?—were writing history.

At the time, even more than "I" it was one woman or another to whom the whole thing meant "onward!" To them, these tireless couplings represented a goal for the entire human race next to which every other activity shrank to insignificance. And any man vouchsafed the image of such a being—transformed into a queen? a guerrilla? the woman from Revelation?—had to feel allied and complicit with her. These women had right on their side, for the moment and for the future.

All the more terrible, then, my letdown when the magic faded, the first time and likewise the times after that. The woman and I would be laughing heartily at the coup we had pulled off against the stick-in-the-mud rest of the world, and two floors farther up in the elevator I would find myself trapped with a stranger inside the most impenetrable cliff. After a cheerful parting from the next of these huntresses, at an international airport, both of us convinced that over the last few days we had inscribed each other feature by feature into the book of eternity, I was sitting on the plane, with the sea far below, the foam on the crest of the waves still visible, and wishing the window would give way and hurtle me into the abyss.

In these situations my sense that I deserved to be executed became stronger and stronger, and I was also grimly accepting; saw myself stepping in front of the firing squad and tying the blindfold over my own eyes, as tight as it would go.

But all of this happened in another country, not a trace of it in my home, in the suburb.

That was taboo. I did not even work there, hardly wrote a line in the years that followed. First of all, my books had brought in enough so that for the time being I could afford this, and then I felt, unlike after a period of letting myself drift, neither the desire nor the need (both had to be present) to sit down at my desk.

My chief occupation for years was leisure, which, however, was not the same as doing nothing. I was taking time off, though in a different sense from working-class people when they take time off. At the beginning of my residence in the suburb, I still looked to the great city of Paris for evenings out or special occasions. Then, disappointed by my cosmopolitan acquaintances, all of whom found the area where I lived lacking in interest—otherwise they would have followed my example!? —I no longer had the slightest idea what to do there, and took my leisure alone, going from one suburb to the other during the day, in summer as in winter, and in the evening stayed at home.

What absolutely had to be done I did myself, hit or miss. I let the grass in the yard grow until only the top of my son's head showed above it, even when he was standing up, and then I cut it with a scythe. Likewise in winter I pushed the snow, which tended to stay on the ground longer than down in Paris, off the sidewalk, and in the process exchanged my first words with a neighbor who was doing the same and who had until then always seemed, in his silence, the epitome of a small-town crook, yet now turned out to be the soul of innocuousness and gentleness. I went shopping, cooked, ironed, darned, sewed—here my years in boarding school came in handy—washed the windows, at least before Christmas, Easter, and the birthdays of those living in the house, scrubbed the floor, also to smell the water drying on it, and promised myself to be the first in my family not to let himself be bent crooked and stooped by physical work, but rather to use it to straighten my back permanently and inheritably. To be sure, my activities were not the same as the grinding labor they had done as hired men, which even the strongest will could hardly transform into something positive.

B ut primarily I walked the entire area; lived with my son; read. And I thought I was close for the first time to the right life, and not just for me. Vanished from society, gradually forgotten by my former world, I felt as though I could finally be pure there, and even now I still wonder sometimes why I did not stick with it. Then again I tell myself that in that period I was near madness and that this life was as wrong as it could possibly be. And even then I knew: as it was, it could not bring fulfillment.

Yet that was something I always had before me, day after day. It was an utterly serious life, very different from the interludes, elsewhere, with the new breed of women. Busy with nothing but leisure, I thought at every step that I was entering an advent period, which I scented and sniffed as a child does snow in the air. Today I see myself there, off the beaten track, behaving more like my own god, in proud anticipation of perdition, which at the same time would mean ascension. What did come seemed at first exactly the opposite.

I often walked through the hill forests extending as far as Versailles, which, seen from Paris, began in my suburb.

Curious that Marina Tsvetayeva, who had lived in Meudon and then in Clamart and was a person in great need of walks and forests, should have complained so bitterly in her letters that there was no forest in the vicinity. Yet I also understand her. For the forest out there began fairly surreptitiously, and a stranger to those parts standing on its edge was more likely to be repelled. As a Russian she was used to the evergreen forests of the east, while here a pine or even a spruce among the oaks and edible chestnuts was a rarity; and her birches, less rare, seemed in size and appearance to conform to the predominant varieties of trees, their trunks unusually thick and their bark more black than white because of the cracks. The white showed up only at a distance, in the depths of the forest, when a swaying passed through the dense ranks of trees there, which then brought the birches' whiteness into view.

Yet the wooded borders of these suburbs hardly allowed such glimpses. A person coming from elsewhere would often hardly even see them as borders, but rather as mere outcroppings of dense vegetation, between houses, with barriers in front of them, mere hiding places, strewn with litter as in no other country, the dog feces, always forming a little pyramid, a sign for turning back at once.

If you manage to overcome your distaste and push onward, the beaten track does widen into a path, the bushes draw apart and shoot up into trees. But nowhere the depth and spaciousness that creates the feeling of a forest. A stranger to the country has the sense instead of being in what remains of a forest that was gobbled up—it gives this impression— by the suburb's structures, which, wherever he looks, are so close that here and there they seem to cut the last tree trunks in half.

Nothing would be more understandable than for a person to give up once and for all, coming to the conclusion that in this country, tidied up by the Enlightenment, propped up by reason, systematically planned and unified by grammar, there is no room for a forest; the unchanging sounds of civilization, of cars, trains, helicopters in this remnant of forest seem to offer confirmation.

But as I kept walking—who knows why?—it happened one time that there among the trees I could feel the deep woods as much as ever before. As I turned off, once, and then again, a door gave way, and after that the area in which I wandered for hours was nothing but a forest, or woodland. (Similarly, time and again in dreams I am in a house I have known for years, and I stumble upon an unfamiliar, empty, yet comfortably furnished lower story that has always been there, ready for me, and then each time for the length of the dream I wander through the adjacent, still-undiscovered suites that open up around every corner.) Even with a few highways to cross in between, along with occasional hammering, rattling, and rumbling from the world outside, the silence gained the upper hand and kept it, up and down over the hills, along the sunken roads, on the paths along the embankments, on the paths along the ridges.

At the time I had the sensation of being constantly shoved and carried along, whether simply out walking or collecting chestnuts to roast at home in the evening, and continuing when I stopped at the inn at Fontaine Ste.-Marie, whose clearing marked the middle of the forest.

As never before, nature revealed itself to me as my measure. To take in nature's sounds and finally become completely immersed in listening was what constituted for me at the time fulfillment. And it even seemed to me I was in the process of pulling it off.

When I nevertheless felt drawn to my desk, I already hesitated in the next room. Having been out and about for all those hours, permeated by the silence, its modalities, creations, styles, and examples, I had already done my work! I felt reluctance about writing it down, which seemed to me an unnecessary, and an unseemly, variation.

Such silence I experienced not only out in nature but likewise on the paths that ran along the rail line between here and Brittany. And the sounds of the suburbs formed part of it. Sometimes I would have liked to live even closer to the tracks, and every time I walked by, I peered at a certain grayish-yellow sandstone house that stood directly by the embankment just before that railroad bridge, at the height of a dam, that linked two suburbs. I wanted to see if the house, with the whirring of passenger trains and the crashing of freight trains right outside its windows, might be for sale someday. Not a few of the older people living along the tracks in shacks, with one main room and a kitchen but with oversized yards, kept chickens, and my ears were more attuned than decades ago in the village of Rinkolach to the crowing of the different cocks, which I could tell apart while still in half-sleep in my bed before daybreak. The occasional barking of dogs, quite far apart, created, not only when I was out walking but also in the nocturnal stillness of the house, along with the trains, a further sense of spaciousness in the landscape.

Most silence, either rural or urban, had oppressed me up to then or made me restless. But this type of silence suited me.

As a result of my long time abroad, away from speaking German, I had fallen into the habit, without noticing it, of using the various foreign languages even when alone with myself. In the suburban silence I noticed how often these idioms found their way into my monologues, indeed already predominated, not as a result of my personal watching and listening but simply as standard phrases. And I realized what had given me that soothing sense of my snapping into place every time I had picked up my pen: it had been a homecoming, to my work and, just as powerfully, to my native German.

If I ever thought I could achieve harmony with—with what?—no "with," simply harmony, it was in my early years there, when I was unemployed, unsociable, out in the primeval forests and the cultural desert of the suburb.

Having only fleeting contact with others, surrounded by a peace I wanted to defend and cherish just as it was (at any rate not phony), I saw myself as leading a life of epic proportions, despite its uneventfulness, along with my son and several ancestors, long gone yet dreaming on in me.

The harmony went deepest for me in the face of those happenings that, in and of themselves, seemed mainly without resonance. From the motion of a suburban cloud, the way a snowflake hit the red asphalt of the sidewalk and turned into a cherry stain, I could pick out a sound and listen to it fade away. And that was all? Yes. And at the same time I knew I was in a phase of preparation; I intended to use my walking, observing, and reading to sharpen myself into an arrow.

Another little metaphor on this subject (which again will not fit perfectly): the Brittany line ran along for a stretch in a concrete-walled cut. Despite the slight distance from Montparnasse, their station of origin or destination, the trains whizzed through there as if already out in the open countryside, and the air current they created always buffeted the luxuriant vegetation that hung down over the steep walls of the cut. The same thing happened with the occasional bushes twisting their way up from below. Even the ivy, which had managed to worm its way into the concrete, was torn loose in the course of the years by the gusts, and floated after the trains as they sped by.

Time and again the vegetation was removed, and then, before new vegetation maybe took its place, a pattern of rough semicircles was revealed on the wall, often layered on top of each other, light patches scratched and etched in the concrete by all the bunches, fans, trailing streamers as they brushed back and forth. If that stretch of wild growth had earlier appeared random, when it was cleared away the half-ring or half-moon forms left behind in its absence appeared entirely orderly. They differed only in size, and were rounded off either at the top or the bottom, depending on whether the plants had been growing up from below or hanging down from above.

And from time to time, when I stood there by the railway cut and no train was passing at the moment—if it remained that way for more than a minute, it could mean only that there was a strike on—contemplating at my feet these chalk-gray, swooping etchings of something no longer there, something from before, so much more powerful than if the growths themselves had actually been present, being whipped back and forth by the trains, I had an experience of massiveness, tension, movement, wild goings-on. In that pattern of shrubs and wind at the railroad cut, past, present, and future became interwoven and spoke to me.

The ornamentation on the ancient city walls of Ecbatana in Persia would have revealed to me something great, as it did to Flaubert when, dreaming of an epic, he became lost in contemplation of it, but unlike to him, the wall would have seemed to me ineffable rather than epic. Here and now, in the ordinary world, grandeur and beauty finally appeared to me describable, as they had not been in the Gobi Desert, at the Lion Gate at Mycenae, at the pilgrim's portal in Santiago de Compostela. And a few steps later they became completely inaccessible again. What had I seen there?

And the more I tried to brood it back, the more meaningless it became, and at the same time more uncanny. Don't try to make something of it, I resolved. Experience grandeur and beauty and then leave it in peace. It does not want to be described. Or not by you. It is not material, not narrative material anymore.

———

It was fine with me that during those years I was not merely idle but also experienced no pressure from imagination or inventiveness. For the way I lived there seemed at certain moments close to perfection, especially when I stopped and became all ears. All that was missing was a little push, a mere wisp of something, a pinprick—but of what?—and it would have been the longed-for merging with the surroundings, with the treetop, with the curved space, the bay between the wings of the swallow.

But by way of compensation for having not the slightest spark of a conception of the future, I now wanted to know things. In the evening I would wait impatiently for Valentin to fall asleep so I could make headway with my studies. I had a telescope there, good enough for an observatory, and with it I looked at the sky, which even there in my first suburb, closer to the periphery, was less polluted by light than in Paris; I traced the deserts of the moon, dotted in Orion's belt (and in between lowered the instrument and counted up the day's receipts with the pharmacist, who, far away at the other end of the street, was staying late to balance his register).

Above all I studied from books. I read word for word and picked out only works that lent themselves to such reading. I soon set aside the local chronicles and histories because they made the region seem sadly diminished in contrast to the greatness, however undefined, of which I daily became conscious there. What was merely worth knowing or interesting did not satisfy me.

On the other hand, I was filled with a steady warm glow from studying the earth's forms and their interactions, no longer merely those of this place; and I could follow best when the textbook contained only key words, rather than complete sentences.

Mountain cirques, alluvial terraces, shifting dunes thus became living images. Coming to understand them lifted all my weariness from me; I felt absolutely clear in the head, as previously perhaps only when I was studying Roman law, and I felt at one with the planet, and vice versa.

Sometimes, late at night, when I was already asleep, I was filled with such burning desire to know more that the urge itself woke me; I switched on the light, and, sitting up in bed, went on puzzling out the explanations.

It was sheer pleasure. I understood the term "morphological diversity": the morphological features on which I was reading up, including those at the ends of the earth, were waiting for me, tomorrow, and each corresponded and responded to an as yet undiscovered vein in my body.

It happened more than once that the sheet I was lying on, with its folds and bulges, took on the relief of the landscape I was studying just then. The landscape seared itself into my memory by way of the sheet. Then I wanted to lie without a blanket, with the light on. And something similar happened to me on those nights when I sat there deciphering old books from classical antiquity. It was in fact a kind of decoding, for with the help of my boarding-school dictionaries I was cracking the Latin and Greek words to make them yield a sentence, and that alone, before any particular meaning emerged, could vitalize and refresh me as much as any adventure. I saw myself as a hairsplitter and since then have never viewed that as a defect in anyone.

But there was even more in the verses of Homer and Heraclitus; it was no accident they had survived the avalanches and floods of history. One phrase after another brought me face to face with a sun that did not blind me, and also never set as long as someone was reading that way. And if I opened a newspaper or turned on the television afterward, I could follow current events effortlessly. Completely alert, I took an interest in what was going on, at the same time without being surprised at anything, unmoved, prepared in advance for the worst. Afterward I sat in the dark, with a goblet that I held at the very bottom, by its foot, as I had seen it done in paintings of French peasant families from a century long past, surrounded by the suburban night's silence and the presence of my son asleep upstairs, at the heart of time.

Why couldn't my life go on this way indefinitely, the life of an anonymous person in an anonymous suburb, with my crisscrossing the area during the day, my hairsplitting and contemplation of word-suns in the evening, with my sitting bolt upright, and with the small, quiet sleeper for whom I performed an easy night watchman's service? Now that certain branch is brushing the window on the west side again, the uppermost one, in the gable. Now the furnace is switching off until the next morning. The wind must be from the north; otherwise the mail train, all its cars windowless and painted yellow, would not rumble so through the house. This now is the moment of the piles of coal way in back of the railroad station, now, with the falling moon. And tomorrow I shall again do nothing! We will go up into the forest, past the standing stone, from under which the spring may be trickling again, after the rain, and then, on the other side of the highway, check to see whether the strawberries are ripe at that particular spot. We will eat, my friend, by the ponds of Villebon, and meanwhile observe what is happening on the water. Then I must not forget again to pick up Valentin after school. And in the evening, my dear fellow, we'll experience the bifurcation of the Orinoco and then work through twelve more hexameters in our *Odyssey*.

Incidentally, it did not strike me as at all strange to see myself, perhaps more than ever, as someone from an Austrian village, then as now almost completely untouched by the outside world, and yet to have found the way of life most suited to me in a hinterland like this, more foreign than the most remote place from my years of travel. In this sense I viewed myself as a modern, one of the first in a series, in an avant-garde.

In various parts of the world I had run across one person or another from this avant-garde, almost always a stranger, and each time I had seen this person as my model. One time perhaps he was sitting in an outdoor café by a railroad station on the border, and amid the natives and the foreigners he stood out as a third type, who, without specifically looking at anything, was entirely caught up in what was going on; in spite of his large knapsack and his ankle-length coat, he seemed to be in camouflage (he was the one whom the patrolling border guards gave a wide berth); and with his untouchability I felt I was in good company with him, and went looking for it, though in vain, the following evening as well.

Years later I encountered my model again in the form of someone else, on a bus trip through the Yucatán, and knew afterward only that he came from Australia; we were on the road together for no more than a day, in a small, cobbled-together tour group. When the bus stopped, he was always the first one out, as if he already had a direction charted inside him, and involuntarily I followed, though whenever possible choosing my own path; I simply felt the urge to have him in sight, for wherever he went, away from the Maya pyramids, toward ash-darkened and glowing-hot present-day burned-over rain forest with almost nothing else, there had to be something to discover, and without attaching myself to him I wanted to see it from a distance.

A third time I even came across my model in the form of a fellow countryman, from a neighboring valley. He still spoke its dialect, though only when he slipped briefly back into German from English. Otherwise he had become a well-adjusted resident of the American Midwest, at the same time remaining the spit and image of a Carinthian villager, whom I could imagine pulling the rope of a church bell, a heavy one, or as an adolescent suffering from raging hormones, spittle gathering in the corners of his mouth as he stood before the girl of his dreams during the "begging-in" customary in our area, at least in those days. He seemed perfectly at home in Minnesota, so established in and familiar with the place, and also in charge of his domain, to judge by his outstretched arm and the space between his firmly planted legs, like a local lord. Yet he did not exaggerate or imitate anything. I just saw him as more alert than the natives, more on the make (without being called Schwarzenegger), at the same time more thoughtful than his fellow Americans and more contemplative, like someone leading his life on a sort of rampart or fort, a quality indeed possessed to some degree by his house, far from Minneapolis, alone on a prairie, on top of a little mound of fill, with an almost endless view in all directions. And in the city of millions where he worked as a physician, "more or less with my left hand," but what a left hand, he remained just the same. At the time we were both young, and I was convinced he would make a great name for himself. "I escaped from home, and it's right here!" he said. "With the smallest sip of coffee I drink, far from my Maria Rojach, not seen or thought of by anyone in the village, I make a contribution to the future of the world!"

I have not heard from him again. Where is he? It has been a long time since I last met the modern person in whom I thought I could anticipate a new world. And I, too, have not stayed the same as during my years in that first suburb.

Without especially holding myself aloof or participating, I learned just enough about people to have life brush me in passing and hardly exert any pressure. During those few years I did not hear bad things about anyone (it was quite different for my son in school, but he did not tell me about that until much later).

The settling, spreading uphill, hardly noticeably yet steadily, was dense and at the same time scattered, and I felt as if my house were protected by the many harmless strangers and their almost constant presence, as quiet as it was palpable; I often forgot to lock up.

The majority of the residents were older, yet quite far from being frail; primarily former retailers and railroad employees, who lived for their inconspicuous, yet on closer inspection practically sculpted, vegetable gardens, and otherwise, too, seemed to be constantly out and about, going for cigarettes or the paper, betting on horses in a certain café, then streaming together from every direction for the Sunday market in front of the station (as now in the bay), knowing in advance and in detail what would be there, and where; I once heard two local people exchange in passing what still echoes in my ear as the customary greeting of the place: "We have it good here, don't we?" — "Yes, we have it good here!"

In my memory at least I have only people like that as neighbors, and there was a similar couple, a man and his wife, who took care of Valentin when I was away, with whom I sometimes sat for a while after I got back, and not merely out of politeness, also enjoying the apples from their own trees that they served (while on the other hand my son later told me story after story about the mustiness peculiar to their house, a different kind in every corner).

In my imagination they are all still alive, even though most of them meanwhile are probably in the ground, and when I occasionally venture across there, over the two hills, I no longer encounter a single one of them; the greeting, if I get to hear it at all, is different from before. The descendants of the Portuguese, the largest foreign group there, often no longer use their language with each other, or speak it with a French accent. The graves of the Armenians and also the Russians increasingly display, under their own, far-traveled script, lines of the locally customary Roman script.

And the few people from that population of whom I had perhaps a less good opinion during my time there must be doing worse things today, yet even they cannot have turned into complete villains, but at most, appropriately for those suburbs, stock types or minor characters from gangster comedies: for instance, the doctor, the only one in the neighborhood, who filled out prescription after prescription, never really looking at the patients, and in the same breath wrote out a bill, to the bottom line of which would be added, as I said to myself, the profit from the volleys of medications, especially for small children, shared, according to a secret agreement, with his accomplice, the proprietor of the pharmacy, two streets over and around the corner, where, even without my telescope, with the naked eye, I could see the parents of the district coming out, laden as if for all eternity with accordion-sized boxes (and at least once I was one of them myself).

But what do I really know of that place today? Other than that the brooms of the still mostly black street sweepers are now made of plastic rather than of twigs; that the photo automat at the railroad station now takes colored rather than black-and-white pictures; that the one homeless person who used to sleep up in the woods has meanwhile become several?

All that time the shelter up on the railroad platform had no glass in its door, and once, when I went to push it open, I tumbled into dead air. Now glass has been installed. And from the upstairs apartment where I dragged my son to his piano lesson no tinkling can be heard now.

I, too, did no one any harm there, did not get worked up even once, and wanted it to be that way always.

On the other hand, I gradually came to recognize that I also did not take anyone seriously, and this was true not only of the local residents filing past but then also of my absent friends. I hardly wanted to hear about them anymore. I was dissociating myself. My going it alone, in my place and domain, seemed so much richer in content than any togetherness. I barely skimmed my friends' letters, and then did not answer them. The simple fact that they were constantly doing things and appearing in public made me indifferent to them; if one of them had appeared before me with his activities, I would have scoffed at his scheming.

Yes, from a distance I was unserious, and at the same time hardened toward my friends. And at the side of my son, too, toward whom I outwardly seemed so attentive and patient, I quite often caught myself merely feigning interest. Certainly I listened to him, but I had no heart for the child. Did that not become clear from the fact that I would forget him if he was away for more than a couple of days? Why did all the world treat me in his absence as a single person, someone without attachments who could be enlisted for the craziest adventures?

If I seem to be making myself out as worse than I was at the time, my intention is not to ask to be refuted but rather to have something to tell. Can it be that this was the only way for me to get started? When I was in boarding school, crammed in like a sardine with the others at Mass, didn't I invent sins or upgrade venial failings to atrocities so I could slip away to the confessional in back, from which I would emerge energized and proud of my stories?

But then I did become more closely acquainted with someone in the region: the later petty prophet of Porchefontaine.

At the time he was proprietor and chef of the restaurant in the hollow of the Fontaine Ste.-Marie, by the clearing in the middle of the woods, as now at a restaurant by the railroad embankment in the suburb of Versailles: since then both of us have moved our base of operations two valleys to the west in the Seine hills, and each of us still finds himself at about the same distance from the other. Between our houses there is a similar set of foothills to cross.

In that period in my life—which, for all my idleness, was a time of preparation—he became for me something that meant more than friends: an adversary whose acumen awakened my own; a misanthrope on whose rationality I honed the substance of my illusions; a tester in the face of whose deliberate heartlessness my own heart opened up as if in the presence of a secret.

The entire person attracted me as just such a secret. He was as he was; in contrast to me, he did not merely feign disgust and distaste; and yet that could not be all there was.

Even though he was my double as no one had ever been before, and finally the one I welcomed, there had been a time when he had made entirely different choices. At moments I was convinced my thoughts mirrored his exactly, yet when I articulated them, the tone was wrong. Only when they came from his mouth did they sound authentic. Again unlike me, he stood by his condemnation of the world. No, he was not my mirror. And at the same time, when I was by myself, I experienced—a word that otherwise only my friend the priest can use without embarrassment—longing for him; likewise for his place.

The stone cabin there on the edge of the clearing, long since gone without a trace, is still for me the most charming tavern on earth, the epitome of an inn. The first time I approached it, after a two-highway, three-secondary-road, four-forest route, I took it for a snack bar, or, with the ponds nearby, a fishermen's pub. But then there was a door, of glass, with a lace curtain; and the Egyptian standing outside, seemingly moving in his motionlessness, like a dancer, in combination with his black suit and white shirt, transformed the barrack, and my long journey there contributed to the impression, into a caravansary.

Its proprietor did not, to be sure, return my greeting, and I had to go around him to enter, and same with a Doberman that unexpectedly, soundlessly, rose from the threshold on long, gangly legs. The dining room, one step beyond, was bathed in green from the forest outside all its windows. The few tables stood well apart from each other, with light tablecloths and napkins artfully swirled in the glasses, in which candle flames were mirrored, although guests were sitting only in a corner in back (in any other restaurant they would have been given a table by the window, also to make it look inviting to passersby).

I stood for a while, and when no one came, I picked a table. I waited patiently. No matter what happened now, I knew I was in the right place for a meal. If not today, I would eat here another time, and then again and again. Unlike in other nice places, I felt no immediate urge to ascertain the particulars. I simply waited, deaf to the conversation at the table behind me, tired from my long walk and happy.

The *patron* appeared, the man with the Egyptian profile, coming now through the swinging door from the kitchen, and wordlessly set before me bread, wine, water, and olives with stems, and had no sooner given the bread basket another turn toward me than he was already out of the small room. The bread was warm, saffron yellow when broken open, with a fragrance of the Orient that went with the pattern of the dishes. The courses that followed, likewise presented in silence and without my having ordered them, on ordinary plates, were classic French cuisine, and yet they seemed different by a degree. There was something more to them; later I noticed that, on the contrary, this effect actually came from something's being left out. Besides, each dish, served by the chef, the proprietor, was sliced and arranged in a way that brought to mind the story of a Chinese butcher: this butcher had learned how to carve in such a way that in faithfully adhering to the original shape he created entirely new shapes.

Thus it was as if I found myself sitting down to a meal that would have been equally suited to the Mongolian steppe or to a salmon river in Alaska, and as if I were also that far away, out in the open. I had not been particularly hungry. But even before the first bite it occurred to me, just at the sight of the modest dish, simply presented in the right light on the scratched cafeteria plate, that something had been missing up to now. Why else should I heave such a great sigh of relief? Why else should I have to keep such a tight grip on myself so as not to cry? Did this mean I had been miserable all this time, and had not realized it until this moment of nourishment?

Then the proprietor's voice made itself heard. He admonished the guests behind me, whose clothing hardly differed from his, to laugh less vulgarly, also to speak more softly, and about something other than food, wine, politics, business, and winning games, for instance about the eclipse of the moon last night or the biography of Pythagoras, which he strongly recommended for the way of life it depicted.

The group seemed accustomed to hearing such things from him and hardly paid him any heed. Nor did it bother them apparently that he then remained standing by their table, arms crossed, as if to speed their departure from his place, and, while they were still making their way to the door, was in a hurry to set the table while still clearing it, to eliminate every trace of them.

And no sooner were they outside than he laced into them, as if talking to himself: They were like everyone nowadays, synthetic human beings, placed in the world to wreak havoc and cause commotion; conceived without love; instead of being born innocent from a mother's body, extruded somewhere, ready for use and for molding; their youth devoted to sharpening murder weapons; their maturity, behind their human masks, an endless massacre; and in the end they would just splinter, unseen and unheard, canceled out, wiped off the radar screen, neutralized.

I only half listened, not knowing whether I should take this seriously; objected, feeling it was my duty, that an innkeeper was there for everyone and should keep his opinions to himself. I did not allow myself to be deflected from my enjoyment of the meal, my delight in this out-of-the-way spot, and I thanked the chef and proprietor for it. Without looking at me, he said that it was not for the sake of me, the chance guest, that he had served up this meal, but rather to pay homage to the good things to eat and to celebrate the day as it came. And after he had poured me mint tea, in a high arc from an oriental-style onion-shaped pot, I had no sooner stood up than he slapped the seat of my chair with a thick waiter's towel, as he had done with the others while they, too, were still there.

After that I stopped in there regularly, also because of the view. It was as if the dining room had neither walls nor a roof, and as if outside, amid the heavy foliage of the mammoth oaks, dots of the sky shone like bluing onto the set table, and as if the clay path under the trees were the picture into which not the painter entered, but his people, and without disappearing into it.

Once, when a light rain was falling, the *patron* barked at me that I should go out onto the terrace; because of the trees I would not get wet, and besides, looking and listening, in combination with his dishes, slowed down one's breathing and kept one warm.

And in fact his inn in the hollow seemed an oasis of summer far into the autumn; as one came up the path, a curiously dry air crackled through the oak leaves, now riddled with holes, which apparently dropped only in the middle distance.

Since in the meantime the proprietor had offended his usual guests for good, and the most recent edition of the restaurant guide now warned people about his gruff manner, there were only a few of us left. Yet even if the place had been packed, running at full steam—which I sometimes wished for—the experience would always have been the same for me there.

The sound of the trees in the clearing, a seething, swelling, blazing, made me understand why one of the auditory ossicles is called the "stirrup." I felt something tugging at me; gratitude galvanized me, followed by an exuberance that wanted to go somewhere and then nowhere at all: I was there, and I was innocent.

And one day the proprietor stood next to me and said, his hand on the back of my chair: "Sometimes when it gets quiet in the clearing, a fist seizes me by the scruff of my neck from above and hoists me off the ground like Habakkuk in your Bible, one of the minor prophets. I, on the other hand, am the petty prophet, and insist on that."

From then on we no longer dealt with each other as host and guest. From time to time he sent me handwritten invitations to his place, with descriptions of dishes and wines. Or, when I could not get away, for instance because my son was sick, the restaurateur from the clearing would come to my house, in the evening, on his (very flexible) days off, bringing his pots and pans, and would cook and serve a meal. He would lock himself into the kitchen, and except for faint Arabic music we would hear not a sound from him, and he always took a very long time. Afterward we would play chess in silence—something he nowadays always invites me in vain to do—he with grim intensity, I casually, while inside us, it seemed to me, it was often actually the other way around. He was a stern winner and a laughing loser.

I admired him for his implacability, just as I was annoyed with myself for my readiness to relent after an initial burst of rage. To this day I have not fathomed his secret. And I always feel a kind of uncertainty toward him, going back to our very first shared moment, or perhaps the opposite thereof, that time at the door to his caravan stopping place.

And soon he had to move, after going bankrupt, to another cabin, beyond the next knoll of the Seine hills, by the upper pond in Villebon. And where this second little restaurant stood, there now grows, like the grass on the site of the first, a tangle of stinging nettles and wild blackberries. From its windows I could see the wind rippling the water down below, just as now, in his third place in Versailles-Porchefontaine, I can see on the embankment the long-distance and local trains speeding and rolling by, overlapping and blocking the view of one another.

Sometimes I set out for there for dinner, taking a roundabout route through the forest, and each time get up disappointed, without having had any complaint with the food or the table by the window. For sitting, resting, meals, pursuing my thoughts, I am constantly on the lookout for an inn like the one at Fontaine Ste.-Marie. And I do not intend to stop looking. Perhaps my friends on their various journeys will tell me about finding one.

But as for the clearing, with the bulldozed terrace area, I now avoid it—like all clearings, by the way. It seems to me that nothing more can grow there: as if today's clearings, even including the jungle of the Yucatán, belonged to the runners, gymnasts, fitness freaks, dogs, bombing squadrons, and poisonous mushrooms. All the entrances to them could be called, like the one here in the bay, "Allée de la Fausse Porte," the avenue of the wrong door.

And at the same time I think at least once a day of my inn in the clearing: what a lovely, eternal, simple sitting one could have there. All the things that had been studied and understood the night before forgotten, and yet close at hand. The breath of wind moves the space between one's fingers—a snapping. Reminiscent: only this word for it comes to mind, an introductory word that calls for a noun, in the genitive, the generative case. Reminiscent of what?

And of course there was no staying there (although the solitary proprietor had his room over the kitchen, as if for the long haul).

Those were the years when, without working, I was riding high as never before and hardly ever afterward, and at the same time feeling more threatened and on borrowed time than ever.

Each time I went to bed after midnight, I had the distinct impression of having survived another day, and I actually painted the date of the new day, the only thing I entered in my notebook at that time. I understood the complaints of various involuntary (unlike me) residents of the suburbs, who saw themselves cut off there from the world as it flowed by, consigned for a time to an evacuation or pre-death zone—particularly on certain evenings when, beyond the gates of the metropolis, an uncontoured brightness settled over the streets, on which the newly leafed-out trees shriveled into wilted cemetery plants, and far and wide a queasy silence reigned, the window shutters closed tight on every side, abrupt chirping of sparrows, the wail of car alarms, and the barking of watchdogs.

That became perhaps most tangible in those suburbs greatly in demand as places to live, on the slopes above the meanders of the Seine, where one had a view of the whole city of Paris, as in Garches, Meudon, or St.-Cloud. From Paris down there in its basin, scattered over the landscape as far as the horizon like millions of bright, crowded dice, only a rustling reached the silent hills and panoramic terraces above. Down there was where everything *was* happening. That was where it was.

The metropolis shimmered, glowed, and way down there, inaudible, was a steady, nest-warm thrumming, and the person who had moved away, way up with his hanging gardens in the fresh air, must have felt he had no hope of ever returning there.

And even I, in my much humbler suburb, in the house from which only the tip of the Eiffel Tower could be seen, found myself thinking at night, perhaps in view of that magic triangle sticking up far off in the gaps between the houses next door, where the lights had been turned off long since, and their dark and dreary cabbage gardens, whether it wasn't an outrage to be away from that light over there.

It was very fragile and threatening, my grand time, back then before the midpoint of life, in my first suburb.

And then one day I really did go mad. My madness remained inside me and did not last. But if it had broken into the open, there would have been no going back for me. I would have murdered my son—and was afraid I would do so, fled from myself into the remotest corner of the cellar—would have set fire to the house and would have run out on the street with a knife and an ax, striking blow upon blow against strangers, until the end. It was as if I had to destroy one thing after the other, just because it was there.

At intervals I was overcome with ghostly calm and thought all the rage of my serf ancestors, which never had an outlet, had collected in me and had now been transformed into the ravings of a madman. I went to my son, caressed him, pushed him to the ground. The child understood, and avoided me for the rest of the day, but he also did not lock his room; otherwise I would have broken down the door.

When I got to the clearing the following day at noon, having groped my way there step by step, gasping as if I had been short of breath for a long time, and told my *patron* about it, he responded that I had just had an ordinary tantrum, the kind that made one's appetite return with fresh vigor. And yet I was sure that I had been in a state close to a new kind of madness, as yet not described in the literature: an interminable raving, wall-to-wall disaster, and at the same time, in distinction to the megalomaniac figures in history or drama, lacking any variation, completely monotonous—the peculiarly modern feature of such insanity being the fact that it was so boring.

M y one-day insanity in the suburb now lies almost two decades behind me, and it has never recurred. And nevertheless, in contrast to other guises in which I once appeared, in my memory this one has not become a stranger—the one in which I went around and around in a circle, my hot head in my correspondingly colder hands, to be jolted out of it only by a series of violent actions, and yet far too weak to so much as lift a finger. This is one *I* I will never put in quotation marks.

2

The Story of My First Metamorphosis

Something had to happen. Something had to be done. What I was experiencing in my idleness cried out for that. I decided to take the plunge and write a long story. Was this really the only way I could accomplish something?

I sent Valentin, my son, to my childless sister in her small town in Carinthia and prepared for my work by crisscrossing Europe.

Among other things I made use of my friends, who at the time were pretty much the same ones as now; for a long time I have not added anyone to the list.

I remained without a permanent residence and accompanied the architect on one of his observation excursions, in the course of which he now and then earned some money as a carpenter, or even just as a day laborer.

With the singer I went over my first song lyrics, which he wanted to try to make singable (the phrases were too short for him, or, I am no longer sure which, too long; the song did not suit him).

With my priest I parsed the epistles of the Apostle Paul, who according to his own words was a difficult writer, his clauses more complex than those of the Greek Thucydides and even the Roman Livy, and in contrast to the two historians, he did not even have anything to narrate, only something to preach, and that had never been my thing, had it?

I stayed away from my woman friend, as indeed from every woman.

From the reader, who could often go for days on nothing but air, I received his "Survival Catalogue": showing how I had to make my way alone, at war with the world.

And with my painter I went out drawing in his various regions, but spent more time sitting in his studios, especially during his protracted periods of getting ready to work, also during his periods of distracting himself, very thoroughly, by dint of shining his shoes, sweeping the floor, trimming his toenails, carving a walking stick, until suddenly he would pick up a brush and start painting, undeterred by chain saws, jackhammers, and bluebottle flies.

L ikewise I conditioned myself physically, convinced that to design the New World I also had to be armed in this way.

In the European countries that were still Communist at the time, there were already Western-type fitness courses, on which you could have seen me running and jumping with the best of them. I, who as a child had never got beyond clinging to the broad back of a draft horse, now even tried to learn to ride, but appeared to myself so odd up there that I felt as though I should dismount for every pedestrian, and at least, if one came toward me on the path, always greeted him first (the same thing happens to me now with horseback riders here in the forest). And for the first time since the Gobi Desert I drove a car, across the summery tundra, and after a few days skidded off the crushed-rock track into a swamp, my head striking the windshield, which cracked in the shape of a star, while I merely bled a bit on my forehead, yet immediately had a thick furry covering over the blood from the mosquitoes. And while hiking in a ravine on the karst I looked for a shortcut, went in the wrong direction, and could get out only by climbing, increasingly enjoying the necessity of keeping my wits about me, and since then I have not actually taken up mountain climbing, but when I am out walking immediately feel myself becoming completely alert in unanticipated tight spots where, in order to get to safety, I have to rely for the moment entirely on my sense of touch, my body vitally connected from my toes to my fingertips as in no other situation.

When I swam upstream in the bright, clear upper reaches of the Alpine rivers, occasionally poked by the cartilaginous mouths of fish, the mountains and the sky moved in very close and seemed, together with the waters, which streamed, like Wolfram von Eschenbach's Tigris and Euphrates, "from Paradise," elemental and epic as they could hardly be in a dream. Once summer snowflakes swirled around the swimmer. Once perpendicular arrows of hail plunged into the river next to him, making fountains spurt sky-high (the former in the Inn River in the Engadine, the latter in the Tagliamento near Tolmezzo). In the Val Rosandra, surrounded by the limestone mountains of Trieste, I stood and stood under the waterfall there and let the stream of water, not great in volume but falling all the harder, drum my brain clear. Back there soon!

And one late afternoon beyond Tamsweg, when I was making my way uphill on skis, in my exhaustion I saw the white of the snowdrifts as that brilliant reflection in which Faust tells us we capture the world, and over my shoulder, the Austrian town far below in the dusky valley, with its oversettled outskirts, seemed to have levitated to my eye level, and both of these sights were not hallucinations.

And most of all perhaps, and everywhere, I practiced for my epic outdoors in the night, pitch-dark if possible, unknown, confining, through which I moved as if nothing were wrong.

And finally I had my teeth taken care of, had new heels put on my trusty shoes, had my hair cut to a stubble, celebrated at a little farewell party with my friends in Rinkolach, and in the fall withdrew to the place I had long ago chosen for my work, the Spanish (Catalonian) enclave of Llivia in the highlands of the eastern French Pyrenees.

I took a room in what at that time was still the only hotel there. My room was the highest in a large new building on the edge of the settlement, which had called itself a city since the seventeenth-century Treaty of the Pyrenees, and was both more and less. Against my better judgment, I had once again chosen a view, without streets and houses, a view of the open highland countryside, with the meadows and trees along the Río Segre, and beyond them the desertlike faded reddish-brown badland cliffs of Santa Leocadia, and beyond that, as if in another world, the jagged Sierra del Cadí as the vanishing point.

Not until I was there did I buy myself a typewriter, for which I had to leave the enclave again and go over the border to Puigcerdá, the only real city in the Cerdagne or Cerdanya: a machine with the Spanish arrangement of keys, on which, since some letters were not in the accustomed place, I constantly made typing errors. The foreign accents also disrupted my rhythm, likewise the upside-down Spanish exclamation points and question marks.

What did not merely trip me up but threw me off track, after the very first sentence, which I had written down, reaching in all directions, with the stored-up élan of the past months, was something else entirely. I should never ever have been allowed to know the first sentence of my epic project in advance and carry it around with me for so long. This sentence made a continuation, of whatever kind, impossible.

You have seen this, no doubt: I cut a figure like that slalom skier in an international competition who goes shooting out of the starting posts with total concentration and in that very moment wipes out at the first pole and is out of the race—yet remains on the screen.

But this analogy does not work (and it seems to me there are simply no even moderately accurate analogies for the vicissitudes of writing): for I did not want to admit defeat. First came a dazed feeling, then alarm, then a new start, although, according to the prevailing rules of the game, this seemed impermissible.

I crept out of the light and tried to continue in the dark, just as in childhood, when I had failed in front of others, I would imagine that off somewhere by myself I could cancel out my failure by starting over (and this analogy, too, is wrong).

At any rate, I started again and again in the days that followed, absolutely without hope and equally stubborn, and with the tenaciousness of a descendant of small farmers.

And yet I never got beyond my preconceived first sentence, which I could not or would not give up. This sentence, at first a simple main clause—subject, verb, object—now grew from day to day, called for additions, concessions, boxed itself in, bulged out, sought to break out into the open with a consecutive clause, came to a head, sharpened its focus, strove for lightness, also for fading, for inarticulateness, demanded, above and beyond narration, to address itself to someone (no one in particular), in a little twist to one side, then already in a subordinate clause, until the entire sentence looked like something between the onset of the long story I had planned and the convoluted salutation of a Pauline epistle, although certainly not addressed to a community, or even to an individual, and I, unlike the apostle, had not the slightest awareness of having been sent forth by anyone.

And when, on the evening of the third or fifth day, the sentence stood there without any continuation in sight, it was clear to me that the world-embracing epic for which I had prepared so thoroughly in spring and summer, as I had never prepared for an examination, was a failure, a bust. All the strength I needed for it had abandoned me. The notebooks I had filled in the previous months, piles and piles in front of me on the table, were utterly useless, as were the detailed maps, some of which I had drawn myself, held down by chunks of the yellow-and-gray stone from the area around my suburb.

I lay down on the floor and slept, or lost consciousness, until the following evening.

Then I casually followed the windings of the one and only sentence that went on for several pages. When I took my eyes off it, absently, a few very short, almost unconnected sentences presented themselves quietly, like "He went shopping. The tree was very beautiful. The summer came," which I immediately added.

And then I realized I was going to have to write something entirely different from what I had planned: something for which I was not in the least prepared and also felt quite unsuited: the story of, or the research report on, something that did exist inside me but was untouchable: my religion, or, as the resulting work then turned out to be called by others, "a prayer in narrative." And although I considered such a thing hardly possible in this day and age, not amenable to being expressed in that rational language without which, in my eyes, no writing and no reading could take place, my few sentences inspired a kind of trust, entirely unparalleled, as never before, in words, in myself, in the world.

As I then went out walking in the evening landscape of the enclave, there swept through me, as novel to me as the word that went with it, ecstasy. The low walls of cut granite that bordered the roads there glittered, and bathed my face. I was looking forward to my one-man expedition.

And with that began what was called at the beginning of these pages a metamorphosis.

It was the loveliest time I had experienced up to then, month after month, then on through the years, and my most difficult. It was the struggle I had always wished for, the war of which the reader had spoken, yet not against an external enemy, out there in society, but rather against myself.

I sensed the existence of rules almost impossible to satisfy, of which I furthermore had no knowledge, except perhaps that the process had to be very different from my usual writing, which, for instance, required that I repeatedly make blunders in order to get on with the story and maneuver it toward my original conception. Here, without an initial conception, without any conception at all, my trusty technique of doing it wrong would not help at all. On the contrary, a single wrong word that I let stand would block all progress on my project.

To put it another way, I could neither have recourse to my experiences, dreams, and facts nor invent action, plot, or conflicts. The book, or whatever it would turn out to be, had to be created out of nothing.

I was in suspense. The struggle seemed unwinnable; at best it could be drawn out as long as possible. And yet I was often also hopeful, could feel myself, as my own enthusiastic opponent, closer to myself than ever before.

Thus I sat from morning until usually late at night in my warm, quiet, bright writing room above the Pyrenean punch-bowl landscape around the enclave of Llivia, in the light of autumn and then already winter.

I ate less and less, often only zwieback with the tea I brewed for myself now and then. There were hardly any people in the "city," which consisted chiefly of vacation houses, whose owners at that time of year, since there was no snow for skiing yet, were in Gerona or Barcelona. And the few local people, in the morning in the bar or sometimes driving the cows home toward evening from the pastures on the highland slopes, were so laconically cordial that they made me look forward even more to getting on with my work.

This was not to involve anything more than narrating happenings, peaceful ones, which themselves were everything, and taken all together perhaps constituted the event itself: the streaming of a river through the seasons; people moving along; the falling of rain, on grass, stone, wood, skin, hair; the wind in a pine tree, in a poplar, against a sheer stone face, between the toes, in the armpits; that hour before dusk when the last swallows swoop across the sky, while the bats begin to zigzag about; the traces of different birds in the mud of a puddle on a dirt road leading through fields; the simple coming of evening, with the great ball of the sun still visible in the west, that of the moon exactly opposite in the east.

It was that fullness of the world, as I had known it during my years off from school, so to speak, in those suburbs of Paris, except that, contrary to my plan, it had no dramatic plot or particular incidents, purely variations, nuances, more and more of them. And nevertheless all that was supposed to appear as interconnected and vibrate, with the intensity of a treasure-hunt story.

Nor were heroes lacking, a group of friends, men as well as women, who, embarked on a common journey, primarily had to serve as eyes, ears, and language for those other stories of the world. In between, the most that would occur would be things like playing cards, dancing, sewing on buttons, or someone sleepwalking, singing an original song, perhaps suggestive of Eichendorff's *Ahnung und Gegenwart*. They all had names from classical antiquity, jumbled up by me so as to seem contemporary.

I transposed the quintessential events from the populated hills of the Seine to the region of the Orinoco in Latin America, which I knew only from directories of subject headings. Snowing in Clamart now turned up near the springs in the mountainous region of Guyana, although there, so close to the equator, it had probably never snowed. Borrowing from the rivulet that emerged from the woods at the foot of the menhir— and immediately ran dry again—I described the origin of the mighty river. The people on the clay path near my inn in the clearing became Indios following a trail through the rain forest.

And the journey on foot was to end at that bifurcation of the Orinoco that obsessed me even in my dreams, where the river, in midcourse, for as yet unexplained reasons, split and went rushing off in opposite directions.

N ever during the writing had there been any thought of its earning money. And here, after the first sentences, it became unimaginable that this story, if I ever brought it to a conclusion, would be read by so much as a single person, and that did push me into forlornness. As I forged ahead, all the more stubbornly, I forgot this thought at first and then found myself enjoying a new kind of freedom.

F or a long time I continued in this way, sitting at my table. Even when I did nothing but wait, there was this sense of symmetry, with the snowflake dissolving on the edge of the balcony, with the strip of condensation behind that. It seemed as if I were ridding myself once and for all of my impatience, and finding my own speed.

And because it was so unprecedented, I can say this: I was there, word for word, in time, as if this were my place.

Quite often, too, the thought came to me that no one had ever experienced any such thing; with me something altogether new was beginning.

In place of my forgotten body I felt a sensuality that I liked because it was simply there, without wanting anything. And then again I became strangely conscious of my body, as a whole, the way usually only a part of the body, a tooth, an ear, a foot, enters one's consciousness, as a bothersome weight, or sometimes an absence of sensation, just before an incredible pain manifests itself there. Along with this freedom I experienced daily an equally new type of anxiety.

What made me anxious was my impression that in the process of being written down the material I was narrating was not expanding, but shrinking more and more, not what I had been accustomed to up until then. And besides, I was treading water with my story: the tour group that was supposed to have set out after only one day at the sources of the Orinoco was still stuck there, with half the rainy season gone and almost two hundred pages. The sentences with which I was circling around them, wanting to do justice to each happening—heat lightning, the sound of the rapids, the shifting sill of the river, marked by the first shadows of fish downstream—were becoming thinner than the air in those parts.

But it was not permissible—that was one of the rules that had emerged in the course of my work—for a single sentence, once it was on paper, to be revoked, at most a word or two. If there was to be any progress, then only by following the thread of the sentence, becoming more frayed from day to day.

I hoped that simply from fingering and fanning out the phenomena that nature presented I would come to a decision that would enable my heroes and me finally to take a leap and start anew. But another rule was that I could not invent such a decision, whereas every other time I had felt firm ground under my feet only when I was inventing.

The decision then turned out to be this: one day, in midsentence, my material ran out on me. And with my material for writing, my material for living. I keep brooding over that moment, and to this day do not know why the certainty suddenly came crashing down on me that I had blown my chance and that it was all over. Who can explain it to me? (No one, please.)

Those prayer books in boarding school had covered every single day, one saint after the other, and for each a miniature biography in the smallest possible print was supplied: these I had always read all through the Mass, not because they were about saints but because, compressed into all the prayers and invocations of the Lord, whose meaning remained closed to me, were, quite simply, stories. That shows how much I have always craved storytelling.

And now this, too, was closed to me. Even now I still do not know why I received this breaking of the thread as a verdict of annihilation, executed immediately.

And again I fell to the floor, but this time did not go to sleep; instead, I had to get up at once and sit down at my desk.

And for the following months that became the last of the still-usable rules. Even when I did not get out a single line, merely this staying at my desk provided a little bit of certainty. When out walking I epitomized the psalmist from whose abyss no tone issued forth. Running water, always such a reliable help in the past, whether out in the meadows along the Río Segre or in the shower in my hotel, made me gag. Among the trees in the meadows down by the river wandered the beasts, and in the eyes of the people on the street below lurked yellow-and-black hornets. Wasn't Spain the land of death?

I set out for the so-called Chaos of Targasonne, a desert of crags, intending to get lost or even fall off a cliff, for all I cared. But I did not succeed. I did not get lost, not at all.

And equally in vain I wished I would get sick, or the Third World War would break out, so that I would at least not be so alone with my very own war (previously I had thought that even in a world war, even if my child died, I would go on writing).

And the others sensed the state I was in. My current publisher, who blew in on his way from a book fair in Barcelona to a skiing vacation farther up in Font-Romeu, beat a hasty retreat, fled from the despair I exuded (to that degree he had a good nose), and patently gave up on me—which for an evening allowed me to take heart again. I understood him, too, in fact could smell the odor on myself.

Then something changed, with the couple of sentences by which I eventually moved on.

First of all a new title for my book thrust itself upon me. From "Prehistoric Forms" it was renamed "The Chimerical World."

What a wonderful aura or addition emanated from a mere two words when they presented themselves in context. Holding firmly on to that, I was circling far outside with the eagle above the highland plateau.

And moments later, when again nothing happened, I became the fly lying on its back in the corner of the room and spinning in place. I had just been at the core of the world, and now I was catapulted into an outer space that was really no such thing. One morning I was thinking again that no one had ever experienced anything as glorious as I had, and in the evening of the same day I would have given God knows what to take the place of anyone else, the boil-studded beggar outside the church in Llivia, or a man condemned to death: at least he would have been declared guilty properly.

Hour after hour I sat motionless, facing me only that cloud with which there could be no conversation, filled with viper's blood that darted its tongue into me from time to time, and unexpectedly I sat up straight and then traced out word for word the source, still so uncertain, even to the explorers who go out looking for it, of the Orinoco in the mountainous region of Guyana where my story continued to spin its spirals.

A mid this constant back-and-forth, my longing was focused only on the smallest, most ordinary, most everyday things.

All I wanted was to be able to bring my son to school again, stand idly on the suburban railway overpass, take my place in line at the post office, the bank, the movies. For the first time I felt a need for salvation. And I visualized it as embodied in everydayness, in its services, manners, and commonplace expressions.

I cursed myself for running away, seeking out an exceptional situation and exclusivity. If my work required that, something was wrong.

But now I likewise had to stay here, could not leave Llivia. Never again will I get out of this damned enclave, I thought again and again, and yet, with the next sentence that got me off dead center, I would have loved to give a party for this heavenly place and all its blessed inhabitants.

A s I fought thus for life, in my own way, day after day, I came to accept myself as never before. I discovered something like a fondness for myself, a kind of brotherliness or friendship with myself.

It seemed to me that I was no I, no body anymore—which at the same time was uncanny—and had finally received, as one in need of salvation, what I lacked: a culture; precisely in my near-helplessness a spirit.

In this way much that was unthinkable became possible and playable, such that I once even let an itinerant soothsayer tell my fortune. She did not manage to lie in my presence, and foretold for me, holding my unabashedly needy hand in her own warming one, even worse and more worrisome experiences.

And once I sat all day at my desk imagining that at my back a camera for a blockbuster film was set up, and each of the letters I was to type would be projected onto a gigantic screen, before the eyes of a mass audience on all continents. I felt the suspense with which the completion of a word was awaited, groaned in relief with the entire theater when finally the connecting word came, and then, when long after midnight the sentence was concluded with a period the size of a planet, I jumped up from my seat, together with the rest of the world. Nothing could be quieter than another sentence after that, a transition, a ford: no sweeter silence.

I simply had to follow this method of finally forgetting any audience, nodding and rocking my head, so that at the first light of day a page was covered, as had not been the case for weeks, an image in writing. I washed myself in the water of the Pyrenees, full of enthusiasm for this me-without-me, and animated by love for my lot, which was something fundamentally different from acceptance of fate or inner tranquillity. (The peace so indispensable to my work was not foreign to me; yet I have not learned to this day to hold on to it, once achieved.)

Occupied with writing, I shuddered at the thought of going out into nature. The clanging of the river against the granite sills made me anxious, then even snowflakes bumping against my ear.

The very isolation of my study, with its view of the Sierra blue in the distance and the red earthen pyramids in the foreground, also became threatening to me. I moved to a room overlooking the highway, and opened the window, no matter how cold the weather, to the sound of the—unfortunately too infrequent—trucks and buses, preferably with the rattle of snow chains.

My daily walk, by roundabout routes through the enclave to make it longer, took me not out into nature but instead into the church of Llivia and even more often into the enclave's little museum next door. It was as if I expected to find a sort of way out through contemplation of the objects, for instance the centuries-old apothecary's cabinet displayed there. At least these handcrafted objects made me forget how things stood with me.

And likewise I wanted only light-colored foods; I had a horror of dark ones, for instance venison. For a time my only beverage was milk, with the thought that the viper-blood black would be forced out by the milk white.

But all that worked for only a day, and not even for that. I was cradled by the world, and went to hell. I conjured up a god *ex nihilo*, and then could not find the right word and the consecutive clause for him. I expected help to arrive, kept my eyes peeled for anyone, on earth, in the sky, around the corner, and then I was again the one who said to himself, "Look here, there goes someone who doesn't need anyone!" I wanted to be taken away by one of the airplanes flying over the highlands, then found myself, in order to get another paragraph done, as I had wished, in the cockpit, which, the next time I got stuck, turned out to have no pilot and no instruments. During a storm I placed the manuscript pages by the open window and went off, hoping they would be blown away forever, then rushed back in a panic. At the sight of a butterfly I felt the fluttering of the wings all the way into my heart, at the sight of the next one, the dusty body between the wings appeared to me as that of the perished caterpillar. Who or what was chimerical: the world? the era? I?

Then a clarification was achieved after all. (If not, I either would still be sitting there at the scratched hotel table, having just reached the place where the first black-water tributary flowed into the Orinoco, or would be part of the musty air up in the crevasses of the Puigmal, the "Evil Peak.")

It was the fault of a day after which I thought I was finally out of danger with my book. After over a hundred days, often spent from morning until late at night at my table, I decided to let the writing go the following day, and merely polish my shoes in my room and then immediately set out across country.

It was a clear day in early spring at thirteen hundred meters above the level of the sea at Alicante, which is how the altitude is measured everywhere in Spain, and soon the high plateau of the Pyrenees stretched at my feet, a sparsely populated scene in a natural amphitheater, whose terraces I mounted, going up the mountainside from one granite block to the next. I moved in a daze, as if released suddenly from intensive care directly into the sunshine.

Yet I could not achieve high spirits or pleasure. And with every step it grew worse. It was far too late to return to my writing table, and not merely for today. The deferment had run out. I would not even make it into the evening on this day.

Although I pushed on, with the world panorama below me, it was a mere wandering in circles. My pencil fell from my hand. My story did not continue. In just this way a person I had seen die was still moving his lips to draw in air long after he had died, or kicked the bucket.

I, who knew of nothing more worthwhile to strive for than to become a part of the world, to see through the eyes of another person, to land with a drop of rain on the dust in the road, now experienced myself, no matter where I turned, as such a part, but in a completely opposite sense. How sweet and kind the planet showed itself to be, and at the same time I gagged at any phenomenon. And it gave me not the slightest relief to tell myself that this was nothing compared to the children dying at this moment around the world. I saw down below in the distance, from the city of Puigcerdá, the smoke rising from the highlands hospital, found myself transplanted into the bone-hard suffering there, and even so would much rather have been lying there myself.

And just as little was achieved by the rebuke: in view of the millions of years represented by the granite cliffs at my back, what did I count for? And I also knew that even in a merry crowd, even among all my friends, I would not be any less on the brink than alone here by the garbage dump on the mountainous steppe of the enclave of Llivia.

Twice in the past months I had been thrown to the ground. Now I threw myself down, face to the ground, and experienced a previously unknown masculinity. But the earth did not help me. She did not take me in. She even pushed me away. She had nothing for me.

Eyes open, look, straight ahead! And I had no choice but to look straight ahead from where I was lying on the ground, at eye level the ruins of a house of the steppe. And my gaze did not let go, and did not let go, and did not let go, and surrendered all hope, and was no longer waiting for any sign.

A rusty stove was lying among the ruins, with an oven from which old newspapers and books stuck out. I eyed the book on top, actually more a large brochure with a picture on the cover that still had some faded color, a princess surrounded by dwarfs, with the Spanish words "Los cuentos de los Hermanos Grimm," The Fairy Tales of the Brothers Grimm.

Venerate the unfathomable in silence. But isn't the act of circumnarrating it an essential part of that? Suddenly I was seized by the certainty that my book would remain a fragment, and that that was as it should be. And that was not yet all: it was not even a fragment, but, unbeknownst to me, narrated to the end.

New lids grew over my eyes. I leaped to my feet. For a while nothing more could happen to me. I ran up hill and down dale, my first time running in how long? And at the same time I remained rooted to the spot: everywhere it was the same, one place. The little brooks in the pastures, together with the granite-glittering fence posts along their banks a sort of signature of the Cerdanya highlands, were rushing, wherever I looked, as though just thawed, and the randomly scattered turret blocks of the Chaos of Targasonne, above the tree line, likewise looked as though they had just been melted free of the glacier, long since gone.

And I swore fidelity to such a picture of the world. Never again should it change suddenly into a chimera, and that was within my power. It was my gaze that made it this way. It was my blinking that divided it up and organized it. But now I had to get going, down to where people were. From now on, that was my place.

Without suffering any harm, I let myself drop that day from a cliff higher than I, stuck my hand into the thorns of a juniper cypress, waded through the icy waters of the Río Mahur along the border. On the last stretch, going uphill again to the terrace of the sturdy little capital of Puigcerdá, I was accompanied by a shaggy dog, which then kept close to my side until late that night. In the local movie house, the Avinguda, more roomy than almost all movie houses in large cities nowadays, I saw a sequel to *Jaws*, whose adventures, so harmless or peaceable compared to those I had just survived, gave me a warm glow around my heart. Afterward, with the dog tagging along, I followed in the darkness a woman who I thought had given me a sign with her hip, and at the very moment when I had decided to accost her and broke into a run, I fell flat on the street, tripping over the dog or a loose shoelace. Satisfied, I then dropped into the municipal casino, at that time still a traditional male stronghold, black with men's suits under white neon patterns on the ceiling, and, standing beside a stranger, I played pool with a sureness of aim and a casualness such as I otherwise have only when I am throwing something or sometimes selecting a word. I kept one eye on the always busy television screen, felt as caught up in the advertising images as in the reports of terrible events from around the world, absorbed it all with grateful gusto. Then I invited my partner to dinner, whereupon, on the terrace of the Maria Victoria Hotel, with a view of the snow-glowing highlands and the railroad station at the border, with the dog between us under the table, he told me his entire life story, including the bombardment of Puigcerdá in his early childhood, in which the casino was almost the only building left standing. I decided that if I wrote anything at all after my book, it would be simply as a chronicler. And then we went down the steep slope to the station. I had the choice of traveling from there either to Barcelona or to Perpignan, or, by way of Toulouse, to Paris or God knows where. In any case, I would leave the enclave the next day. Extraordinary how the world was open to me, into whose neck, just a few hours or moments ago, that string had still been cutting by which, according to an old custom of Cerdagne, killed moles are hung up in a row. That was the first time I felt balls of air swelling in my armpits.

It is another story altogether that the mutt ran off on me as I was making my way home in the dark, that when I passed the lonely border station in the no-man's-land just outside Llivia I wanted to be there in place of the uniformed guard watching television in his bare room under the stars of the Pyrenees, and that I choked on the final sentence of my book all through spring and summer, from one city in Europe to another, with the last line finally typed in Munich or somewhere or other, on the day of the Blessed Virgin's birth or some day or other, in the garret in the house of my reader, who later told me he had just made up his mind, after days of silence behind my door, to break it down, when finally the typewriter started up, then again nothing for a long time, and then Gregor K. with a packet of manuscript and his traveling coat asking where the nearest post office was.

And it is also another story that for at least the following year I considered my salvation or release into a new freedom, or this change, a delusion; I thought the verdict on me was still in force, and now, right now, the time to execute it had arrived.

That this relentless pressure finally let up I owe to reading, not Holy Scripture, but the poet Friedrich Hölderlin, who filled my veins with new blood, and then Goethe, who could be counted on to raise my spirits. This reading provided me with roots in the air and the light; and only on this basis did I then develop a sense for the Gospels, and not only the Christian ones. And simultaneously, although at the time I clearly understood religion, no matter which, as a given, even in previously incomprehensible variations, I still felt it was the highest calling to be a storyteller.

As for my book on prehistoric forms, alias the chimerical world, I thought during my relapses that I had ended it wrong, and was thus a failure and at the same time finally in the place where I belonged, and then again that I could build the rest of my life on it, or at least a piece of my life.

My notion that no one would read it was not borne out. To be sure, many people, especially members of my own generation, distanced themselves from me and my project, wordlessly as a rule, almost considerately, and when someone did say something, he said he found the sentences too long, the words too archaic, the focus on nature too exclusive. But then, with the passage of time, new readers turned up, younger ones, and, something I had always wished for previously, above all older ones. The reviews were nothing special. Only one of the critics, the cleverest

and at the same time the most limited, a man who presented his limi-
tations as simplicity, sniffed out something and offered the opinion that
the longing for salvation that presses on one of the heroes' eyelids was
an infelicitous image, and wondered whether falling to one's knees,
which happens to one of the characters in the course of events, provided
a suitable position for thinking.

During the following year I remained in my birthplace, Rinkolach on
the Jaunfeld Plain, taking shelter like a child in the cottager's house
that had belonged to my parents, recently bought back by my successful
brother, my almost-twin, the uncrowned king of our family, and yet
again and again the loser (at the appointed time perhaps I shall write
my first play about him, with the title "Preparations for Immortality,"
a tragedy?).

Earlier I had thought of the house, which belonged to us three siblings, as my last refuge. Now it felt as though there I would finally make
a real beginning. In my ancestral region, the world in the form of details
now opened up to me as it had revealed itself to me in the suburbs of
Paris. The way of seeing I had developed there had become so much my
own that it persisted in this area, similarly simple and unpicturesque, as
I now realized. At last Austrian objects, along with the spaces between
them, showed themselves to me, and spread out to form an environment.

None of these things forced themselves on me any longer (which in
my childhood had often made the impression of hypertrophy). Now on
the plain the pines and firs stood there, and Globasnitz Brook and Rin-
ken Brook flowed as all over the world, as above them much more than
a purely Carinthian sky hovered blue.

And thus the place names in my more immediate homeland also ac-
quired resonance and rhythm, even if only those of the villages: Dob,
Heiligengrab, Mittlern, Bistrica, Lind, Ruden, and of course Rinkolach.
The names of the towns, as small as they were—Bleiburg, Völkermarkt,
Wolfsberg—remained mute, not to mention Klagenfurt or Villach. Only
on the other side of the borders did it continue, with Maribor, Udine,
Tricesimo.

And likewise the natives, though again only those in the villages—

which in any case were almost all I saw during that year—struck me as people from anywhere, with the appropriate horizon as a backdrop.

All this I took in, and yet for a long initial period I was utterly incapable of having dealings with anyone. Even with my brother I could hardly get out a word. It was a kind of violence that forced me to hide myself from him as from the others, or to turn my head the other way.

And even the simplest daily tasks I seemed to have to learn all over again: to put my jacket on a hanger, to make my bed, to get on a bicycle.

Once, when I was swimming absentmindedly, I paused and almost went under. Another time, when with my brother I had set out after all for the town of B., he sent me off to do an errand, and secretly watched me from outside on the public square, and afterward described how I had suddenly stood there with a package of butter in my hand, not knowing what to do next, and the cashier had had to reach into my pockets for the money, and, when I finally found my way back to him, the butter had melted between my fingers.

That I finally got my bearings can be ascribed, I believe, to the location of my bed or sofa, in the back corner of the entrance hall, under the stairs leading up to the former granary. My brother had hung a lamp for me there, with a switch next to it, and a table and stool also graced my little realm. Here, while reading, looking up through the cracks and knotholes, and likewise while sleeping, I was plainly gathering strength for the world outside. What a relief, simply to have the top of my head touching the underside of the stair treads when I sat there.

During the day I then sat more and more at one of the windows, which as in all the old southern Slav peasant houses was very close to the ground; leaning one elbow on the unusually broad windowsill, the grass of the little orchard in front of the house at eye level, I was merely an observer; I did not touch a writing instrument once during that year, and even longer.

And just as on that evening among the blocks of stone along the harbor of Piran when I was a young man, I had forgotten all knowledge and also no longer had an opinion or a judgment on anything. My brother teased me for having become so tolerant. "Where's all your anger gone?"

And it was a fact that my way of just staring resembled that of a village idiot. Whatever I saw, I liked. And in the same fashion I accepted everyone and everything I could. In this I felt not limited but slow-witted. Only as one who was slow-witted—this I had experienced again and again—did the person I was awaken in me.

It implied no contradiction that I continued to enjoy studying, even if that was confined to the leaves and blossoms of the weeds in the area, which altogether, the longer I bent over them, swung into motion in a marvelously varied and yet symmetrically delicate round dance. They had names—spurge, valerian, hemlock, plantain—yet for now I wanted only to take in the colors and forms, all intermingled. "Remain impression-able" . . .

The out-of-the-way and rather inconspicuous vegetation was almost the only thing in which I became engrossed during this time.

So how did I define my metamorphosis? There was hardly anything from earlier, from childhood, to see anew—this I recognized. The old mushroom places in the woods, for instance, were bleak and bare, and the clearings, if any forest was left, had shifted, like moving sand dunes, often without the strawberry and raspberry patches that had previously been there. Even the field paths, along with their deep dust, had disappeared or now took an entirely different course; on the other hand, they had cleared even more logging roads through the hills. The Crab Pond was now that in name only, just as the Inn on the Bend was now located on a straight stretch of road and is supposed to be renamed the Trout.

And in spite of all that, in my eyes nothing about the area had changed. And just as before I was reluctant to block my view of these things with historical reminiscences. Of these, practically the only story people still told was the business with the American soldier, a black, who was dropped by parachute almost at the end of the Second World War, and got so hung up, head down, in a tree by a field that people came running from all direction with flails, scythes, and sickles. I went

only so far as to examine, in the rectory, that turn-of-the-century chronicle in which house by house the occupations of the inhabitants were
noted. Again: what was Gregor Keuschnig's metamorphosis?

Since during this year he understood everyone, even the former SS man
and the future one, he soon enjoyed an uncanny general confidence.
He joined in all the celebrations, was a favorite partner at card tables,
and the fact that later on he often confused himself in his memory with
one of the others—"Was it me or was it you who was drunk and fell
off that ladder in the apple tree?"—proved that he really was part of
the village community. (On one thing he even became the expert: on
lost objects, in particular the small and smallest ones. He could be
counted on to go straight to the right spot in the general area, bend
down, and even in the thickest gravel come up with the lost bead or
contact lens.)

In his black rubber boots and floppy blue pants, cinched at the waist
with a length of rope, he more and more resembled a native, one from
earlier times, and he himself, when he sat there with his palm turned
upward or sternly looked up and inspected the person facing him, sometimes saw a double image of himself and his grandfather, which the
third party then also noticed.

In this region, as out-of-the-way as ever and lacking a middle class,
he became a sort of authority, and not only as a finder of lost objects.
Finally he was even offered an official position; don't ask me which.

At the same time he remained aware that he did not belong among
people. The same thing would happen to him as in elementary
school when he had his only role in a play; as a dwarf among dwarfs in
the background, he had nothing to do but sew, and kept pricking his
finger (which, to be sure, only his mother noticed), and then in boarding
school, where he was chosen to make up the rules for a new game, which
turned out to be completely unplayable, and then as a magistrate during
his year in court . . .

But only the children caught on to his chronic unreliability, for instance the child next door, to whom, while in the next room the child's

father lay dying, gasping for breath, to calm the child down he read a fairy tale in which someone's heart was torn from his living body.

The person who at that time understood almost everyone, disarmed, reconciled, convinced people—that was not me. So, for the third time: That was supposed to be a metamorphosis?

Certainly, all that year I felt an authority in me, but far from the community, alone, as I remained for the most part, and often half asleep. If a metamorphosis, then one without deeds; without external consequences.

And at the same time it was the year during which the Rinkolach chess club won the Jaunfeld championship, during which in Carinthia a former partisan was elected head of the provincial government, and the Blessed Virgin appeared to his defeated opponent in the Bärental, during which, on the other side of the border, representatives of the youth of all the southern Slav peoples gathered and sang "Jugoslavija!" again, during which in Germany part of the population committed mass suicide, during which Japan erected its Great Wall, during which the world acquired a second moon, and at the end of which, on the highway bridge over the Rio Grande between El Paso, U.S.A., and Ciudad Juárez, Mexico, for the second time, after exactly a decade, one and the same Austrian from a South Carinthian hamlet and the same Spanish woman from Catalonian Gerona, after both had in the meantime gone or stumbled their separate ways, were reunited.

It had become time to leave Rinkolach. Now my place of birth was to be only a temporary stopping place. What else could I do there, aside from whitewashing rooms, chopping wood, picking fruit, except let the sun shine on me, let the rain splash on me through the open front door, let summer and winter come (although I had a special liking for all that)? What did I write there except perhaps, and that merely dictated to my brother—anything but touch a writing instrument!—one report for the community news bulletin on the annual meeting of the local water company (although I had a hard time with it, cold sweat and groping for words as always).

And the villagers, despite their tactfulness, a characteristic of small farmers, were relieved to be rid of me at last (although one—the innkeeper—then sent word that the village seemed empty without me). At last they, even the priest, even my brother, could be by themselves again. My presence made me the superfluous one; I was all right in their eyes only when absent. Even Filip Kobal in the neighboring village of Rinkenberg, already a popular figure there, found it embarrassing after a while, despite all the cordiality with which he received me, not to be the only writer in the region, and I could understand his feelings.

Only the dead seemed to need me there at home. At any rate, every time I left the cemetery they fell upon me in the form of an angry swarm of flies.

I had a wife, and now I had to go back to her. Without her as my Other, it was all over; this was my thought, an entirely new one for me.

I asked my sister if my son could stay with her a little while longer —or was it she who asked me?—and set out to find the woman from Catalonia, who in the meantime was back at the United Nations in New York. She knew of course that I was on my way to her, but not that I would take a detour by way of the bridge over the Rio Grande, which I did with no purpose other than to catch my breath before our reunion, just as with everyday appointments I had the habit of loafing around beforehand. It was always as if I wanted to gain time that way, but for what?

And why even now, when our reconciliation was overdue? All this while, I had been enthralled by the thought of my distant wife. Compared with her, even my childlike son was only incidental. I had very persistent dreams about us, in which we made love and just stayed together all night long, in majesty and affection. Similarly, during that period of separation, I often felt the woman from Catalonia there with me, invisible, for days at a time, and whether alone or among others, I would again and again turn toward her, looking over my shoulder into the empty corner; unlike in her presence, I made an effort not to do anything that might displease her, and when I did not succeed, my look over my shoulder became a plea for understanding: "Look homeward, angel."

Later, when we were newly together again, I had such a conviction that she had been with me in certain situations that when we wanted to recall them together I complained each time about her poor memory.

And now our first exchange of glances was repeated when we met, a day before the appointed time, far from the appointed place, I coming from Mexico, she coming from North America. Although preoccupied with her in my thoughts, I did not recognize her at first, and turned to look at her perhaps only because this woman appeared to me so amazingly "pale and young." But afterward: heaven help us! And she, too, she told me, had recognized me only when she looked back for the second time at someone who, literally, "looked so pale and young." How tired each of us was then, how tired.

But only her return banished the last vestiges of the crotchetiness I had developed during my period of solitude. She loosened my knotted limbs and relaxed my false fists, and through her new presence I learned to be there with my entire body in every movement, a forcefulness that at the same time could be as little as a gentle touch.

In the Japanese imperial city of Nara we made up for our skipped honeymoon, and then I lived in her two rooms high up in the Adams Hotel on 86th Street in Manhattan, with a view of the reservoir in Central Park. Our harmony there had a trace of amiable irony about what had been done to each of us by the other during the previous decade, and that seemed to make it durable. (And yet a decade later we lost each other for the second time.)

Toward the end of winter I then had the courage, with her in the next room, to sit down at a desk again. All the snowing in New York also made me want to write, especially in the evenings when the lights of the constantly landing airplanes were switched on and in them one could see from my skyscraper window the snowflakes whirling from the potholes in the street up into the heavens.

It turned out to be my shortest book, also because at that time I expected the narrative to unfold more from my groping my way back and questioning myself than from a masterful windup and playing of my trump card, with all the components that had seemed to me to have been part of my repertory far too long.

My piece, although ultimately it was supposed to be nothing but a story, was called "Essay on Neighborhood," and was a sort of description of the life of one person through the voices of the various neighbors with whom he had had dealings since childhood, and then, privately published, under the pseudonym Urban Pelegrin, by my friend the reader, a printer by trade, it became my worldwide success. The Peking *People's Daily* called me a progressive humanist focused on the here and now; the *Osservatore Romano* (Via del Pellegrino, Città del Vaticano) recognized in my language something related to the gaze of a rural laborer, to whom, sitting on the edge of a field after many hours of toil, the only pleasure left is to gaze at the sky; *The New Yorker* printed it in English translation before the book appeared, and invited me to a party at the Algonquin Hotel (except that by that time I was long since here in my Paris suburb bay, and did not want to leave anymore). Only *The New York Times*, swollen with daily reality, could not find its reality in mine, and on the other hand saw my way of writing as too emotional, or too cold, or too subtle, or too old-fashioned. And my enemy in Germany, who meanwhile had become the much-flattered first-name buddy of my former publisher (but even before that, whenever I went to see the publisher, my chair would still be stinking hot from the other man), exclaimed, when I crossed his path—no, he had no path, he was everywhere and nowhere —as he deviled by, with the rolling eyes of a mad dog that to his chagrin was kept away from the object of his rage by a fence: "So, Herr Pelegrin-Keuschnig, how's sales?" (Once again he thought he had outsmarted me; what he did not know was that Keuschnig was also an assumed name. And as always he, otherwise so adept at sniffing out and tearing to shreds, lost the scent when it came to things that mattered, for these have almost no smell.)

I had actually written my little book simply by lying down and snapping my fingers. All the sentences took shape when I was half awake or dozing, drifting in and out of consciousness, and whenever a sentence came clear, I would jump up and write it down. Word after word emerged as soft as it was immutable, and up to the final sentence, when in the next room, where my wife and lovely neighbor was sitting, a summer wind already wafting through the open window was rolling the pencils back and forth on the table, not a single one needed to be changed.

When the woman from Catalonia and I, on the evening of the same day, were waved by the elevator operator on the top floor of the Adams Hotel into his brass cage, and on floor after floor during the leisurely trip down, more of the monthly and yearly guests got on, until at the end all races and ages were represented, it was decided that the moment had come for us to be with our child again.

New York at that time was the last big city in which I felt at home. But in the meantime every town offered itself as the hub of the world—much as more and more individuals, without particular deeds or natural gifts, took on the roles of heroes and stars—including Sp. on the Drau, renamed on the signs Sp./Millstätter See, where I went to pick up Valentin, while the woman from Catalonia, who could break out in a rash at the mere sound of Austrian dialect, waited for us in Paris, deserted now in August.

My sister lived in one of the satellite developments in Sp., built in what had once been the meadows along the Drau, now officially called the Drau River, and with her husband operated the only restaurant in the area, located in the next block.

On a late afternoon, in unwaveringly harsh light that reflected blindingly off the densely parked cars, having reached this wasteland, covering the last stretch on boards laid over mud, after I had got lost again, the same as every other time, and had asked myself why in such places, despite the impressionability I was always cultivating, I immediately lost my keen eye, I saw, sitting under an umbrella on the concrete terrace of the Blue Lagoon Bistro, the only guest, a young man whose face from a distance immediately came within a finger's breadth of me, as sometimes faces do that bend over you in the moment of waking up, and only when he jumped up, with a long-contained cry of dismay, did it turn out to be the child's. It was the last time up to now that at the sight of me Valentin came running, and from a standing position, and how he ran.

(Much later he told me that at that moment he had finally seen me in my weakness; he could never stand it when I acted strong; even when I held out my arms, he wanted to push them down.)

He was wearing glasses, and the once-dark gaze of distrust had been transformed into the calm, watchful gaze of a researcher. My sister stepped out through the beaded curtain in the doorway, invoked the name of the Madonna, and disappeared, for much longer than necessary, and that, too, was something new: that she, so alien to every tradition, having renounced any origins, voluntarily and self-confidently nothing but a figure in this no-man's-land, here manifested the ageless behavior of Slavic village women: in her surprise and pleasure she first went off and hid. It accorded with this image that she then returned with bread and smoked ham, served up by her husband, a former ship's cook, whom my sister constantly put down in my presence, so much so that it was only from quick looks they exchanged that I could tell how much they loved each other. (Though he later left her alone in her hospital room on the day she died; he said she had already long since been unconscious—but I am certain that she was conscious to the last, that all the dying are conscious up to their last moment.)

While we sat there together, until long after the first bat—they had them even there—the first mosquito, and the first star, I secretly resolved that if "my sales" allowed, I would help her buy another eating place, on a public square, like the Fontaine Ste.-Marie, or, if she preferred, at the end of a dock on the Wörther See, with Udo Jürgens as a regular guest arriving in his motorboat and with me as silent partner.

And once during this evening I asked my son, "Where are you?" and he, who in between was serving the few guests, pointed by way of an answer at himself, with both hands, but not at his chest but into his armpits, and even stuck his fingers in there.

And then he described, with my sister as a witness, how I had done everything right as a father. But I knew better.

What has always suited me best is to narrate from one day to the next, as the *Odyssey* goes from dawn to the rising of the stars, and to continue this way the next morning, or in general just to treat a single day in this fashion.

But how to narrate the decade from our reconciliation to the beginning of this current year, since which I have been sitting here at my desk, and in the briefest way possible, for the story of my seven friends scattered over the world, as well as the chronicle of my year here in the bay, has been crowding in and knocking all this time, at every threshold? I shall try. I will do it.

As my, and our, future landscape, now mine forever, only the hilly suburbs here, open in all directions, could even be considered, with their unstuccoed clay-colored sandstone houses, the settlements poking like long or short fingers into the forest dunes that defined the visual image, and with a silence that made one prick up one's ears.

Nobody would know us there, and we would be all the more available to each other. The woman from Catalonia wanted to be separated from Paris by one more range of hills than the previous time, my son wanted to go to a "school in the woods," and my final choice of a place satisfied even my stern ancestors: on a day early in the spring of the following year, instead of falling upon me again as a swarm of flies, they peeped out at me somewhere among the hills in the form of pussywillows overhanging the path, and amiably reached out to shake my hand as I passed.

That was the day on which, after a fall and winter spent searching, I had found the house, but was still in doubt, not because of the house—I had immediately felt at home in it, along with its hollow, as the only right place—but because of its more immediate surroundings. It put me off that houses of the sort that attracted me were so much in the minority. Only en masse, one next to the other, street after street, did these fieldstone structures, in their slight geometric variations, retain a powerfully fairy-tale-like, very immediate character. Here, however, where they were few and far between, they seemed like leftovers from a bygone time, set apart from the mostly stuccoed, yet grotesquely different blocks from the periods between and after the world wars, many with names legible from a considerable distance (although I immediately scraped the name off my house, in the meantime I have come to be fond of some of them after all, for instance "My Sufficiency," "My Cottage in Canada," "Sweet Refuge," "Family Ties," "My Horizon," "Our Sundays," "My

Parachute," and recently I dreamed of a house in the bay with the name "My Births").

And once during the decade a crow's feather landed on the Absence Path; the older men in the bar called Fountain without Wine smelled snow one wintry evening, but it did not come; my petty prophet, who had meanwhile moved to yet another restaurant, scared off his guests with a tin cutout of a Moor by the front door, which blew over in the slightest wind; the Three Stations Bar was gutted by fire; a military airplane crashed right nearby in the forest before it could land at Villacoublay—beforehand its huge shadow over the house; I boxed the ears of my almost grown-up son after I had picked him up at the police station, where he had been taken for shoplifting; I threw a burning branch over the fence of a neighbor, the noisiest of all; during the Gulf War no trains passed through the tunnel to Paris for so long that the suburb seemed cut off from the city, as if at the end of time; my son left immediately for Vienna after his last examination at the Lycée Rabelais, halfway into the forest of Meudon; my sister died; the frozen-over Nameless Pond pinged from my skipping pebbles by myself; the woman from Catalonia left me for the second time; having reached the top of the transmitter here, the highest vantage point around Paris, for which I had special permission, I confirmed for myself that my suburb actually did cut into the wooded hills in the form of a bay, more remote than a village on a fjord or a research station in the Arctic; and this morning, in the construction fill of the Absence Path, I came upon the fragment of an inscription with the very words I recall from a tombstone, meanwhile disappeared from the graveyard, back home in Rinkolach: "Returned to His Fluid Ancestral Home."

That was more or less the story of my metamorphosis. When I reflect upon what I have experienced in my existence up to now, it was neither the war during my childhood nor our flight from Russian-occupied Germany home to Austria, nor my youth-long imprisonment in the boarding school, nor, after many feverish attempts, that first quiet line that made me certain I was now on the right path, nor being with my wife or my child, but only that metamorphosis.

Why does it seem to me that this is the only thing I have ever experienced? I do not know, just as after writing this down I do not know any more about it than before. At any rate, the other happenings came about like something that had been foreseen, while the metamorphosis seized hold of me—like an accident? an assault?—no, as a completely unknown force it seized hold of what was deepest inside me, which only in that way became distinguishable, like something in the dark lit up by lightning. There was no deeper inside than that.

And what else? Nothing else. Even the word "metamorphosis" came only long, long afterward. But then why am I convinced that it is the only major thing worth telling about that happened to me in my fifty-six years of life, on five continents, on two moons, on the highest peaks on Mars and in the hottest springs on Venus, and why does everything else, no matter how inspiring or devastating, strike me as incidental?

How wretchedly cut off from the world I found myself time and again, how blissfully at one with it, and yet only yesterday I thought: "I have never deserved to be hurled to the ground except back in my metamorphosis period!"

At intervals I continued to view myself as the only one with such a story, for otherwise wouldn't it have been told long since, and have become a classic? Or had I, on the contrary, had innumerable forerunners, and was I perhaps merely the first who had not perished in the process?

But didn't my story therefore cry out all the more urgently to be told? Or, again on the contrary, had all those who had had this experience survived and yet found nothing to tell? Or were they afraid to try?

Hadn't I, too, felt a great deal of resistance to continuing the narrative, as if it were somehow improper? And is it not true that I got into this only against my will?

What I do know: that metamorphosis, or expulsion, or merely a new orientation, has been used up. It seems to me that I have lost or frittered away all of its benefits: patience, mental acuity, magnanimity, boldness, empathy, receptivity, tolerance, ability to disarm, to forget. Or have I just muddled along halfheartedly? Failed from the beginning to make the right start?

———

This morning I saw the first hazelnuts of the year here on the edge of the woods in the bay. The little ovals in their pale green neck ruffs reminded me of the same hazelnuts from my metamorphosis period, as one of its visual images, and I thought: "That was a time of freshness! Now is not a time of freshness anymore, and not only for me. But who knows? *What does a foreigner know?*"

On to the story of my friends! Let them surprise you.

PART 3

1

The Story of the Singer

The singer was about my age, and wanted to go on singing as an old man, like Muddy Waters and John Lee Hooker.

And yet there had already been quite a few moments in his life when he would have been ready to die on the spot. This happened to him once after a night without sleep in a one-engine plane over the source of the Mississippi, in a morning blizzard, when, thinking of all those before him who had perished in this manner, almost customary for singers, he wanted to give the plane an additional jolt, as it tossed about in the darkness, so as to hasten the crash and be scattered in all directions, with the snowstorm outside so thick that even in the long-drawn-out flashes of lightning, prolonged further by the whirling snow, one could not make out whether the flakes were falling down or up. Instead, he promptly composed a song, his ballad, which had to be screamed almost from start to finish, with the title "Why Are You Not Serious?"

Another time he had been similarly willing to die in blissful exhaustion after a concert, not even a very large one, in the school auditorium of a midsized city in Switzerland, where (after that unfortunate period when people kept throwing themselves at him, he played at an even greater distance from them, often even with his back to them) for the encore he unexpectedly mingled with the audience, hoping a knife would be thrust into his heart, sensed that one person or another in the crowd might be the one, recognizable by his tense absentmindedness in the midst of all the elation, and even challenged him by stopping just far enough from the would-be assassin to give him room for the windup, and proffering his chest, as if that were part of his song; even at the exit, not a private one but the general one, he looked around, unprotected, in the lingering crowd for the "disturbed yet purposeful face" one could count on in such situations: "And in Switzerland my stalker was a woman every time"; and such a woman actually did pull a knife on him—except that the singer, prepared for this as he was, including dying, in that same breath, not at all bereft of will as he had thought, knocked it out of her hand. (The song occasioned by this incident began with "I'll die at the hand of a woman.")

A similar openness to death also took hold of him on that January day during his solitary trip through Scotland, as he was making his way on foot through the hilly fields above Inverness.

He had been working all fall on an album, was exhausted, yet also in a good frame of mind—less or differently irritable than usual—but still had enough breath, as was generally the case after an effort that excluded everything else, for a further undertaking, which promised for once, in contrast to his trademark works—ballads, angry tirades, sung narratives—a pure song, in fact "The Last Song."

For now, however, he was simply glad to be out of the studios and the big cities. Precisely because of his (powerful, not loud) music, which he wanted to authorize to be played only in places where it belonged, he was elsewhere extremely sensitive to noise, and he found it soothing to be away from the clacking and scratching of high heels on the streets of Paris and London and, after a short visit to his mother in Brighton, to have escaped to this Scottish rubber-boot landscape. Even the women, the young ones, came toward him here in rubber boots, and not just in the fields, and from their footsteps there was a sighing behind him, and accordingly he, too, went about in rubber boots.

It was a mild winter day, then warm as he mounted the slope, and he, in Scotland for the first time, at least out in the country, thought at the sight of the grovelike rhododendron bushes along the path, blowing in a southerly way and greening in the rainy wind, that it was always this way here. At the crest of the hill he spread his arms, turning his palms upward. The ridge was broad, almost part of the highlands already, and he still had to swing himself over several granite walls, chest-high because he was so small, until, in the narrowest sheep pasture, he stood facing the stone circle of the Celtic burial ground.

He did not approach it immediately, even avoided focusing on it at first, just gazed around for a long time. A couple of oaks, the only ones in these bare surroundings, groaned, and in the northern distance, beyond the arm of the sea, or firth, by Inverness, snowcapped mountains shone clear. In all the pastures roundabout were sheep, but in one, just as crowded and of about the same light color, was a herd of swine, munching away, on muddier ground; and instead of the usual dog among the sheep, there were several hares, distributed evenly among the herds.

The singer took off his woolen cap, stepped up to the one stele that stood twice as tall as the others, outside the circle, and leaned his head on it. Against his forehead he felt not so much the stone as the lichen, spreading, rust-colored, and scratchy. The predominant sensation became the beating of his heart, noticeable at the spot where he was touching the rock, filling his entire body, pulsing, pounding, as if passing into the interior of the column, and at this moment it would have suited the singer if the tall stone had given way and crushed him. He even shook it, without success. But this time no line of a song came to him instead, or only a word for one, "present," or a fragment, "On the road . . . practice the present."

When he opened his eyes, two sheep with raven-black faces were staring up at him from the grass. He squatted down at a distance from the circular cairn and shared his provisions with them, bought in the railroad station of Inverness; the apple he ate himself. Thus removed from the burial place, he became witness to one of those tenths of a second from so-called prehistoric times when the main stone, set up by the Celts or someone, became perfectly perpendicular, as it had remained standing through the millennia to that moment. It grew quiet on the knoll, including the bleating and grunting.

Still expectant of death, the singer, much later, set out to return to the valley, again cutting across fields, without paths or even wild-animal tracks. He crossed in a zigzag, from one field to the other, every thickly wooded gorge, where one false step in the slipperiness could have made him disappear, never to be seen again, on the bottom, under the unbroken canopy of leaves over the bog. And on the other hand he took each step carefully, and if he had fallen he would have kept his balance and would, broad as he was, have rolled over and over like a ball and landed softly on his feet.

He moved through the often thorny thicket in such a way that he did not receive so much as a scratch, and in his folk-dancer-like agility he would not even have been prey for one of the descendants of the pumas once released into the Scottish hills and surviving in these almost inaccessible gullies. The singer made his way along his path with the help of only his two legs, for he needed both hands to strike the Jew's harp, the only instrument besides a harmonica that he had taken along on this hike.

Down in Inverness he fetched his backpack from the locker and took a room in the hotel that formed a part of the monumental granite railroad complex and had a suitably fine lobby with a grand staircase and chandelier.

No one recognized him, and no one would recognize him. That was his decision.

When after a shower he stepped out onto the square in front of the hotel, it was already long since dark, and it was raining, heavily and at the same time inaudibly. Having ducked into a rear courtyard to listen, the singer said to himself that he had never heard such a quiet rain as this Scottish one. All the louder the cackling of the sparrows, which were fighting head to head for a sleeping perch up on the ledge of the main church, or were chattering with each other before going to sleep. Like the plane tree here by the suburban railroad station, in Inverness the ledge was far and wide their only place for the night. There as here

the sidewalk underneath was encrusted with their thick white droppings.

In a pub he leaned against the bar like the others and drank a beer,
glancing occasionally at the bull's-eye when a dart landed in it. As everywhere, the singer could not be distinguished from the local people, except that he might be from farther out in the country. When he heard
"Mr. Tambourine Man" coming from the jukebox at waist height, he
thought that the songs of thirty years ago had painstakingly worked
things out, while in the meantime they all sounded so glib, his as
well? The beat he tapped on his thigh with his fingers did not fit the
song.

He consumed his evening meal deliberately, with a bottle of wine
over which he sat for hours, almost alone in the dining room at the
window of the best restaurant in Inverness, as the new justice of the
peace? architect? soccer coach?, directly before his eyes the river Ness,
which seemed disproportionately wide for this rather small town. Besides, the river was rising and seemed to be galloping toward its nearby
mouth at the North Sea. The water was of a blackness that did not come
merely from the darkness outside, and also merely as the color of moor
water would not have had such density and brilliance. The rushing from
the January rains had to contribute to the effect. To accompany the
mighty current, which he felt at the same time in his arms, the singer
beat out the steady refrain "Winter–water, winter–water, winter–water."
Then he reminded himself that he was on an island, though not a very
small one, and that for him, a person from the continent (with an English
mother), an "island river" was a child-wondrous concept, especially one
that raged this way.

The waiters, of whom there were several, had meanwhile not budged
from his side. Instead of with a credit card he paid in cash, a thick
packet of which, damp at the edges, he had loose in his pocket; the clip
that went with it was dangling from his ear. He did not want anyone
to be able to trace his whereabouts.

On the wooden bridge outside, of a length suitable for a metropolis,
staring at the peat-black turbulent water, the singer recalled how once
before, after a sort of concert on a cruise ship with a group of rich
Americans in a Turkish bay, fairly far out, he had jumped overboard at

night in his clothing and shoes and had swum toward land through all the lively motorboat traffic, looking neither to right nor to left, coming up for air with eyes closed, over and over again, in defiance of death.

On the opposite bank of the Ness the suburbs began immediately. In one spot the sky had cleared, with a star so bright it had a ring around it like the moon: Sirius. Below, in one of the huddled suburban houses, a window was open to the mild air. An old woman in a housecoat was leaning out as if for a long time, and out of the silence she and the singer greeted one another.

Up the hill, along the Caledonian Canal that ran along halfway up, he stepped into a suburban pub, still open, though probably not for long; inside it looked like someone's living room, with a fire burning in the fireplace, on whose mantelpiece stood a collection of books with the *Pickwick Papers*, one of the books he had in his tower house, *Uncle Tom's Cabin*, and *The Bobbsey Twins in Echo Valley*. He sat down with a glass of whiskey in a wing chair and gazed at the only other guests, a very young couple who kept sticking their tongues down each other's throats, undeterred by the coughing and choking this caused. Having finished with that, they promptly moved apart, as if their game were over. The girl leaned back in the shadows, and the boy turned to the singer and asked him, out of the blue, in a perfectly calm, also polite voice, whether he was one of the lumberjacks. In response to his nod, the young man told him that he was a Gypsy, had come here as a child from Poland, and was in the process of training as a forester near Inverness. But in Scotland there were hardly any forests left, whereas after the Ice Age the entire land had been covered by the great Caledonian Forest, first bright with birches, then darkened by the Scottish firs, then mixed with oaks. Probably he would be the first Gypsy forester.

Up by the canal, the door to an automobile repair shop was still open, and the singer, who liked to look into such places, saw in the brightly lit bays a few young fellows at work, with a song coming from the radio of a car being repaired, accompanied by the clang of tools.

He listened attentively, clenching his fists in agitation, and only when he was back in the darkness again did he realize that the song was his.

Through his sleep whistled the trains down below in the station, and he dreamed the usual dream about his children, scattered across the countries and the continents, who, entrusted to him, had under his very eyes torn themselves away from him and disappeared for good. This time, after a few swimming strokes, they sank in clear water, knee-deep, and remained impossible to find there.

The next morning there was a rainstorm, and although it was part of the singer's routine to expose himself to something unpleasant, to withstand something each day, he did not set out on foot as planned toward the snow-covered mountains in the north, but took a bus of the Highland Terrier Line, with Dornoch as his destination. In such a storm, unlike in high wind, there were no sounds to be heard while walking. And besides, it was coming from the west and not from the north, where he would have had it blowing beautifully in his face. From Dornoch he would tramp westward.

If he had to ride cross-country, then it should be by bus, and not because he was accustomed to that from his tours. In Plato's *Critias* there is mention of the melancholy, who should be sent on a journey by ship to lift their spirits, if possible when the sea is turbulent, so that the atoms in their bodies will be shaken up and can find a healthier arrangement. This effect, and an even better one, could be achieved by a long bus trip, preferably on winding mountainous roads.

An additional factor for the singer was that on the road this way, always in a window seat, either way in front or way in back, drawing the curtain, even in his own tour bus, only to sleep, he could sink into himself, down to a point of complete tranquillity, and at the same time see himself as connected with the surroundings outside, of which he, without even having to turn his head once, could also keep a large portion in sight through the front or rear windshield.

Here, too, he could not tolerate any music, let alone a television above the driver's head, as had become common elsewhere on cross-country trips. In that sense Scotland was probably too backward, for on this trip from the beginning there was only the landscape outside, seen through untinted glass, and the humming of the engine. The stormy wind, gusting and subsiding, seemed subdued in the rocking interior space. There was plenty of room.

The singer sat, together with one or two other passengers, on the east side, where the windows received the least rain, and from looking out he soon felt warm, although down below rain was blowing in through a crack, and instead of dribbling and trickling, swelled up with foam, blackish, as from a moor. And right past Inverness, on the suspension bridge over the firth, at the sight of the strangely curving, rounded waves down below, on closer inspection seals, he felt as if he had been cast among the animals, and spouted water, tumbled, let himself drift as one of them.

He was alert and feeling irrepressible. An element of pain, an openness, had to be added, and the song would come, he thought.

And then he thought nothing more during the entire trip. Although, besides him, no one on the Highland Terrier was looking at anything in particular, it was as if he were looking in consort with someone else, or as if he were following someone else's eyes. The region, rolling off into the distance, was so bare that Mongolia came to mind, a place to which his travels had never taken him. The hero of *The 39 Steps* was fleeing through rain-drizzled rounded mountains, chained by handcuffs to an unknown woman, who was stumbling along behind him. A pheasant fluttered into the air and with its heavy body promptly thudded to the ground in the storm, as if shot down. In moments of clearing you could see, farther off in the North Sea, dusky oil-drilling platforms, like temples. And a year ago on the square in front of the bus station in Cairo there had been a sleeping place for the sparrows just as the night before in Inverness, in a single scraggly, mangy cypress there, and each time, approaching his Nile Hotel by a roundabout route, he had gone toward that shrill racket the birds made as they battled for a spot, audible above the roar of the entire city, so that at least he had something to orient himself by amid the African, or Arab, or whatever chaos. And the one old woman on the bus made him think of his mother, as did so many old crones in the country, although his mother was neither from the country nor a crone, and had not even been present at his first major performance. Whereas his father, who to this day, when his radio in the retirement home went even a week without playing something by his son, would comment that it had been a long time since they had heard anything by him, his mother had been concerned even back then, with his sporadic singing engagements at suburban summer festivals and graduations from Ville d'Avray to Courbevoie, that he was constantly being heard from.

At the sight of the stepped terraces in the craggy landscape, he felt in his own body the jerks with which aeons ago the glacier had withdrawn from there until it was gone from that area—that was how low the Scottish mountains were. All that had taken place unobserved. But someone must have observed it, with eyes that could still be felt? With what eyes? "I'm searching for the face you had before the world was made," was a line in one of his songs.

Perhaps the singer was also lost in thought during the trip, brooding, bad-tempered, more than anyone else. But that was nothing compared to the moment when he was in song, as another might be in the picture. This being in song was very rare, rarer than a poem. Being in song was the original condition for him.

In the storm a sheep dashing across a pasture now, its damp fleece flying behind it like a coat.

In Dornoch, where the singer was the only passenger to get off, it was almost dark again. The gulls, for whom it was a struggle to fly forward, toward land, appeared black against the sky. The rain had stopped, but the storm from the west would blow all night. The cloud in the band of light left by the setting sun had the shape of a deeply frayed, broad-branched cedar, which, uprooted, came gusting through the air and then disappeared as if in a puff of smoke.

He gave up the idea of continuing his hike today, indeed forgot any plan for the time being. Here in Dornoch the singer felt as though he was already on his way. Was this a seaside resort? a town? a farm village? Except for him there was no one out on the street. Yet in the squat houses and the yards with storm walls he heard heavy steps, echoing, as if on the planks of a boat.

He stood still and watched for the moment when the now-clear firmament would reveal the glitter of the first star. He even knew the
approximate spot. And again, as each time previously, in Archaia Nemea
in Greece, on Mission Street in San Francisco, he must have blinked at
the decisive moment. For there Venus was now, gleaming as always
against the horizon, blue-black like a lining.

Below, almost out in the dunes, in the glow of the last streetlight, in
front of a flat-fronted wooden house, the figure of a young woman appeared, who, out of breath, as if she had run toward him, invited the
singer to spend the night in her house; the hotels in Dornoch were all
closed during the winter. He could tell immediately that she did not
recognize him, and accepted. He merely said he wanted to stay out until
midnight, set down his backpack on her doorstep, and let her give him
a key.

Then he made his way, up dune and down, to the North Sea, which
came crashing up to the crown of the farthest dune; at first he felt as
though he did not belong there, as with every ocean.

He went down into a crouch. Everywhere along the shore little seaweed fires were burning at regular intervals, with not a person in sight,
crackling and sparking, intended as light signals out to the high sea. In
the glow of such a flame the singer examined a plant sunk into the sand,
around which a miniature dune had formed. A single kinked leaf still
poked out, lance-shaped, rotated by some storm gusts almost around
itself and snapped back into a resting position in between, whereupon
the sand around it showed very delicate patterns of the quarter, half, and
whole circles it had described, like a wind clock, with the seaweed frond
as its hand.

Who in the world needed another song, his song, a new song?

The singer fell into a sort of brooding, trying to picture to himself
those who stood between him and his audience—the record company
executives, the booking agents, the copyright holders. No, he could not
picture them, they offered no image—so repulsive were they to him. He
was not a businessperson, would never be one, and thus everything he
had done since youth and had intended for his own people belonged to
these others, who were not his people. They held the rights, and he was
the supplier. Accordingly they were convinced, nowadays more and more,
that they were the ones creating the event and its heroes. What had one

of them said, the one to whom he had "supplied" his biggest song, around which he had been circling for months in a chaos of words and notes and which he had written down in a moment without sound, between fear of death and joy? "Let's see what I can make of this!" Jettison the middlemen, the singer brooded. But how? It's the system, and any other, no matter how different, is still the same. Act as if nothing were wrong. Those people between my creations and the world don't exist. They aren't there. With a snap of the fingers I make them disappear. I decide: everything I have done up to now and will do from now on belongs to me and no one else.

And he could say what a song was: "In it the most distant streets flow into each other." With this line he leapt to his feet and shouted or murmured names into the dark surf, as at the end of a concert he announced the names of his backup singers or band: "Orpheus in the Upperworld! The fish, rain worms, and snakes lamenting the Buddha's death. Moses piecing together the Tablets of the Law. John Lennon, Liverpool. Van Morrison, Dublin. Blind Lemon Jefferson. John Fogarty. Lao-tzu. Blaise Pascal. Baruch Spinoza, who sang that human wisdom consists not in thinking about death but in living! Marsyas pulling off Apollo's skin!"

On the way back, again beneath the village streetlights, a storm gust was so powerful that in a series of puddles the rainwater jumped from one to the other, and so on in this way as far as the horizon. And now he had the desired wind in his face, in which it looked more than usual as though balls were rolling in his armpits as he walked.

From the dark building at a distance from the others, tall and narrow, an old folks' home, came angry groans. At the same time the Pleiades sparkled above, initially all seven stars crowded together in a little heap, from which then each emerged separately, glance after glance. And here in Dornoch he also listened for the birds' sleeping place: too late; the sparrows, wherever they might be, were silent.

When he had walked around the night-dark church, which stood in the middle of a grassy area, inside the church the stone sarcophagus of the crusader, who lay with legs crossed and his dog beside him, the street was suddenly thronged with local residents, leaving a choir re-

hearsal. No matter which way one of them went, the same snatches of
song could be heard from all directions, and if one of them launched
into a new song, another singer over there, already out of sight, would
promptly join in, and he wondered why he had never had a singer as a
friend, except someone he did not really know, from afar, and why, when
he was put in a chorus, he always sang out of tune. But whenever stars
were gathered to sing together for some cause, didn't they necessarily
produce cacophony, starting off wrong, one too soon, one too late, each
with a different version of the lyrics?

Following those choir members who formed the only small group, he
found his way to the village pub, where everyone shook hands with him
as if he were an old acquaintance. A drunk, already more falling down
than just swaying, was playing pool, and made each shot with hairline
precision. Above the wooden floorboards, which had been cleared, with
tables and benches pushed to the sides, a tape was fiddling a square
dance, to which no one was dancing, and the singer, for whom his ancestors had been looking for the longest time—"Where in the world can
he be now?"—saw himself finally discovered: "Ah, so there he is!"

Outside, a few bars on the Jew's harp brought air into his lungs. The
song felt so close, and then again so unattainable, that it frightened him.
He had been away from population centers and the news only a couple
of days, and already they did not exist anymore, or at most in casual
thoughts, detached, never serious.

In his northern Scottish lodgings all was sleep-still, only a couple of
lamps to light his way. For what had looked at first like a cottage, the
corridor was unusually long, as the room was spacious, the ceiling high.

It was deepest night when the singer, whom even a lightning strike
would not have awakened, was shaken out of his sleep by a child
crying. It did not stop, and he got up, put on his ankle-length raincoat,
and made his way through the house until he came upon the crying
child, alternating between the highest and the lowest notes, in a crib on
casters, which, being pushed back and forth by the young woman, added
its own screeching and creaking.

The singer asked the mother whether she would mind if he tried to
quiet the child, too, and she gave him permission. With his hands on

the headboard, he did nothing but, without moving it, give the bed tiny shoves, invisible to a third party, at first unevenly but with all his strength; all one could hear was a series of sounds consisting merely of rustling and scraping, which, now longer, now shorter, insinuated itself into the bawling and, when that first paused, could become regular, rhythmic, and articulate, like a piece of music. To make the child keep on listening and at the same time calm down, this sound had to hit the right moment with each note, and the whole time he had before his eyes the billy goat in a burning barn who had not followed him out into the open until he had seized his horns in his hands and neither pulled nor pushed but done almost nothing, yet with the utmost patience and attentiveness!

When the infant had finally sighed himself back to sleep, the mother was long since asleep, and the singer, too, soothed by his own lullaby, sank, the minute he was back in his guest bed and had closed his eyes, into the sleep of a newborn. He lay there with his face close to the window, again amazingly wide for a cottage in the dunes, through which the winter constellations shone all together into his dreams, and thus themselves were already the dream. Orion, the Hare, Castor and Pollux, broad-thighed Cassiopeia, the veil of Berenice, and then as yet undiscovered ones called Weymoor, the Headless Woman, Iron Gate, La Grande Arche, and finally the morning star alone moved through his innermost being with the slowness of the universe and penetrated it. Such a caress the singer had never experienced before.

This was accompanied now by the very high notes of a saxophone, which, when he had opened his eyes, went on playing in another room. The wind had fallen. The sky above was bright, the gulls below still raven-dark, and they really were ravens now.

The woman playing the saxophone sat, the child at her side listening without stirring, in the dune-sand-yellow kitchen at the laid table, in an even longer dress than the previous evening and rubber boots with high heels. He silently joined her, drank a cup of coffee such as he had tasted neither in Italy nor in Hawaii, until she put down her somewhat battered instrument and without much ado, as though she were simply switching from one language to another, told him that in her childhood she had once spent a summer at the ferry station for the Hebrides, Kyle of Lochalsh, about a hundred miles to the west, on the other side of the watershed, on the Atlantic. She came from Dornoch, here on the North Sea, and had made her way halfway around the world, but only at the ferry in Kyle of Lochalsh had people been good to her. "Dover, Vancouver, San Francisco, Valparaíso are nothing compared to Kyle. When I'm an old woman I'd like to lick the salt from the windshield of the ferry in Kyle."

Not for the first time the singer noted that people who did not get along well with the place they came from did not really long to be off in distant cities; they longed instead for something they had known early in their lives, only a few hills and rivers away, which with the years had become legendary.

And he felt the urge to get to that Kyle of Lochalsh, if possible entirely on foot, even if it would take him until spring, until fall; he wanted to set out at once, told the two of them that, bowed to the child, kissed the woman's hand, received from her a rain hat to put on over his cap, laid a banknote on the doorstep, and that same afternoon was standing somewhere in the interior, between the two oceans, on a southeastern slope sheltered from the wind, facing the banana palm that he had been sure grew even here in the north of Scotland, hidden in the tangle of wild rhododendron.

The singer continued his westward journey into the spring and summer.

He went astray at least once a day, in spite of maps and compass, often willingly, and when he no longer knew where he was he became all the more sharp of eye and ear.

For an hour he would move along as if on wings, the next hour would draw him, head down, toward the mud, impossible to get past on the high moors, and not only in winter. Sometimes in the evening his head would be bursting from the roar of the brooks all around, and the next morning the racket would draw him anew. Again and again he almost fell, or he slipped and tipped over, and each time the twitching that went through his body was followed by redoubled alertness and mental acuity. He recognized that the apparent obstacles in his path were nothing of the kind, at least nothing significant.

He took an ownerless boat lying by a lake in the moor, seemingly since prehistoric times, with as little hesitation as he headed over a pass that appeared on no map. In the morning, with his sleeping bag rolled up, he struck out from the tumbledown hut, stinking of sheep droppings, set in a wasteland of heather, wiped his behind in the morning with a fan-sized bog leaf, damp from the rain, sat in the brief midday sun with his bread and apple on the throne formed by a stray boulder, stumbled in late afternoon into a hailstorm with stones so hard they pounded down his outstretched fingers, and in the evening lurched like a vagabond, impossible, with that hat over his cap, to identify as a man or a woman, along an illuminated avenue leading through a park toward a highland castle-hotel, called, for instance, Ceddar Castle, where, without his having a reservation, the double doors swung open for him at a distance, showing the torchlit, fireplace-warmed great hall, and then, combed, parted, in necktie and custom-tailored suit, he took his evening meal with the family of the Japanese crown prince on his left, the stars of the Glasgow Rangers on his right, at the head table the great-great-grandson of Sir Walter Scott and the heirs of Robert Louis Stevenson, but he belonged there a bit more than all of them, and the next day continued his game of—what?—of getting lost. And at the same time he never felt alone. "I am with my song."

And just as he presented a different image from hour to hour, the seasons kept jumping around, winter appearing in the middle of summer, spring leading back into fall. In the last night of January a cuckoo called, then none again until sometime in June. In May on the heath out of a clear blue sky a great many leaves fell, but from where? And in a cold dusk a snake crept toward him on a patch of snow.

Altogether, just as in dreams, at one moment almost nothing was impossible, and then again everything seemed to be over and done with. The torrents, which, seen from a distance, gushed from the crests of the mountains, a host of them, in white, long waterfalls, reminded him today of a medieval, no, of a prehistoric time, which, however, still lay ahead for humanity, and on the following morning the entrails from the nocturnal slaughter of a small animal by a bird of prey at the foot of a lonely church tower were enough, and the only things that seemed valid were the bestial and barbarous, even if only until he caught sight of almost the only reliable thing, the red-and-yellow van marked "Royal Mail."

I received my most recent picture of my friend after the beginning of summer, when he had finally put the watershed between Scotland's two oceans and then also Kyle of Lochalsh behind him and, having taken the ferry over to the Inner Hebrides, within calling distance, at least for his voice of thunder, was now crossing the island of Skye, mainly on foot.

This picture again had to do with the Royal Mail, on a day after a day of heavy rain, since his walking until then had been almost entirely a slipping and sliding, initially down in a fjord amid the knee-high shore seaweed, now high above along a treeless alpine slope on a crisscross pattern of sheep terraces, churned into deep mire; he had willingly strayed up there, believing from afar that it was a multitude of mountain paths, all coming together in a single broad path leading up to the peak of Ben So-and-so.

But the network of paths beaten into the mountainside by the sheep hoofs turned out to be even more impassable than that peculiarly Scottish tracklessness, which, with the rounded, disappearing mountain shapes, at first seems as if it can be crossed effortlessly and then turns out to be a highland moor, its steep slopes, where the ground should be firm, as deceptive as the flat areas; the sheep slopes, too, were moor, and before each step he had to test the ground ahead. And furthermore, the animals whose terrain it had been, had, because of their jumpiness, unlike cows, dug or stamped out an extremely uneven, nervous zigzag. Time and again, at the places where the sheep had leaped, the apparent tissue of paths tore, and the singer had to become a moor mountain climber, which, by the bye, gave him a certain satisfaction.

When he reached the top, bareheaded, his cap and hat long since tucked away, suddenly the path led, instead of toward the peak, over flat surfaces, as if into infinity, and on firm, dry, even ground, high above the tree line, with a few pines huddled together.

From them, too, came the unanimous roar that he had previously, when he stuck his head over the crest, taken for a personal greeting from the spirit of the mountains. Winds from different directions met there. One minute it turned cold and dark, the next summery warm. The tooting of the second ferry, the one from the island town of Uig to the Outer Hebrides, was the only sound that wafted up from the foggy depths and seemed at the same time to come from the clouds above. The dots of foam in the grass, which was delicate as only grass under alpine firs can be, puzzled the singer: had they dropped from the mouth of a rabid fox?

Now the clouds took on two different shapes: some, formless, drizzly, drifted in from the west and were rain clouds, and the others, from the east, formed windrows, brighter, with space in between, and carried snow. And at the moment when the two types of clouds encountered each other, they merged into a great uniform glowing haze. And now the western clouds also carried snow, and from both sides a curtain drew slowly and steadily across the entire sky, reaching down to the earth.

The hidden highland birds cackled, barked, neighed. The snowing created a sphere in which colors emerged, the brown of the pines, the green of the heather, the black of the rubber boots. The flakes, clumped together but still with individual crystalline parts, melted on the mountain climber's nail bed, hot with exhaustion.

And now in the tracklessness way up there, the red-and-yellow vehicle with the postal horn comes rolling out of the curtain of snow, this time a jeep. On every weekday during his journey he had been able to rely on it; out of affection he had even counted the patches on the mailbags; and one time, when the storm over Kyle of Lochalsh had ripped a card addressed to me out of his hand as he made his way to the mailbox, and he thought it would never be seen again, the card actually reached me, though with a few puddle stains.

So was there a house on the plateau at the peak that had mail delivered? Perhaps in a eucalyptus grove? He quickly wrote another card, with the snow crackling on it, to the Queen of England or someone, finishing just as the mail vehicle came rattling up. It stopped, with a robust gray-haired Scottish woman at the wheel who reminded him of his mother. And he placed the card in her outstretched hand, and she shoved it in among the other pieces of mail, held together with a rubber band.

It seemed to the singer as if something in him were beginning to heal, something which, although he had sung about it again and again, he had not even wanted to have healed.

2

The Story of the Reader

W here had that been?
He was sitting with his girlfriend by a swampy pond in
the forest near a city. Dusk was far advanced, and the two
of them had not said a word for a long time. Instead, from the small
round body of water, light rose, the only bright thing all around, a
reflection of the last bit of daytime sky, or of the night sky as above
large cities?

His entire life up to then had been marked by a sense of futility. This
did not leave him even during this one hour, yet was accompanied by a
tranquillity or feeling of safety that was new to him. The girl beside
him felt that, and bowed before this realm. The back of a fish arced
soundlessly from the surface and dove under again, a dolphin. The musk-
rat, about to scurry from one hole in the bank to the next, stopped in
midcourse and sniffed the air, standing on its hind legs, its tail broadened
into the shape of a beaver's. After all, nothing was happening, with the
forest darkness all around, but the light at their feet, the water and the
light.

His entire childhood and youth he had spent in Germany, in the
Reich, then in the state in the east, then in the republic in the west, in
the country and in cities, from the Mittelgebirge down into the ancient

river valleys and up into the Alps. But here by the swampy pond was
the first time that he had seen a world open up in his country, if not
for him then for someone else, for instance his descendants.

Where had that been? And what was her name again, the young
woman from that time? And if he had children perhaps, why were they
even more hopeless than he had ever been?

And where had that been again? After wandering around all day—
while always, in accordance with the traditional German parental
admonition, "staying on the path like a good boy!" through high-rise,
villa, and allotment-garden suburbs, all equally inhospitable and unreal,
as were the forests, the village squares, and even the vineyards or the
slopes with apple orchards, he had, again toward evening, found himself
in a town whose center was built in a hollow, and suddenly in the
stillness—of midsummer or deep winter?—had seen himself generously
and cordially received by the solid mass of half-timbering erected there,
whose network of beams had struck him until then as the epitome of
confinement or narrowness.

The town seemed no less deserted than the villages he had gone
through to reach it, and yet from its crooked streets, as he descended
into them step after step, something like a cheerful expectancy emerged
and leaped the gap to him. And that was no momentary deception. The
alley dog, the kind that usually made his neck stiffen with fear, licked
his hand as if it were seeing him again for the first time in seven times
seven years, and then ran on ahead to show him the way. And there it
was: the welcoming garland, especially for him, in the form of plastic
flowers in a tin can above the door to the house; the summer or winter
garden that had a view of a volcanic cone with a petrified prehistoric
horse in its basalt wall, and Condviramur and Percival, in the form of a
North Hessian or Westphalian innkeeper and his wife, as his hosts.

Were the German fairy tales in force once more, in defiance of history?
Was it in his, the reader's power, not exclusively his, but his as well, to
awaken to life a place thought to be dead? And why had he been successful in doing so in his Germany only that one time, which now had
again been "over" for far more than seven years? Was it his own fault

that it had never been repeated and renewed? What was the name of that town again?

And where had that been? During a long winter he had gone to his workshop every morning to print a book that was causing him particular trouble and pleasure, and back home in the evening, through a city of millions, though always taking only side streets.

And each time he went out it had snowed, day after day, through the months. It was a light, dry snow that hardly ever stayed on the ground. At most it slithered over the sidewalks and road surfaces, like sand over the ripples of dunes. The system of side streets leading to the central axis, not always parallel to it, that he used, now seemed profoundly silent, and if yesterday it had belonged to the evil Germany, today it belonged to the world at large.

Snow and epic narration. Yes, what opened up before the reader was no longer just a short tale or a fairy tale, but rather an epic, and it was even set in this typically German area. Was set? No, would be set there in the future.

The German epics familiar to him appeared starkly contrasted to the one the reader saw taking shape at that time through the veil of snow, from the *Nibelungs*, in whose heroes, according to Goethe, unlike in Homer's, no reflection of the gods was at work, to . . . And Wolfram's *Percival*, did that take place in Germany? And Keller's *Green Henry*? (An episode.) And Stifter's *Indian Summer*? And wasn't the location of Goethe's *Elective Affinities* and *Wilhelm Meister*, the two narratives that most closely approximated the one envisioned by the reader during his walks back and forth in the snowy light, instead of a factual Germany, the province of a solitary powerful mind, a province cleared inventively and energetically for development, dramatization, and intensification, even in a tragic mode, of his ideals?

The epic tale of tomorrow—this is how the reader saw it before him in the slowly falling snow—would, as in the work of Johann Wolfgang Goethe, as far as a certain Germany was concerned, definitely behave as though this Germany did not exist; on the other hand, it would not locate the events in an ideal country, dreamed up in isolation, but rather in that worldwide Germany, employing a host of German things and place names, the few that had remained untainted as well as those fraught with guilt, particularly these!

At that time snow fell for months around a pub on Schellingstrasse where Hitler had often sat and where at the moment the hand of a young waiter from Bari could be seen, through the almost opaque windows, dicing truffles; it fell on Amalienstrasse around a woman who snapped at her child: "You stay here!"; it fell in the Adalbert Cemetery around the statue of the dancer Lucille Grahn, in an appropriate pose, now mimicked by a young girl passing that way; fell far out by the moss of Dachau around the bench on which the reader in earlier times, as an adolescent, after wandering through the concentration camp, had sat engrossed in Grass's *Cat and Mouse* until just before the last train left; fell around a loden coat, the Milan cathedral, the Kalahari Desert, meat hooks, the Three Kings from the Orient, idle snow shovels, newspaper vending machines, on sidewalks as everywhere in Munich, with the same headlines from morning to evening, which in those winter months, in view of the epic narrative, meant precious little to the reader, otherwise so easily distracted by anything in written form.

And where was the epic of Germany now? The books that had talked about the country had again in the meantime, as always before, disheartened him—and precisely, as exciting as some of them were, because of the German names in them. Because of them he could not believe in even the most extravagant flights of fancy. It seemed to him as if there were an epic curse on "Berlin" and "Flensburg," on the "Weser" and the "Zugspitze," on the "Black Forest" and "Helgoland," even independently of his century's history. And there was no question of his writing himself. He was the reader.

So his winter day's dream of a great story that would bind together and at the same time thoroughly air out his fellow countrymen, and not only them, had blown away with that snow? No, he was convinced that any day now a new Wolfram von Eschenbach would—not appear, no, simply be there, drifting in from a side street, with a wealth of purely epic place names, of which the first might be, for example, Respond/Upper Bavaria.

Although my "Writer's Tour" is studded with South German to West German place names, the reader felt less constricted by them than usual, because for one thing the story is short, and it also looks more like a notebook. He understood, too, that I could not be the one to write the book he was longing for, that demon-exorcising book about the other Germany. First of all, I would have had to spend my childhood there and remain in residence here and there a long time, instead of merely making the tour; I would have had to sit and wait for such an epic, like a piece of property. "And then you're only half German and decided against your half-Germanness. You renounced your father, very early on, in the first disappointment after your search for paternal salvation, and later, on your tour, you also renounced your fatherland, and have not set foot in it since, have even avoided the river that forms the border, which, with its broad, bright, gravel-covered banks is like something from antiquity, where both of us used to swim, with unalloyed pleasure, avoided it out of fear of crossing the line down the middle and thus ending up in German irreality. At the same time you swore fealty to the German language, and many reproached you for that as a contradiction. What you write in any language other than your German does not have the value in your eyes of something written. What you think in French over there in your foreign land carries no weight for you. To be sure, even if you undertook to return to your fatherland, I do not believe that someone like you would succeed in writing the book of conversion that I envision for my Germany. Not even Friedrich Hölderlin, with all the power generated in him by initial concurrence, then near-despair, then sober illumination, managed to get past the Germans in their country and their cities in favor of a larger, more broad-minded, and at the same time solid epic concept. In *Hyperion* his German contemporaries loom large as the sheer counterimage to his heroes, the Greeks, who immerse themselves in the common struggle for restoration of the realm where the decisive factor is the idea of the sun, embodied in books, trees, a table, a plate. What seemed impossible for him to narrate in prose he invoked in his poems. He challenged German youth to take up the legacy of long-lost Hellas and establish an equally brilliant empire, specifically by force of arms, which his poems now called holy, as previously air, water, the vine. According to Hölderlin, after the Greeks it is now the turn of the youth of Germany to take their place in history. They, and they alone, epitomize the world spirit, and they will celebrate their sacred slaughter, on the banks of Father Rhine or on the Elysian Fields, as the legitimate successors to the Hellenes. No, these poems were bad enough, even without being misused in the following century. And anyway: my wish for Germany, which actually seems possible, since I can wish it, is not a poem but precisely that long, long narrative. When it comes to narrative, the rule is: no misuse. An epic cannot be misused. No, it can be used again and again, and the user is amazed each time at what he missed the previous times, and pities the animal at his feet, whether cat or hedgehog, because it cannot read! O narrative, exhaustive, of German lands, different from anything found in newspapers and previous books, where are you? And in my imagination it is not a young man who will presently approach bearing it in his hands, but a saucy, wonderfully beautiful young woman, not blind in the least."

The reader kept sending me such letters from his travels through Germany, once following the route of the tour described in my occasional story, then again in any direction that suited him; in these letters, in typical fashion, he could not refrain from taking the stance of a prophet, toward me as well as toward the world.

The one just quoted he wrote at the beginning of his travels, still in midwinter of the current year, as he rode in an almost empty passenger train from Oldenburg to Wilhelmshaven, where at twenty I had first looked up my father. And although it is true that even when I think of Germany here, from afar, my imagination fails me and the images refuse to coalesce: when I felt my friend setting out with such anticipation, I was happy to travel at his side, thinking of him instead of the country, suspended in a more innocent, purely momentary present.

I see him in his train, which stands out sharply illuminated against the dusky North German flatlands, high up in the all-glass cabin of a suspension railway, or of a carousel as big as Germany. And besides that I see the dark silhouette of a horse in a pasture, its motionless head bent to the ground, as if rooted to the spot.

In Wilhelmshaven on Jade Bay the tracks ended, and when a train pulled out, the loudspeaker would announce, "Attention, the train is backing out!"

The reader went to the hotel right next to the station, which catered to salesmen and itinerant workers. While in the stairwell and hallways only the night lights were on, it was all the brighter in the taproom, and in a silence like that of a waiting room, for instance at a ferry slip, along with a couple of sailors a policeman was sitting, very young, with a voice so gentle that the reader, at the next table, fell to wondering who the patron saint of policemen was, like St. Joseph for carpenters and St. Christopher for teamsters. Yet the other man had merely looked over and asked what he was reading. He held up the book: the *Novelas ejemplares*. And as always happened to him with Cervantes, he was not really succeeding in getting into the stories, and not merely because he was reading them in Spanish, one word at a time, and also not because he felt the policeman watching him.

After an hour of catching his breath by the pitch-black bay, while runners still panted past him constantly, and eating his evening meal at a Turkish restaurant in the pedestrian zone, which seemed to be all there was to Wilhelmshaven, he sat on a bench at the railway station, and later, until long after the last train's departure, on a baggage cart by the bumpers where the tracks ended. The row of shrubs over there was the only thing still stirring around midnight. The rounded, slightly convex bumper beams gave off a calm reflection. A railroad car, which had been standing on a siding for a long time, wheezed. The waxing moon was now bright enough so that the objects on the platform acquired an additional shadow. It was not cold, and the reader had taken off both his shoes, whose oval, blackish openings down by his feet, as he gazed at them, more and more took on the form of mouths opened in a death cry, and then were nothing but his shoes again, at the end of a long day.

The following morning the reader set out for that pond in the Wilhelmshaven hinterland where, according to my story, I had planned, at my first reunion with my father, to let him drown.

The water was still there, out among pastures with mossy hillocks, on the edge of a birch forest. But it could not be seen until he was standing directly beside it, because it lay so deep in a hollow below ground level, such as one otherwise finds only with groundwater lakes in old gravel pits. It also appeared as large as a lake, and beyond a bend it seemed to extend much farther, with an arm in horseshoe shape, like the cutoff meander of a river, peat black, impossible to see into from above.

The only way to get down the steep bank was by two overlapping ladders of white-barked birch, not nailed, only joined. Once at the bottom, the reader suddenly understood the expression I had used, "sound horizon," which, in the context of my usually rather simple vocabulary, had startled him as he was reading the story. Every distant sound was inaudible in the hollow, that of cars as well as any other machinery, and there was nothing to be heard but the interior sounds, which, however, were amplified down to the most delicate by the restricted sound horizon, such that the silence round about took on audible form—the rolling of a clump of earth, the fluttering of loose birch bark, the lapping of one of the infrequent waves.

It was only the reflection of the winter-black earth banks that made the water seem so impenetrable. From a squatting position one could see clear to the bottom, which, at least as far out as the end of the dock, was lined with the same white pebbles as the narrow beach. Now it made sense to him that in the summer people from town would walk out here occasionally, instead of along their everyday Jade Bay with its powerfully changing tides and often overcast horizons. And there, as if camouflaged under the dock, was also the boat, of which he was certain at once, even if it did not fit the facts at all: "It's the same one in which you invited your father, who can't swim, to go for a ride."

Paddling out himself and venturing into the arm not visible from the beach, he also saw that my murder plan made sense. Today as then there was only a narrow canal leading into an extensive sea of reeds, with so many twists and turns that even if any swimmers had been there he would have been out of their sight in no time.

Yes, in that bayou-like corner, beneath the reeds, which formed a roof overhead, in that closed sound horizon, I had intended to make the boat capsize, in the deepest part, with me and my father. Even today I am surprised at myself, for I was dead serious.

Yet it had begun as a mental exercise, without any basis. For at twenty I did not hate my father. At most it bothered me for a moment or so that he avoided the sun, or that he could not be serious, especially in company. If he was ever the center of attention ("as you would have liked him to be all the time," the reader wrote me), it was on the strength of his joking around. I saw him as frivolous, and at the same time as a spoilsport. And what bothered me most was to see him as the exact opposite of that father of my daydreams, who until then had been my invisible guiding image, my only one, someone mysterious, my sovereign. And although the Germans' actions during the last Reich had forever made me the enemy—of whom? yes, of whom, really?—I never held it against my father personally that he, at least according to his role, had been one of the perpetrators. He must have been as unserious about that as about everything else (except perhaps sometimes when he sat on the sidelines and watched quietly).

My decision that he should disappear into the reeds came perhaps merely from a summer whim, born one night when I was on a walk with my father and pointed out to him a cluster of lightning bugs deep in a clump of bushes, massed together into a glowing ball and seeming to revolve in the dark, and he did not respond with so much as a word. But when I invited him to go for a ride with me in the boat that afternoon, I realized there was no turning back. I had to push him overboard way out in the reeds. I had been planning the invitation all week long, word for word, intonation for intonation, and when I finally got it out, my voice was shaking and very soft. So: this would be it! What followed was easy to narrate, for a change: my father was not in the mood, and I felt infinitely relieved.

"But how you missed your father during the years before that!" the reader wrote or transmitted to me from the reeds. "The thought of him was closest to your heart. Your allegedly lost youth: you did have it, you were a youth without a father, and to that extent a young person if ever anyone was young. Your thoughts about the future circled not so much around a wife and child as around your absent father. And your thoughts were directed upward, from far below, such as come only from a son in need of a father. The time when you were waiting for your father was the only period in your life during which, instead of being blissful intermittently, as was later the case, you were consistently devout, almost like the child of Siebenbrunn. The image of your father, destroyed by your mother and for a long time not inquired about by you, was, as became clear as you grew up, innate. If you ever expected salvation, it was from your father's turning up. At the slightest hint of a father, you would have been ready to set out in search of him. During your time of growing up: your father was it. And his image grew along with you. And one day you told your mother to her face that you were not fatherless, as she and the entire village had allowed you to think, but had a father. He exists. He has to exist. My father exists. Tell me who my father is. And where is he? And your mother burst into tears and said: Yes, you have a father. And your father is alive. And there, in the burning silence that followed, you experienced the greatest sense of triumph in your life and also for the first time pictured your life as an adventure. The far side of Eden was to become the here and now. And part of it was that when your mother admitted to you that your long-lost begetter was not a native, not a Slav, but rather a German, you felt proud of this father from the great, unfamiliar country of Germany, and it gave you a further incentive when your mother, whom he had loved, told you your father was not a villager, always spoke High German—not dialect!—and had always led her as light as a feather when they danced, and lived way up in the north, by the ocean!"

The reader had time. In the following days he not only returned several times to the scene of my near-crime in Wilhelmshaven, where the wintry desolation made him feel less like murdering someone than like hugging someone, but also visited the area on the edge of town where my father lived.

Since the death of his lawfully wedded wife (whom I sometimes think my father poisoned), he had been living alone for a long time in his little, pointy-gabled row house, and the reader watched and followed the old man until the lights went out at midnight (after that, in the stairwell, where the steps could be dimly made out through a high milk-glass panel, from time to time a ghost light would go on to frighten off invaders from the planet Mercury).

My father hardly went anywhere on foot anymore. He rode his bicycle to the Rathaus tavern for his early-evening beer with the two or three pals still alive, and on weekends drove to Oldenburg to see his lady friend, who was his own age, in his Mercedes, the new model of which he had already ordered from Untertürkenheim for delivery in the spring. During such drives he would pull over to the side of the road several times and take a catnap; or perhaps it only looked that way. In the company of his elderly friends, he, although also elderly, seemed by far the youngest, and when he spoke they tended not to register it. Each time he began with a stutter that was not a speech defect; it sounded as though it came from a schoolboy, the type who always contradicts and knows it all. But when they drank he was the one who replenished the others' glasses, always to the rim. One time he unexpectedly took a young woman in his arms and danced with her through the pub. And one time the eighty-five-year-old mentioned, without being asked and again almost unheard, that he had a son by a foreign woman, his great love, and his son was a joy to him. The reader reported to me that my father had said this without any stuttering.

Keeping himself in the background this way was something at which the reader had less and less success during his travels. Otherwise, wherever he was, he managed with his way of reading to achieve more than merely being overlooked: he created a zone around himself, just wide enough for turning a page, where even guests at a stag party would give him a wide berth. He became taboo, even directed the happenings around him.

But this time, as the days passed, he became downright suspect, except in the vicinity of my father. For he merely pretended to be reading, or he did read, and could have, if asked, recited every detail of the exemplary tale in question, but he remained uninvolved, receptive at most to the elegant structure of the Spanish sentences, and this was not his way of reading. It was like the repeated attempts he had made since childhood to read *Don Quixote*. He could neither take seriously nor find comical these self-anointed heroes and their flailing around. And yet he kept trying. At some point he had to enter into the world of Miguel de Cervantes. He believed, if not in the author, then at least in his, the reader's, predecessors, through the centuries. This time he would find his way into the book. The wintry light on Jade Bay, clear, dark, as if from below, would help him.

One time, to make himself receptive for reading, he even swam in the cold February sea, and then thought, with one stroke: "Now!" No. The book remained mute. And afterward, as he ran over a bridge that crossed the locks, he, this corner-of-the-eye person—he picked up things more quickly this way than by looking at them head-on—who had been a goalie in his youth, caught sight of a car following him at a snail's pace, and the merest thing would have had to snap inside him for him to toss the book into the canal and go after that metal hulk with an iron rod. The car was a police car and in it the young policeman with the gentle voice, who asked if he was still working his way through *Novelas ejemplares*, whereupon my friend discovered that the person in uniform was a lovely woman.

The reader tried to make headway with the book on Helgoland, and back on the mainland in Delmenhorst, Buxtehude, Hameln, Wunstorf am Aalmeer, during Carnival, on Palm Sunday and Easter Sunday, on Ascension Day: Cervantes's sentences galloped, bounced, and danced, but they did not carry him along with them. Meanwhile he carried on his business, inconspicuous to an observer, yet when the moment came, completely focused, a dedicated businessman.

In a church in Hildesheim, looking at the roundheaded figures from the centuries of a very different Germany, and even looking at the Gothic ones, he wondered how Goethe could have been so disdainful toward such luminous figures and found them distorted and barbarous, he, for whom the human skull matched the vault of the heavens.

But without his reading my friend saw his Germany as more desolate than ever, and himself along with it. Without his reading his Germans appeared to him as usurpers in their own country, either hacking the air space apart with their excessively loud voices or whispering as mythological ear lindworms. When he still read, then under duress: "Liposuction," "Utilization Factor." And once, in another German pedestrian zone, he read a sign that beggar children held up to his chest, read it from top to bottom, only to find that they had stolen everything off him but his paperback book.

But he had time, after all. And thus on a day in late spring when he was watching a national soccer match in Frankfurt's Waldstadion, he saw at halftime, out of the corner of his eye, a person next to him who picked up a book. It was a young woman, in profile. And she held the book away from her, at first still closed, which somewhat resembled the initial position in a wrestling match, also because her shoulders were leaning back and her eyes lowered. The woman's entire body was involved, and remained so when she began to read. It became just a bit quieter, at the same time more mobile, with the addition of silent exclamations or breaths, as if she were cheering the book on.

"All right, and now I shall read, too," said my friend next to her, and spelled out in one fell swoop—that was no contradiction—a page on which a Cervantes hero is finally taken seriously by another character in the story, whereupon the reader likewise could finally take him seriously, and read, and spelled out, spelled out and read, on and on. Then he looked up. He had read enough for today and was looking forward to tomorrow, with the book. And he looked at his neighbor, who now, at the end of halftime, closed her own book. Yes, wasn't it the pretty policewoman from Wilhelmshaven on Jade Bay? She had been following him all this time!

And she turned to him, and the two readers edged closer to each other, and then watched the ball together, which, when it went in the wrong direction, forced them to pay attention, and when it went in the right direction, on the other hand, lifted their spirits. And that was where? Where am I? And the reader could think there was a Germany still waiting to be kissed awake.

The thought formed such a clear image that he believed in it.

3

The Story of the Painter

Meanwhile late summer has come, or early fall already, and the painter is lying, his materials next to him, facedown on a bed of flint in the shade of the only bush at a bend in the Río Duero, at his head the steep, high, reddish-yellow sandstone terrace overlooking the river, and up above, already far off, Toro, with its façades of the same color, in the province of Zamora on the *meseta* of western Castile, about seven hundred fifty meters above the level of the Mediterranean at Alicante, while the painter is lying about one hundred meters lower.

The large birds surrounding the painter now in midafternoon are not ravens; they also have beaks too straight and too long for vultures; are they pelicans?—one of them is holding a fish crosswise—flamingos? no, they are storks, which, with their heads bent over their backs, burst out in squawks, one after the other, so that in the deserted and quiet river landscape it echoes like the so-called *Ratschen* back home on the Jaunfeld, the rattles that replace the church bells during Holy Week until the celebration of the Resurrection.

At some distance from the painter, down there by the bend in the river, on the almost white, almost glassy expanse of flintstone (I have a few lumps of it here on my desk and can smell the sparks in them), are lying fat dead fish, carp and pike, both gleaming gold from the solid coats of flies covering them; the gills of one of the fish are still pulsing, but they, too, are already swarming with flies.

Every morning, upon making his way down from Toro, the painter wanted to ask the fishermen why they simply left some of their catch lying on the bank, and precisely the finest specimens; to this day he does not know. Although he is a Spaniard—he never calls himself Catalan—there are many customs in his own country that even now, when his hair has turned gray, remain a mystery to him, one he is reluctant to solve.

Meanwhile the fishermen are having their meal at the barrackslike bar under the poplar trees on the other side of the Roman bridge, whose low, squat, round arches let through the Río Duero, here white with cataracts, with a roar that scales the steep banks and penetrates far into the streets of the town, but at the bend where the painter is lying is audible only as some soft, windlike sound belonging to the expansive, bald Spanish or Indian summer silence.

It is already approaching evening, and at the foot of the earthen terrace, hardly visible for a moment between two of its foothills, as in the gap in a canyon, the storm-dark Talgo flashes by, the daily express from Madrid to Vigo and La Coruña, which does not stop in Toro, glimpsed just long enough for the silhouette of a passenger to appear behind the tinted window of the bar car; and then, at the next curve in the tracks, which follow the river, between the cliffs, again that Mississippi-wide tooting in the echo of the roar and whistle of this railway thing, as graceful as it is heavy, from which the entire fisherman's pub on the other side jingles and jangles; this now you see me! now you don't! is something the painter has not allowed himself to miss once in all his weeks here; and the way it slices through the alluvial plane appeared to him daily as a plowing up of the entire earth and at the same time catapulted him into a previously unknown loneliness. Up! Back to work!

So was it still possible, now near the end of the twentieth century, to be motivated and stimulated, as once in the age of the great engineers, by a machine, the sight of it, its sound, its speed, undeterred even by the thought of a catastrophe right around the next corner?

Was he still "the painter"? (He allowed himself to be called a "film-maker" or "cinéaste," despite his film, long since finished and even shown here and there, only with a modest step to one side, as if to make way for someone else.)

He had begun to paint long ago with a particular notion of distance, which, however, did not then become a feature of his paintings. The distance was there beforehand: his original image—the thing that motivated him—his starting point. It determined him.

And now, as a result of his one role change to filmmaking? as a result of all that went with and came after it? as a result of what? he had lost that distance, his material? Once and for all? So what had this strange phenomenon, about which he had found nothing, not even in the textbook on "psychogeometry," meant to him in the past?

That distance had appeared to him way back in childhood as the blackness he saw when he closed his eyes.

Yet since birth he had fixed his gaze on the most distant horizon possible: from Tarragona in the direction of the sunrise, out over the Mediterranean, overlooking which, people said, the city lay as a "balcony." The sense of distance he got from this was, however, one of apprehension, in the face of the emptiness and the height, and the infrequent ships or boats in the middle distance did not suggest safety. The inky or steely or leaden blue also contributed to his impression that in this boundlessness there was no destination, or, if there was, then over in ancient Rome, where, he was sure, one of his ancestors who had been dragged away from his coast had ended his life as a slave or as lion fodder.

With eyes closed, he saw an entirely different distance. In all the blackness something like a harbor took shape, where he saw himself safely anchored.

And it was even more: in the black expanse, which did not seem all that black, but shot through with thousands of variegated little brightenings, without movement, something was constantly being danced, played, sung, narrated, drawn, as a model for him. "Model for," for it was not a question of images copied "from" anything. Besides, copies consisted only of foreground, and moved, vibrated, shrank, grew, as if on their own, while his stories in the blackness took place in the most distant background possible, and the movement he perceived in them seemed to come from him himself—from his heartbeat? no, for that it was too light, too disembodied—from his lungs? for that it was too quick—from his brain? for that it was too even, too powerful in imagery, too comprehensive, too intimate, too childlike.

It was even stranger that closing his eyes, without crossing them in the least, he could look away from the distant black happenings and then continue to watch them, except that the distance now shifted from its place behind his closed lids into his innermost self and became something whole, "one and all."

To be sure, that happened during his childhood only when he was lying in bed, as he was waking up in the morning. So were they images between waking and sleeping? No, neither copied images nor images between waking and sleeping. For the distance behind his eyes, he had to have had a good sleep and be well beyond the boundary of dreams, clearheaded, and the distance also did not create concrete images, as the state between waking and sleeping created still lives, for instance, especially of landscapes, and it also dispensed with the succession of spaces characteristic of that other state, indeed with space altogether; the distance itself was enough. And nevertheless it was active, and what it did was to produce an effect. Produce what effect? This constant, marvelously delicate movement in him and at the same time independent of him, without beginning or end, a sort of motionlessly moving repeated figure in the blackness, drawn to guide him.

And then with the years, he could say, paraphrasing Paul Klee, "The distance and I are one, I am a painter."

Yet it was something else again to get down to the images and get down to work. That was where painting began, art. It was not reproduction that counted but metamorphosis, or reproduction through metamorphosis. The starting point disappeared into it, or was absorbed into it. What was drawn for him, his model, formed only the bottom layer, and with scraping would perhaps have actually come to light sometimes, the mere appearance standing in baffling contradiction to the completed picture. For this he not only had to displace the original image, set it on its head, but also, so far as it was within his strength, invent things to add as well as subtract, so that as a rule something entirely new emerged in the end.

Precisely through such energetic distortions he could then, with reference to the distance, say of each picture: "I have reinforced a presence." And it had been a long time since the painter experienced his source of motivation only with eyes closed, when lying down. And on the other hand, he still found nothing in just any old distant blue, or red, or yellow. The location of his particular distance was somewhere nearer, could shimmer out at him from a clump of earth, mixed with stones and wood, at the tips of his toes, or when the colors of someone's eyes transmitted themselves to him from close up, also, in the mirror, his own (Black Sea black).

This distance could be most reliably tracked down, at least before his involvement with film, in a very specific visual realm.

That realm began at a certain remove from the eye, and yet long before what is commonly referred to as distance. The path leading to it was difficult to measure; earlier people would have said, for instance, "a stone's throw" (how large was such a stone, and who was throwing it?). And then the sense of distance was limited to a rather narrow strip or spot; if he looked out past it, just a bit, that promptly put an end to the distance, even if the high sea spread before him or the grassy lane swept into a savanna.

Thus distance appeared, just begging to be circumscribed and conveyed to the surface of a picture, at the end of a garden, for instance, in front of that wall and the bushes over there, on the ground, in the grass. It revealed itself thus on a pond in the forest, just before the barway on the opposite bank, as a delimited place there on the water, almost no more than a little tip.

And curious, too, that an ordinary meadow was already too spacious for such a unit of distance, while an ordinary backyard was too small. And the same was true of a lake on the one hand and of a mere puddle on the other. To offer material for an image of distance, the yard had to be larger than usual, just as the pond had to extend farther than a pond usually does—both, however, by just a bit, "to be recognized," "by a factor of one." And that, to be precise, was the measure of distance.

Only in this way did distance seeing come into being, as was fitting for a law of nature.

At the same time a displacement occurred such as no other distant horizon could bring about, neither that of the Himalayas nor of the Amazon delta: as a result of its limitation or framing, this particular distance drew the painter into a scenery, with a light on the water, on the grass, on the treetops like that in a mirror, and distance literally put in an appearance: there! It will start right there, there is the place to board, it will take place there, it will play itself out there, it will be hatched there, it will become concentrated there, it will catch fire there, it will be spread out there, right over there, in that narrow, limited patch of distance it is clear again, everything is being freshly polished, is gleaming as on the first day of the Creation.

And remarkable again that such distance occurred as if without movement, at any rate with hardly anything's moving noticeably in it. It seemed to the painter as though quiet was a prerequisite for this effect: that the distant grass tip, the distant coast of the forest pond, the distant interwoven pattern of the treetops had to remain nice and still.

Yet the distance over by the garden wall or elsewhere moved him as nothing else could, even the most remote curvature in the universe, and in its presence he thought, "There the world is at peace!"

And it also set him in motion, not toward it, not to circle the pond, in order to dive like a mystic into the distant glow, but in a sidelong direction to appropriate action, creation, spreading the word.

People, many of them, were moved to reflection by his pictures, at first sight so gloomy, and they were happy, even as a crowd, not merely the individuals. Each of his pictures had the same title, *La vega negra*, "The Black Meadow." Their unusual format, much wider than high, was simply about twice that of my slate in first grade—exactly right! was my immediate reaction—and likewise every figure or every squiggle, that is, every darker or lighter shading, clearly had its place, its proportion, its distance, just as in classical paintings.

And yet the painter had long since begun to wonder how it happened that, with the passing millennia of human history, distance and images of distance had become more and more significant in this way, whereas, for instance, imperial Rome, including the poet Horace, whom the painter knew somewhat by heart, had had no interest in such things.

Or was it that the current distantness did not yet exist in the spiritual geometry of those times, or merely as an incidental, or only in slaves (but hadn't Horace's father been a freedman?)? Had it become fundamental only today? As fragments of distance? fragments, yet fundamental?

That he earned a good deal of money with what he did was something the painter took for granted. He had it coming to him, and every time a head was shaken at the sums paid by collectors, he countered with his standard "That's the price." He was "my rich friend"—and doesn't everyone have one such, more or less?

And yet you could hardly tell by looking at him that he was wealthy. (Only certain women spotted it immediately, and by dozens of indications, from the expression in his eyes to his socks.) The apparent apartment house in which he lived in Paris was a little lower than the others next to it, and still looked like one downstairs in the lobby, except that from there no staircase, only an elevator, took one upstairs, with the entrance to the living area directly outside the elevator; and only later, when the guest was escorted downstairs by way of a spiral staircase concealed behind a door in the wall did he recognize that this upper floor had been merely the dining area, followed, a flight down, by another floor for sitting, conversing, and reading, then one with paintings by old masters, then an entirely empty floor, brightly lit into the farthest corners, and finally the ground floor, taken up entirely by a palatial white-tiled kitchen, with a cook: from top to bottom the tenement was the urban pied-à-terre of the painter, who finally came out with the admission that at the very top, to be reached by a sort of fireman's ladder, was the bedroom floor, at the same time his observatory, and the acquaintance who had assumed the chore of carrying the meal upstairs?—"he is my servant"—no, he said "factotum."

It was similar in whichever of his studios you visited, the urban ones as well as the others. In the company of a visitor he could hardly be distinguished from the former. Like him, he could be a dealer, a buyer, a speculator, a critic, a patron. In a dark pinstriped suit: he stood thus, arms crossed, at a distance from the pictures. In the presence of his guests he did not touch them. The actual displaying was done by stooped young people in gray lab coats, not students but assistants, employees, helpers, while the one responsible stood in half-shadow and with a stream of chatter seemed to want to deflect the observer from his creations as if from some awful deed. Only his sidelong glances at the works, from a distance, expressed something different. And not until the observer voiced an opinion—an exclamation was sufficient—did the painter step forward and acknowledge his work, also join in the enthusiasm, show a pleasure in what he had made that often hardly left room for that of the person standing next to him.

Not the fact that he earned so much, and, when he was without his work, outwardly had something of the air of an entrepreneur or a gang boss, secretly disturbed the painter, but rather the thought, which grew more powerful as he got older, that he had won. Merely to be secure was itself uncanny. And a winner, too: self-disgust. If he ever wanted to do away with himself, it was when he imagined that he had outdone or trumped "the others," "all of them." To be sure, for him every "Victory!" was immediately followed by "What kind of victory?"

It was something else again that he had got involved in the film. It was by no means a mere whim or an interlude. For one thing, he was not unfamiliar with the cinema, both as a moviegoer of many years, one of the most faithful, passionate, and knowledgeable in all of Spain and France, and as an actor, trained at a school in Madrid, after which he had performed in a few films, in larger supporting roles.

And then the painter saw his film as a variation on his paintings, or an added dimension.

Instead of with his color, black, on a pictorial surface, he now felt the urge to tell about his distance in a film for a change. He was not the first painter to do this, and his dream was a powerful dream. In it, regions and people appeared with an impact very similar to the shadings and figurations of black in his paintings. And the people moved; above all, they spoke.

The painter had a story to tell with his film, a story rich in both events and images, created for the large screen and a thousand-seat theater (such as still existed everywhere in his Spain, at least until this year, even now in the small town of Toro).

And this story had long since been available as a book, one of decisive importance to the young and also to the now almost old painter, William Faulkner's *As I Lay Dying*. Time and again he had been astonished that in the almost seventy years during which the farm family from Mississippi had roamed about, having various adventures as they carried the coffin of the dead mother, so as to lay her to rest, as she had requested, in her place of origin, no one seemed to have narrated the film of the story. He, at any rate, felt the need for it. He would have been the first to go to see it. And since the film did not turn up, he wanted to make it, for himself, the moviegoer.

He bought the rights, wrote the screenplay, traced on foot the stations of the coffin expedition, Castile, Galicia instead of the American South, and put together a team consisting of professionals—the technical crew—and nonprofessionals—all the actors.

The problem that arose during the shooting was the painter's or filmmaker's decision not to show, as originally planned, the transportation of the mother after her death on a first, long zigzag course through the Spanish interior provinces of Soria, Valladolid, and Zamora, but to jump immediately beyond the Cantabrian Mountains into stone-gray-glittering Finisterre by the sea: for one thing, during that early spring it was raining far more, and also heavily and unceasingly near the Atlantic, which was necessary for it to be visible on film; the rivers were overflowing their banks and thus cutting off the pilgrims' paths to the grave, as the story required, and forming, like the Mississippi in the book, that great floodplain where the coffin was supposed to disappear in the mud, in danger of never being seen again.

Furthermore, the filmmaker did not recognize until the test shoot in the Castilian highlands that the light there differed in some decisive way from that in his dream. To be consistent with that dream, an entirely different light had to prevail in the next sequence, after the family set out with the corpse of the mother—which, like the living, joined in narrating one phase or another of the journey, from the coffin; the light was to be that of the "Land Behind the Mirror" (the film's title).

It had to do purely with sense impressions that were missing from the Iberian interior with its lack of water and its almost nonexistent cliffs (those that did exist were dull yellow and hardly reflected anything), but not from the sparkling granite areas along the coast, where in the heart of Galicia even seemingly dry brook beds and mere mud puddles that looked like cattle watering places would swell up in the flooding and spread out to the width of the rivers or lakes they really were: not small meadow brooks, not merely damp, naked earth between two fields, but arms of the sea with salt water.

And there was another reason for him to have his film take place in that light, besides the most obvious one. When he, already no longer young, had first found himself in Vigo, Pontevedra, and La Coruña, he had moved through the area from beginning to end with the sensation of cities behind a mirror. He had certainly known their names all his life, but not been able to imagine an existence to go with them. For him Spain ended long before that, with the Sierra Cantabrica or at most with Santiago de Compostela. (Similarly, in his childhood, in his own house, there had been forgotten corners, which, when one entered them unexpectedly, appeared brighter than the rest, with everything highlighted and graphic.)

Something was behind the mirror, it was said, had been there all the time, and very close by, too. And nevertheless one first had to get through to it, who knew how? at the suitable moment, when was that? But then there were revealed, and as a rule precisely in one's own country, on one's own continent, as if independent of it and self-sufficient, as if completely on their own and also quite healthy and sturdy, existing settlements, entire cities or city-states, in whose polished mirror surface a new world could be deciphered. At least that was how it had seemed to him that time in La Coruña, and even more in the larger town of Vigo. And all this was perfectly natural.

So for the film it was merely necessary to soften here and there the gleam in the foreground and add a glow in the background. The technical crew, uncertain at first because he, allegedly a painter, did not lay out for them a single camera angle or light setting, soon got used to being, like him, only somewhat prepared instead of completely. It even electrified them when he came up with a surprise at the last minute.

And with the passage of time they, too, seemed happy that he was not narrating his story as they were perhaps accustomed to; he allowed the images to follow each other in such a way that it looked more like a frieze than an ordinary film, and background noise, of planes, of trains, was as welcome to him as the sudden shadow of a cloud on the face of the actor who happened to be speaking. Finally a sound engineer took it upon himself, after the end of the workday, to go, in pitch-black night and heavy rain, out to the lighthouse of La Coruña because he was not satisfied with that day's recording of raindrops falling on an empty soda can out there among the cliffs; he wanted to catch the sound between the drops that fell into the can through the drinking hole.

And the actors, a family of Castilian villagers, to whom the coastal region was also new, recited their story, or watched and listened to it with a complete, almost imploring solemnity, which came perhaps from the fact that the moment of shooting was the first time all of them were speaking their monologues—the script had nothing else—learned in isolation, each of them alone.

Things changed when the film was finished. Even before that there had been hardly anyone who seemed to be really looking forward to the film, and those who said they were curious did so in a tone that made it sound like a threat.

At a first screening for his acquaintances in the interior, they avoided his eyes when it was over, and those who opened their mouths spoke of something else entirely, or praised the shot "where the fish leaps over the coffin." A few complete strangers had wandered in off the street, one of whom began to clap at the end but stopped at once in the general silence.

Of a second screening, for a couple of potential distributors, at which the painter was not present, he heard only that one of them had had tears in his eyes, and had at the same time given the thumbs-down sign. Then some viewers had their praise conveyed to him, and a short while later expressed to him their disappointment at his failure to respond.

Having believed that his film was for the whole world, my friend felt mute anguish at his lack of success, anguish that stemmed from the thought of having done something that hardly anyone needed to do anymore; the times—or who or what?—needed stories other than those in *As I Lay Dying*.

His loss of distance had a different origin, however. The origin lay within him. It seemed to him as though with this film, for which he had seen himself as responsible, he had lost his unity with himself, his identity; only when it was no longer present had it been transformed from a word into a thing.

That he had made a fool of himself was something he welcomed; from the beginning that had been characteristic of him, had meanwhile become, to an extent, a sort of duty, which enabled him to carry on. The waste of money was a matter of indifference to him. And if the notion of defeat came to him, he thought, "What defeat?"

Yet no such redeeming contradiction presented itself in response to the thought: "Distance and I are no longer one, I am not a painter anymore." The question "Who am I?" had ceased to be rhetorical for him. It was he who had driven himself from his special place, to which he had laid claim from very early on and had occupied with an assertiveness unlike that of any of the painters around him. It had been said of his paintings that in them, specifically with the many variations on black, perhaps for the last time in history the coasts of the Mediterranean had been brought to life, from Gibraltar by way of Sicily and the Peloponnesus to Crete and Phoenicia, as only once before, and then by all the peoples together, in classical antiquity.

No longer to know who one was also implied culpability, incurred anew with every step. Since his transgression he was an outlaw, not vis-à-vis the world around him but vis-à-vis himself. To be without identity was not something he experienced as blissful extinction. It was a stigma he could not hide, for it was visible only to himself.

The loss of distance meant at the same time a loss of images, in the sense that without that feeling for distance he could no longer paint—could not send his color off in any direction. Whenever he looked around for his material, as now on the Duero, light did radiate from the spot, to be sure, but it was whirling and frightening as, in his childhood, the snakes on the Medusa's head in the Roman museum in his native

Tarragona had been. Hadn't the gaze that allegedly turned people to stone looked to him more like one that summoned people to reflect? Thus in his months of confusion he thought one time: "It may be that I have blocked my way back home." And then another time: "That's fine. What an adventure. Finally out in the wild world."

Medusa was a beautiful, solemn young woman whose head was later cut off, and from this sprang, instead of snakes, the horse with wings, Pegasus by name.

That he had formed the habit of stretching out on the ground in the course of the day was not merely the result of his great tiredness. Had that been the case, he would have changed his position and would not have lain facedown the entire time, motionless, his eyes open. He lay this way on purpose, somewhat like one of his forerunners, the American Sam Francis, who, when he was sick once for a long time, was supposed to have looked for several months at nothing but the floor under his bed, through a hole in the mattress—or had he pushed the mattress off the bedspring? Except that at that time Sam Francis had not yet been a painter, and he himself now?

He sprawled there on the river-bend pebbles, these so close to his eyes that when he blinked, his eyelashes grazed them. The flint bulges appeared dark, with a shimmer of light only around the edges. To think that he expected to be strengthened less by looking up into the heavens than by looking down at the ground! And who else would have been able to give himself over to lying down this way? Not Picasso, not Max Ernst, but probably Matisse when very old, Cézanne obviously, Poussin, especially in his in-between period, when he was unhappily painter to the king, and even persnickety Braque.

Except that this grouping no longer had anything to do with him. None of what he had produced out of himself previously in his life could he now claim as his work. What he was trying out at the moment was amateurish drawing after nature, and on every sheet only one thing, a flintstone, a shrub, a pyramid of earth, a wave in the river. With determination he set himself up as a Sunday painter (daily), working with ordinary pencils on writing paper, and their little sound meanwhile

meant as much to him as his earlier stroking, rubbing, scratching, scraping.

And thus he wanted to continue wandering and hiking into wintertime, going upriver from one drawing station to the next; he had started
out in Portugal, behind Pôrto, where the Río Duero flowed steeply
downhill into the Atlantic, had then crossed the border and continued
on until he was below Zamora, in front of the ruins of the church on
the little island in the river that had almost been washed away, while
on the other island, around which the current swirled, a dog that had
been abandoned there in the wilderness or had found its way there barked
and barked for a week—then nothing more.

The feelings on this trip were new to him. Although they resulted
from tiredness and were called sorrow or desolation, he experienced them
more deeply and lastingly than those from his glory days. Weakness and
defenselessness conferred a strength all their own, or so it seemed to the
former prince. He felt compelled to see, precisely because of his repu-
diation; to take things in; to act. And thus he might shake his fist in
space or spaces and say, "A new kind of painting must come! For which
the peoples will mobilize. In the face of which they will fall silent and
then go away, go and go. A kind of painting as festive as life. No more
pictures hidden away in museums. Cliff painting."

The sketcher on the field of rocky rubble at the foot of the great Duero
terrace sees above his sheet of paper a flash of lightning from a
cloudless sky. It has already gone out of his mind when a peal of thunder
follows. Or does this come from a shot fired by the two hunters, father
and son, who for hours have been lying on the other side of the tracks,
their sights trained on the badlands with all the rabbit holes?

No, it thundered and lightened, again and again. The hunters disappeared, running. The frogs jumped into the river, the wind died down,
and autumn leaves fell, straight down and heavy. The lightning could
be seen not in the bright blue sky but rather only in its reflection on
the scree; each new bolt seemed to shoot out of the hummocks there.

In the confusion my friend sniffed his pencils—the scent of thyme—
and continued sketching his object, a single pebble, shaped like a viper's

head. The drawing done, he set out for his camper, up on the chamomile-covered steppe just beyond the town. But first, after traversing a stretch in a sandstorm, with hares, storks, and rats scurrying back and forth across his path, and a sense of well-being from the grains of sand striking his cheeks like sharp blows, he stopped in at the barrack bar, where all the river fishermen and hunters were crammed in together, and there he stayed until the other express roared by, the last of the day, from La Coruña to Madrid, announced long before between the river terraces with a bull-like bellow.

As he continued on up the mountain, the first drops fell from the still-blue sky, and on the entire stretch such first drops again and again. The old cobblestone pavement on the serpentine road was darkened by them to a fresh black and wafted a fragrance up at him. If he painted again, he thought, it would be in camouflage colors like this.

If anyone was out in the open, it was alone on each of the slopes separated by precipices, searching for mushrooms or simply out there, the old men, "like me," he thought. But he had not even entered school when they were fighting the civil war, that man there against that other one? And now? Tomorrow on up the river to Tordesillas.

But for today to the clay-yellow church of Toro, where with his eyes he traced the masons' arrows, keys, and circles etched into the blocks of stone. Then to the Alegría Bar on the Plaza Mayor, where at the moment of his entering the glass of fino was already waiting for him, and on the television, just before the coup de grâce, torero and bull began playing with one another, seemingly cheerfully. Then on to the Imperio movie theater, where he was alone with the lighting strips along the aisles, like those on a runway. After the film, which he did not watch to the end, it was already night, with the rushing of the Río Duero in its deep chasm echoing through the town, and up here almost no other sound than the din from the pool halls, as if people tended to disappear into their houses more in Toro than elsewhere in Spain. Then for the late evening meal alone again in the innermost room of a little inn, with a view of a trompe l'oeil window, including curtains over the opaque glass, lit up from behind. Then, after the proprietor's hand on his shoulder in farewell, lying, no longer on his stomach, at some distance from town, in his camper on the savanna, and reading Horatius Flaccus by the oil lamp: "What? A criminal gets up at night to strangle someone. And you, to save your skin, remain at home?" While turning down the light, brooding over the masons' marks, and the thought: "Arrows in those days still had feathers! And ours today still have them?" And in the dark then a woman singing on the radio, "*¿Quieres un lugar?*"

4

The Story of My Woman Friend

She had always wanted to return from her solitary journeys with a treasure. Yet every time she came back empty-handed again, and not because her searching had been without success. Each time she stumbled upon amazing things and took them, bargained for them, or, more often, stole them. She was capable of dragging them around with her on hikes that lasted for weeks, and then leaving them behind somewhere, one after the other, at the latest on the final leg of her journey, the last item perhaps just around the corner from her house.

These found objects did not lose any of their specialness in her eyes; they merely revealed themselves toward the end of the journey as something other than the treasure she had had in mind. Over the years they were then brought back to their original place if possible, as now, on her southern Turkish excursion, the old milestone or marker from near Ephesus, which she had laboriously dug out and then rolled for hours with her hands and feet, with a Greek inscription of a fragment from Heraclitus: "The nature of each and every day is one and the same." Once she had it in a different setting, this object had come to seem like a mere theatrical prop.

Yet as always in the presence of such a presumed treasure, out of enthusiasm or feverish excitement she could not refrain from promptly removing it from the spot, getting her claws into it. "Here it is," she thought each time, "I've found you at last," and hurled herself upon it as if upon her destiny, finally discovered, which would bring the solution to the riddle of her life that she had long since ceased to expect from any man or system, and why not in the form of this unique wooden cudgel on the alluvial cone at the base of the coastal mountains, let's say near Bodrum, alias Halicarnassus, although almost only the husk was still wood, while the inside, the core, was packed lengthwise with shells or fish bones? shaped like drinking straws and open at both ends, so that she could imagine looking through the wooden pipe as through a particular prism that broke the light as nothing else would and had been lying in that very spot just for her. "And now tell me, precious thing: Who am I? What should I do? Where is my place? How will I come into possession of my power? What is going to happen to me next? Light my way."

That piece of wood had long since been rolled back to the rubble cone, just as later the salt-white erotic three-legged stool, break-in booty from a saltworks distillery, was returned the same evening. But this morning, after a night in her sleeping bag up on the boat deck, at the first call of the muezzin (or his voice on tape), still in darkness, beneath the stars, from the distant land, along with the first cock's crow, which reached her at the end of the bay, over the sea, she again awoke with the sentence on her lips, "This is the day for the treasure; I will have hunted it down before sunset, and the world will share my amazement."

Who was she? And how did it happen that each time she set out searching anew it was in the Middle East of all places, in Turkey, whose inhabitants still lurked in the minds of her southern Slav contemporaries as arsonists, throat cutters, and stomach slitters, even though their domination of her part of the world had ended long ago?

I read once in an article entitled "Speech and Silence of Women in Medieval Epics" that women at that time avoided any speech that threatened or exerted pressure: orders, directness, and questions that expected an answer. And in an article on "Interrogative Intonation in Various

Languages" I once read that German questions were marked by an interrogative intonation, whereas questions in the Eskimo languages managed without; where do you fit in, my dear friend, in this respect?

I do think I know a few things about her. To begin with: of all of us, she is the only one without cares, sometimes to the point of being infuriating. For her, only the present seems to exist, whatever is more or less peaceably there. Anything that is not there, if it does not attract her, she considers a nonthing or nonperson. And even if her conversational partner knew otherwise: from her face he could never imagine her living with a man, let alone having children, being a mother. Even when no longer all that young, she still seemed, to use an image from an earlier century, virginal, at least at first glance, transient, and likewise for the person who saw her again after a long time, always swept away into the prevailing daylight, surrendering to it as the most crucial factor, something also visible in the angle of her head and her posture: for this she could forget even her searching, with the greatest of ease, without transition.

And she knew no fear. Whenever she heard about a fearful person, her eyes would stare in incomprehension like a cow's, and her face would become beautifully clueless. Equally foreign to her was any compassion, and far from despising a compassionate person, she would be angry at him: if anything could be done to help, she did it at once; if not, she ignored the other's misfortune.

And she was the one who did not have a name for anyone or anything, or if she did, not the original one. Her using a name was such a rarity that the listener would experience either disenchantment (probably initially hers) or a solemnity unusual for her. But as a rule, for her nothing in the world had a particular or unique name. "Dalmatia," where she had been living for a long time, was not allowed to be called that, but "the coastland" or the "steep coastline" (even "karst" was too specific for her), and equally impossible were "thistle," "hemlock," "Tito," "Ephesus"; only words such as flower, bush, marshal, city, perhaps "philosophers' city" could cross her lips. She usually did know the various particular names, but it was as if she were saving these for a special occasion. Or at first she did not even want to know the names, especially place names; her letters carried place names only in their cancellation stamps, and at most she might ask the recipient long afterward what the "village on the lagoon with the miniature turtles" had been called, where she had spent a week in the "half-moon country."

The most noticeable feature of her speech, however, was that she did use names, but ones she had invented, in the form of circumlocutions or images. Just as her "container," "river beyond the mountain," or "conifer that loses its needles in the fall" resembled the clues in a crossword puzzle, I found myself time and again trying to guess what she meant by her "fruit that makes you sleep well afterward," her "day on which the trees with the white bark stand next to the front door," her "star with a belt and the male sex organ beneath it." Maribor, where she had been born, was always referred to by her as "the town with the red tiled roofs" (although that might have long since ceased to be true), and the Drawa, which became wide there, as "the river with the smoking ice floes," simply because once as a child on a particular winter day she had observed this from the great bridge, when it was so cold that everything seemed rigid but the huge, wild ice floes galloping along with much crashing and banging and smokelike frost clouds that rose from them, from which all the pedestrians on the bridge fled, except her, of course.

Those tiled roofs, stacked in layers all the way to a distant horizon, had been, seen long ago from the window of her room during her childhood and youth, the entire city of Maribor, with the addition of the long mountain ridge in the south, which only in a moment of impassioned homesickness was given its name by her, "Pohorje!" And from tile to tile the red had often changed its shade, so that in her eyes an eternal writing, which did not begin or end anywhere in particular, spread over the roofscape, formed by the darker patches, in curlicues, waves, loops, crosses, indecipherable, which she nonetheless never tired of reading; the longer she let her gaze travel back and forth over it, the purer she felt; and when later, in another Slovenian city, was it Ptuj?, with a similar roof map of the world before her eyes, in the midst of it, on the largest of the roofs, was it the cathedral?, real writing, monumental, dark on light red, leapt out at her, "IHS," she saw such obviousness as positively barbarous.

And the ridgepole tiles on those roofs had also been something special, she said, one long hood after the other, and thus in many rows, often a little irregular, as if slightly bent, marching in procession toward the four points of the compass, which for her at that time had all been called "Land of the Rising Sun," "Orient," "Levant"—not names but images to evoke. And if names, then only those derived from the sun, or from its reflection, the colors (when a cow was called "Brownie"), or from the forms of the earth ("the High Road," "the Deep Ditch," and all the capes of "Finisterre").

What encouragement it gave her when she learned that somewhere in the world something was publicly and compulsorily known only by its generic name, where, for instance, a forest was known as "the Forest," a delta "the Delta," a hilly area as "Collio," a lake as "Jezero" (that could also be the name of a village on a lake): "I must go there!" Such designations were never deceiving; things with names like that, such as the hillock named "Hillock," the bay named "Bay," fulfilled what their names promised, did them proud.

Or didn't the image of originality and exemplariness that emanated from the brook "Brook," the place "Kamen" (stone), the desert "Le désert" (even when the place marked thus on the map was only a sandy field in the midst of the bush), come instead from the power inherent in names and markers? How had that ancient debate as to which came first, the things or their names, been resolved? At any rate, as far as she could say herself—and I never heard anything from her mouth but her own thoughts—although the Turkish Mediterranean was not half as wild as other oceans, it, which was called almost exclusively "Deniz," the Ocean, without all its nicknames, officially as well, billowed up before her every time as only a high sea could, and whenever she reached the top of a range of foothills she took it at first sight for an even higher range of foothills in the distance. Yes, this ocean with the name "Ocean" seemed original to her in the sense that the word is also applied to a human being; he is original—thus an original?—no, *the* original.

Almost all the given, arbitrary, specialized names sounded to her by contrast like diminutives, unsuitable, almost as idiotic and embarrassing as all dogs that were not simply called "Dog." If it had been up to her, she would have had her children baptized only with the name "Child," and she stubbornly referred to them, even in the presence of close friends, in just this way, calling both of them "otrok," without "my" in front, but also not, as I did with my son, as a way of conjuring them up, but rather as a given: that is what they are called, and that is what they are, and vice versa.

Time and again I heard her reply, when asked her own name, especially by people on the street, where many thought they recognized her, not only in her Yugoslavia, "I have no name!," triumphantly self-assured or furious, and each time believable.

Yet twenty years earlier, just out of school, she had been "Miss Yugoslavia," and although every year a new one was crowned, for many in her homeland she remained the one and only beauty queen, not forgotten even at the Albanian border, at Lake Ohrid—especially not there. On the magazine covers with naked women that in the meantime have become common, but were not in her day, not a few Balkan adolescents apparently replace the faces with cutout photos of hers, and just recently I heard a boy from the Hungarian minority in Croatia who was going blind say that he had studied every single feature of her face with a magnifying glass, day after day, with the world of light gradually disappearing, so as to have a concept for later of how a woman can look.

On the other hand, it has happened to me not infrequently that in her presence I thought I had never encountered such an unprepossessing, ugly creature. Whereas it was only later that I dismissed various other women, including some described as beautiful, she was "the broad," "the crone" only at first sight. It was her intention to make such a first impression; she actually enjoyed going unrecognized as much as possible, even now and then by those closest to her, such that they looked away from her as from a man-sized wart. To disfigure herself in this way, all she had to do was change her facial expression a little, not even twist it, and this, practiced before the mirror during her year as beauty queen, she could accomplish at will. And a kerchief over her head, nothing more, provided the appropriate disguise.

Memorable events in her childhood were the Catholic prayer services in the cathedral of Maribor during the month of May, where she floated up to heaven with the hymns and litanies to the Blessed Virgin. An event of another sort was that afternoon under the apple trees in a school that trained nurserymen when two of the young trainees there and she had shown each other their private parts, after which the three of them had tried to kill a stray cat, with almost no fur and looking as if it were about to die, "out of pity," as the brats said, driving it with stone after stone, stick after stick, to the farthest corner of the orchard, where the animal was still alive and howling, while one of the boys was already in tears and she and the other were becoming more and more silent, "inside as well."

Then she was the national youth champion in sports, in track, especially hurdles—they had that for women, too, there—in the broad jump, in swimming, in volleyball, and the movements of each continued to vibrate inside her for a long time afterward. It was not only the torn ligaments, the pins in her bones, the stitches that made her give up competitive sports. The only thing she continued to practice was parachute jumping. Yet she did not view that as a sport, and she also kept it as secret as possible; when she described her jumps, she seemed to disbelieve herself, and only when one believed her in spite of that and responded was her enthusiasm kindled.

It was an athlete, after all, who then married her when she was a beauty queen, one of the stars of the Yugoslav national basketball team, a dark, handsome Croatian workingman's son, who had become rich from sports, always alert even when not on the court, as if ready to go after the ball, and yet, "but not because of his height," shy and with laconic good manners, always greeting people first or letting them go ahead in hotel hallways and entrances; he and she, the daughter of a shabby inn in Maribor (that was where her room under the eaves was), made a dream couple. She described how people underwent a metamorphosis in every place they entered, even if they did not recognize him and her as so-and-so. In the most dreary people's meeting hall on a Sunday evening, with the cold December rain and wind outside, with the waiters baring their teeth at the darkness and waitresses showing at most the white heels of their stockings in their clogs, from the moment she appeared she caused great sighs, beaming smiles, straightened backs, welcomes, people taking their seats. Suddenly invisible lights were switched on or lit, also a fireplace fire, and that in Yugoslavia, and then musicians stepped forward, who had been waiting specifically for her in a back room. People clustered around the couple with great emotion, solicitous and childish; at last they could show their best, their true side. Who were "they"? — "The peoples."

Later the two of them set out together for Arabia, where he worked as an engineer building a pumping station along an oil pipeline and after a few years committed suicide, or, as she said, "went of his own accord." She told the story that way so that the listener, instead of asking why and how, would merely nod.

She returned to Yugoslavia, to the city of her birth, for a time managed her parents' inn, engrossed anew in the citywide roof-tile images, and the processions of ridgepole tiles heading toward the Orient. Either she was seen only in the taproom, now in heel-revealing clogs herself, and with grim, dark eyebrows, intentionally penciled in this way, or far away on the wintry back roads, recognizable by her rapid pace, almost like the jerky movement of a speed walker (an athletic discipline), shoulders back and rolling.

Then she became, the first woman in Slovenia to do so, a forester, no, godzar, whom, almost as famous as the former Miss Yugoslavia, no one connected with the latter, superior to the men because of her sharp eyes and ears, especially in the forest dusk and night; then married again, a local "co-worker," both of them in uniform and studded with decorations from the Communist Party; then she returned alone, "single," without work, to her room under the eaves, where she made herself, as she said, "beautiful again," simply by looking and reading, and began to draft maps of imaginary countries, on a very small scale, painstakingly precise, with every watering place, cave, pier, cliff, following the example of the map in her copy of *Treasure Island*, which had remained more deeply engraved on her memory than the entire story; drafted, measured, outlined, entered; otherwise did nothing besides her work in the taproom except, on her morning walks along the edges of the fields, dig out *hren* (i.e., "horseradish") to be used as a seasoning for the "cold-cut platter" in her restaurant, long, always amazingly white-white roots, until one day we met on the bridge over the river and each of us reminded the other of someone else, she me of no one in particular and I she perhaps of everyone but her first husband. With our shared story consigned to the past, my friend married for the third time, after an interval long enough, she wrote me, for her to feel "pure again," and she moved to join her husband in the "city where the cathedral is an imperial palace" (Split) and gave birth to her children (two).

Not only did she take on nothing from her new status in life and continue her solitary trips as well as her Treasure Island studies; her children even seemed to be born without her, slipping from her body without labor pains into the world, and this, it seemed to me, was how she dealt with them later, more than merely unconcernedly, I thought, roughly, irresponsibly—but who knows?

It was similarly disquieting that in the intervals when she assumed the role of a housewife she became one with a single-mindedness that left no breathing room for anything else. She would be constantly cooking—and overcooking—washing laundry—washing out the color —washing the dishes with such forceful motions that they broke, and she went around, even on the street, along the pier, in felt slippers, every inch the slattern or the caricature of a concierge, with the two ends of her headcloth sticking up like rabbit ears. But might she not be on her way to a parachute jump in this getup? Yes, who was she?

And then again it sounded believable when she said, "The supermarkets and shopping centers are my native turf." And once she also let fall, as if it were to be taken for granted, that she, who hardly had to worry about money, participated in a housewives' circle like those in American suburbs, in which the women took turns inviting each other to their homes, and combined a convivial afternoon, with no men around, with the selling to each other of plastic kitchen utensils, like peddlers, except that it was in their own houses, she! and in "our Yugoslavia"!

She had come to Turkey this time in response to a classified advertisement, either delivering or smuggling to someone in Izmir a Ford Mustang, the luxury car with the galloping wild horse as its insignia.

After this she continued to head east, almost exclusively on foot, not only from bay to bay but just as much through the interior of the country, where on a single plain there were often numerous little brooks and rivers—marked by a succession of high natural fences consisting of reeds—often in the middle of nowhere, each like a living thing, flowing side by side toward the sea, slowly, and easy to cross (for her).

To stroll across such deltas, to wade, to swim, to dive, with a new watercourse every couple of stages, without bridges or boardwalks—of all the varieties of being underway she found this the airiest and most lofty, "my golden proportion." These plains were similar to those of the Isonzo, Tagliamento, and Piave rivers in northern Italy, which streamed toward the Adriatic in parallel, each one as the other's neighbor, only the plains here were far more remote, and smaller, and the watercourses, often nameless, were closer together and simply more ancient-seeming, and that not only because of the older history of the region.

It could happen that she did not cross such a brook immediately, but continued in it and with it—she was equipped for that, or sometimes not—to where it flowed into the nearby bay, where the ocean was often so still that there was a clear boundary between the two types of waves, those of the brook and those of the sea, their encounter with and merging into each other as gentle as imaginable, or that even the individual waves came from the fresh water streaming out into the salty deep, or at least the individual ones that made themselves heard.

For her it was something special to feel this borderline, slightly rocking, against the backs of her knees, at her hips, or on her thighs, one water in front of her, the other behind. (And although she subsequently referred to herself only in the singular, I think she was not always alone, "not absolutely alone.")

In such spots she also regularly found, underwater, something resembling a treasure, which, however, soon lost this aspect once outside its particular zone.

She was even more powerfully attracted by such river-mouth areas, the miniature ones, than by the ocean.

In the meantime, along the paths, in the Turkish villages, she transported her few things on a cart she had "borrowed" somewhere, and thus gave herself the appearance of a pilgrim to Jerusalem.

Then, too, sometimes, when it was already spring, not in order to disguise herself but for protection against the sun and the dust on the road, she went along with a jacket over her head, pulled down over her eyes and mouth, looking thin and so black-clothed that she appeared more peasantlike than any native woman. In the light shining through the material, filtered by it, the most harsh and naked landscapes were softened as if by an eclipse of the sun, a different sort from the kind we associate with certain battles during the Crusades: a calming one that sharpens one's powers of observation, and she wondered why no one wore sunglasses made of this different kind of transparent material instead of glass.

If she attracted attention at all, it was only because of her bare legs, which, from her knee breeches down, were scratched and rough, even revealing the beginnings of varicose veins, "appropriate," in her words, "for a Slavic woman."

Then one morning she was jolting along, her heels almost in the dust, on a mule; trotted by toward evening on a horse; was sitting the following day behind the windows of a bus that were shaking like a kaleidoscope, which also made the countryside look kaleidoscope-like; turned up by the sea a few days later in a thickly wooded, seemingly uninhabited bay, high on the hump of a camel, looking from the other end of the bay like the advance guard of the scattered "Orient Circus" that had lost its way, appearing from close up, with her sooty cheeks, like a guerrilla or simply a charcoal burner's wife—higher up in the forest a charcoal pile really is smoking—who now settles down with all her earthly possessions on a dock in the reeds, by a carefully carved-out channel, little by little joined by similar figures loaded down with bundles, who, like her, seem to emerge from the underbrush, several children in tow, all of them now waiting, in silence, for the weekly motor launch that will carry the group on to Fethiye or Marmaris, where they will change to the bus to Istanbul or to the steamer to Antiochia, Alexandria, Heliopolis, Leptis Magna, while the camel, now riderless, already far away, circles the bay at a leisurely pace, and a child who stayed behind on the shore fills with stones the shell casing found by my woman friend on her way there but then left lying on the beach.

Although she did not keep notes or make sketches or take pictures on her trip, sending her husband and children only picture-postcard greetings and sending me, in loose imitation of Heraclitus, only fragments like "The village of Kokova shouts its poverty out over the sea," it seemed to her as though all her movements, back and forth across the country, were being recorded.

With her peculiar style of being on the road, always and intensely focused on the subject at hand, prepared to let herself be surprised and to surprise others, she pictured herself making tracks not only through these regions but simultaneously on a particular map of the world. There each of her present steps seemed at the same moment to be placed as a marker, like the markings of an explorer, and ineradicable, which gave her a good conscience in addition to the pleasure she could experience alone with herself this way: as if her crisscrossing were now a form of work, for the common good if any work ever was.

In addition, as she saw it, not a single step in the course of her journey could be such that it contravened that transfer onto the "trail map" as she pictured it. One false step or thoughtless action, and the entire marker script that she had paced out would be eradicated; her work, her oeuvre, would have been in vain.

From such consciousness she then derived something like an ad hoc ethical imperative: "Conduct yourself on your journey in such a way that you see nothing you do as a violation of your leaving traces."

But then why did she still expect that the next time she came around a bend she would finally have before her eyes that which she found sorely absent from such a way of life, scandalously lacking? Why did she search, and search, and search?

And from time to time she thought that what she would encounter around the bend would be the ax murderer intended just for her, and her presumed leaving of traces was merely a sickness, part and parcel of that irresponsibility that led her to tell herself that what she was doing should not be judged and punished like the actions of others, simply because she was the one doing it?

And with the outer-space-blue Turkish sky above her, she saw herself as far from where duty told her she should be, indeed as torn away from it, never to return. No matter how faithfully she continued to follow her personal rule, which, again paraphrasing the stutterer Heraclitus from Ephesus—a place already irretrievably left behind—went as follows: "Go well!" and which she had mastered and now modeled for the world around her as otherwise only the woman apothecary of Erdberg (from my unwritten novel) could: in such moments she was behaving, in the eyes of the agency responsible for her, like a vagabond, as a disgraceful neglecter of her main concern.

But what was her main concern?

The others, even her children—thus experience had taught her—were better off without her constant presence; her long absences did them good. Her assignment—thus experience had taught her as well—was her way of being on the road in this original fashion. "My way is my assignment, nothing else!"

Yet now that was no longer valid—for hours, even days, at a time. No matter where she struggled along, eyes opened wide to the millennia-old life of the Orient, her graceful movement providing at the same time an example of pure presentness: nothing more of it appeared on that map that required no reprinting, located—plotted—recorded— transmitted. Among thousands of good news items this was the bad news from this journey. She did not feel herself to be either in the Orient known for its patriarchal atmosphere or in the Levant fabled for cinnamon and clashing cymbals. Spaceship Earth did not answer any-more, even to the most imploring SOS scraped by toes and pounded by heels.

Carefreeness: was my friend in the process of losing it?

It could even be that in the course of the summer, in some city on a harbor, in the bars and bazaars, she was listening for sounds of home: except for a bit of Russian, nothing. During this year she seemed to be the only person from her country spending time in this area, or abroad at all, and for the first time this was not a matter of indifference to her. For the first time she felt something like fear, or a prelude to fear.

One day she could be seen among the yachts, where, without needing money, she offered to help the crew with shopping onshore; and the next day she rented for herself, for continuing her trip eastward, a light cayman with crew, she being the only passenger, in which role she then stood erect in the bow, which was decorated with nothing, nothing at all, and sailed into a bay accessible only to ships and already sparkling festively when she arrived and filled with the sweet scent of wood fires, tying up in the last berth there, to the sound of "Death and the Maiden" drifting across the water from the most distant of the boats. And on a third day, still in the depths of night, she created a silhouette, standing before the glow of a village flat-bread oven in the interior. And in the first gray of dawn she was darting along a path through the hills, whose earth was cracked from dryness into an endless hexagonal net; she walked ahead of a herd of goats, the males' horns clashing against each other. And that same morning, in a town already up in the mountains, she had a tooth extracted, and at noon stood in a house entryway without a door, contemplating a pair of canine lovers, glued together, no longer able to break loose, howling with strain and pain, tumbling around and around each other, until she felt hungry. And that same afternoon she crossed a mountain village, deserted except for an old woman and her hens, and robbed of its access road by an earthquake; she had to practically scramble over the village, like a wall of rubble and boulders, then wished a good evening to a soldier on patrol with a walkie-talkie, on a rise, in the icy wind, the eternal Taurus snow before his eyes, and then ran downhill, ran and ran, until she reached the next harbor, where the cook on her hired boat was already waiting for his queen of Sheba with the evening meal, while the helmsman lay on his back next to the cayman in the extremely salty water and by the light of the full moon read the news-paper spread wide between his arms, or made it look as though he was reading.

This particular day occurs in the August heat, when even the wind is blazing hot and makes breathing difficult, and my friend has had a taxi drop her off before sunrise near the ruins of an ancient temple to Leda, who was ravished by the chief god in the shape of a swan. Actually the temple was dedicated to Zeus's lawful wife, his first, whose name was similar, Lato, but the traveler had decided to rededicate the temple in honor of the woman who bore Helen, which happened to be my friend's name as well.

And indeed, in the darkly shimmering light of dawn, more part of

the marly furrowed land than of the sky above it, in the midst of a
heavy, soundless stillness, the swan in question swooped down among
the fragments of columns, in a sudden dive, casting its shadow ahead of
it, like a bird of prey about to pounce on its booty, landed amid splintering and cracking in a puddle, flapped its wings furiously in the air,
and promptly lifted off again, vanishing immediately behind the dike
along the nearby river, and in the temple precinct, as a branch usually
bounces after the departure of a winged creature, the water rippled in
widening circles, with the disappearing swan's flight creating a sound
like an immense coughing. "On with the day!" (Another of her favorite
paraphrases of Heraclitus.)

After hours of heading inland in the heat, quite often running to make
the breeze feel cooler, far from any water, once passing fleshy, hip-high
stands of wild sage, once passing stinking sheep skeletons, she found
herself marching through a broad stretch of hinterland, where, again for
hours, all the umbrella pines and scrub chestnut oaks stood charred,
which afforded a view of the world very similar to the one she had had
with the black jacket over her head. For a long time she encountered
not a single living being, just as the soot colors, up hill and down dale,
remained at a distance, and, in the absence of wind here, the only sound
came from her footsteps. She waded through ash mixed with pitch. The
smell of burning brought back to her nostrils the remembrance of the
smokehouses of her childhood and thus now and then provided a sort of
cooling by way of memory.

Once, when she crouched down to relieve herself, there appeared unexpectedly, from all sides, butterflies—small ones and large, blue, white,
multicolored; in no time they had swarmed over the spot of urine and
were drinking it. As she held still, all around her in the charred landscape
she heard the very delicate chirping of crickets, which, like no other
sound, wove together or dissolved proximity and distance, a welcome
sound after the cicadas' racket, which here in the dark light was absent
for a change. And close enough to touch, glassy in the dull ash gray, a
snake glided by, slithering in a zigzag, its head slightly raised, as if
looking for its family after the fire.

On with the day. And toward sundown she came to a strip where
finally some growth was beginning again, first in the form of blackberry

canes, clambering green up into the dead branches, and their berries, which in such a setting somewhat resembled animals made up of thousands of black-gleaming eyes, for which she stood on tiptoe, jumped, took a flying leap. She followed the green strip as it widened, and descended by the steep path, with now and then a breath of ocean air from below, for a while adhering to the rhythm with which a long-bodied Mediterranean hornet flew time and again at a snail shell on the ground, pushing and rolling it along, until the house was finally lying with its open side up, into which the hornet promptly slipped, and my friend recognized, and heard as well, that inside it was now ripping and stripping the rotten flesh from the walls.

The water of the new bay, which she reached as the last swallows were still swooping across the sky, again at a run, in loping strides, was —without a ship, hardly even a boat—thickly populated by swimmers, probably from the village nearby, all generations together, their heads gazing out over the still, bright surface of the ocean as if everyone were present.

She joined them, swam as she had previously run or strolled, and the sea, which at the same time did not make her feel wet, buoyed her up under her arms, embraced her, mothered her, as if celebrating the return of the Prodigal Daughter, and as if this were all that had been necessary to quench the thirst of her many days' journey. She dove down, saw on the ocean floor, half buried in sand, the sarcophagi of a sunken ancient cemetery, or petrified boats, their keels pointing up?, and afterward she sat down on the shore, her face turned inland, from which now, in the katabatic wind, parachutists, an entire squadron, facing toward the coast and, some of them linked together in figures as during an air show, float down onto the "Bay of the Prodigal Daughter": from close up, the wings of linden blossoms, with the fruit capsules dangling from them, and swarms of bats zigzagging around them.

And my friend murmurs half out loud, turning to no one in particular, including herself: "I've never seen anything like this. It's all over with me. I shall die soon. Today was a happy day. Thank you. When was that? It was a long time ago. I am mourning. Ah, movement! What do you want to search for? Look. One must look. Sweet life. I am afraid. Is anyone there?"

And she listens to her own voice and is amazed at what comes out of her when she simply talks to herself this way.

And she longs to perish, longs for glory?

5

When I was in Japan, in every new place, in the cities and even more in the countryside, I imagined undertaking the journey with a farmer from my Central European village, Rinkolach, and a woodsman from the same Jaunfeld area.

I would have been the tour guide, so to speak, but one who kept silent if at all possible, and in the presence of the wooden temples, the fields and trees, would have been merely a witness to the exclamations, the observing, the touching, the describing, the comparing, perhaps even the theorizing of the two others with their expertise.

With their calm, endless capacity for wonder they would have, I thought, kept my own wonder alive; without them it pretty much dissipated after a few days. Instead of taking in the differences, as at the beginning, with refreshed eyes, thoughtfully, I found myself observing almost exclusively the similarities, which manifested themselves more and more concentratedly with every day that passed, and from which, unlike in Europe, there seemed to be no escape into unpopulated areas or into nature (at most in the national parks), such that at times I actually felt like a prisoner on the Japanese islands.

If I set out to get productively lost, I did not once succeed, blocked as I was on all sides by barriers or impenetrable thickets. If, on the other hand, I set out with a destination in mind, also in a hurry and short of time, for instance trying to make a train, I would get so hopelessly lost that in the end I did not know anymore which was right or left, had two left hands or feet for every movement, and collided with all the passersby in Japan, who without exception took the shortest route and also never stepped out of a person's way.

Without the woman from Catalonia at my side sometimes—this was our honeymoon—I might perhaps have knocked down one of these millions of prison wardens, who acted as though I did not even exist, and embarked on a meaningless flight.

But with my two fellow villagers I would have found constant pleasure in Japan. Every day they would have grasped and explicated in my presence things that could not be found in any guidebook; they would have been the right teachers for me, their unhurried eyeing of an object and then of the relevant subject matter, articulated in astonished conversations with themselves; in no time flat they would have been on intimate terms with the local folk, without imposing themselves on them and without even exchanging a word, with construction workers, cottagers, priests, drinkers, women at the market, gamblers.

Imagining their company did help me now and then, but did not replace their physical presence, the actual expert fingering, sniffing, measuring.

The carpenter and architect did not need such companions. Wherever he was in the inhabited world, when faced with any questionable phenomenon he could summon and deploy from within himself an entire team, as it were, in which one complemented the other, helped him along, took over his role. If he was constantly talking to himself on his trip to Japan, it was a discussion, usually in question-and-answer form, between not merely a builder and a woodworker but also, for instance, a geologist and a well digger, a teacher and a road builder, a photographer and an ironworker, and, last but not least or in between, an actor and a nobody or a ne'er-do-well. As he learned from unfamiliar objects, he learned from himself.

Yet he accomplished hardly anything, and did not even much care. When he built something, it was almost always without a commission, without a client, for himself, or for no particular reason, on the piece of property he owned, a scruffy savanna on the Italian karst, above Trieste, which he had inherited from his parents, or secretly, on no-man's-land, especially that of cities—to the extent such a thing could even still be found anywhere nowadays.

That these structures stood there unfinished, one and all, was not his intention, at least not his express intention. As he said, he wanted to leave himself as much time as possible for each, and it did him good, he remarked, to start something new in the meantime, and besides, it was a pleasure to do everything himself. And furthermore, he had no money.

So for a house on his land (he acted as though he did not know whether it was intended for himself), he had dug out a small sinkhole to create a cellar, but since then nothing had been added: only the hemispherical form, hollow, its walls like its rounded floor finished with the local white, gray, and bluish limestone, lay there sunk into the steppe under the open sky, and a spiral staircase built from the wood of the narrow, tough karst oaks, without a railing, stuck up out of the hollowed-out cellar, rose above the earth's surface, and ended at about the height of a diving board, with a final, thicker, threshold-wide step leading out into space—that was where the entrance level of the house was probably supposed to be, with a round floor plan, eventually or never?

To be sure, he had already erected a doorframe made of the same weather-resistant wood as the staircase, broad like a portal, set into a marble base, but it stood, and apparently not only temporarily, somewhere else entirely on the lot, with nothing else around it, and seemed to belong to a second house or a future courtyard wall; and the ramp of tamped red earth, located somewhere else again, gently mounting into nowhere, was perhaps conceived of as the approach to a barn, or at least such a thought was suggested by the ladder wagon left from his parents' days that stood there, with stone chucks behind the wheels, the shafts stretched forward as if in anticipation of a new draft animal—though he then put the barn somewhere else entirely, at first nothing but four tall poles set in concrete, topped by the ridgepole and the rafters, uncovered to this day, through all of which the air whistled, except in the entryway built down below, its boards tightly joined, with two completed doors and even a glazed and puttied window, an entryway large enough to sit in—but what did that have to do with a barn?

A trench from the First World War ran right through the builder's work area; his parents had filled it with rock and especially brush when they cleared the land, and he piled more on top of the juniper, grapevine roots, blackberry bushes, interwove the whole thing, stuffed the interstices with the tough savanna grass, the hard, clumpy red earth, smoothed and rounded the top, creating, along the former trench, the longest, most curving, most elastic bench for sitting on that I have ever encountered, although it was not certain that this structure had been planned as such: would he raise the bench later to the height of a wall, perhaps even studding the top with bottle shards?

At first sight someone might perhaps have mistaken all his piecework for a movie set. But for that the individual elements were too solid. A set designer or builder would never have been capable of designing and devising actually usable nooks like the craftsman and master here. And in distinction to a movie set, with these structures the adventure being played out or the relevant story would remain utterly mysterious, or, on the contrary, would not pose the slightest mystery.

His architectural works outside of the inherited parcel, in hidden no-man's-lands in the four corners of the globe, stood there unnoticed. Aside from his friends, hardly anyone knew that those mounds that could easily be confused with local piles of rubble and soot were, under their camouflage, bake ovens, cisterns, root cellars, and woodsheds.

This notion stemmed from his childhood on the karst, in a borderland, which additionally had the "Communist threat" on the other side of the border, against which a third of the entire Italian army was massed, with weapons and tanks, all camouflaged under fake woodpiles, from which, when he was on his way to school, he would suddenly see a tank's gun thrusting, under fake igloos of stone, which would unexpectedly flip open, revealing the nose of a rocket, inside a lone tree of the steppe, from which, through a sliding door, a heavily armed guard would emerge: the architect and carpenter's later structures were the reverse of all this.

The only money he earned, in addition to that from odd jobs, came from a position at the University of Udine, where, for one hour per week, he taught the architecture of Greece and Rome, and his earnings went almost entirely on his building projects, or, as he called them, "void building," "memory building," "attention building." That he could spend this year in Japan was a birthday present from us, all his friends, and to reciprocate he had promised us a sort of photograph album, with the working title "No-Man's-Land Strips in Japan."

Yet up to now, the middle of autumn, he had hardly taken a picture, although the painter had given him a camera that could take pictures with the most accurate long-distance focus, and although, contrary to expectation, here and there among the Japanese subdivisions, which were built up almost solidly, something similar to *terrain vague* had turned up; he had hardly taken a picture either of the theme of his journey or of anything else typically Far Eastern, but instead perhaps a picture of a motorbike wrapped in a silvery tarpaulin in Yokohama, the hands of three children, one on top of the other, on an umbrella handle on the tiny island of Izu, a wooden rack for drying rice straw, similar to the hayracks in Carinthia and Slovenia, at the turnaround in a field in the north—and that could have been anywhere in the world.

The moment was gradually approaching for fulfilling his promise. But, as he just wrote to me, he still feels reluctant to take pictures. And the photograph he did send along, of the Ryoanshi Temple, which he had just visited for the second time, of the "nothingness" or contentlessness of Kyoto, did not show the famous empty pebble garden with mossy boulders (and in addition perhaps the rake belonging to the monk-gardener), but, as a wobbly snapshot, merely the masses of visitors, sitting head by head on the balustrade around the square, their legs dangling down, apparently talking loudly, laughing, squinting as they faced the expanse of nothingness.

The handwriting in the architect's letter was certainly not that of a person who had been sitting idle. It was that carpenter's writing that I take as my model now and then. By that I do not mean the thickness of the carpenter's pencil, intended for marking and numbering pieces of lumber, but rather the heaviness of the hand, perceptible to the reader, from which I sense: the man who wrote that must have been working just beforehand, using his entire body.

Not that the writing is shaky. Rather, it is rounded, the fingers, just washed, rest on the paper, except the index finger and the thumb, blood coursing through them from the manual labor in which he was just engaged, and the joints follow accordingly, and with them the lines, loops, connections, and transitions among the individual letters. The carpenter's writing has something about it as handy as it is hearty, it is painted and built, and it breathes like the thing written; I decipher it as a document.

Thus I have likewise developed the habit of seeking out some physical work that involves the whole man—not a sport—before I get down to writing. Except that my raking, sawing, chopping, cropping, thinning is different from the carpenter's painstaking fitting, joining, measuring, nailing, bracing, and more often than not I fail to achieve with my gardening that pulse of variety that would make my hand not only heavy but also flexible.

And as I look again at my distant friend's letter, I picture him that same morning, on a vacant lot in Kyoto, onto which, overgrown as it is, he fought his way with the help of a bamboo knife, and where he has gathered and piled up stones to make a hidden fireplace, from the outside merely the empty base on which at one time, in the outer courtyard of a now vanished holy place, the demon of deterrence once stood. For secretly the architect has an entirely different project in mind than the aforementioned photo album: to leave behind in a Japanese no-man's-land another such camouflaged structure.

Back there in the winter snow of Morioka he was already close to accomplishing it. After weeks of searching from south to north, he was standing, not all that far from the center of town, at the first break in the rows of houses that otherwise stretched unbroken across the long island country of Japan.

The sight of the windy strip, with nothing but a clump of bamboo poking tall and narrow out of a puddle frozen solid, down to the gravel at its bottom, without a sign that new building activity was in the offing, for the moment did him nothing but good. A very long time ago something must have been built in this opening, of which now only a certain artificial unevenness, its forms blurred, served as a reminder. The wire fence that separated it from the street had gaps where one could slip through; it had rusted out long ago, and no sign either indicated that the place prohibited entry or announced new construction. From the crown of the bamboo, whose shafts were bluish, came a seething and humming, and the listener wished the sound would resolve itself into an utterance that he could take away with him.

Instead a little plane broke through the clouds above him, and from it boomed that martial loudspeaker voice that had accompanied him, so to speak, all through Japan, in which a nationalist party was demanding the return of the islands lost to Russia during the Second World War. And the following morning, when he came to his project site very early, still in bitter-cold darkness, equipped with a tinsnips and the many pockets of his special jacket stuffed with the necessary tools and materials for erecting the planned enclosure—a space in which the rustling of the bamboo in the midst of the emptiness could resonate—he found it illuminated by spotlights, the bamboo hauled away, the first holes bulldozed, and the area swarming with workers in blue overalls and yellow helmets, like all over the world, and even the Keep Out sign had English subtitles. And so he watched the workmen, dark like Mongolians, until the sun rose (late and very slowly above Morioka, already very far to the north): the first thing they set up was a tall wooden partition, a sort of screen from the street. And although they appeared to overlook him, in time it seemed after all as though they were following, as with a foreman, his eyes' silent directives, which, because he knew what the next step had to be, were always one step ahead.

The medium-sized high-rise buildings around the center of Morioka looked hardly any different from those in Udine, for example, and the many sparsely wooded hills reminded him of those of Friuli, from between which, just as here, the snowcapped mountains in the north gleamed. What was so different from home in this remoteness, except perhaps that instead of the accustomed clanging of bells a gong sounded? And the carpenter felt compelled to get away from the cities, in the opposite direction from most architects.

At the railroad station in Morioka, while he was waiting for a train to take him farther north, where the couple of falling snowflakes collided in the air, for the first time on his journey one of the natives approached him, a young boy, and requested permission in English to ask him a few questions, but then could not stammer out even the first question.

To get out into the Japanese countryside, into a village, into nature, then became more tedious than tracking down the last hiding place of vagueness in the cities. But since he was fired up with enthusiasm for such a destination, it had to exist, as he told himself. And since he had unusual patience—"refresh your heart, be patient" was his motto—even the routes he took gave him pleasure.

Yet as a rule he had to plot them out himself, especially where the plains thickly dotted with settlements and cultivated fields met the mountains. Here he suddenly encountered virgin forest so dense that he could move forward only with the help of his special folding hatchet. How had the itinerant poets of earlier centuries made their way through here? Or had it been easier to cross the Japanese countryside on foot in those days? But hadn't almost all of them died young, and in the course of their wandering?

He then recognized that the quintessential rural and village settings were very like the Japanese urban no-man's-lands: they, too, often existed only for a single moment, though in different form. On yet another morning, now much later in the year, having arrived, as it were, by the back way at a mountain temple, and then been for hours its only visitor, squatting in the dim outhouse there, hidden in a remote spot behind plum and cherry trees, for a moment he had again experienced the sense of security he had had using the privy on his parents' solitary farm near Aurisina, reachable only through the barn or by way of a long, roofed wooden gallery; whereupon he wrote to me that it was time for my long-promised "Essay on Convenience Stations."

It was conspicuous that he usually stumbled upon such spots near temples, specifically in their far-branching, always narrow, tapered hinterland, carved out of virgin forests, here a small vegetable garden, there just such a cemetery, connected by an old wagon trail; and the couple of Buddhist monks, always busy, appeared there in the role of farmers.

And again one morning he saw in such an area a cluster of people who did not merely appear to be country folk, men and women, but were the spit and image of those from home, with stooped backs, prolapsed knees, gout-ridden, and this group of village pilgrims broke out in a unanimous cry of astonishment at the sight of the temple bell, at which each one straightened up from his stoop, stretched, stiffened, snapped upright, and one of the farmhand types almost tipped over backward.

That he almost always saw such no-man's-lands or villages only from the exterior was something he found perfectly all right. Remarkable architect that he was, he almost never felt drawn to interiors. He even avoided these wherever he could.

The many different voices speaking inside him did not interfere with one another. Each one—that of the wood inspector, the wind expert, the acoustical engineer, the vagabond and dowser—could have its say, at length, was distinct from that of its predecessor, which it took account of, continued, supplemented, grounded. That would yield an entire book (and someday he means to write it himself). And in between, and often for a very long time, the voices also kept silent, and he was, again as since childhood, just someone or other, feeling invisible.

In time many of the Japanese appeared to him more like travelers than himself. He was the native. Having set out with a swarm of them before dawn to climb Fujiyama, he went off on his own before they had even reached the tree line and spent the day searching for mushrooms, in the course of which he came upon a deer, small and stocky, almost like a wild horse, like his deer on the karst. And in Yokohama, where he lingered for an entire day on a slope above the harbor in the "European Cemetery," with the graves of the first traders to come in the nineteenth century, he sat or walked, like the cemetery watchman of many years, behind native visitors, who photographed each other in front of the mostly English inscriptions, and here and there young people, as dusk fell, kissed; and then another time he stood in one of the temples of

mountainous Nikko while the priest deep inside called out "Amida!"—
that single word that was supposed to secure eternal blessedness—but
how he called it out! He stood in the background as the temple servant
on duty, one step away from the group who had come by bus from
Tokyo and seemed more amused than anything else by the priest's cry.

Only the Japanese children violated from the beginning his imagined
unobtrusiveness. He was the one on whom rested the bright black eyes
of the infants (one of whom was always crossing his path, although
during the entire time he never once saw a pregnant woman), and in
front of the giant Buddha of Kamakura, enthroned out in the open, so
large and heavy that he positively radiated peacefulness, he, the observer
half in shadow, became a more significant sight for the children filing
past all day than the colossal statue. And although he not once caught
an adult passerby looking at him, afterward he sometimes carried glances
inside him, especially from women, deeper and more durable than anywhere else: and each time he realized how much he had needed to be
noticed after all.

Thus from time to time he himself was responsible for his plunging
again into the world as it streamed past, not only by making himself
noticeable but also by noticing things himself, and not merely various
no-man's-lands or the bare countryside.

On the day of the great Buddha of Kamakura, he stood there until
evening on the shore of the Pacific amid a group of girls in dark blue
school uniforms who, one after the other, tossed long-stemmed roses like
spears out into the ocean, and then danced until the flowers were carried
out to sea and night fell. And then again schoolchildren, adolescents, in
the railroad station of northerly Sendai, running in swarms alongside the
train departing for Tokyo, in which sat their teacher, who had just taken
leave of them forever; they were uttering wild cries of dismay, wailing,
their tears visibly flying, their half-raised arms like stumps, their weeping
spreading through the entire station, while at the same time the teacher,
sitting in his compartment, wept silently in unison with them, something my friend had not experienced in any other country on earth, and
also not in the land of dreams—only in the portrayals, everywhere in
Japan, of the various animals mourning the death of the Buddha.

———

In early summer, back in the north, to which he felt most powerfully drawn, while crossing on the former ferry, now converted
into an excursion steamer the size of an ocean liner, from Aomori
to Hokkaido, he caught himself, shortly before docking, under the
still-bright midnight sky, in the dense crowd of passengers on deck
who were taking flash pictures into the void, running his hand from
behind over the hair of a beauty, a tall woman with a very broad Mongolian face, as previously he had now and then run his hand over the
head of one of the children. And she, too, let it happen, except that she
turned toward him and did not smile. Never had anyone looked at him
that way.

The horizon all around displayed long, smooth strands of clouds, almost horizontal, floating, just like the hair of his fellow passenger,
though instead of black they were snow-white, and the ship's arrival
signal was still that of the former ferry, the only long-sustained note
that had reached his ears up to that point in Japan, where from the traffic
lights to the gameboys everything merely peeped and trilled (the temple
gongs always died away too soon for him, and the dark drumming of
water as it shot out over stones poking up through a cataract, a rarity
everywhere in the world, was even more rarely to be heard out in the
Japanese countryside, so difficult to get to).

On the island they became lovers, and he spent a few weeks with her,
during which hardly a word passed between them, in a fishermen's village, where they occupied a hut built on stilts among several similar
ones, each standing on its own spot and painted in its own color, there
along the steep, rocky slope.

During the day, when they went outside, they touched up the paint
and improved the dock, which was given a slight curvature, and who
has ever seen two people, both in overalls of the same whiteness, working
so close to each other and never getting in each other's way? Only people
who had grown old together in house and garden could sometimes
achieve that—but these two were still far from old.

The carpenter's heavy hand became, in loose imitation of Vitruvius,
my friend's Roman ideal, identical with the architect's elegance. When
the two of them, finger to finger, pulled the skin off the fish they had
fried together, squatting hip to hip, the bones formed an arrowhead
pattern in the pale flesh, and in the dim light of the narrow pebble

beach, after midnight a single shell, the size of a fist, shone iridescent in all the colors of the spectrum.

When he set out to leave her, it was understood that they would meet again by the year's end at the latest, and from then on would do every-thing side by side. Through her, the rest of the natives had become more accessible to him (sometimes even too much so for a reserved person like him). After that he had only to seek out certain places—not only the farmers' or fish markets, or the strange village on the northern sea where there was hardly any transition between the boats and the cottages—and the Japanese would reveal themselves in what was to him—this vigilant man from border country—an unfamiliar rootedness, even im-pudence, and, what is more, out of the public eye, lost the tormenting fear of failure they usually displayed there; when among themselves, they cheerfully made mistakes, merrily did the wrong thing.

What he had initially read in a travel guide now acquired another meaning for him: "You cannot get lost in Japan."

This morning, already in mid-autumn, in Nara, the original capital of the empire, where he spent the night in the suite made almost entirely of wood that the woman from Catalonia and I had occupied during our honeymoon, the corridor outside as broad as a street, my friend found the courage to take his first picture of a Japanese no-man's-land, then passed part of the forenoon lying on a temple balustrade facedown, his gaze through the gaps in the floor focused on the reddish, shimmering earth below, just as in childhood he had looked down from the gallery of the house on the karst into the chicken yard below, and in a residential quarter he again witnessed even the natives stumbling over the high threshold of their dwellings, and later he marveled for days over the course he had taken, not merely during this year in Japan but from birth.

He was born at the bottom of a doline, above San Pelagio near Au-risina, on that land he later inherited, a stone's throw from the barriers on the Yugoslav border, brought into the world by his mother during an air raid while she was working in the fields far below, at a turnaround, and he imagined that his birth and childhood in the great hollow of the sinkhole, with the unique sounds characteristic of the place and the very round horizon above his head, had provided a sort of outline for his future life and his profession, also simply when, in his few earlier attempts at building houses, he had always left the roof uncovered—strange carpenter!—open to the sky, citing the example of the Romans, who did not allow the temples to Jupiter, the sun, and the moon to be roofed over.

And furthermore—while here in the bay, amid the leaves blowing in from somewhere all year long, this autumn's first are falling, softer than the others, coming down perpendicularly, at the same time more slowly—he thought today in Nara about how the unvarnished fir planks of the ship and the dining table of nutwood back home had smelled after being washed down with hot water: how spicy, how appetizing. And about the pile of firewood out in the courtyard that reached up to the eaves, stacked almost without gaps, and how he had seen the only hole, down near the ground, triangular in shape, not as a hiding place for the cat but as the model for some future human habitation: he would sit in there himself someday and watch from the warmth the earth being swept clean by the north wind, the Bora, whom his parents called "the purest of women."

And for years he had stared transfixed into the pit right behind his parents' house where there was a bubbling, hissing, spitting, steaming from the lime being slaked, and for years he had also cracked the whip in the orchard on the steppe, using the juniper handle he had carved himself.

And then that cold morning in July when he no longer sat on the bus to Aurisina and Trieste as one commuting student among others but as a first-day apprentice, apart from the other passengers, in his still new-blue stiff work overalls. And how he then, in the Don Bosco Home, felt such homesickness for precisely the shabby spots at home: the worn linoleum under the table, the hot-water reservoir in the woodstove, encrusted with mineral deposits, the burn marks under the ash box, the pitted enamel of the washbasin, the scraped wooden threshold with the rusty nailheads.

And then the years during which he worked alongside his father as a carpenter, outdoors, feeling uneasy only on the day of the topping-out, not because his father would get drunk again, but because his father would not be as jolly from the drinking as all the others.

And then another such cold morning before he set out for the university, across the border to Vienna, when his parents planned to dress him ceremoniously in the cutaway of the godfather who had died in the war, which they had been keeping in a trunk up on the wooden gallery for just such an occasion, black with fine gray stripes and heavily padded shoulders, and this often tried-on garment, which previously had always been still too big and heavy for him, when it was unfolded this time suddenly hung there in tatters, shredded by moths.

Then came the many years until the moment, when, on the great plain down below by the limestone base of the karst, in Aquileia, which had been so close all the time and had once been very familiar, and not only from school excursions, behind the basilica that stood all by itself back in the grasslands between the mouths of the Isonzo and the Tagliamento, at his feet the former Roman harbor filled with the frogs' gentle evening croaking, he found himself completely drawn into that antiquity of which he had previously been conscious only in bits and pieces, actually only a single piece, from a homey, swamp-black corduroy road, a section of alder, particularly swamp-resistant (according to Vitruvius)—the one moment when those couple of logs half buried in the path, which every time had announced something to him rather than reminded him of something, now became one with the once-mighty city of Aquileia, the metropolis of the ancient world, which at that moment did not seem at all vanished to him; it was now, it had arrived, it was his world, his future field of work: "Classical antiquity and I are one."

And then waking up early today in Japan's oldest city, where not even the temples struck him as ancient, for the wood, even on façades thousands of years old, had, as everywhere in this country, been replaced during this century. And looking down through the knotholes in one of the temple galleries, he saw, lying on the ground, the pine needles mingled with chicken feathers and corn kernels from the courtyard at home in San Pelagio or Šempolaj.

And from one of the pagoda towers, story after story, an unbroken chirping of sparrows, of whom only now and then a little flurry became visible, gray on the likewise gray roof. The doves tripping along in the gravel like first drops of rain. At the sight of the nostrils of a Buddhist holy figure, a desire to see a forest filled with apes the next day, for instance in the mountains around Kyoto.

On the way to the station in Nara, my friend encountered a Japanese woman with freckles, at which he thought, "I have a woman!" A sidewalk sweeper crossed the entire broad street to sweep up a single grain of dust on the other side. Behind a bamboo fence the first Japanese dog growled at him. Many of the passersby were carrying on silent conversations with themselves, which, to judge from their hand gestures, consisted chiefly of mental arithmetic. And, as everywhere, children balancing on the curb. On the evening train to Kyoto, talk going across the compartment, as if from starting blocks.

During his walk on the bridge over the already familiar Kamo River, the night wind billowed the sleeves of the mendicant friar there, his face invisible under the rim of his hat. From the open entryways of the buildings, especially the restaurants, wafted the smell of freshly washed floors. On all the city bridges traffic similar to that in Hong Kong or elsewhere, but under them, among the pebbles on the banks, here and there a frail elderly person, and the thought: "When I am that age, I, too, will go under the bridges."

The no-man's-land he had photographed that day had been marked by the concrete foundations of a long since dismantled barracks, emergency shelter after an earthquake, lying there a single stick of wood that was on fire, sending up a tall column of smoke, repeatedly decapitated by the wind. And then, at an afternoon No play, in which the actors kept speeding up their monologues so much that his heart began to race, he had seen another mask that showed him a self-portrait: that of a man caught up, according to legend, "in a one-second dream encompassing his entire life and at the same time aware that, on the contrary, this entire life itself is such a dream"—the expression on the mask one of tremendous astonishment. And outside the city again, on the edge of the wilderness, a Buddha lurking behind the jungle foliage appeared to him as the image of his parents involved in their almost silent work at the bottom of their cultivated doline, where even he, the son, had for decades been surprised and also startled by the faces of the two of them, behind sunflowers, pole beans, cornstalks. And at the end, at the stage of going under the bridge?, it seemed to him as though on this day his many voices had come together into one—if only a rather feeble one.

Yes, the time was coming for his building. Except that on the journey he had little by little lost all his tools. And not for the first time in Japan my friend thought, "I'm not even born yet!" It was certainly the first time that he then thought, "I haven't been anywhere yet!"

6

On an autumn evening in the current year, he, who otherwise dreamt consistently only on the nights of hoarfrost between Christmas and the festival of the Three Kings, had had a dream that stayed with him, in which he was not a priest but a nobody, a creature, his naked self. He stood there in harsh artificial light before the altar of his parish church, and unexpectedly there came from the sacristy a villager who had recently died, after a miserable death struggle lasting several days. He was larger than life and ordered him to his knees to receive the host. In the dream he had not knelt since his childhood, let alone received the "body of the Lord," and for those very reasons the moment became special to him. In addition, the voice of the deceased, who, in priestly garments, had become the administrator of the sacrament, was commanding in a way that he had never heard in a terrestrial being. What this voice told him in the dream it immediately confirmed for all time: no way led around this food; to consume it was absolute necessity; without it you are lost! And although upon hearing this voice for the first time in much too long he felt a shudder of awe go through him, it was not just a bad dream; he did not wake up, but slept on, at first trembling and quaking, then peacefully, and finally blissfully.

That night he got up even earlier than usual, also because he had to work on his sermon for Sunday. From his desk he had a view of the back of the rectory and an orchard, which then, as was usual on the Jaunfeld, merged into meadows and fields without more ado. After morning Mass and his morning classes at the school in B., he planned to pick apples that afternoon and take them down to the cellar, without help, all by himself. And what else today? Lunch with the much younger priest of the parish on the other side of the Drau, in an inn halfway between them; another visit to a dying parishioner; an evening Mass for one who had passed away in Rinkolach.

If he looked in another direction, he could see the unmade bed in his bedroom, which would remain thus until late at night. It was cold in the two rooms, the only ones that were still lived in; no housekeeper to light the stove; and he himself did so only when company came, and even then often not.

In his sermon he wanted to challenge the Pope, in all seriousness, and that soon warmed him. For not long ago the man in the Vatican, in connection with a war in which enemy soldiers had raped and impregnated women, had called upon the women in question to love these children and bring them into the world and raise them in this spirit. What upset the priest was less the assumption that the women would carry to term these embryos conceived in violence than the command to love them. Could something like love be imposed from without, and furthermore from on high, publicly? To praise love, as the apostle Paul had done once and for all in his epistle to the Corinthians, was one thing; but to declare it a law and proclaim it as such, wasn't that entirely different? Certainly he could well imagine that one of these women gradually, or more likely suddenly, might be seized ("surprised"? "afflicted"?) by a sort of love for such a fruit of her womb. But first of all, wasn't that her own business, yes, her secret, and no one on the outside, not even the deputy of God on earth, could presume to approach a human being with a commandment to love. Or at most in private, as priest and pastor, like him, and then not in the form of a commandment but perhaps as a mere possibility, a little pointer.

He, the priest, was angry at his Pope for speaking of something like love in prescriptive terms, and he wanted to express that openly in his sermon (although precisely thereby his outrage would be perceived as part of a game). Wasn't the love of a violated woman for this alien seed more the stuff of a story, a novella, than of a sermon from the pulpit? To be told only long, long after the event? Or perhaps not even in eternity? Something to keep unspoken, a matter only for the mother herself? And might not such love, in the cases in question, have long since gone silently and fervently to work, only to be desecrated by the papal edict? But was such a love even capable of being desecrated, by no matter what interference?

The greatest outburst of anger he had witnessed up to now in his life had come from a priest. It had happened during religion class, in the school in his native village, and the perpetrator had been that priest who was the epitome of gentleness, and not only in the eyes of the children. Instead of singing a psalm as usual, to put himself and the class in the right mood for the reading and narrating from the Bible, he posted himself in front of the class, at first without a word, his briefcase closed and his face disconcertingly red, and it became redder and redder as he broke into shouts so loud that they shocked even these farm children, accustomed to quite a bit from home. Every single one of them cringed, and was overcome with fear and horror, which grew from moment to moment, for the entire hour; for that was how long the priest screamed at the assembled children, without pausing for breath. At first they could make out only individual phrases here and there, like "Judgment Day," "brood of vipers," "end of the world," "wailing and gnashing of teeth," "spew forth!" and only near the end, when he began to tell a story, though still full of wrath, raging and yelling, did it become clear what this was all about: the previous day, upon entering the deserted church, he had caught one of the village children in front of the altar, thumbing his nose and sticking out his tongue at Christ on the Cross. But it was not a simple childish prank; the longer the priest raved, the more the listeners came to see it as the worst offense possible, which could lead only to eternal damnation. Although he indicated that he had recognized the blasphemer, and he was seated there among the others, he did not name him and even avoided looking at anyone in particular. Even though the last word he spoke in this hour was "Vengeance!"

repeated several times, he stressed that the avenger would be someone else. And they all felt implicated; each one slunk away, sure that he was guilty of sticking out his tongue at the Lord from the shadows, and maybe even spitting at Him; even he, who later became a priest himself, and in those days was already the "child of Siebenbrunn," the one with natural piety, had at the very least been an accessory to the crime, and from now on it was all over for him with what had been in his eyes the "greatest fun," the Mass?

Not only a believer but also a little propagator of the faith, or one who animatedly told anyone who would listen about his faith, that was what he had been as the child of Siebenbrunn.

The church, at some distance from the village, at the foot of a hill from which, as the place's name indicated, in bygone times seven springs had actually burst forth, next to the farm of his father, who was also the sexton, from the beginning represented for him an extension and special part of the family holdings; very early on he was entrusted with the key to it: over the centuries erosion had piled up earth around the little sanctuary, more and more cutting down the size of the door; the threshold had been raised, and as a result the keyhole was low enough for him to reach. But for a long time he kept his distance from everything inside the church, and touched nothing. It was his father alone who rang the bells, laid out the priest's robes for Mass, changed the flowers, lit the candles. The boy did not even feel drawn to be an acolyte, and whenever he substituted for someone, finding himself unexpectedly too close to the altar, especially the gilded tabernacle, in whose hollow interior he could actually sense the Holy of Holies, he would feel like an interloper; and he became terribly clumsy, pouring wine on the priest's fingers, spilling incense on the altar steps, and during the entire Mass was scooping up the pellets there before the eyes of the congregation.

The child of Siebenbrunn felt at home only way in the back of his church, whether during Mass, in the course of which he regularly experienced an altered state, by the "Kyrie eleison!," if not sooner, or when contemplating the old paintings, also the frescoes and wood carvings. Before he even learned to spell, he took the situations they portrayed as fact: that was how it had been, that was the only story worth telling, and even if he later found that it was not documented in the specific wording of the Bible, he continued to read the pictures from his church as piously as the Bible. It was thus a certainty that when Jesus was baptized in the river Jordan, an actual dove spread its light-radiating wings in the clouds overhead, that upon Jesus' entry into Jerusalem a youth waved to him from the top of a tree with a palm frond, that when the Blessed Virgin breathes her last, her soul will escape from the lower part of her body in the form of a tiny child, who will in the same moment have already taken his place on the lap of the Almighty up above in the firmament.

And the child of Siebenbrunn told these stories to others for years and years, including to those who passed through that desolate place by chance. He invited the other person, the adult, into his church, so to speak, positioned him in front of the pictures, and recited and intoned their stories from the background, in a voice that emerged from an uninterrupted conversation with himself, which simply happened to become audible from time to time. He believed without reservation and serenely in these pictures—there could be no greater serenity—and lived in a continual state of joy, perceptible also to outsiders. Nothing could shake the faith of the child of Siebenbrunn; it was innate. With its first mirroring in the pictures of faith, life "was manifested," as it said at the beginning of the First Epistle of St. John, a saying he later adopted as his motto. With him, at any rate, a loss of images remained impossible.

Or perhaps not? That "life was manifested": did it not apply to "the Word" rather than to images? Had he, the priest, kept joy alive for himself? "Not really" (he now thought, in the middle of morning Mass, at the admonition "Lift up your hearts!"), "or at least not always."

Did the child of Siebenbrunn still exist? Where was he? And what had become of him? No, nothing could become of him other than what he already was in the beginning! But then how did it happen that nowadays, if he returned to the area of his childhood at all, he tended to avoid his Siebenbrunn and instead sought out the church in the neighboring village, which was almost devoid of pictures, a church that had Job as its patron saint?

Not once had the child imagined in those early days that the priest-hood would be anything for him, although that gentle and hopping-mad local priest had had an eye on him in this respect for a very long time, and then even treated him openly as one of the chosen, for instance because in catechism class he had answered the question as to where the Blessed Virgin had carried her son after the Immaculate Conception, not as the other children did with "in her belly," but with "under her heart."

Only a kind of yearning, unspecific, also undimmed by any trouble-some hopes, was there. No question but that he would become a farmer right after finishing school, since his parents had both died young and his sister could not run the farm alone. Thus he lived for a decade, and then also fell in love with a girl, in fact from the village of Job, and the two wanted to marry. That he was always slightly absentminded did not trouble the young woman; she liked him that way.

What finally brought him to the priesthood was a lecture by an agrar-ian engineer for the young men of the area, given at the local community center and sponsored by the Agriculture Bureau. The title: "A Vocation for Farming." First of all, it dawned on him that he lacked all the characteristics of a future farmer: unlike the others around him, he did not feel at all attracted to the fragrance of livestock; nor did his heart swell at the thought of ripening crops; nor did working outdoors make him happy or even proud; instead, he went about his work as if it were a sideline, like any day laborer, and his thoughts were usually somewhere else entirely.

Once he recognized his lack of vocation, he was seized with a burning restlessness. Instead of to his priest, he turned to the agrarian engineer, whom he looked up in the city of K., to tell him about his fatal lack of interest in farm work. To this day he thought it must have been simply the way he told the story, imploringly, that made the technical expert ask out of the blue whether he had ever considered becoming a priest.

The moment had come. At last he knew what he had to do. Yet he would have kept on farming if it had not also happened that his fiancée understood him instantly—"with glowing eyes!," as he told us—and even encouraged his plan, and that his sister around that same time met a man with whom she would run the farm.

In the beginning he, already an adult, attended a boys' seminary, where he sat in the back and off to one side at a single desk, avoided by the adolescents and mocked as a "manure farmer" (although as a rule these children's parents were farmers, too), and then he transferred to a special school for those called late to the priesthood. There he noticed that all the men, from the most varied walks of life, had at least one thing in common: like most ordinary priests, they had experienced while still children something like a summons or a vocation; except that they, unlike the others, had not felt that it applied to them, and had instead followed a course previously laid out for them. And to find their way to the priesthood they had all needed a second impetus, much later, well beyond their childhood. Things became clear to them and the picture came into focus only the second time around. They had had to rely on that second manifestation of life, which thenceforth remained immutable for them in a way that hardly anything did for the other priests—weren't they, the latecomers, the ones most likely to stay with it for the rest of their lives?

After saying morning Mass, a silent one, in which his lips moved and no word was audible, it seemed to him as though he had taken a breath that would last him all day.

He went, in mufti except for the stiff white clerical collar, which, unlike his fellow priests, he never dispensed with in public, out of the parish church and across the already heavily traveled highway to the Inn on the Bend (on the long since straightened curve) for his café au lait, shoved across the counter to him without his having to order, stood there among the handful of workmen out early, men of few words, clearing his throat like them, and skimmed the already wrinkled newspaper, unmoved by even the most terrible events in the world (just as "his" dying parishioners never haunted him, even in dreams; once out of the sickroom he never returned to them in thought, and also calmly said so to anyone who wanted to know). According to the paper, a recent survey showed that the majority of the population considered priests useful to society, even if they seemed to have disappeared almost entirely from public life; except that, the article went on to say, in the eyes of most people they no longer spread happiness or tidings of great joy.

Then he set out in his forester's vehicle, whose back seat had been removed to make way for a duffel bag, a pair of rubber boots, the slice of a tree trunk, all lying loose like the few tools and apples, which during the trip overland to the secondary school in B. caused a constant rattling and bumping.

It was a dark day, one on which small things showed up as if lit from within, and the world, with the sun in hiding, lay open for a new beginning; the rattling of the tools behind him provided a musical accompaniment. It made him think of the painting by Brueghel in the Museum of Art in Vienna, his first picture outside of a church (seen on the only field trip taken by the latecomers, otherwise always penned up in rural Horn, in Lower Austria), which had filled him with as much astonishment as the portrayals of the Gospel in Siebenbrunn, perhaps also because of its title, but who had given it that name?: "The Dark Day."

But that picture in Vienna had been melancholy and almost menacing, especially because almost the only bright thing shining out of the gloom of late autumn was the ax or knife blade, with which, if he remembered correctly, an almost faceless peasant silhouette was pruning a bare tree, while the brightness of the present dark day appeared now in the round shape of an apple, now in the oval of a corncob, now in the rectangle of a many-colored beehive standing alone on the edge of Rinkenberg Forest, now in the triangle of a chapel's shingled roof.

These objects, registered just this way in passing, brightnesses even for their form alone, appeared regardless of season and had, in their substantiality, in the wood, the fleshiness of the apple, the mealiness of corn, something ethereal as well, which allowed him to feel himself become, for the moment, fruit, silvery shingles, thin air.

Only once, and then for a long stretch, did that brightness disappear, when a series of unharvested fields intervened, filled of all things with sunflowers, probably self-sown, on this farmland that was more and more being abandoned here, each of the many flower heads, which turned or drooped in every direction, darkened, and this black-in-blackish extending all the way to no horizon.

He stopped then, although the children were perhaps already waiting in their classroom, by an abandoned farm along the way, half in ruins, in whose chimney cap on this chiaroscuro day the old live owl was sitting again, even if the only part of it that moved was the amber eyes, following the smallest motion of his finger as he walked back and forth before it, constantly looking up.

Unlike most teachers, the priest did not try to remember the pupils' names; barely glanced at the individual faces. When I was back home for a visit one time and he took me to class with him, the way he ignored the children annoyed me at first. It reminded me of all the priests I had known since I was very small, in whose eyes I, and likewise those next to me, did not exist and at the same time had a duty to be there.

But then it appeased me that my friend at least did not impart religious instruction to those entrusted to him. Not only did every child from the outset receive the same, the very best grades: he also did almost nothing but have the children take turns reading the Bible stories aloud, during which he gazed not at the reader but out the window. At the beginning, he said, he had been the expert on the text, and still the reader himself, and then he had recognized how hollow it sounded coming from his mouth, compared with such first-time readers. Often the children did not even need to puzzle out the text, but came out with it fluently, as if nothing in it were foreign to them, and in the process they captured the nerve of the whole in sentence after sentence.

After that one hour in school, setting out with him on foot, I noticed on the other hand that he knew almost everyone, or everyone past school age, greeting people from afar, and loudly, calling them by name: many of the local people, however, including beyond the town limits, did not return his greeting, not even when he waved and gestured. "They don't want to know me!" he said. And those who responded to him did so without a smile, and hardly anyone stopped to talk. He commented that it was their "guilty conscience," while it seemed to me, on the contrary, that these passersby did not derive any real joy from their priest, and not because he was this particular one. His showing up resembled that of a keeper of public order, whose way of keeping order was not needed, not by the young people, and also no longer by most of the older people. Always he had been well received only when he did not present himself as who he was. And now and then he even enjoyed being a kibitzer for a while, a participant, or a first-name friend to the people in his congregation, in pubs, outside shops, at soccer games. As long as that was all there was to it, and he, laying aside the priest, contributed nothing but his share to the conviviality, he was well liked; others interacted with him as they had perhaps always wanted to interact with a brother.

But every time the moment came when he viewed their continued familiarity as inappropriate, and tacitly expected them to consult him as their priest. And because that hardly ever happened, except far off in the villages (did such places even exist somewhere?), according to circumstances he would make a point of calling attention to his profession himself, no, his position, and so abruptly that his previous comrades would turn away from him in shock, seeing him suddenly as a man of the cloth.

He insisted on it, however. To present himself as this kind of authority from time to time was his duty. Of course he considered himself one of them, if anyone was. Yet it was not acceptable for them to keep letting themselves go in his presence; they had to give heed to his central concerns, at least now and then. In the long run he preferred to be cursed as a preacher than to be their pal. It filled him with conflict that, except perhaps when he was celebrating Mass or writing his sermons, he appeared outwardly to be anything but a "Reverend."

How he loved driving, and fast, especially on this broad, rather deserted plain along the border, where during the period when he was engaged to be married he had even participated in an amateur auto race, with the same number painted large on the Volkswagen that he later used for his laundry in the seminary for latecomers.

Yet Carinthia north of the Drau, where he was headed today around noon, remained, as in his youth, a cold, unfriendly region, almost enemy territory, as if—though this was actually not true, if you looked at it the right way—southern Slavic soulfulness and earth-dreaminess came to an end there, and starting with the northern bank of the river, the landscape, including the fields, which were really no different, and the scattered church towers, were pierced by the gaze of the Germanic front soldiers, extinguished by a word-rattling German-speakingness that kept

everything else at bay. This image—where did it come from?—he had
still been unable to exorcise entirely; not long ago he had looked at the
faces of schoolchildren from the capital city bouncing along in the back
of army trucks on the tenth of October, the anniversary of the referendum
that had joined the southern region to Austria in 1920, and had seen
the faces of these children, obviously gleeful at having a day without
school and high-spirited because of getting to ride in such a special
vehicle, as those of grim volunteers, or at least children who were up to
no good.

Such moods, which he called his "daily dose of dementia," were
calmed now by driving, also by the sight of snow high on the Sau Alps,
which ran across the entire countryside to the north, and finally dissolved
in thin air over on the other side of the rift carved out by the river, at
dinner, where he sat with his "brother in office," simply by virtue of his
now having for the first time that day, not shadowy ghosts, but a person
with clear outlines sitting across from him, and quite a young one at
that, his mouth, cheeks, eyes, forehead nothing but young.

And thus, when his neighbor told him that the sole remaining Slavic
grave inscription in the Ruden cemetery had now been removed, or at
least hidden, squeezed in between the wall and German-gold stones, it
was he who said that did not mean anything; to overlook it would be a
form of strength; what mattered was something else entirely!

And he continued talking, about how urgent a German translation of
the New Testament was, one neither as colloquial as Luther's nor like
one of the more recent ones, pitched to the understanding of the average
newspaper reader, but one that was as literal as possible, from the Greek,
which was akin to German, heart and soul, as were no other two languages he could name.

On his way back he thought he heard from a house standing alone at
the bottom of the rift a loud sobbing, which turned out to come
from the television there.

Out of the river rift, up on the Jaunfeld Plain again, back in his south,
open in all directions, he saw from the highway, at the foot of Rinkenberg's hill, which seemed closer on this dark day, the ancient priest from
the village out walking; he had recently gone completely blind, and was

being led across the fields by a child, his outstretched hand on the child's shoulder, a gesture with which the blind man continued to celebrate the Eucharist in his church, proclaiming the texts from the *Introibo* to the *Ite missa est* by heart.

My friend turned off to the east, to the village called Dob, or in German Aich, where his parishioner lay dying and at the same time a single figure stood waiting at the edge of town in front of that railroad station he had always associated with Westerns, those films he had watched in his youth, and not merely to kill time; in his thoughts he got out and waited there with Jimmy Stewart.

In the heart of the village—there still was one here—by the outdoor clay bowling alley belonging to the restaurant now no longer in operation, he actually did stop, simply to roll into nowhere the one mud-encrusted, half-rotted wooden ball lying around.

Only after that did he enter the house next door with the dying man, who was fully conscious and at first shrank into his corner at the sight of the man in black, hair and eyes also black. What calmed and strengthened him at once was precisely the odd scorn in the priest's gaze, which certainly did not pertain to him, the invalid in the last stages. This man facing death asked for the priest's blessing and did not want to receive it lying down, but instead got out of bed and knelt for it; and thus received Extreme Unction, this sacrament that has almost gone out of use, practiced now simply to ease the conscience of the relatives, to whom the priest in departing indicated outside the door that their father would not die during the night, but tomorrow morning—for a long time now he had had a sense for the moment. And what if he himself died now, this very evening? they asked. He was indignant. "I'm not finished with myself yet."

Alone, heading back to his car, he found the remote village in mid-afternoon still permeated with the freshness of morning. In the courtyards turnips were heaped up; a pear, at eye level, felt heavy in his hand; the mountains forming a great circle around the arena of the plain stood there in a color for which the name "Wyoming blue" came to him out of nowhere. How long had it been since he had gotten away from this region, the entire year thus far. He ordered two youths who were

sitting on motorbikes and talking at the top of their lungs, while repeatedly revving their engines, to turn them off, went to his car without
trying to hear what they were saying about him behind his back, and
himself stepped hard on the gas.

T he only walk he took this day that deserved the name was on a path
through the fields, back to the edge of the Dobrava Forest, his destination the roadside shrine there, from which, on his instructions, a
stonemason was removing the stucco and also the postwar frescoes—in
the priest's opinion not only clumsy but also mindless—so that the little
place of worship would once more have nothing to show but its medieval
stonework, at least for the present.

Now he had his rubber boots on, and also a mason's jacket and cap,
and joined the silent workman in hammering away, one of them outside,
the other inside, and the mason was then fired up by his employer's
encouraging shouts, growing louder and louder as the original structure
became visible and began to shine through (hadn't it originally been his,
the mason's idea?).

And later, wearing the same outfit, my friend back home in his orchard picked clean the one apple tree that had not yet been harvested,
until the last glimmer of day, when, from the foot of the ladder, a man
in a necktie inquired where he might find the priest here, saying the
Eternal Light in the church was not working; he was a traveling candle
salesman, and also sold electric ones (now preferred by acolytes as better
for their lungs). "The priest is on a round-the-world journey," my friend
replied, coughing from the phlegm caused by the candle soot, which
would get worse during the winter, and laughed at the salesman's departing back, neither maliciously nor kindly, just determined to remain
uninvolved, decisively unmoved, as the child of Siebenbrunn had been
taught by his father the sexton.

W ashed and changed and then out again! already in darkness to
Rinkolach, the village at the end of beaten paths, the village
through which no street leads onward.

The affiliated church there was open, except for the commemoration of its consecration, held on a Sunday in summer, only for the few Masses for the dead. On this particular evening it was for a small farmer or occasional farmhand, without any family, who had died a long time ago, from the windows of whose former cottage turkeys now looked out, being raised by the neighbors who had ordered and paid for the Mass for him. Aside from the almost obligatory stranger who had somehow wandered in and sat off to one side, these were also the only people waiting for the priest in the dim church, praying, in Slovenian, the long All Souls' Litany, actually more a sort of invocation, close to singing, and finally, very gradually and very delicately modulating into singing. At first, after entering through the open door, he had merely stood in the background, and they did not notice him until he joined in the last apostrophe, addressed not to the saints but to the Holy Trinity, at a terrifying volume, and also in another key.

The church of Rinkolach (Rinkole in Slavic), on its patch of meadow in the middle of the village, looked from the outside to be about the size of a hall; the inside, of the dimensions of a living room, though for a large family, did not provide enough space in the middle for a so-called "people's altar," and thus he said Mass at a distance from the people, raised above them on the stepped platform, usually with the nave at his back, from which, to be sure, the dove of the Holy Ghost embroidered on his vestments kept an eye on the congregation.

For each sacramental act, performed alone, without an acolyte, he stretched his arms wide, summoning all his strength, as if he were doing work that required muscular effort. At the same time he moved along briskly, without prolonging any gesture; even the pauses during which he collected himself or simply waited showed him in a sort of activity. Just as he spread his arms like a weight lifter, he also snapped open the book for the reading of the apostle's epistle, leafed back to the Gospel, jabbed, with his thick finger, at the written text, hammered, gripping the altar slab with both hands, his forehead audibly against it, fell, with a crash, to one knee, pounded himself so hard on the chest that it echoed, unlocked the tabernacle with a powerful twist of the hand, fished out the chalice with his fist, thrust it toward the congregation—"eat!"— and sawed the air as he delivered the benediction.

Once he had even disappeared in the middle, running to that narrow passageway behind the altar where the wooden structure of the altar, without the gilding, rough, in its unexpectedly mysterious form, could just as well be an old, abandoned flour mill, a part of the flour chute; he remained, as during a Mass in Russia, absent from the action out in front, which merely increased the suspense, and returned only after quite some time, again at a run, for the continuation.

Outside the momentary gobbling of a turkey, the drone of a night plane, the seemingly even more distant screeching of truck brakes.

It was perhaps the last mild evening of the year, and therefore he sat for a while afterward with the neighbors of the deceased on their farmyard bench, long enough for an entire tribe to line up on.

With their backs against the wall of the house, half in darkness, half in the glow of the barn light a little farther off, they sat in silence, facing the barely discernible pattern of the ventilation slits in the barn—in the form of solar rays—hearing the rustling and crackling in the invisible famous branching linden tree (and the hundred-year-old cherry tree) in the middle of Rinkolach, and sat and sat, again as in an earlier time, with which, my friend now thought, something could still be undertaken, something could be done; and not at all sure that with artificial lighting of the dead-end street a "long-cherished wish" of the villagers would be fulfilled, as the community newsletter regularly stated.

How he loved the night wind, the black on black. No star was in the sky. No child was crouching under the bench. A riddle from the old days: "What's lying under the bench, and when you grab it, it squeals?"—"A chain." All across the plain ladders were standing in orchards. In the last train from K. the heads of the sleeping passengers were leaning against the windows, and the locomotive's whistle echoed far into Yugoslavia. A palm tree rustled in the sun on the outskirts of Jericho. In a new German translation of the Bible he would put "confidence" in place of "hope." The woman next to him brushed the dandruff off his coat collar with a hand that was neither cold nor warm, more mineral-like, like flintstone.

And again, without any movement, he felt, in the first hour of night, the approaching morning, this time, however, as something ice-cold that reached into his armpits and then alarmed him mightily. At the same time, he felt "longing" coming back, his favorite word. No, it was a hunger, in the middle of his heart, and it was not coming back, but had been there forever. And then he caught himself also thinking, "No, I did not give up today—not yet!"

What? Did he need a third manifestation?

7

The Story of My Son

To be asked about my son, by anyone at all, has always put me in a bad mood, out of a clear blue sky; it has immediately destroyed the harmony between me and the other person. It was even worse when I was expected to tell stories about him. "Tell us!": the very form of this invitation rubbed me the wrong way, and all the more so in conjunction with my own child. At least one way out was to say terrible things about him, to revile him from afar, and in general to invent atrocity stories about him (which also could be counted on to elicit an entirely different kind of sympathy than when I morosely stuck to the truth).

Even very early on, whenever I told a third person something about him in his presence, he himself would break in, as if his father were guilty of betraying him. In his absence I still suffer the effects of this, such that when I am forced to speak of him I vividly picture his disapproval. But the law of silence that pertains to my son's life, including trivial details (these in particular), originates for the most part with me. Already long ago, even without the child's punishing stare, I was usually conscious when talking about him that this was actually a form of gossip, and inappropriate.

I also strenuously avoid asking other parents about their offspring, and when I happen to do so after all, out of politeness or heedlessness, or heedless politeness?, I feel hostile in advance toward any answer they may give, and then I am sometimes surprised at how enthusiastically they come out with the answer, even in the case of bad news, as if certain fathers and mothers found themselves in their verbal element only when speaking of their children—why else would their conversational tone be transformed into triumphal blasts?

My resistance to telling anyone about my son seems therefore not to follow a universal law. Isn't it actually crazy that I already resent it when a person asking me about my son presumes to use his first name?: "So, how is Valentin these days?"

It is something else again when it comes to telling about my next of kin or ward when no one is asking me about him. Then I occasionally succeed in being perfectly relaxed about it, speaking in a voice seemingly made up of several voices together, so that my son, I am certain, would not only approve but would also feel validated. This kind of storytelling I have inside me. Only it comes out decidedly too infrequently, because it is either the wrong listener or more likely the wrong moment (is there even such a thing as the "wrong listener"?).

And telling stories in writing is something else again. There, without a specific audience, without my voice's getting in the way, not forced to wait for the right moment—that is within my control when I write, which unlike any other activity gives me an awareness of having time —my telling stories comes to me in a way that oral storytelling comes only by pure luck, often invalidated the very next day. Only in written form is my storytelling suited to my nature, on the right path, at home, no matter whom it deals with, even my son.

This has meanwhile become a conviction, reinforced by the observation that all my life, whenever I opened my mouth to tell a story, even if I was bursting with it, I hardly ever found a hearing, but instead alienated others and spoiled their fun. Where was the humor I kept trying to slip in edgewise? Only through my writing and being read was a change brought about.

———

This year, when my son was traveling in Southeastern Europe, almost always alone, I did not worry about him, for the first time. Nothing could happen to him, and for moments at a time this very thought made me uneasy again.

Yet wasn't it true that in the preceding years, at precisely those times when I knew him to be in danger, my otherwise constant worry about him had ceased, replaced by a pleasurable sense of acceptance? And since the dangers, always major ones, had multiplied of late, hadn't that very fact rendered me immune to my age-old worry about my closest kin? But: was he really still my closest kin? And: who was I without my age-old worry?

For example, that time when Valentin was trying to hitch a ride on the outskirts of town and his leg was almost torn off by the kick starter of a motorcycle that grazed him as it whizzed by, and he would have bled to death then and there if help had not arrived immediately, as I left the hospital where my son was lying with shattered bones and went home in the middle of the night, I felt receptive as never before to this particular hour of the night, to the region altogether, and grateful; the way things were now was right; I had shed a part of myself, a part that was past its usefulness. Only an adult could be as light of heart and unshakable as I was then—or unmoved? At any rate, that hour, and the others that followed, almost fatal to my son, gave me a standard by which to measure.

It is not entirely accurate to say that Valentin undertook his journey to track down his father's youth. One stimulus, among several others, was a story I had invented out of the whole cloth, a first-person narrative (a form that always suggests itself when the bulk of the task facing me consists of inventing and playing out the possibilities), the only one of my books he read, actually at the suggestion of, no, under orders from his girlfriend, although otherwise he knows the classics, as well as my contemporaries, from Filip Kobal to Kazuo Ishiguro, also Peter Turrini and Max Goldt, and now at twenty-two, out of fear of soon having nothing more to discover, is a great reader, the only one among thousands, but wasn't I the same in my day? And besides, time and again he has knowingly deviated from the route of my story and has picked up the story again only at intervals, as a sort of travel guide, more testing it than using it ("many mistakes, but apparently intentional ones").

And the money for his trip was almost entirely his own, from working as a disc jockey in various young people's nightclubs and from selling his first pictures; a contribution came from my sister's estate, which, because it consisted of almost nothing, struck him all the more powerfully as an omen. My son sometimes makes so much of his frugality that I have come to view it as one of his main characteristics, like his punctuality, which does not stem from a sort of obsequiousness but rather manifests itself as that of a tyrant, whose time one wastes at one's peril; woe unto him who, regardless of the fact that he may be much older and even more powerful, comes even a quarter of an hour late to a meeting with my son, let alone without an excuse.

Having arrived in Ljubljana on a frosty January day by train, by way of Graz and Maribor, Valentin continued on by bus to Nova Gorica.

At first Yugoslavia was merely a country he had to pass through on his way to his site for a walking tour, Greece. It meant as little to him beforehand as his ancestors. Although receptive to and gifted at foreign languages, new ones as well as old, he gave everything Slavic a wide berth, except the literature, as if its very sounds were an imposition; the music, whether folk songs or the works of nineteenth-century Russian composers, even repelled him; he felt as if his blood were being sucked out by those "parallel fifths, which are taboo, and not without reason, in melody" (whereas I at his age had shivered through entire nights in my pitch-black student room on the Kahlenberg with Mussorgsky).

Nevertheless he could do nothing now, as at other times, but keep his eyes and ears open. In contrast to his father, who in something new often notices an incidental or grotesque feature, or nothing at all, he immediately notices the salient characteristics, and quite casually. I have often wondered whether he, who has this eye for whatever is essential to a phenomenon, and yet, it seems to me, is never astonished at anything, is really cut out to be the researcher he wants to become someday. In many respects he is superior to me—but what is his passion? his dream?

Thus he had now set out, almost too well prepared, I thought, on this yearlong journey, had anticipated every unusual situation and had taken something along for it. But was that really true? Didn't his main baggage consist of a present from the petty prophet of Porchefontaine, Valentin's benefactor from the time he was a child, an ancient Greek biography of Pythagoras, in which the philosopher's guideline for life had less to do with tools and measuring instruments than with untrammeled observation of phenomena and committing them to memory?: thus Pythagoras had had his disciples get out of bed each morning only after they had repeated to themselves the previous day's lessons, and then those from the day before; this retrieval of the day before yesterday, without aids, purely from memory, was, according to his biographer Iamblichos, perhaps the essence of the Pythagorean doctrine.

And thus my son, on closer inspection, had his few tools—his army knife, drawing pencils, a geologist's hammer—more as a sort of ballast, to keep "both feet on the ground." Committing the phenomena to memory was not something he set out purposefully to do; rather he brushed by them, his thoughts elsewhere: "If you expect an object to leave a lasting impression," he told me once, "you mustn't under any circumstance stare at it; you should look through it, though attentively, and only then will the impression be reliable and lasting, and its gestalt will give rise to discoveries more readily from an afterglow than from the thing itself!" (His other approach was to turn away intermittently from his object, intentionally immerse himself in something else, so that, when he turned back toward it, he could "catch it as it was!")

Valentin produced that day-before-yesterday experience often on the same day by falling asleep right after an event, for moments that took the place of an entire night, and, after the first waking up and recalling, falling asleep a second time: now, after the passage of barely an hour, he saw the object in the light and form of the day before yesterday. Wasn't that sufficient as a dream?

A trip by bus on a winter's day, through an unfamiliar country, was particularly suited for this kind of brief, two-time slumber. And thus the "day-before-yesterday effect" assured that even before he reached Postojna, the prehistoric dugout from the moor of Ljubljana that he had just seen in the museum there had engraved itself upon his memory for the rest of his life, its length, weight, peat-blackness, fissured surfaces.

On the bus he had breathed a peephole in the ice flowers on the window, through which he looked out in his own fashion, barely moving his head. They entered an area almost without human traces, deserted and more than deserted, leading into an expanse with invisible boundaries, in spite of the cold already green as in spring, as if made for fruit growing, except that no roads led there, and even the few cart tracks immediately came to an end: this had to be one of those areas that at unpredictable intervals, hardly related to precipitation, was flooded, the result of subterranean water pressure, which made it shoot up like jets from holes in the ground, forming large lakes from one day to the next, which could then be crossed only by boat.

Yet my son took in not the image of the strange landscape but a subject for scientific research: nature as "landscape" did not count for him. He was not interested in looking at things, or at any rate he hardly lingered over that. He immediately, as a matter of course, shifted his focus to the particulars, allowed these to impress themselves on him, distinguished them from one another, and looked for what they had in common.

The first thing he had always looked for, beyond the phenomenon, was its underlying principle. And having detected this, as a rule instinctively, in the twinkling of an eye, he was able, as he then once wrote me from his travels, to achieve "an entirely different view." Except that he did this in passing, kept it to himself, explained nothing (at most uttered, more to himself, his one-syllable "Look!"), and only when he was asked came out with his conclusions, inferences, his always convincing theories, which, translated literally, were of course "observations." Thus in his account of that bus trip he merely mentioned in passing, along with Traveling Band on the radio and the way his nostrils froze during the short rest stop in Vrhnika, the gray that altered from one type of tree to the next—thousands of shades of gray, passing, blinking, flashing by his peephole, and only later, in the spring, during a longer stay on Lake Ohrid, did he set about writing down his "Observations on the Variations in Winter Gray."

———

Then the so-called Threshold of Postojna, a threshold also in a historical sense for all the migrations of peoples through the ages, from east to west, actually more flight than migrations, and more a narrow pass or battlefield than a threshold.

For Valentin, however, this was a mere threshold in the rock, a geological formation. For him there was no such thing as history, and in politics he was a self-proclaimed idiot. He did not even know that the Yugoslavia he was using as his corridor had earlier been Communist, had even earlier been overrun by the Germans, had even earlier been a kingdom, and even earlier . . . If chastised, he would at most have responded that such "earliers" were everywhere, extending back into prehistoric times, and that would be all well and good if everyone did not arbitrarily derive from his particular "earlier" all of—what was it called?—history, and then, from that, exclusive rights to the present. "I learned in school that two thousand years ago this was the Roman province of Illyria, and today in Ljubljana I saw in a window the book title *Are We in Reality Not Slavs but Illyrians?* To me what is real should be first and foremost what exists now."

Now, after the Threshold of Postojna, it began to snow, which it had been too cold to do before. At an unmarked stop by a road through the woods, a schoolchild, his cheeks rosy, stepped in the swirling white out of the underbrush, and did not even need to warm up particularly on the bus; while waiting he had crouched in a natural basket formed of branches, without freezing.

And after the next threshold, the one leading into the lowlands along the Adriatic coast, it was raining, and in Nova Gorica, where darkness had long since fallen, a warm wind was blowing, in tune with the palm trees there, which rustled. From the bus station, a glass shed in a wooded park, walking paths radiated in a star pattern, and Valentin joined the largest group. On this evening he walked along among the unknown silhouettes as if he were a local person going home, and not only because he had the address of the place where I had stayed there.

The offspring of a villager, he had none of the traits of one. Where I had stubby fingers, his had turned out long, narrow, and almost oddly flexible; I could not imagine they would ever display hundreds of little scars like his father's. Likewise my neck, which was squat, or perhaps hunched between my shoulders out of old boarding-school habit, had in him grown freely into the air, also strong and straight, and when he was tired his head never drooped to the side like mine, or to the back, like his grandfather's on the farmyard bench of an evening. At the same time, Valentin had larger feet than I, and his soles had more standing surface than those of almost all the cottagers and their offspring in the region we came from, where people stand better on one leg than on two (one immediately notices, whether inside churches or outside at gatherings, that the men as well as the women, the entire population, are constantly shifting from one foot to the other, just like that, standing next to each other and talking, often shifting at the same time, as if in a preestablished rhythm, giving the impression of a regional dance that consists of constant rocking back and forth, swaying, wobbling).

My son likewise shows no tendency, as we do, when meeting even a familiar person, to become skittish (observation in the Jaunfeld villages: that in everyday conversation, even between neighbors who have known each other all their lives, each looks somewhere else—as if they felt brush by them and flash through them that old uneasiness on soil where they were once only tenants).

And it means little to him that he is an Austrian, or a German, and not merely because he has a Catalan mother. He is neither ashamed of it nor is he proud of anything in that connection; he is indifferent toward it, in a way that seems entirely new to me, as far as one's own country is concerned. As a young person I suffered from Austria—I use this expression advisedly—and thought I was the only one, discovering only later: many suffered. Yes, we suffered from Austria, and differently from the way I imagine a German suffering from his Germany. That a person then became head of state who represented to a T the outlines of our perhaps half-forgotten youthful suffering brought all this back and at the same time made it obvious that this was a suffering without hope, for life.

Valentin, on the other hand, who had been living in Austria for years now, had a few places, or rather spots, there, where he liked to go, and that was enough of a country for him, if he even used such a word. And when I visited, if he happened to take me to them, I allowed myself to catch his enthusiasm, for I noticed how important it was to him that I at least approve of what he liked. Although he had spent most of his time in suburbs, dragged out there by his father, and then eventually reconciled to it, all that now seemed as if it had never taken place, and in Vienna he never looked for a possible equivalent to the suburbs of Paris, unlike me (every time on the very morning of my arrival, as if salvation depended on it). He strikes me as the kind of person—and his entire generation with him?—who is less intent on finding a permanent home than on having hideouts here and there, located neither in the center nor on the outskirts, but usually, almost as a rule, somewhere in between.

Also my habit of walking everywhere means little to him. But when he walks, from one hideout to the next, he moves so quickly, without ever breaking into a run, throwing his whole body into it, that I can barely keep up with him.

He traveled south, crisscrossing Slovenia, from the coastal area back into continental Europe, from early spring into winter and vice versa. For a long time he saw the sea, the Adriatic, only for seconds, from afar, from the limestone ridges. Sometimes, after covering a stretch in the dark, when he had not been able to see anything, the next morning, in daylight, he would take the bus back the way he had come, approximately to the place where night had fallen.

It was already February when he found a place to sit by the harbor of Piran, otherwise hardly a day's journey from Nova Gorica, on the break-water there, my stones of ignorance, in the face of which, when I was his age, thirty-five years ago or the day before yesterday, everything I had learned and all my origins had fallen away from me, and for an afternoon and an evening I had felt nothing but that I was cocooned in the world, a feeling that never came back so completely, if at all, after Piran and that first day by the sea.

From this vicarious refresher course, Valentin sent me a drawing of the stone blocks, nothing but these; the bay and the wooded shore opposite he had erased. Seen thus, with nothing around them, filling the

paper and furthermore executed with excessive precision, the blocks
looked unrecognizable, might just as well be animal heads, cracks in a
wall, bundles of laundry, and were, or created, when I held them up
close to my eyes, just as long ago, for seconds at a time, the image of
nothing at all. Yes, I had seen these objects back then, and myself with
them, as just this pre-creational, unformed. But how could one escape
knowledge in the long run? No matter: my stones were still there.

Hardly imaginable that in the calm bay of Piran such a breakwater
was necessary, and yet farther out by the *punta* with the lighthouse Valentin encountered wall-high masses of pebbles, thrown by the most
recent Adriatic floodwaters from the ocean bottom high over the seawall
onto the promenade, up to the foundations of the houses on the spit of
land, much as a previous storm had buried those saltworks in the neighboring bay of Štrunjan, where the youthful first-person narrator of my
much later "Stones of Ignorance" story, aroused by the salt-white emptiness, hounded by lust for an unspecified woman, who, however, never
appears, then decides it is now or never: he must sit down and write a
book.

This sea, calm as a pond today, tomorrow a raging monster, began to
preoccupy my white-skinned son, previously a rather reluctant guest on
the Atlantic and the Pacific. Yet he saw "my" saltworks only on exhibit
in the Piran salt museum, in photos, with the last remaining objects,
the corncob as the smallest sluiceway possible, the bread stamps the
various saltworks families had had for the bread that was baked for them
in the communal ovens, the hats with extra-wide brims that also protected their eyes and noses from the blazing sun there.

He also studied in Piran that particular gray of the palm trunks, and
in the mild evening on the docks for the first time enjoyed a folk dance,
even the costumes; or he caught a sense of how the dancers enjoyed
finally having such a different performance space for their dance and their
music, otherwise always performed only far off in their narrow Alpine
valleys; here their accordions, clarinets, costumes, and limbs were animated by the wind on the harbor square, serving as a great dance floor,
and open besides at the rear to the salt tide.

———

During the first month of his trip he had not always been so much in the thick of things. From time to time he had even been seized with desolation.

Again unlike me and many of my generation, being isolated, alienated, or dislocated did not give him a heightened sense of reality. (At least when I was his age, it was often the odd twist, the element of strangeness that made me feel at home, synchronized.) Only on his first day did all the unfamiliar silhouettes provide an escort for Valentin; then they took on hostile or at any rate unfriendly features; shifting his focus to music or nature no longer created a protective sphere around him.

For the first time in his life he found himself in a truly foreign land, and this seemed particularly meaningless to him, for he had gone there after all without any necessity. This was not his world, not Europe; these Balkans, of which he had had no image ahead of time, did not allow him to form one even now. And if the streets in the couple of larger cities with their hordes of pedestrians had been great centers for stimulation and relaxation well into the century, including for my generation, they were nothing of the sort for my son now: reality for him was assured only by his few regular hideouts at home in the in-between districts, along with the jam-packed crowds of his contemporaries who frequented them—not even friends.

But turning back was not possible. He had told his people at home about the trip, and until it was completed he could not show his face among them. And yet at the beginning, every time he made one of his morning excursions back in the direction he had come, retracing the previous night's stretch, he was strongly tempted to stay on the bus as it traveled north, and flee back to his own world.

During just such a spell of back-and-forth, at the station in Koper, Istria, which on the previous evening, through the steamed-up windshield of the bus, had been nothing but a rain puddle in the drizzling darkness, the turning point came.

Various factors were at work: the transportation center in the freshness of morning, long and low, with lots of glass, in which the sky was mirrored and through which the sea shone, far outside town, the depot for buses, for a couple of boats, and likewise for trains, whose tracks ended at a belt of reeds, showing a new shade of winter gray, among them scattered vegetable gardens and orchards won from the sea, each populated by one sheep; a saying of Pythagoras, encountered as he read on in the biography: "Every place demands justice"; simply counting silently, and perhaps even the local brandy, helpful this time, drunk outside standing up, with other drinkers, older and younger, at the tent-like snack bar between the end of the tracks and the bus platform.

After that he was healed of his foreignness. He had reached the point of no return, and there my son, who otherwise always had a strange look whenever I asked him whether he was happy, could say he was, yes! No more thinking that he was missing something in his Viennese cellars; and before his eyes a wonderfully long trip. Nothing, nothing, would make him turn back now.

First, however, he went to get some sleep, under a cypress in the local cemetery, on the slope just beyond the tracks, boat channels, and streets, and waking up as if it were the next day, although he had drawn only a few deep breaths, seeing a blond young woman in dark clothing watering the plants on a freshly dug grave, he took the local bus to that very Piran where "the day before yesterday" he had slunk around like a total stranger.

From then on, although he continued to dawdle and also returned to his practice of repeating night trips the following day, his journey took on a sort of élan.

Still on the Istrian coast, in Poreč, he copied off the oldest building there a Latin tribute to a famous man; he, until then completely without ambition, was gradually catching fire for some undertaking or other—"I shall do something"—and wanted a similar memorial to himself one day: "In his honor this hall has been doubled in size," and then forgot such dreams again, for instance spending an entire Sunday in Pazin, back in the interior of the country, knowingly missing one train after the other, while he listened to the doves calling through the city and out into the whole expanse of countryside.

He, ever meticulous, positively finicky about his clothes, discovered shabbiness, or the particular form of it characteristic of Yugoslavia, felt

accepted by the deliberately unpleasing, pocket-sized, shacklike lodgings
as by a reality more compact by comparison with that of the Europe he
knew, stood, soon no longer distinguishable from those next to him, at
bars often set up for only a day out in the open, squatted, leaned, and
lay down among the scraps of newspaper, indecipherable to him, in the
dust and weeds outside bus shelters, forgot departure times, slept his
daily brief day-before-yesterday sleep on the floor of public toilets, curved
in a U-shape around the bowl, by train embankments, also in the middle
of a railroad yard.

Letting himself go was not merely a game for my son now. He even
considered it something worth striving for; only in this way could he
fulfill his potential; only by letting himself go would he also belong to
the others, be less conspicuous and alone.

As for his face, it took only a little, a reddening of the cheeks, a
swollen lip, for him to seem on the skids (at least to me). And on the
other hand it took even less, almost nothing, or just that momentary
dozing off, for the apparent bum to change back, into a young man?
No, rather into an ageless scientist, someone untouchable, the very opposite of the genuinely down and out, for whom, according to Pythagoras, no doctrine was even conceivable, because not even a dream could
cleanse their souls anymore.

Roaming over the Croatian island of Krk, in the company of similarly
scraggly figures, when talk arose of cutting off the braid of one of
them, it was he who in the general hesitation flipped open his jackknife
and hacked away until the victim burst into tears. In Zadar, after an
ashtray was hurled at a mirror, he was beaten up and thrown out of the
bar, and then stumbled along for days, now one among many in that
country going around in bandages and dressings, his on his chin, another's above his eye, that of the woman way up front on the bus on her
knee. Then on the trip to Split it was not the driver but Valentin who
picked the music, well received by all the other passengers; he stood
with his cassettes up front by the windshield, as if at his post, calm, in
his mind planning the right transition from the present tape to the next,
unapproachable, untouchable. And at the bus rest stop in Dubrovnik,
on the Dalmatian coast, he amazed those present by doing one-second

sketches of their faces, so good that one of those whose portrait he had done went parading through the bar, sticking his picture under everyone's nose with a triumphant and also menacing "That's me, see!" And in Ohrid, outdoors, with a view of the sea and the almost bald mountains of Albania, he wrote, from memory, his piece on the different grays of the wintry trees (which in the meantime has won a prize).

Now it stayed light in the evening so long that he did not need to retrace his steps the following morning. But near the Greek border, in Bitola, Macedonia, after the middle of April, shortly before Easter, snow caught up with him, actually only the flash of a few flakes at night by the bonfires in front of the former mosque where chess players were sitting, whom Valentin then beat one after the other. On an unlit side street a mule meanwhile stood motionless by a cart, its head lowered, in expectation of heavier snow.

Although it was just as cold the next day, on the other side of the border, in Florina, Greece, he felt welcome there in a different way from in his father's Yugoslavia. That country, he wrote me, was really not for him, or not right now, though it would be later, and that indubitably. The appearance of standoffishness in the people, even toward each other, was too predominant; their friendliness remained to be discovered, behind the stolidness and the embarrassed scruffiness and coarseness. But whoever would be the discoverer?

In Greece he found himself back in the here and now, after the gloom of the previous months, due not only to the winter. What a gleam in Florina from the watches on the arms of passersby. And whereas in Yugoslavia there seemed to be only one direction and its opposite, here he was caught up in a cosmic confusion, a welter of possibilities.

On the day before Easter his travels took him on toward Thessaloniki, for the first time in a long while again on the trail of me, or of the hero of my story "Stones of Ignorance." And again a long bus trip, over mountain thresholds, and again snow, which in the coastal area became nocturnal rain.

The following morning in the city there was so much traffic that getting from the seaside to the church on the slope where I had found the picture of the Resurrection was an uphill struggle. On the Egnatia, the east-west highway as wide as a river, cars flowed in such an unbroken stream, amid the constant din of police whistles, that the other shore with its façades remained not only inaccessible for a long time but also completely out of sight. And having finally reached the steep, winding north-south artery, without sidewalks, one not only had to hug the old brick retaining walls to get anywhere but from time to time also had to make oneself as skinny as possible, one shoulder leading, one's hands in the fissures in the wall like a mountain climber's, to reach the next switchback without being crushed by the trucks.

Valentin visited the fresco in the church of Nikolaos Orfanos described in my story only after all the other Byzantine sanctuaries, no bigger than chapels and squeezed in among ordinary houses, always very hard to find, and this, too, he at first contemplated only with his researcher's eye: What were the paints made of? Where was the variation in the figures and groupings, seemingly the same from church to church?

And in between, in the open air, he had cast an eye over the equally numerous, but dilapidated, overgrown Turkish-Islamic monuments, especially the moss-green domes of the baths, as if to refresh his retina after all the Christian pictorial sequences, or for relaxation he had gone in any direction where there was nothing to be seen, or down the slope, way down to the smoke-shrouded Aegean sea.

That fresco, too, was in the church, or stone hut, one among too many. It did not show the usual resurrection of the Son of God, but one of the moments afterward. It is a scene such as I, although pictorially familiar from an early age with every Station of the Cross, have never seen anywhere else. It does not show the Son of God risen from the dead, floating up out of the open grave; nor does he encounter, as in the usual sequence, the women with the anointing oil running away. The painter shows an episode between those two. The Savior, obviously just risen, is by himself, and is walking along in his billowing white shroud through an unpopulated landscape, in the background dark mounds of earth with scattered trees, and above a deep dark-blue sky, in my recollection as black as outer space. Aside from his finger raised in benediction as he walks, no action is portrayed except this billowing and these vigorous steps in an early morning otherwise devoid of human forms, yet the eyes as well as the shoulders of this figure returned from the dead are receptive and permeable to all the light and morning air of the world. Who has experienced such a resurrection? And my first-person narrator thinks at the sight, "This is the image with which the world will begin anew."

My son, on the other hand, immune to being distracted by the imagination, which he holds in reserve for his dreams, set the record clear: "black as outer space" was an exaggeration, and besides, as far as he was concerned, nothing needed to begin anew; things were new as it was. And then, in full view of that Easter scene in the Nikolaos Orfanos chapel in Thessaloniki, he suddenly fell asleep, there on the bare floor, and woke up even more quickly than usual, and contrary to his custom not in a reliable day-before-yesterday, but in the middle of nowhere. What resulted from this sleep and the shift into a Pythagorean day-before-yesterday was bad, as bad as could be: he was nowhere, had no father and no mother, had never had them; that business about friendship, which, according to that charlatan philosopher what's-his-name, kept everything together, was a swindle, there was no one backing him up, no one he could call upon, the world, everybody, was fundamentally hostile and evil, he had merely managed to stay out of their clutches up to now, had been sleepwalking, and now that was over.

And that was the whole story, the only story. He was lost, had always been, and now he realized that. And half a continent away, in my study here, at my desk, I heard, through the bawling of a small child in the yard next door, the wails of my far-off adult son, and thought: Well, well, and then: That's the way it is. And then I realized that of all my kin the one about whom I knew the least was my son; I knew nothing at all about him.

The following day Valentin traveled from Thessaloniki southwest over the Epirus mountains in the direction of Dodona, where in ancient times the great oracle had spoken, from amid the groaning of the oak trees.

PART 4

1

The Decade

For a long time now I have been familiar with the southwestern suburbs of Paris. But there is one forest bay I overlooked for an entire decade. Even on maps of the area, which more and more constitute my morning reading, in place of the paper, I failed to notice that the area was settled. As I took my walks deep into the forests of the Seine hills, nothing but silence emanated from there; sounds came almost exclusively from the highway up on the plateau of Vélizy, or the military and state-visit airport of Villacoublay on the other side; only much later, as a permanent resident, did I develop an ear, also at some distance, for the commuter railway, a sort of acoustic ligament running right through the bay, and often pricked up my ears at its high-pitched hum.

Or when I was out walking along the roads, I must have bypassed that bay every time, not particularly meaning to, perhaps imagining that there, on that last small spit of houses, there was nothing more to see, except perhaps a couple of cottages and sheds, very like the ones here along my path, only even smaller and more pitiful. But it seems to me I did not even have any such thought, simply turned off before I got there, because the road also turned off, giving a wide berth to this area, whose only remarkable feature was a tiny Russian church—the diminutive does not make it small enough—there as if by a birch grove.

It was late afternoon on a clear winter day when I wandered into this hinterland, and, following a railroad cut, which gradually rose to become an embankment, went under an overpass, and reached a square that in any suburb would have been large enough to make one rub one's eyes, and was also quite remarkable.

On one side it was bordered by the railroad station, on an embankment several stories high, on all the other sides by buildings huddled together, also distinguished from the previous ones by the fact that every single one was a shop. Nothing characteristic of a suburb could be detected around that extended rectangle, emerging from its surroundings brightly lit by the streetlamps, the shopwindows, the neon signs, the waiting room, animated by the trains streaming into and out of the lower level of the station (on the upper level apartments with laundry hanging out to dry), while the sparrows, looking for a sleeping place, were as audible from the plane trees to the newly arrived observer as the cars, the train whistles, and the one-armed bandits in the three or four cafés.

Not only because of its three bakers, three butchers, three flower shops, Vietnamese delicatessen, North African restaurant, its newsstand that carried international papers: this was a real town. I had an experience similar to that of my friend the painter with Vigo, the place he had entered through a mirror, as *terra nova*, which had been there for ages, a planet unto itself, pulsing and vibrating just as now when he discovered it; or similar to that of Filip Kobal with his karst, where he, who for a good part of his life had been on intimate terms with every pile of stones, had one summer evening taken a step off the beaten path in this little highland, usually visible at a glance, and found himself on a "second karst," right next to or behind the familiar one, with similar desert villages, whose lights, reflected at night here and there in the clouds, had always been present, but for him constituted a fresh, a young light.

———

Thus I, too, upon arriving in this unexpected place, was excited and at the same time sure of myself. There was something here for me to do. Yet it did not occur to me that I could ever reside or live in this neighborhood. I wanted only to work here. The square, with the railroad platforms up on the embankment, would be my field of activity.

And my activity was to consist chiefly of what suited me best, as I had recognized in the meantime: observing. Hadn't I always been a good observer? One whose manner of empathizing had often not merely influenced events but actually created them? Whenever I had taken the stage as a hero or man of action or intervenor, I had made a fool of myself, if not in front of others, then in my own eyes. But as soon as I became an observer, I felt that I was coming into my own, and that my way of observing was almost the only action possible for me. And I remain convinced that actors become gloomy without an audience and go back to war. Yes, all those gloomy competent ones: I would rather be a bright spectator, as when I started out.

Yet my observing had never become anything steady, seldom extended beyond an hour, and besides was more a question of luck than discipline (in the sense of an athletic discipline). But now, immediately upon my arrival, I had the idea of steadying it, by making it my work, "for an entire year."

Daily, from morning to evening, I would do nothing but record what took place before my eyes on this suburban square and in its environs. I would spend the nights elsewhere, back in Paris, or even farther out, in Versailles.

And as my place for writing I had in mind a room on the second floor of the Hôtel des Voyageurs, where, as I immediately found out, one could rent a room for several months at a time. I would sit there close to a view out the window through the plane trees, with nothing but paper and pencil, would also need no table; as a writing surface I would wish for a windowsill as wide as the one back home in Rinkolach, where doing homework would pass imperceptibly into looking out, far and farther, and vice versa.

At the window of the Hôtel des Voyageurs my observing, my empathizing, and my writing would be one. My hand would be guided by nothing but the happenings outside, and if an image, a thought, or a daydream interposed itself, it would be welcome material for my notes, provided it materialized or hove into sight only as a result of my attention to the external world and immediately made way again for this and its yearlong annals.

I pictured my project as child's play, as effortless and free of strain and constraint as I had always wished the work of writing might be. Working while at rest, as part of resting, out of restfulness; working as the great form of resting.

And what did I promise myself from this kind of year of simply recording? Something to read; a book, airy, penetrating, full of discovery, oblique as none had ever been; the kind I myself needed to read. And why should it be set here, of all places, in such a place? And furthermore without a plot? Because it was a place in which I trusted myself to spend an entire year as nothing but a hardworking observer, and because I wanted to read a book whose locale would not grow a second head from previous knowledge, not a Paris book, not an America book, not an Arctic book, and also not a book that would dissolve into mere atmosphere for made-up stories.

In this respect I can say that I believed in the place at first sight, and consequently also saw something to do there. In its presence I felt more unrestrained and at the same time more blessed with space than by the Dead Sea or in the Gobi Desert. And I was certain that here I would succeed, if anywhere, in remaining an observer.

The fact that I would be merely a guest, and only during the day, assured that I would not be co-opted by the square in any way; I would not be in danger, as I might as a resident, of finding myself called upon to participate and abandoning my observation post. And aside from that, the place itself seemed ideal for the policy I had developed over the decades: "Participate by observing!" In this place I was exactly where I belonged with my project, and yet it would never become my home. Any such prospect would have been a threat to me. What I saw before me, however, I experienced as a promise, a moderate and nicely modest one.

An additional factor was that while I was circling the square, slowly and unceasingly as evening fell—a brightly lit stadium surrounded by near-darkness, a rump metropolis, New York's Bronx surrounded by chestnut forests—my ancestors, the dead ones, from far away in the village of Rinkolach on the Jaunfeld, also those interred in the Russian taiga, could be felt walking by my side. What a rare occurrence. Otherwise they turned up almost only in conjunction with those images I had of the future in which I was a resistance fighter in a world war, and they gave me their approval there, and almost only there. But this place and my plan for it meant even more to them. This was the place and the approach that would make them most consistently present to me. Here and thus, with my observing and recording, they could be counted on to be constantly and reliably butting in. And those interred in the taiga would also light my way in the form of a bud on one of the wintry linden trees up on the railroad platform. That was how it was.

And I was also certain that I had something even better ahead of me than the resistance struggle I had so often daydreamed into existence. The locale, my future realm of action and inaction, seemed, as the workday drew to a close, as indestructible as it was inexhaustible. Here there would not be the same danger as with systematically recording one's dreams, which as a result of the process became more and more fuzzy and finally ceased altogether, or were no longer worth mentioning. Here, as I envisioned it, recording things would, on the contrary, cause the events to blossom, day after day. All the objects, obscure corners, and likewise people's gestures, as well as their postures, would present themselves to me for the long haul as unspent, imperishable, always good for a new surprise, in bright contrast to not only Austria and Germany. Here I would not have to begin by summoning up and ordering the physicality of the world by means of scientific, religious, philosophical inquiry, would not have to rely on the miracles of the moment. For me something would be happening, taking place, and revealing itself constantly, and that would be true not only for this one hour but for at least an entire year. There, for me and my way of thinking, was where it was. It was there.

And how did it happen, then, that your plan of merely recording turned into a story, and also hardly about the railroad station, whose double name was at first supposed to provide the book's title? And why are you not sitting at a window in the Hôtel des Voyageurs, but in a house a few streets away, and as a resident, a day- and nighttimer, and as a property owner? And why, during your writing year in the bay, have you not remained that pure, strong observer, but have instead participated more than ever? Where are your eyewitness notes, your annals?

I did not take my project to the hotel, first of all simply because, as it turned out, the plane trees blocked the view from every window (at least during their more than half-year foliage time), if not of the railroad yard, the wooded hills, and the sky, then certainly of the square below, of the happenings down there that I was particularly keen for, of the ground altogether, in the form of earth, grass, pavement, obvious proximity. And furthermore, I did not want to attract attention, and as a hotel guest, as was already clear to me after several test visits, my person would not have gone as unnoticed as in Paris or Versailles, and that would have jeopardized the restfulness of my observing, even if I sat there out of sight. And finally, none of the windows had the table-wide sill for taking notes or even just supporting my arm that meanwhile had become an idée fixe with me. And as a result of my becoming a resident in the place, my field of vision has expanded, from the square in front of the station and the streets leading into it to the entire forest bay, to just the degree necessary for developing and enriching my proposed undertaking.

And the fact that my planned recording, reporting, chronicling, remaining on the outside has become twisted into a story, and a first-person one, stemmed from the recognition, at the very beginning of the year, that I, the writer, would fail with this book if I did not in turn work myself into it, to give the project the necessary vulnerability, like an animal, which during a fight leaves its throat exposed at certain junctures (and it always made me, the reader, feel good when in a book this kind of first-person narrator spoke up and validated the project, and also intervened in it).

And the thing responsible for the fact that my planned sketchy recording turned into old-fashioned sequential narration was another "once more," a dream. Tonelessly and imperiously, it outlined a narrative as the only form I could even consider, gave me an order, which at the same time made such good sense to me that I then obeyed.

Yet I ask myself whether the dream hasn't betrayed me. Is it possible that even the kind of dream that happens deep in one's heart, and pierces one as no daytime image or event ever would, can be false?

Sometimes it seems to me that storytelling has been used up, or that there is something rotten about it, and not only my own. Something like the texture has become threadbare over the course of the millennia and no longer holds together, at least not for a larger context, unless it be a question of war, an odyssey, downfall. (And it is not even serviceable for that anymore?)

But on the other hand, the contention that storytelling, the book-long variety, cannot do without catastrophes is something I have never understood. I challenge this alleged principle. It should not be considered valid anymore. I want things to be different.

And that became the source of conflict in my activity. Many features of the area here have lost their original magic over the years, and in the process, the bay, at least in its totality, has come to seem no longer worth telling about, certainly not because I have become accustomed to it or because I am getting older—that with age pleasure wanes should also not be considered valid—but, perhaps, because I, now a resident, have succeeded too little at preserving my distance.

And thus even in this place, ideal for my project, I drifted more and more into the kind of judging that makes me disgusted with myself, and furthermore is destructive to the imagination, the best part of me. How determinedly ignorant I was in the beginning, as far as people were concerned, how wonderfully opinionless. And now? How I left the local passersby alone in my thoughts. And now? Torn between my exuberance here, my distaste there (at the thought of another Sunday with the various generations in warm-up suits on the railroad station/market square, of the thousandth mountain-bike rider zooming through the quiet underbrush, no doubt a great thrill to him), I then see only one possible way: to go back to my initial idea of being purely an eyewitness: look, register, record; the storytelling part as a sideline, and also never pre-meditated, rather, just as it comes, as a by-product of reporting, which would remain the underlying tone.

With my eyes and ears I practice this daily, and succeed time and again in making a snap judgment transform itself into the lasting plea-sure of perception, of having-one's-five-senses-together with the aid of the chronicler's role.

Yet when it comes to writing things down, that has not worked out. Whenever I tried to achieve this kind of objective recording and wit-nessing, in the middle of the first sentence things would twist and turn on me into a kind of premature storytelling, even prattling. Was it conceivable that nowadays there was nothing left in the world to tell, merely the compulsion to tell stories?

On the other hand—my conflict—I encountered here, and again daily, so many phenomena for which inventorying, reporting, noti-fying, in short, any kind of naming, was just wrong or simply impos-sible. The only thing to do was to let them be—by telling about them, or circling around them, or touching on them, or letting them resonate, or letting their vibrations die away. And together with the area itself, these phenomena included, for some extraordinary mo-ments, inhabitants of the place. (To be sure, I have almost nothing of the sort to tell about the usual adults, only about certain children, many old folks, and from one to three joggers or indefinable types.)

Even when telling about these phenomena does not promise any coherent narrative, I still find its preliminary form—observing—fasci-nating as nothing else can be. This is my form of participation, and participation is music enough for me, and storytelling is the music of participation.

The chronicle does not correspond to what I continue to intuit, beyond the profound dream: the chronicle does not correspond to humanity. Only when the facts, the blind facts, thousands of them, can shed their scales, get clarified, and acquire language-eyes, one here, one there, am I, leaving the chronicler behind, on the right path, the epic path, and life, once so deprived, is enriched.

And thus I muddle along, having faith in spite of everything, follow-ing that dream, and continue to circle the epic it called for. If nothing comes of it: that's good, too. I have long since stopped being wild about doing it right. Wrong directions, wrong moves: all the better.

In truth, the situation is more dramatic than that: my panic long ago at what I could only much later call the "metamorphosis" arose, after all, when I, about to write a story, in a flash lost all certainty that deep within me a new story could always be discovered and brought to light every time I sat down to write something, a story that in the course of the sentences and paragraphs would unfold on its own, without my plucking and plotting. And I could not get on with myself, with the book, with the world until I found the other certainty that within me was, if not story after story, then something even more disarming, something that did not merely postpone the end like the stories of the thousand and one nights: storytelling, inventive in itself, independent of particular inventions.

But what if such storytelling, too, stayed away, forever, and that were the signal for the next metamorphosis, again like a fight to the death? Metamorphosis? And what came afterward? If even storytelling lost its universal significance, did anything at all come afterward?

Since the beginning of this year I have been swept back and forth. At one point I see myself traveling along, in conjunction with my undertaking, in some airborne vehicle, brand-new, spanking modern, which for short stretches dives into dark, narrow passageways filled with screeching skeletons, and then again the whole thing appears to me on the contrary as an interminable trip through a tunnel of horrors, with the wide-open, naturally colored outside spaces barely glimpsed as they flash by for an instant before the trip continues for days through nothing but black backdrops with swinging scythes and bared teeth.

I had been living in the area for a long time before it first revealed itself to me as a bay. Previously it had appeared to me this way only in a figurative sense, for instance late at night in the most remote bar, with a couple of silent men standing at the counter and others asleep at

the tables, along with damp-shaggy stinking dogs, when I envisaged a
sort of flotsam that had slipped past all the other massive and more
densely entangled debris and had finally been driven and washed in here,
one piece at a time, to this last station or remote "bay."

That my domicile in fact has the form of a bay was something I finally
saw one day from the ridge that traces a wide curve around it, and in
addition I had to be standing way up on the catwalk at the top of the
transmitter; from its base, even from the middle levels, the settlement
below remains, if not hidden, at least unclear in outline, as a result of
the wooded slopes that run down toward it all around; it looks as though
the large, pale deciduous forest continued through the hollow, rising
on the other side in the west to the next, unchanging, but already far-
off glimmering hill country.

The transmitter, set in the middle of a convergence of roads and wood
roads, is usually accessible only to authorized personnel, but I got in
through the good offices of my petty prophet of Porchefontaine, who, in
between two restaurants while one of them was in bankruptcy, was man-
aging a canteen there in his inimitable fashion.

To have the settlement's houses, seen from up there almost all equally
squat, almost all with light red tiled roofs, at my feet as a bay, thrust
deep into the wooded heights, which were otherwise of an almost unbroken green, mimicking crown by crown the mounting rows of an
amphitheater, arching toward the horizon: that meant something. I stood
before this form of settlement as before a discovery. This bay was at once
so small and so large. And in retrospect it now seems to me as if a
column of smoke were rising from every single chimney, straight, narrow, almost transparent, and one close by the other. A former refugee or
work camp, erected for perhaps a month on an extended clearing in the
midst of the wilderness, had become a permanent settlement, and merely
as such had opened itself up to the ordinary suburban world outside, if
only along a narrow corridor, as an access channel; the streets still recalled, and not merely when seen from above, the grid of the camp, just
as the houses, no matter how solid they seemed, appeared in this bird's-
eye-view borough to have been pushed around like temporary huts or
tents and to be standing every which way.

From the top parapet, dizzyingly high above the treetops, of the transmitter skyscraper (which strangers often take for a second Eiffel Tower, transplanted to the Seine hills), I heard, with all of Paris visible over my shoulder—white on white except for the golden dome of Les Invalides and the iron black of the original Eiffel Tower—far below in the backwoods bay, scattered guard dogs from the camp barking, and also a rooster crowing in response, while the sound of the frequent commuter trains was swallowed up in the whooshing of air currents around the platform; the only other sound that made its way up here was the whistle of the long-distance trains speeding back and forth between Paris and Brittany, on the second rail line, which I now recognized as the bay's tangent, as the divider between it and the open sea of houses to the west, in the direction of Versailles.

The silence there in the depths of the bay seemed at the same time powerfully alive; it was an active silence, on land and likewise on water, on the two fishponds, both taking up approximately the same area as the two other largish gaps in the delicately laid-out thousand-dice game of the houses: the playing fields of the towns that share the bay area. One of the one-engine planes just flying over would lower its landing gear any minute now and touch down on the main pond as in the Alaskan interior, while from the woods along the banks a long column of camels would appear, riderless and unescorted, and by the edge of the other pond, in mammoth oaks, the temple monkeys would be chattering, and from the bus station on the most distant rim of the bay the bus line with light blue horizontal stripes would take you to Providence.

Any longing I might have for far-off places was assuaged by the sight of the bay. And my homesickness was long gone, and now, toward the end of the century, hadn't every kind of homesickness vanished from the world, like a disease that has been conquered? And in that place I would no longer need any distraction or concentration in my life, no movies, no games in a stadium, no strolling down a boulevard, no sitting in an outdoor café, perhaps not even any reading. Compared to perceiving, inventorying, and reporting the things that appeared there, I thought, all the rest was a waste of time.

And finally during that hour, from my lookout on the transmitter, I picked out my own house down in the bay, or just a section of its roof between the chestnut tree in the garden and the pair of cedars just beyond. In the midst of the patchwork of red, green, and gray all around, it was further marked by the dark line of the narrow lane, which, over-arched by shrubbery, led toward it like a tunnel. I was already living alone on the property at that time, without my son and without the woman from Catalonia. Did I also have no need of friends anymore in my bay? Didn't I need anyone anymore?

For years I could not imagine that there might be any palms in the surrounding area besides that one in the otherwise treeless courtyard of a cabinetmaker's shop. It looked as if it were set in concrete, and had apparently been there much longer than the workshop, and not until I had passed the second palm, which I had overlooked day after day, did my search for palm trees begin, with the certainty that there would be no end to finding them, and by now I have reached seven.

It was similar when one day in the local deciduous forest I unexpect-edly found myself standing in front of a larch, looking, with its shaving-brush bunches of needles, as though it had blown in from an area of high mountains; in the meantime I have discovered all around the bay entire groves of larch, seemingly hidden yet out in broad daylight; and similar, too, when one summer evening, by the road, which, if any, is the main road, in the place where it grazes the forest and has a bank, the most splendid edible bolete mushrooms lay, with lemon-yellow flesh, probably scattered by children playing, the special kind called *cèpes de Bordeaux* in France, since which time, in my mind, the bank has always been called the Bordeaux bank: over the years I later discovered that the forest around the bay was a paradise of these mushrooms; in the current year alone I have brought home several hundred of them, and what nicer and better weight in the hand?

And much that I could not have imagined here beforehand has re-vealed itself to me and put me on the alert or made my eyes open wide, and that will continue, not only as long as there are children, who hardly miss anything when they are playing; as if the same thing were true of the bay as of the largest borough of New York, about which someone once said, "Only the dead know Brooklyn."

———

But even though at that time I stumbled upon my house in just that
way—so to speak in the footsteps of the children out playing—in a
spit of the bay that had previously eluded me, to this day I have not
been able to track down another structure related to it. And yet I am
certain that somewhere there must be another house of this sort, designed
by the same architect almost a century ago.

Be that as it may: on that long-ago spring night, after I had turned
off for the first time to look at the house I had always overlooked, which
I knew instantly would be mine, I forgot for the time being my plan of
writing down day by day my year in the area. I stood in the half-darkness
up on the railroad embankment, the only person waiting for the last
train to Paris, and imagined that after moving in I would do nothing
but live there for an indefinite period, and I saw that as an activity that
would occupy me completely. Furthermore, no one, not even my friends,
was to know where I was. No one in the world would visit me here, and
this image, empty and at the same time spacious, branching out, gave
me the sensation of being showered under my arms, and I felt wondrously
refreshed.

From the beginning I thought of myself as alone with the house, also
without the family that we had become once again at that time. Just
me and these night-black rain puddles, as at a railroad station on the
border, and all my kith and kin over the hills and far away. To inhabit
the house and the place in this exclusive way, to do nothing else, also
to make no new acquaintances—how robust that seemed to me, how I
could picture myself caught up in such a project.

The following months we spent waiting for the house to become available; we were living in one of the painter's Paris apartments, with a
tree-rustling inner courtyard, in the midst of the city, the broad Seine
right around the corner, crossed by the Pont Neuf, the bridge on which
the woman from Catalonia and I had once agreed we could spend our
lives, going from one bank to the other.

But I was already feverishly looking forward again to my move into
the suburb beyond the ridge of hills, and every day spent the entire
morning hiking out to my property; when I skipped that, I saw the day
as lost.

I made a point of approaching the house from all possible directions, and then walked past it without stopping. A glance out of the corner of my eye at the place, barely visible from any vantage point, and the day had taken on color.

And each time I set out alone. No one was to accompany me, not even Ana, who had said that the house in its wide, hummocky hollow of a yard looked like something out of a fairy tale, by which she meant she felt closed off from the world there.

From the list of previous owners the lawyer had given me, I knew that the house had been occupied almost exclusively by retired folk—a general, a plumber, a professor of ancient Greek, a gravestone maker. My immediate predecessor certainly appeared to have been constantly busy in every room, with shelves of binders, computers, specialized maps of the most distant parts of the earth. But I later learned that he had been unemployed for years. Along with the house I bought the garden tools from him, not only rakes, shovels, and hoses but also the power equipment—lawn mower, chain saw, hedge clipper, even something like an edger—only Flaubert knew the proper name for it—the smallest of the power tools, which at the same time made the most noise, and that was how it was meant to be, as I was told later by a neighbor who worked in a factory that manufactured such tools.

I did this with the firm intention of taking care of things as much as possible exactly like those before me and those around me. Yet to this day I have not even started up most of these instruments, and various neighbors, seeing me hacking away again with my bare hands, have offered their help with the words "I have power tools!"

A m I entitled to call that first evening in the house "ours"? On the one hand I saw myself as having arrived as never before —the opposite of what the woman from Catalonia had hinted about the building and its location—in the external world. On the other hand I felt hostility toward the presence of my son and my wife. I wanted to be alone with the house, bare yet livable, the doors and windows wide open to the warm July night, its darkness so uncitylike. Or at least no one, not even one of my near and dear, was to obstruct with face and voice the admission of the outside world into the house, the lights from the transmitter flashing in from the eastern hill, the rustling of leaves in the garden and of the trees in the forest wafting toward the house, late trains chiming in, the coolness from the pond waters drifting by.

I turned off all the lights in the house. Valentin went up to his room. I sat at some distance from Ana, on the floor by a window. I had forgotten those entrusted to me. They did not exist.

From the darkness outside the silence spoke to me, on and on, and breathed in, from room to room. That was how it should go on speaking forever. And my house should continue to be as empty as this. And on this night I would not touch that beautiful strange woman somewhere over there.

It did not work out this way, however, and even before winter the house had lost its initial emptiness. If during those first weeks my only connection with the everyday world had come from listening to that transistor radio no bigger than my hand, and then almost exclusively Arab music from Radio Beur, from the metropolitan nowhereland beyond the hills, from time to time we came together of an evening in front of a television set; the turning of the pages of a newspaper, even if it was my own doing, sounded to me like the crack of a whip; books piled up wall-high, when I had wanted to have an armful of them at most in the house, and those as much out of sight as possible, in the closet under the stairs or in one of the many wall niches, of which I still cannot keep track; my wife's things spread from one bare spot to the next; on the table the tiny little garden flowers and wildflowers were elbowed out by florists' bouquets, which, furthermore, against my intentions, were purchased not here in the suburb but in the metropolis; and the lamps, hardly larger than clothespins, and also like them clipped on here and there—a temporary arrangement that I as usual had thought of as permanent—were replaced by lanterns, "remember the ones on the bridge between El Paso and Ciudad Juárez?," and a chandelier from a plantation house in the American South.

A friend (the carpenter, the painter, the reader?) on his second visit praised the improvement in livability; one could feel a woman's hand at work. Yes, I had not kept to my resolution not to let anyone in here, or into my new region at all.

And it was not only my friends who came, who were shown around the house by me, who slept in a guest bed (which, now that I am living alone, is mine, because right next to my study), who gave advice, who also blocked out the emptiness round about in bars and on wood roads, but also people with whom I had nothing to do except to let them interrogate me, persuaded to do so by the woman from Catalonia, who decreed that my concerns were public, and it was my duty to behave accordingly.

What about that metamorphosis? Was it even still in effect? (Luckily most of those who made their way here had eyes neither for the house nor for the surrounding area—which on the other hand annoyed me: I wanted even them, the strangers, now that they were here, to be pulled up short at least now and then, to look and listen and then perhaps to let me tell them something about the place.)

No, after the first quiet summer nothing about my life in the remote bay remained the way I had sketched it out for myself. A new publisher stopped by, coming from the funeral of one of his authors, the twelfth in the current year, and on his way to the University of Montana in Missoula, where he was to receive an honorary degree, and sat facing me with barely contained disapproval, directed if not at me then at the too small chair, which squeaked and creaked under his weight. All my Catalan in-laws gave the property the once-over, and Ana's mother was convinced the balcony was about to collapse, while her father would not want even to be buried in such a poorly lit suburb, indistinguishable at night from a Transylvanian forest, and with the strangest bunch of hut dwellers swept together from all over the world, and sang the praises of his Gerona and the Catalan nation.

I just barely managed to avoid being talked into a wine cellar, and remained true to my idea that the birds flying past should suffice as pets (though the house was invaded by the barking of a wolfhound right next door, which my new publisher said he would buy himself, too, if he lived in such an area).

Whereas one favorite saying of the woman from Catalonia was "No, no, no!" I myself could hardly ever get out a single no. I never really resisted that, and in the first couple of years in the bay, with the monthly and then also weekly interruptions by visitors, often from far away, of the invisibility I had promised myself, I took satisfaction in this peculiarity for a time. There were moments when I harbored the thought of creating a center in this area, without a groundbreaking or public announcement, simply by regularly inviting one person or another, whose work or style of idleness appealed to me, to come here over the hills and be put up in my house or one of the hard-to-find inns in the bay, preferably in whichever one was being operated just then by the prophet and bankrupt restaurateur, at that time still a station away from Porchefontaine, who could be counted on to contradict my guests, with me as a mere listener. Even if they happened to be very famous, my visitors would have no need to worry that they might attract attention in this area, and that alone had to yield something positive. No face from film or television would be recognized here. At the very most one of the local residents would be taken aback for a moment, but would promptly calm down, thinking it impossible that the person over there could be Michelangelo Antonioni, or, let us say, Eric Cantona, P. Zaroh, Pedro Delgado, Pane Secundo, or Ama Nemus—for never would such celebrities come to our remote corner of the world, even to drop in. I conceived of this center as neither an academy nor a school, though perhaps Pythagoras' rule about mulling over with others the day before yesterday influenced me, to the extent that I imagined that by retracing our steps this way in our minds, instead of changing fundamentally, which was probably what the philosopher had had in mind, we would see what we were made of. Thanks to my argumentative prophet and even more thanks to his cuisine, this project actually got off the ground, but it soon fell apart, for one thing because by myself I was not enough of an audience for those celebrities, for another because it turned out that strangely enough those who were invited felt a need to be recognized out here after all, and by more than just a few. When they went unrecognized, almost all these famous folk remained silent, actually seeming offended. Or at any rate they were not generous with themselves. Or did none of these people, so dear to me from afar, ever want to let down their guard? That, to be sure, was what I would have wished for, among other things.

Thus during my entire decade here, to the present day, I have never been able to give a party either in my house or in the region for a single visitor—and in the meantime almost none come anymore. That, too, I have not stopped wishing for, if only for just one time.

Never would I have believed that it could be a source of pleasure to live in a house and have the title, the legal title, of owner. Yet that was what it turned out to be in those days, even beyond that first period with the almost empty rooms, and more than that—a joy.

I felt impelled to live in accordance with it, this joy, and that meant more attentively. I resolved to treat my house, just as it was, more carefully than anything previously. I decided not just to treat it gently, but also to give it the benefit of constant observation, including the inconsistent shapes and ill-chosen colors left by the succession of previous owners, along with the harmless peeling and weathering. I then felt annoyed with myself for so much as letting a door slam or pressing a latch without thinking.

My property made me pull myself together in my dealings with it. At the same time, I wanted to use it and make it fruitful (and not only the kitchen and the orchard section of the grounds), and that without adding anything; everything had to remain the same, except perhaps for a fresh coat of paint and a new shrub here and there.

Using it in this sense could mean that I simply went from one to the other of the many nooks and crannies in the house as well as on the grounds and did nothing but let the effect of this spot in the beech thicket, or the shoe closet at the bottom of the cellar stairs, or the room with the stalactite-like plaster, sink in for as long as possible. And time and again it was as though in the process that particular dream of mine was fulfilled in which an undiscovered floor turned up in a long-inhabited house, with rooms like the chambers in a castle, all of them with quiet festive lighting, all of them having stood empty for a long time until I entered them, at the same time filled with an expectancy that now merely strengthened with my presence.

As an owner I also rid myself of certain opinions about right and wrong, beautiful and ugly objects.

Thus among other trees in the yard there was a pine that I would otherwise have judged did not belong there; its place was in a forest. Yet now I thought nothing of the sort, but instead rubbed the smell of the fresh shoots under my nose in springtime or from time to time soaked up the special pine wind rustling through it, no different from the sound I had heard long ago on the edge of the forest in Rinkolach on the Jaunfeld Plain.

That the weeping willow next to it, a sight that would earlier have made me gloomy, now appears differently to me, I owe to what I heard a workman in the bay say one Sunday evening about such a tree as he stood in front of it with his family: "They're lovely, these weeping willows" (although his voice sounded subdued).

I wanted my fellow residents in the bay to see the owner in me, yes, in their eyes I should be nothing but the owner of this house here, of these grounds, of this narrow, gorgelike lane, in the same sense as on quite a few tombstones in my place of origin, instead of the person's profession, beneath the name was inscribed "house and property owner" —except that in my case they would not even know the name. The most they would glimpse of me was a silhouette at the window, by the garden gate, in the lane, and they would say nothing but "Ah, there he is, the owner, the same as yesterday, the same as always!" with an undertone of relief, as if my being there like this contributed to their daily sense of security.

It may be that all this led me to feel, if not like the owner of the entire area beyond my own property, then at least responsible for it, especially since hardly anyone else seemed to care about the place, to see himself as one who also had something to say and some say, if only "Out of the way!" "Don't build here!" "Don't you dare cut down this apple!" or even just "Quiet!" Although not borne out by the facts, it seems to me as though my chief occupation during that first period in the bay consisted of such using and cherishing, guarding and defending.

When did the woman from Catalonia disappear for the second time? One can almost describe it as "an entire lifetime" that we have been playing the game of losing each other. Perhaps we are both convinced that nothing can happen to us, we will never be finished with each other, and thus push the game to the limit, keep putting off the serious part, or what is real in us, longer and longer, until suddenly there will be no going back, and one of us will be irrevocably lost to the other.

It is a dangerous game, a sinful one (it was not my friend the priest who said so, but I myself); for we see that we should stay together, even without the formal sacrament, in glory, and that it would be a dreadful shame to spoil it. "Fragmentary experience—complete dreams": in this belief, too, one of my favorite mottoes for many years, Ana resembles me.

So it was always for only moments at a time that we were serious with each other. And but a moment after such a repeat honeymoon we might run into one another, coming from different directions, and cringe; so thoroughly had we forgotten the other person's physical reality in no time at all.

Very often the intimacy we had just experienced would be transformed abruptly into mutual rage. Who was this man? Who was this woman? The house in the bay, not so much roomy as full of odd corners, favored such estrangements, and as far as I am concerned, so did the fact that I was infatuated with my property, or, to use an old expression, I "had a fancy for it." Such a fancy tended to have a paradoxical effect. And once more Ana and I used the game of loss to put off thinking about our true relationship with each other, put it off until the relationship was over. With each new day of grim dissension she and I both thought to ourselves that there was still time to find our way to the relationship we had had before, and one day: too late. It was the end not only of the game but of the two of us. And now, in retrospect, too late, I think: we were not really those two who once walked toward each other on the bridge to find harmony, nor those two who wanted to destroy each other with their bare hands, but beings of a third sort who had not yet been discovered for one another.

2

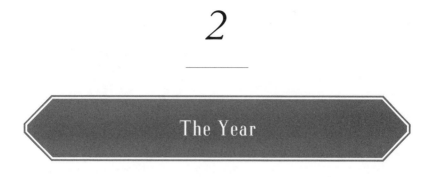

The Year

I almost missed the right moment for telling the story of or reporting on this particular year in this region.

For one thing, it seemed to me that simply by living, walking about, taking things in, I had already written the book, that each day in itself was at the same time the day's work, and explicit word-making was more like a superfluous addition, a retracing, that would result in gratuitous ornamentation; for another thing, now that I had already spent several years in the bay, it was too late for such a one-year report, because, always thinking "too soon, too soon," I was waiting for the aforementioned right moment, instead of simply beginning at some point.

This is what I finally did, actually with little faith, half convinced that the execution of my plan was a mere re-presenting, and was also taking place at the wrong moment, too late, or perhaps too soon after all. But I did it, and with the very first sentence all these hesitations were gone. (They were replaced and intersected by others.) I, the writer, was now the one who decided; and if I was ever anything, it was the writer. I experienced that once again simply by sitting down, as after every longer intermission, and writing—from the activity itself.

First of all I decided what would not be included in my notes on one year in the bay. And what would be included would not be decided in advance; to paraphrase Wittgenstein, or simply to play with language, it would dis-cover itself, and in my writing down of things I would follow it.

What would not play a role but at most be mentioned: anything I had not experienced myself as an eyewitness, or verified, at least after the fact. Thus in the course of this year the statue of the Blessed Virgin was stolen from the pilgrimage oak at the edge of the forest. And upon hearing the news I went there and first observed the empty spot up in the fork between the branches, then, a week later, the plaster replacement figure, obviously mass-produced, and finally the original, which had turned up again. And I found out only from the bay's weekly newspaper about the old lady who left her house one morning and with her diamond ring scratched the paint on all the cars parked on the main street, and yet I felt as though I had been there.

What they call world history was also to be kept out as much as possible, less because of my dislike or distrust than in recognition of my weakness where not only that but also all major events are concerned: I do take an interest—and television does not prevent my feelings from being profound—yet I could hardly say anything about these events, let alone write anything. Not that the world's seemingly endless obstacle race leaves me speechless. It is only that in this connection images very seldom occur to me, images which, I sense, I would need in order to say anything, and when they have occurred to me, they have not once provided me with the necessary opening bars.

My weakness, with regard to both the horrors of history as well as the things that occasionally move me profoundly, is that I cannot transform them into images and cannot fall into a rhythm, as for instance William Shakespeare could, and who else? History becomes an image for me at most later on in my dreams, often even a compelling image, but then without a context, and if there is a beat to it, it breaks off every time in the middle, and furthermore the period in which the action occurred has never been my current one, generally agreed to be certainly epoch-making, but each time a past period, already almost legendary, once with Goebbels as the protagonist, transformed into a saint, during his last days in Berlin, another time with Nicolas Poussin as the main character, during his unhappy year as court painter in his native France; or the dream took place at the end of time and of history, on the day before Judgment Day.

But I persist in my weakness. And who knows whether things may not be different someday? Whether world history will not eventually give me a coherent dream? And who says I have to wait until night for that? I'm thinking incidentally of my brother, probably the only master our village of Rinkolach has ever had, master in a trade, and his lifelong struggles with his country, his religion, his contemporaries, himself, his desire for victory, his desire for self-destruction, his ghosts—indeed his "preparations for immortality."

A long time before I set out to record this year of 1999 in the bay, visits to me had already become fewer, and in the last months, the months of preparation, they ceased altogether. As a result of my son's moving out, then my wife's, the house gleamed freshly in the emptiness, a little also the shabbiness, of this new beginning, and I asked myself whether it wasn't being completely alone there that I valued above all else and for which I had been fiendishly scheming all the time, not unlike a long-premeditated crime. ("You can't share your rustling of the trees and your trembling of the grasses—except in the book": Ana.)

And after the initial befuddlement, then desolation, then longing for death—no, it was thoughts of doing away with myself—I was in good spirits, nothing else. I undertook no more journeys, not even short ones within the country. Instead I set out on foot every morning, even often in the winter rain, beyond the area, in all directions—except toward Paris—farther than ever before, and undertook actual marches through mud and night away from the bay, also as though I had something to be afraid of there.

I read hardly any newspapers anymore and no books, except the pamphlet in which the stonemason from the transitional period between the Romanesque and the Gothic told in fragments the story of his Middle French forays: "The New Cathedrals, Building the New Tower of Babel."

Likewise I stopped making notes, put the pile of filled notebooks away in the most inaccessible cupboard, took down the maps of the Seine hills and the aerial photographs (smuggled by someone out of the air base up there for my purposes), wrote no more letters, removed from my desk the stones, wild apples, falcon feathers, and other fetishes, leaving only a row of pencils almost the width of the surface, most of them old and used up, and the ball of clay, scooped up from a sunken road here and long since become hard as rock (even paper—this above all—I banished from my sight), and then in the week before beginning I avoided any kind of preparation, forbade myself even to break into a run, drank before going to bed more wine than usual, expressly to distort and muddy my dreams, usually so clear and incisive, especially in the dark season, turned away when I felt drawn to look at something, and finally was waiting only for the first snow.

The last thing I did was sweep and scrub the house, even into the out-of-the-way corners—the housekeeper had given notice after my family moved out, explaining that there was nothing further for her to do with me there alone—and pruned the trees in the yard, more than necessary, so as to have additional spaces and openings to look through from my window; even opened with my clippers a small, round breach in the hedge, which, from my ground-floor study, was to serve as a peephole through the garden next door to the road I had declared the main one.

The bills were now paid in advance, as much as possible; the heating-oil tank was filled, the lane freshly strewn with crushed rock. And the first snow fell, if initially only, as I heard one morning on the radio, in the highlands of the eastern Pyrenees: I saw it from afar on the crops of the short-legged dark horses in the meadows by the Río Segre in the enclave of Llivia. And that was enough for me. I would begin the next day with my year in the no-man's-bay.

On the evening before the beginning, the blade of a jackknife with which I wanted to tighten a screw snapped back and cut me in the index or writing finger, so deeply that for a moment, before the flesh closed up again, still without a drop of blood, I saw the white of the bone flash. In the hospital, outside the bay, where the wound was sewn up, the doctor said the finger should be kept still for weeks, and "What is your profession?"

That was all right with me. All the better: I would make do with my other fingers, thus avoiding the familiar pitfall of false dexterity. No more postponement.

In the hour before I went downstairs to my study, I started a fire upstairs in the fireplace, of beech wood, as my grandfather always did before the Feast of the Three Kings, except that he used the glowing embers, and like him I then held my hat over it, and pulled it, still smoky-warm, over my head, for that kept headaches away for the rest of the year.

After that I went out to the yard, got up on the tallest ladder, and sawed a funnel-shaped opening in the top of the spruce, imagining that the mythical beast hiding in the woods, of whose existence I am convinced, would, if it were winged, build itself a nest there in the course of the year, to serve as its outpost in the bay, and I could have it and perhaps its brood in sight from time to time during my writing.

Then I went to the Bar des Voyageurs at the station, read a letter from my carpenter friend from Morioka in northern Japan and my favorite paper, *The Hauts-de-Seine News*, suburb by suburb, on the way home took a roundabout route, so as to pass the dog next door, locked in the garage during the day, and let the massive animal, which repeatedly jumped at the steel door, bark at me and bark himself out, and finally squatted in the yard by the open door to my study until, in the sparse grass at my feet, a path through the fields appeared.

The first sentence after that, not thought out in advance, promptly led me deep into the forest bay, and only now can I return there.

A stranger crossing the bay on the rather leisurely local train, traveling for example from the center of Paris (which is almost everywhere, after all) out to Versailles, will, at the sight of the expanses of hanging vegetable and fruit plantations to either side of the tracks, interrupted at first by no houses, only toolsheds, at most be surprised at suddenly being out in the countryside, the more so since during a 3,200-meter stretch in the dark just now he may have thought he was in the subway (the supposed subway is in actuality the tunnel through the barrier formed by the Seine hills). The stranger will hardly be likely to get off at the station with the plane tree, unless he has time and no particular destination, and unless the surprisingly rural quality or rather the sudden indefinability of the landscape reminds him of something and holds out the promise of some curious excursions.

When I hear other languages in the bay, it is almost always from residents, especially the Portuguese—no, they actually tend to conceal their native idiom, speaking in public more the language of the country—the North Africans, the Asians, most of all the Armenians and the Russians. Pretty much the only foreigners who are here intentionally, also of their own accord, come from nearby Paris, and can be recognized as outsiders precisely by their not presenting themselves as such, but instead as people from the capital in one way or another, including having the accent to match; and then they are not in the area for its own sake, but are using it only as the starting point or end point of a hike.

Otherwise I have encountered in these ten years almost exclusively foreigners who found their way to the bay either by chance or even involuntarily. One evening a couple from a provincial city came into one of the few restaurants, sought out, if at all, only by residents of the bay; they had wandered in from one of the industrial exhibitions on the periphery of Paris. The couple immediately drew attention to themselves there, in and of themselves and then also because of their completely different, louder, gesticulating, space-grabbing self-assurance, and finally they expressed in such clear signals and utterances their superiority to the region, also their disdain, in the presence of the scattering of brooding, seemingly hunched-over local folk that I, if they had not wolfed down their food and disappeared quickly, would have got up from my seat and, as a representative of the place, barked at them to behave themselves in a manner appropriate to strangers and guests here among us.

It was far more often than once that I heard people who had strayed into the region asking from their cars, "Can you please tell me where I am?" and when a car with a strange license plate pulls over to the side of the road, I am almost sure in advance that someone inside, looking quite lost, will be unfolding a map. And one time, when I was heading home long after midnight, several people came running toward me over the dark square in front of the railroad station, waving their arms and uttering cries of dismay (I immediately picked out my son in the group): as it turned out, a group of Chinese, who had mistakenly not got off the train until after the tunnel, and had now spent hours, meanwhile seized by panic, running back and forth like headless chickens, trapped in this indecipherable, night-cold no-man's-land cage, without taxis and without any passersby at all, without an open bar or police station.

But hadn't things been this way since long ago, not only in this current year of 1999? This year only one foreigner has stuck in my mind thus far: that almost-friend, a journalist, who changed his specialty from sports to war. When I, meanwhile more receptive to visits, perhaps precisely as a result of my months of activity here, showed him around the region, he considered it very special because he saw in a store window "souvenir" plaques of marble—in reality grave plaques in the stonecutter's display. He has remained in my memory because he, still a very young man, was dead soon after that, killed in the German civil war.

It is not just since the beginning of this year that I have spent early evenings now and then standing in that bar, also a tobacco shop, that for me marks the last spit, the *finis terrae* of the bay. But only this year has it become an observation or looking post.

It happens that two major roads from Paris to Versailles meet there, one of them formerly the route that kings took over the chain of hills, both ascents very steep, with an actual top of the pass up there; the other, Route Nationale 10, leading from the great bend in the Seine down by Sèvres through a gently climbing, meandering, gradually broadening valley, in my eyes at the place in question already an upland valley. The acute-angled junction of the two roads is officially called a *pointe*, a tongue, or, as I call it, a spit. Certain buses of line 171 have POINTE posted as their destination or last stop, whereas the majority continue on to the palace of Versailles, and likewise almost all the nearby facilities are called after it: Ambulance de la Pointe, Garage . . . , Pharmacie . . . , Video . . . , Tailleur de la Pointe (specializing in alterations).

———

In the Bar de la Pointe I avoid standing directly by the door, located right in the spandrel of the junction, and instead seek out the back of the bar and gaze through the gaps between the others at the counter. And time and again at nightfall I had the image of a particular darkness, in which cars on the former royal road that cuts across the bay were all in a hurry to get onto the decidedly brighter and also wider highway, the Nationale, and as they accelerated it sounded like the squeaking of rabbits in flight, while the vehicles approaching in the opposite direction seemed to hesitate before the already palpable wooded darkness of the bay.

Yet not only in my imagination is this Pointe something like a place of transition, or actually more a line of demarcation. On old postcards it is also represented as such. On one photograph of the two-road spit of land, taken facing toward the east and the metropolis, what is today the Route Nationale still has trolley tracks and plane trees along the sidewalks, then as now the width of a boulevard, seeming even wider than in Paris, because so much less crowded. Only an old man is walking along, on crutches. The road from the pass, on the other hand, already part of the bay, initially more a path through the hollow, has trees only in the background on that turn-of-the-century postcard, the hillside forests, which at that time extended farther down, and for pedestrians on both sides, then as now, there are only slats, boards set on edge, balance beams. In those days the present junction or fork or bifurcation café, was, in accordance with the significance of the spot, an *auberge*, and why shouldn't the innkeeper of Porchefontaine, as his last undertaking, someday open a very special place with a view, here on the spit of land?

I act as if the bay had fixed boundaries. In truth these seem to me to have become fluid during the current year, also because I have undertaken a kind of survey. One day a spot that I previously included as a matter of course falls out of the picture, on another it is reincorporated, and another that had previously gone unexamined reveals its bay character. There is a constant shrinking and stretching going on, and on some days outside the bay I have even circled around little enclaves, and likewise here in the bay, on the contrary, enclaves of other realms.

A factor contributing to such changeability is probably also the way in which I approach my writing terrain. Sometimes, in order to get closer to the original image, I have moved away from it and then approached again in a wide arc. But precisely in this process, as a result of the different directions from which I returned to the bay, its boundaries became most fluid. And my inner image of the entire region also changed and jumped about, depending on the path I took to get home; and thus I came upon it every time as a new arrival who knew nothing about it, which was fine with me for this year, without a trace of memories from my decade-long life here.

A newcomer of this sort turned off the Route Nationale one rainy evening and promptly found himself in an abandoned coal-mining area in the Ardennes. In the former miners' settlement, a village along a street that stretched farther than the eye could see, the doors of the few still-occupied houses were slightly ajar, and the road surface, rumbling from the heavy traffic, had blackish streaks and potholes, from whose huge splashes one escaped only into the half-open entryways of the houses.

This bleak, unchanging highway finally dipped under a railroad overpass, on one side of it a bunkerlike concrete protuberance, the Rive Gauche (Left Bank) station, on the other side a building whose ridgepole hardly came up to the height of the railroad embankment, the hotel (with bar) of the same name. A woman, shadowy, ran inside, and in passing he heard her asking for a glass of water. And after her, out of the darkness under the bridge, came a pack of derelicts and inquired, one more addled than the next, after the Route Nationale or the Rive Droite station.

The underpass, then, barely lit, nothing but pale, crumbling concrete, some of it already fallen, had a ceiling from which thousands of whitish nails were sticking, at second glance stalactites, deposits from the concrete, of which drops landed on the asphalt sidewalk, falling onto the corresponding stalagmites or ground dripstones, tiny mounds, glassy cones, which could now be felt under one's soles. The rattling of trains overhead interjected itself into the sound of trucks crashing along, and a squad of soldiers came by at a run, loaded with heavy sacks, almost knocking over the stranger to these parts.

On that evening this was the main access to the no-man's-bay, in the form of the gate to a dripstone grotto, with the rounded mounds below as its threshold; since then, whether returning home or setting out, I have always made a point of rocking and swaying on them for a moment on the balls of my feet.

After that a leap to another image: in front of a dense, lumpy-wet stretch of woodland along the road, a longish, dim rectangle of light, the across-the-way bar, with the name Little Robinson, a sort of log cabin, surrounded by junk and even more by tree trunks, more higgledy-piggledy than stacked, but protected by tarpaulins as if for several rough winters; the silhouettes inside less those of patrons—the proprietor seemed to be alone there with a shaggy dog—than again those of branches lined up and halves of tree trunks. And smoke puffed from this shack. And then in the woods something rare after all, bunches of rowan-berries, in a resolute red.

And again the image changes. The entry had not yet been negotiated. I had not yet turned into the bay, as I usually did at that spot. The previous highway, after an unexpected curve, cut across a hollow and became a nocturnal landing strip in a penal colony, far from the rest of civilization. Although the inmates could move about relatively freely, they slunk past the wire fences and piles of muck with heads either bowed or turned away from each other, and though the paths were wider here, each walked at a distance from the next person, including the couples, and not only the old ones, to whom it was probably not a new experience, for either the man or the woman, to be a few steps ahead of the other.

There were hardly stores in this sector; the one supermarket, like those otherwise found on military bases, was without displays, without price lists, with sight screens, and if a product was visible, then only its back, and the cashier's head itself seemed to be that of a prisoner, just as the children sat there trapped in the bare neon-glare-lit room, in a deeper cut in the hollow, in a camp school, born already unfree, the offspring of the banished.

In addition, out of the hill-darkness all around, the watchtower loomed, many-storied, huge, each story shining down fixedly on the isolated stragglers and slinkers along the track, and only from the top of the tower a restless flashing and smoldering.

On that evening I did not feel I had arrived in my bay until I reached the square in front of the local railroad station, full of motion from the shadows of the plane trees, whereas usually the bay began way back at the Route Nationale and sometimes even before that, for instance at the Armenian church, or at the shop of the alterations tailor beyond the junction, the Pointe.

On another such day during this year I returned after tracing a similar arc through the woods, from which far more wood roads and hiking paths led to the settlement than streets from anywhere else. And just as I daily had the experience of noticing something I had previously over-looked, it was the same now: by a clearing deep in the forest, among the oaks and edible chestnuts, a palm tree; and one of its fronds, on an almost windless day, was rustling and rattling like a sail on the high sea. An owl hooted, and yet it was the middle of the day, with the bells of the Catholic church chiming noon, and the almost simultaneous siren from the roof of the only official building in the bay—a mere annex to the main building somewhere else—an indication that it was the first Wednesday of the month.

In the distant outlet of the forest, directly facing it, stood a house, framed and overarched by the last trees; the path led directly to the door and the few steps up to it. It was a sight so different from that at the other end of the forest, up on the plateau with the office complexes, which as a rule displayed only their often windowless side elevations to the roads there, and then only parts of these, the edge of a wall, a ventilation pipe, a propane gas tank, their colors also clashing with any of those in the forest. Perhaps, I thought, this impression of the office buildings' defiantly confronting the trees stemmed not only from the fact that the buildings towered above the latter, but also that one had to go uphill to reach them in the end, whereas the wood roads more or less gently descended toward the houses in the bay and merged with the side streets or even pointed toward a particular door, as though that were its destination.

Yes, the houses down below, the great majority of them, were pro-portioned to the forests around them, and not only when glimpsed mo-mentarily through the trees. I have never seen woodlands and human dwellings achieve such a vital and beautiful communion anywhere else. That comes, I saw, specifically from the bay character of the settlement, extending deep and with every glance deeper into the otherwise intact primeval forest—an illusion renewed almost daily and perfectly fine with me—and even more from the wildness, no, the aboriginal quality of almost every individual shape amid the hodgepodge of houses, comparable to the trees in the forest primarily by virtue of a similarity in the spaces between them. And to me, the new arrival, even when I had long since passed the outer edge, and instead of on the wood road was walking down the side streets here, which I hoped would go on forever, the robustness and simultaneous delicacy of the arboreal structures and the residential structures seemed similar.

On that day the boundaries of the bay thus extended to include the last houses up on the opposite slope, and the intrusive sounds, almost the only ones in this great expanse, were the shouts of children playing, dogs barking, hammering, while behind me, from the woods, the owl could still be heard.

And on yet another day, as I was walking home toward midnight, by full moon, on the wood road, no owl was hooting anymore. Instead a fox was standing in front of the house at the forest outlet, and stood there, and stood there, a fox profile as never before. And when it ran then, showing up in a flash several gardens away, it appeared to me as a ghostly flitting through all the fences and walls and house foundations, whereupon it just stood still again, its entire silhouette horizontal, from the bushy tail to the perfectly pointed nose, its head over its shoulder for a long, long stare at me, at no one but me, and from there it dashed on again, fleeing or directly toward me? A shudder ran through me. Where was that? Was that even here in the bay at all? And in the current year?

As for this, the first thing I recall is the bats, again in a clearing in the forest, at dusk up in the hills of the Seine, and that was in January, right at the beginning of my sitting down, during a hike over the hills to Meudon, and a warm wind was wafting. The bats did not show their faces again until late summer, and then only for one evening, flying by rapidly in a zigzag through my yard, above which a few swallows were still swooping.

It was likewise still January that time I stepped barefoot into the grass outside my garden-level study to sharpen my pencils and then spent a good hour walking back and forth between the pear tree and the cherry tree, the ground was so warm under my soles. But it was probably only my imagination that at the same time crickets were chirping from the forest preserve, the result of the great winter silence there sometimes. (More later about the sounds of the crickets here and their connection with the silence.)

No hallucination—although I took it for one at first—was seeing a little snake creeping along the sidewalk at the foot of the Bordeaux bank on the bay's main street, on a winter night that was damp and cold after all, no, not an earthworm or a novelty store item, and it really moved, though in very slow serpentines, and when I crouched down beside it, it raised its head weakly in the lamplight, flicking its tongue with its last strength, or not at all. The lone late passerby to whom I pointed out the snake was not surprised for a moment to see the animal at this time of year, and altogether the people of the area seemed to find hardly anything astonishing. And as several boys approached from the floodlit athletic field, I pushed the dying snake over the bank into the thick-layered fallen leaves of the forest.

And it was also in the depths of winter that I became a witness to the removal of a ninety-year-old woman, who, alone in her house up on the plateau (part of the bay on that particular day), had caught on fire from her gas stove and had burned up in her living room: when I passed again later that afternoon, pelt-black smoke was still puffing from a smashed windowpane, being photographed by the chronicler of *The Hauts-de-Seine News*, too late on the scene as usual, and a village expression acquired new meaning for me: "Your place is as cold as a burned-out house!"

And even before the onset of spring something unprecedented happened in the bay and the surrounding area, an earthquake, still inexplicable even to the geologists, also, these say, because so little research has been done on the area: only a small one, to be sure—the rattling of glasses was mistaken by most people for the doing of one of the bombers

from the air base again—and yet, in the gypsum-rich part of the circle
of hills, the underground tunnel of a former quarry is said to have collapsed, putting an end to mushroom-raising there.

If the earthquake hardly jostled my handwriting in my study, something else did so all the more. I, so dependent on consistency and daily
routine, was threatened with being brought to a standstill and almost
compelled to give up my undertaking, as yet so up in the air, also because
I was still only at the beginning. (And where am I now?)

The woman from Catalonia, my wife, who had vanished long since,
suddenly reappeared, but not to live with me again, for a third time,
but to forestall my, our, book. At least that appeared to me to be her
intention during those winter weeks when time and again but never
regularly, and also at no particular hour, she would block my path in
unexpected places.

It did not solve anything that I fled in between to Salamanca in the
Spanish highlands and continued my work there, the Plaza Mayor, seen
below in bird's-eye view from my attic room in a pension, merely pretending to be the view from my study (those weeks seem so distant that
I am not clear as to whether the dying snake here wasn't actually dragging itself through the wet leaves down there on the bank of the Tormes
River, and altogether whether the person squatting by the animal isn't
actually my friend the painter): I had to go home to the bay; without
my presence there throughout the year the book would lose its locale
and its basis.

And on my very first morning back, as I continued my work, "that
woman" descended on me again. Actually I merely saw her running away
down a side street when I went to my mailbox, located at the end of
the lane, as if for a farm, fastened to the lamppost there, and then found,
my only mail, a picture postcard of the medieval bridge over the Tormes
in Salamanca, the back side left blank.

Ana had keys to the house, and some days I heard her banging around
above me. Later she also came downstairs to the study and sat in a corner.
I avoided speaking to her, recalling the phrase an almost-friend had used:
Let the will-o'-the-wisp have its way; otherwise all that will be left to
it will be its substratum, melancholy. (Earlier, when I had repeated that

to her, the woman from Catalonia had replied, "But beneath my melancholy my joy may be waiting!") And she spoke no more than I did, merely watched me in silence, hour after hour, and hadn't there once been a time when I had wished that of her for my work? Then, as if she sensed that the day's quota would soon be polished off, she would get up and leave. But on occasion she would come storming in, especially when, increasingly exhausted by the situation, I would be trying to sleep in the next room; she would shake me, still without saying a word, and then be gone again.

And on a spring day she appeared in the backyard and pounded with her fists on the study door. I went out to her. She had the ability to acquire tremendously broad shoulders all of a sudden, and with these she rammed me to the ground. I stood up, and she rammed me again, except that this time I was ready and stayed on my feet. I would have defended myself, but then I would have lost the sentence in the middle of which she had interrupted me, and with it my ability to continue the book. And so, with the woman from Catalonia one fingertip away from me, eye to eye with my enemy, I silently spelled out the next sentence, and likewise the one after that, and at the same time was close to seizing this giant dwarf and spiking her on the fence pickets, longing at the same time to unite instantly with this female body and give Ana a child, wanting at the same time nothing but to put my arms around my wife, and fearing at the same time that one of the neighbors might see us like this.

And what finally did happen: as old as I was, I began to cry, and in the process became as old as I was. And it seemed to me that her hatred was now being transformed into scorn. Yet as I then looked at her, she had disappeared again. And I squatted down on the spot where we had just almost killed each other, became lost in contemplation of the overlapping traces of wallowing and stomping, along with the uprooted grass and clumps of earth, thought that no human race was foreign to me except sometimes my own white one, and even more that of women; thought, "One day we will kill each other"; thought, "I shall find us once more," and then continued on with this year of mine in the no-man's-bay.

Since that day my wife has not appeared again. Instead, when summer came there were other threats and hindrances. But don't you need those, too, for your writing, as the outward calls to order, without which you would inwardly let yourself go?

From time to time, yes, from time to time.

It is the moment for focusing on the houses in the bay, which in the beginning looked so odd to me, and meanwhile stand there so naturally.

Only in this process of writing things down, which sharpened my senses, did I become more attentive to the buildings here. That happened in an almost time-tested way: since I am incapable of forcing myself to perceive something, I would first note down at home at my desk what, without specific observation, had caught my attention about one house or another as I passed it. This allowed me to get away from my little memory trail; I became concrete, described as completely as possible, made up details at random, drifted into make-believe.

With such descriptions of a house and its surroundings in black and white in my mind, actually more like guesses, I would set out a second time in that direction. And only in this fashion did I become capable of seeing how it really was. And far more powerfully than what I had got right my mistakes impressed upon me the real character of the place. Except that in order to achieve that I had to have interjected something in writing between the object in question and my senses, if not something wrong, then something half cloudy, and in any case something in writing. Then all I had to do was go home again and correct this where necessary.

And sometimes I allowed the mistakes to stand; who could say that the telephone booth I had hallucinated onto a certain street corner would not in fact be installed there the next day?

Nowhere else have I seen such houses as those in the bay? Yes, and I have never yet seen houses like those here.

And again it was only during my writing year that I began to distinguish: it is not merely because of the particular building style. It also has to do with their location in this remote spit of a settlement, cutting deep and narrow into the forest. (The solitude or remoteness helped create this world—and what besides?) Not a house there which, observed from a distance—and the majority reveal themselves thus—does not have as a background, high above the roofline, a wooded ridge, which then extends over the roofs of the other houses as well.

The chain of hills round about not only provides the frame for the houses of the bay, but even more forms part of their image. Without it, marking the curved horizon floating gently above them, the houses would stand as if alone, each an incomplete phenomenon, so to speak. Without this omnipresent background of wooded hills the settlement would lack something that constitutes the unique solidarity, if not of the inhabitants, then of the dwellings there.

It has sometimes happened that I have looked out my window and pictured the wooded heights as gone from behind the near and more distant gables in the neighborhood, the eastern chain of hills with the transmitter, the southern slope, called Eternal Slope, of Vélizy and the Poussin Meadow in between, the western heights, now at the beginning of November already shrouded in snow clouds; and each time a sense of uneasiness, almost of horror, has seized me at such hilllessness round about, with all the buildings in the fore- and middle ground continuing on into unbounded, drizzly, identical plains.

No. Even by themselves the houses of this region, without the green and gray arc of hill forests above their roofs, are a force, at least many of them. Even on the plains they would assert themselves, and would form lovely and spirit-lifting horizons, one in conjunction with the other, as well as with the front and back yards, around corner after corner, off into mirror-polished depths.

And again, only as a result of this year have I recognized that the city of my childhood longings was not exotic but one exactly like the settlement here in the bay; that those white cities I later chased after through the decades were not the right thing. Or: the White City is nothing for me.

The bay also has white houses, but they are rare, and in contrast to the White City, which begins to glow only from afar, here the last white disappears at a distance, or one has to search for it. A century ago there was only one such building, which was also called La Maison Blanche.

The façades display concealing colors, so to speak. Although yellow and red, even purple paint also occurs, nowhere does it make an impression of brilliance, or even of colorfulness. Yet the houses do not seem camouflaged in any way, but rather embody, in their distinctness and clarity, the fact we know as a house, and these house-facts stand, according to Karl Valentin, out in the open.

But isn't it also thus in other suburbs? Perhaps. Except that the houses here appear more forcefully, precisely in that they are almost without exception smaller: if just as broad as elsewhere, they are lower; if as high, decidedly narrower. And since, on the other hand, the yards are often larger than elsewhere, the space between houses is entirely different from there. So much more air is visible, no matter how narrow the gaps, between and above the houses' smallness.

It was this play of staggered in-between spaces that first brought back to me childhood images of a place of the future and rendered them concrete. And the play developed even more drawing power from other unique characteristics of the bay's buildings. Almost every one of the thousand little houses, strangely angular or strangely spreading, had a form different from the one next door, and when two similar ones did occur, it was as rare as twins, and they always turned up far apart. Besides, they did not stand in a row anywhere, but rather each at an angle to the next, the barracks-flat one close to the street, the next one, towerlike, in back at the end of a bowling-alley-length vegetable garden, and then vice versa, and so on. And at every step you found the façades pointing in different directions, not only around the one pond or the one round, always unpeopled plaza called Place de la Concorde.

The yellow-and-gray sandstone, that common suburban building material, did not occur in the bay all along a street as elsewhere, but in isolation, likewise buildings of red brick and pale limestone, and the few stuccoed houses displayed from house to house not only different shades but also different pebbliness in their textures. Thus far I have encountered one or two whose walls reveal a pattern like the first application of mortar with the trowel, and just as many, each time again at locations far apart, where the stones, cut into hexagons, were accordingly laid in nature's basic pattern, most noticeable otherwise in the cracks the earth develops during a drought.

Otherwise the houses tended to have no decoration, except for the chimney pots, often a veritable collection on a roof, one like a pretend factory smokestack with an upside-down flowerpot on top, the one next to it a many-winged miniature pagoda: hamlets in their own right. And on two southern façades thus far, separated by several streets, sundials revealed themselves to me, so unusually tiny—like insurance company decals—that they were a discovery if for no other reason. And on a garden wall, that row of concrete blocks, set on edge, in the form of dice whose black dots had meanwhile been whitewashed, and on a house wall a relief representing billiard balls and a queue.

All the houses in the bay huddled together in the broad hollow surrounded by wooded hills; none stuck up from a rise. None had a tower, an oriel, or turrets, or imitated a palace like quite a few in the neighboring suburbs, and none could be called a "villa," except by a real estate agent. The one house that was somewhat more imposing resembled a forester's lodge; the one, the only one, with an arched portal had probably once been a rectory. And in distinction to the other bays in the Seine hills, where one can repeatedly see, when out walking in the cookie-cutter side streets, a rounded Romanesque form here, a Gothic pointed cap there, in none of the established buildings here could I discover a single imitation of another building style, and probably nothing resembling a style at all.

For the architectural style of the Paris suburbs, the expression *pavillon* has been introduced. But for most of the local lodgings here that is not applicable. They look too unplanned, too little thought out. They are simply residences, or buildings of convenience; yet there is nothing provisional or hasty about them either. They have been standing and existing there in the forest bay since long ago, and are meant to last. I keep seeing them anew, singly and all together, as classic, less in the sense that they are timeless than that they are original, and then, too, in that they gave me a concept of everywhere, not just any old one, but rather a central one, particularly rooted in that place, indeed animated by it.

And I would never have assigned the population there to any particular people or any specific social class. A short while ago I read the remark of a famous architect from the metropolis beyond the hills, who, on the subject of the pavilions in the suburbs, whether ironically or seriously, praised the good taste of the petty bourgeois revealed in them. I do not know. At any rate I have never had any such thought in connection with the inhabitants of those classic residences in the bay here, to my delight.

As a result of the reserve the longtime inhabitants of the settlement brought to each of our encounters, I experienced all of them the same way I did their houses: as modest and untroubled—which is different from humble, or obsequious, and carefree. Each time I want to greet them, even though I do not know them, when they show themselves at their windows or garden doors, which occurs infrequently, and at times I have actually succeeded. And what a glow, a quiet, laconic, also playful glow, I received in return. I can say: In the old people in their cottages in the bay, and most of them are old, I have faith (I cannot say that of the other generations, certainly not of my own). If a single term for them ever came to mind, it was certainly not "petty bourgeois" but "cottager," as they would say in the area I come from. And in their discretion, I thought, they combined the characteristics of saviors and the saved. Most self-deceptions are more farfetched.

Whether I am walking down the main street or down the hundreds of side streets: these residences appear to me every morning as houses in the purest sense, and still with the freshness of morning in the afternoon. And they form such varied in-between spaces with each other that the things within these spaces—the bushes, clotheslines, benches, and, way in back, the woods—or simply the empty space itself, can walk, drive, ride, or move along with me as I pass. The cheerfully rhythmic glimpses or onward-onward gestures form courtyards between the houses, if only with the breadth of a crack, and, when there is a little more room before the next house, they actually are that as a rule, rather than gardens, grassless, paved with crushed rock, occupied by rabbit hutches and chicken ladders (and soon I will also discover the first beehive there).

With the help of such interstices, the image becomes sharper from one step to the next, like the opening of a curtain, then another and another, back into the deepest background, accompanied by a constant shining forth of individual parts of all the other houses, worked in relief, of a window over there, a gable one yard over, a porch there around the corner, a steep exterior staircase up to an attic room—every separate part recognizably an element of a human habitation, and the entire thing housing in the most fundamental sense, and not a schematic drawing but in the proportion of one to one, also not dreamed up, but entirely real.

An unusual feature for a town was also that the vegetable gardens and fruit trees were located more in front of than in back of the individual houses, whereas from the backyards only a basic element or nothing but pure green could be glimpsed between foundations and edges, with the feeling of a secret meadow spreading out there. I merely intuited this. Merely? Intuition comes to life: hardly anything has a farther reach.

Untroubled, yet with constant modesty and care, would also describe the style in which these original settlers added on to their houses in the course of time. Often close to blocking off the in-between spaces, but never entirely doing so. Without fail there always remained a slit, dark, to be sure, but letting one sense all the more powerfully the greening behind at its outlet. And untroubled, too, the way in which some of the additions jut out onto the already hardly present sidewalks, and one balustrade, hardly wide enough for a cat, and one door high in a wall without stairs up to it. And each addition, even a crooked or a sprawling one, merely reinforced the original harmony.

So, is there nothing at all about the buildings in the bay that disturbs you? — Well, perhaps I notice the absence of something: for instance, larger roof overhangs, to allow sitting outside when it is raining, which instead of soaking a person would only spray him now and then.

And probably for longer than just my decade here, but obvious to me only since I began my writing year, something has been happening in the bay that upsets me more than an interruption: the closing of the little vistas. At least once a week I stand in front of another such in-between space, which last time I looked was still part of the spirit-lifting back-and-forth game running deep through the settlement, and it has been walled up, specifically by one of us, those who just moved in, the buyers-up of property.

This year's wars in the world were civil wars. Yet as a rule the contending parties hardly knew what they were fighting for. It was not that part of the population of the country at war did not live in freedom, or that its language was being suppressed, and also the inequality of

opportunity was no longer so egregious as at one time, or was it? At
any rate, such things were not cited anywhere as causes. No one cared a
fig for causes, or if so, then only for show.

At last there was war in the world again; that was its natural state,
that was how it had to be, for otherwise where did those dreams come
from, even in lifelong peace, in which it was a reality that my sister put
out my eyes, my brother kicked me out of the house we shared, my
father ripped my flesh from my bones with his teeth, gazing at me with
the eyes of a murderer, and when I came home, my mother, in the form
of a giant avenging witch, jumped me. This contradicts those psychol-
ogists who declared that within the human race any material for making
war had been used up for all time. (I had believed them, and in a way
I continue to believe them.)

As wild and cutthroat as these wars were—as they say only civil wars
can be—those who waged them had none of the characteristics of close
relatives. Instead these were wars among distant cousins, and it seemed
as though even in the long peacetime actual brothers had become as alien
to each other as though they were separated by ten degrees, and then
enemies. Even where no war was taking place: how often in the last
decades I have heard someone speak of his brother in a tone that suggested that as far as he was concerned the brother could not only drop
dead but also go unburied—and if he were to be buried, then in a grave
with another name. After the outbreak of war they went at each other
accordingly: bloodthirstily, and at the same time with an "I'm not touching you!" Slaughtering, shooting down, blowing sky-high, yes, but all
that only with the fingertips. Devastate and destroy, yes, but at the same
time with an expression as if it were all for show.

At least that is how it was with the German civil war, not even the
East against the West, but almost each person against every other, and
finally more and more often massively against oneself, a threat to the
economy and combated by the professional army. This war, which suddenly broke out, in all the countries, early in the spring of 1999, has
meanwhile long since ended, and it is as if Germany were finding itself
at something like a beginning for the first time, without ghosts, healed,
if shaky on its legs and bemused, "I hope for more than just the moment"
(the reader); as if now its entirely different history were going into effect.
And the other peoples of the earth seem gradually to be following this

into a peace that is not even phony, in the sense that for them, Germany, to paraphrase Jorge Luis Borges, is the world consciousness. In contrast to that period before the first millennium after Jesus Christ, now, before the second, ominous signs as well as promising ones are on the increase (except that for many countries a time-reckoning different from the Christian one is in use).

In that spring my almost-friend had dropped in on me in the bay, only yesterday the author of sports reportages as light-footed as they were stirring, and in the meantime, still as young as ever, only pale, with a stubble of beard and a black shirt, a war correspondent in Germany, exclusively for a paper specializing in war in its everyday variations, a paper engaged in passing on news, as even the sentence structure revealed, less for the purpose of informing and explaining than as a power game and profit-oriented business, without a hint of an eye or compassion: my young acquaintance's very first article was veiled by those employed there and turned into a sort of mask, and he did not get to write any others.

On his brief detour from the fronts to the isolated bay, he was, to use the expression that instantly came to me upon catching sight of him, "full of war." So instead of letting him come into the house, I promptly walked with him from the doorstep out into the landscape. We then sat down on the far side of the body of water with the name Etang des Ecrevisses, Crayfish Pond, at a picnic table by the edge of the forest. This morning, over half a year after his shot in the head, I sat down alone in the cold and emptiness of that spot to recollect better the hour we spent there.

He was constantly snapping pictures, though not of the region but exclusively of himself, and they were also the only ones he included in his war article. The old fishermen, the former Crayfish Pub, the palm tree back in the in-between space of a freshly turned-over root-vegetable garden, the constant trembling or bubbling of the water, like that of the palm fronds, the taiga birches at our back, already with a hint of green, the trumpet blasts, monotonous, curt, muffled, from the track workers on the horizon—to me the music of the bay—the great sky, the broad earth, this quietly vibrating peace certainly did not go unnoticed by him, but he despised them. Somewhere else was war, which counted, and through which he, as young as he was, had finally established a connection with the world. Just as certain characters in animated cartoons had the sign for money (dollars) in their eyes, so he had in his eyes, as if black-ringed in mourning, the sign for war. Relaxation and pleasure now meant to him, and he was not the first: lying on his belly on the ground between two battle lines, barely protected from the hail of ordnance, and feeling his own heartbeat. It was almost as though these very eyes pushed my hand away, when I casually, more for myself, tried to point out something in our surroundings or offered him a few hazelnuts from my garden.

But what came to my mind this morning by that pond, at the sight of the blackish, pre-winter-bare table with carvings left there by lovers and single individuals? I should have waved him into my house, or given him a kick in the pants. How his face came to life for a moment when over there, on the pond road, a parachute-green military vehicle rolled by, with a machine-gun muzzle sticking out through a gap in the canvas.

Later that spring Mont St.-Valérien above Suresnes, the only elevation in the hills of the Seine known as a "mountain" because it stood apart, was transformed overnight into a volcano, again to the amazement of the geologists, who would never have guessed that the magma, thought of in the region as more harmless than almost anywhere else, under all the soft, quiet layers of sand, sandstone, limestone, and gypsum, would ever find its way through them up to the surface.

The eruption was not exactly powerful, no mountaintop was blown off, no rock thrown up, the liquid earth just bubbled up as if from an underground oil tank, though one that was boiling hot. After the one hour of volcanic activity a crater hardly formed, or if it did, it was half filled up again by the rock rubble rolling back down, which also stopped up the magma shaft for the time being.

The flow of lava down the mountain in the direction of the Seine was, however, no trickle but a small stream; the contents of the burst tank were plentiful. The only thing destroyed by it was part of the fort on the peak, used during the war by the Gestapo as an execution place, now a memorial, in whose inner courtyard the new volcano had opened up, and the edge of the famous vineyard of Suresnes, whose delicate yet robust wine bears the designation "Vin du pays des Hauts-de-Seine":

there the magma came to a halt; today, long since cooled, having fused with the sand and gravel it swallowed up on its way down Mont St.-Valérien, it forms what looks from a certain vantage point like a glassy flank—the ground in which a handful of vintners there will cultivate a special basalt wine in the next few years, a red, as a varietal of the wines of the Seine hills.

That vantage point is located here in the bay, at the highest point on the wood road that I call the Absence Road, a point that lies several stories above the extinguished volcano of Suresnes, which in that spring could be recognized through the sprouting leaves by its white smoke, and now, through the bare trees far and wide, by the gleaming tongue below the pale fort, with the platforms of the towers of La Défense in the most distant background. Simultaneously with the brief volcanic activity, the entire hilly area, in its great arc around the Seine, is supposed to have risen by several millimeters, and it actually seems to me as though I no longer, as in previous winters, have to stand on the very tips of my toes to catch sight, from my highest elevation in the countryside, through the myriad of treetops, of the glassy stump of a mountainous cone there on the distant bend of the arc.

Usually it rained so hard for a while in springtime that some of the former brooks, without which the fairly impenetrable network of valleys, often actually ravines and gorges in the suburb's landscape, would never have formed, overflowed the sewers of which they had long since become a part, and on the surface, if only fleetingly and quite harmlessly, traced out their old meanders: for instance the almost forgotten waters of the Marivel on the boundary between the bay and the upper valley, a name now attached only to an apartment complex, a résidence. Some writers of letters to the editor of The Hauts-de-Seine News offered the opinion that this was a bad omen, while others took it for a good one.

Likewise leaves wafted and whirled, without a real storm, from the woods, long before summer, for days, flying high through the bay, as if to blot out the sun, not withered leaves from the year before, but the pale green leafage of the current year, barely sprouted from the oaks as well as the edible chestnuts, birches, beeches, and again that was interpreted one way or another (for those who had seen it as the handwriting on the wall, the summer foliage that followed, more luxuriant than it had ever been, was a miraculous sign).

As for me, the summer was remarkable particularly for those legendary lizards, the central figures in the coat of arms of the bay town, to which, by the way, a coat of arms was as little suited as a castle or any kind of overlord.

When I came upon them, on the gray-sanded sunny bank deep in the forest, I at first mistook the two animals for pieces of bark, and then for dead, because they were lying on their sides, close together, their whitish bellies almost skyward, and, unheard of for lizards, did not dart away the moment they were prodded but remained motionless, completely lifeless to the touch. And only after that was there a pulsing in their necks, increasingly powerful, and finally I noticed the foot of one of them on the other's body, tiny and yet pawlike. I sat down on a tree trunk on the other side of the path, which since that time I have called Lizard Way, and watched the couple, as I have subsequently done every time there is still, sunny weather, play dead while copulating—apparently? didn't lizards conceive virginally?—while above the treetops, through the great blueness, the transmitter sent out flashes from its upper deck, like a lighthouse operating by day.

With the passing weeks and months, the two animals moved, each on its own, into holes in the bank, side by side, in which they lodged like giant cave dragons of old, only gradually discovered by me amid the camouflaging shimmer of the clay, with their rigid, scaly triangular heads, from which only rarely their tongues darted out.

For this attempt at a chronicling of one year in the no-man's-bay I have not yet looked even once at my notebooks (although they fill the two upper drawers in one of the few pieces of furniture in the house, the dresser, to the point that they stick). In my storytelling I am following only my memory, and would like to keep it that way.

And with the help of—or according to the measure of—my memory, it is again animals, when I recall how the spring continued, as Pythagoras' pupils recalled their day before yesterday, that determine my image of the bay at that time.

First, even before the lizards, on the days that did not get a little warmer until around noon, on another path by a bank in the forest, I came upon a colony of wild bees. These had their holes, numerous, honeycomb-close, like an earth city, in a zone of the gray-blue sand that is called here Sable de Fontainebleau, although the Seine hills are far from the town of Fontainebleau. The sand dug out by each of the bees, forming bulging ramparts around their holes, seemed to come from a considerable depth; it looked so unweathered, unwintry fresh, and pale as wood shavings, providing, along with the barely noticeable yellow of the pussy willows, the first spring color in the great expanse of tree gray.

Those hundreds of circles of sand on the mossy bank first drew my attention to the craters in the middle, which, when examined from a squatting position, turned out not to be empty at all. Hairy black heads with antennae filled the openings, at first only here and there, and then, after a warm hour of sun, in almost every earth comb. Fine sand blew and slithered in all directions, along the entire bank, and finally here and there a couple of bees flew out of their grottoes and took off, some black-armored, others red-pelted, toward which pollen?, while the majority who remained behind, merely crawling around their holes, were now pounced on by slim, all-black flies, at second look also bees, only of a different gender?, which circled and rolled about with the bigger, more colorful ones as if in foreplay.

That was repeated several days in a row on the Wild Bee Path, except that more and more of the plump chief bees were left lying as cadavers next to their holes. (I explained this to myself as the result of the persistent nighttime frosts; they had frozen to death.) And in spite of the stronger sun, the thousand-grotto city seemed to be dying out more and more; a rarity now when a hairy black head slowly struggled up to the light or landed with yellow-dusted legs; and the dive-bombing small bees had completely disappeared. And only later, when I turned over one of the curled-up putative frost-corpses did I see an empty thorax, as if sucked out, and it was exactly the same with all the others: only the back held together for appearances' sake; underneath nothing was left.

The legs of the dead, gilded with pussy-willow pollen, thus became for me the next color of spring. And even later, when I pushed the dead

leaves aside one at a time at the base of the bank, I discovered under
them the main deposit of mining-bee corpses, heaps of them, all topsy-
turvy, on top of and underneath one another, swept together after the
slaughter as if in mass graves, and all the cadavers were completely
without flesh between the head and the abdomen.

Since then, for the rest of the year, I have not seen any mining bees,
either murderers or victims, either at the long since flooded settlement
in the grotto bank or anywhere else. In the summer I was stung a few
times in my yard by bees, true enough, but those were the usual kind
(which, however, likewise in summer, for an incredible, sun-darkening
moment, whooshed through that same yard, no, roared, a swarm-cloud,
in flight).

Only once, also in summer, did I have an experience with perhaps
similar wild bees, but I hardly got to see them. And my experience was
then entirely different.

That was the day when, in one of the bay's forests, on the edge of a
ravine, I finally found my way to the cliffs I had been missing in the
area as a sort of nourishment for the senses. I had been following the
upper edge of a brook bed, during a hot noon hour completely free of
wind—and there: the cliffs, in which I had almost ceased to believe
anymore, after all the terrain symbols for *roches,* which then turned out
to have been blasted or built over, now only names on maps.

I stopped in my tracks, on a path overgrown with beech seedlings, at
the foot of the row of massive rocks, emerging so unexpectedly out of
the forest, with the sun shining on them and the trees at some distance.
These were cliffs as cliffs should be, for climbing, for hurling oneself to
one's death, for taking shelter under in a storm.

And then I again heard a roar, but different from that of the honeybee
swarm and that of the warplanes that were still tracing their practice
loops more often than usual from Villacoublay to the Ile-de-France: it
was very close, and also, unlike the bombers, had something profoundly
even about it, and came from the cliff in front of me.

For the moment there was no other sound. The entire stone face, as
high as a building, and smooth as a pebble, was thrumming, and not
until I was within a hand's breadth of it did I notice the crack from
which that mighty sound surged—I almost had to put my ear right
against it to be certain. Surged? It surged through me, swept me away,

and I allowed it to surge through me. And at the same time I was almost gripped by fear, and not only because of the occasional bee that came shooting out with its lone buzzing, which once out in the open promptly dissipated or sounded like nothing worth mentioning.

That there was such a roar inside the cliff had to do not only with the population of wild bees in there but also with the way the fissure probably widened out inside into a cave: the bees returning home sounded as shrill as wasps in the moment of squeezing into their refuge, and a moment later their sound was swallowed up in an entirely different sonority, the roar from deep within the cliff. As close and threatening as the sound was, I had, on the other hand, never heard anything come from a greater distance. If this was a trance, there was nothing more real than a trance. Only this made presence of mind possible. If ever there was a music of the spheres, it was resounding from the earth here.

In that hour with the cliff bees, the noon stillness did not last very long in the surrounding area. On that very day in Paris another peace conference was taking place, in connection with one of the civil wars, and the airspace above the seven-airport region was soon filled with the rattling and rumbling of helicopters ferrying representatives of the warring parties back and forth between Villacoublay, Buc, Toussus-le-Noble, Guyancourt, St.-Cyr-l'Ecole, and the Elysée Palace. But even while the squadrons were flying uninterruptedly over the treetops, I was listening only to the roar of the wild-bee colony in the cliff—like the humming of my childhood in the telegraph poles, except that it was a live sound if anything ever was, a sound before every other sound—and I tapped my foot to it and wished we might all have such a ringing in our ears, in our skulls, in our hearts, for me and you in the hour of our death.

It was not yet summer when I then went to the woods to write. On the one hand I had long had in mind to sit out under the open sky with my stuff, as I had during my time in Ulan Bator. On the other hand I left my study not of my own accord but as a fugitive.

To be sure, there had always been noise around the house now and then, but in the meantime it had become so bad that even in unsettled weather I ran away from it. By noise I do not mean children crying and sounds of work. Although high-pitched whines, drilling, hammering, and squeaking could get on my nerves, I knew I had to put up with it, and battling my way through even seemed good for the text: as if it were to be tested for accuracy that way. There was a crash with whose help I found my way back to a train of thought I had lost during a period of too much stillness; wasn't there a danger of letting language run away with me in the stillness? This other noise, however, was dangerous in a different way. It seemed malevolent to me. It was not even that the noisemakers were taking aim at someone else—someone else, anyone else, did not exist for them.

In the last few years I had acquired some new neighbors. With the many trees and dense hedges, I hardly saw them, and merely heard, all the more clearly because I could not see it, that things were being torn down, built, rebuilt. Some evenings it was actually a relief when, in place of the earlier pitch-blackness and desolateness, from the area around the yard here and there another illuminated window shone. To be surrounded at a distance by the silhouettes of small houses, their roofs hardly visible through the treetops, was nice. It was as if a village had sprung up around my property, or a circle of wagons.

The nights in the bay still kept their spacious elastic fragrant peace. The problem was that I had to wait for daytime for my undertaking, or my observing. And now there was hardly a day without this noise, which left room for nothing else, and all the more noticeably in that it disrupted the very special silence of the region, and always without reason.

There were days when I was surrounded by it so completely and complicatedly that the only thing I could do was laugh and quietly keep plugging on. While one of the faceless neighbors was assaulting his environment through wide-open windows and doors with every madness aria ever composed—any music, no matter how lovely, blared this way now—the one next to him was blasting away—with an air gun? but then where did the smell of burning come from, penetrating into my study?—tirelessly at the swarms of pigeons in what was not even his grass, and the invisible third neighbor around the corner was trying out one of his ever-increasing number of fiendish machines, using the acquisition of the week to go at the not terribly old apple tree in his pocket-handkerchief yard—which he wanted to turn into a raised barbecue terrace?—instead of digging up the tree, grinding it to bits, on the spot, stump, root, and branch.

To this day I know hardly anything else about these people except that they have some of the attributes of campers (but aren't there quiet campers, and nice stories about them, and don't campgrounds have their rules?), and at any rate none of the attributes of residents, either of their houses or of the bay. Never have I encountered them except on their properties, or by their cars, which are always ready to start up, whose engines are also often running when the owners are somewhere else, and whose alarms go off at intervals, now here, now there. And never was even one of these neighbors to be found at Mass, or at the local bars, on the soccer field, on the *boules* court, in the handball hall. When the outdoor market opens on Sunday morning on the square in front of the railroad station, they may just possibly pass through the crowd, recognizable by their weekend-only garb, glaringly bright warm-up suits and jogging shoes.

They seem to be of no particular age, neither poor nor rich, and it is uncertain, too, whether they come from the country or the city. If of any origin, then from an alien, extremely alien planet. The only thing that is clear is that they have never had a neighborhood and will never understand what a neighbor is; that in their work other human beings never occur, or if they do, then only as raw material; and that for them Sundays and holidays exist only so that they can broadcast into their surroundings from inside their hedges, as though they were sitting there in its midst, their ever so inventive racket, which always erupts suddenly and at double decibels.

And none of these neighbors feels disturbed by the fellow next door. Each is so engrossed in his own din that he does not even register the other one's. When one of them, again on a Sunday afternoon, out of nowhere, broke the last existing sound barrier, and I, convinced that something terrible had happened to him, wanted to alert his immediate neighbor from my ladder, propped against his fence, there at my feet a shadowy figure, surrounded by a cloud of dust, continued with utmost equanimity to operate a sandblaster, with which he apparently wanted to render his façade as marble-smooth as the palace of Versailles, while to my left a sprinkler was hissing for the benefit of a lone patch of grass with the approximate dimensions of a doghouse, and what to my right was incessantly whinnying behind the shrubbery was anything but a herd of horses, and diagonally at my rear cries of passion continued to blare from a rented video, accompanied next door by the hundredth repetition of the waltz of the fleas or *Bolero*. One of these neighbors remarked once that he did not even hear the noise anymore. So what did he hear? And there had been a time when I thought: If salvation, then through hearing. But what was there to hear now?

An additional factor was that almost every single one of the hitherto remaining interstices, even the most inconspicuous slots, were walled up in no time flat by the new arrivals, used for garages, recreational spaces and various storage spaces, or for enclosures for newly added spiral staircases, so that in the fairly tight ring of buildings around me, instead of the breeze from the woods, a massive echo was created, which made impossible a pinpointing or locating of individual noises, which would at least have provided a kind of reassurance.

And more and more the loudness of these neighbors also came to lack that regularity with whose help one might perhaps have got used to it. The longer they stayed in the bay, the more erratic their world of noise became. I could no longer rely on the initial din. This would break off suddenly, and after a brief, squishy soundlessness, like the sudden cessation of a mosquito's whine in the night, an entirely different one would break out. Something even worse than a roar filled the air: a whanging.

And when all the other inhabitants of the bay had set out somewhere for the day, even if only to the nearby forests: my racket experts stayed behind, at least on Sundays and holidays, glued to the spot, and if they did not create pandemonium outside, they rumbled around inside, armed with machines, between cellar and attic, as invisible as they were audible far and wide. It could happen that in between, exhausted by their frantic activities, they slumped down and stretched out all four paws. But there was always one who kept going in place of all the rest, alone, indefatigable, and it was because of him that I went to the woods to work, even in thunder and lightning.

His new house, with a run behind it for the German shepherd, was the structure closest to the study that had been meant to be my place for the year in the bay. And although there could hardly be anything left to do on his almost immediately clear-cut property, I heard, especially with the onset of spring, my unknown neighbor constantly busy there: if on the other side of the hedge, a few steps from my desk, peace reigned for a change, it meant he was away, the dog shut up in the garage, where it made all the more noise.

The man had a special piece of equipment for each of his gardening activities. There was nothing he did by hand. And each of his equipment sessions took at least as long as the equivalent manual operation. He went about them with grim thoroughness, yet afterward the soil or plantings, viewed through my hole in the hedge, looked exactly the same as before: barer, more monochromatic, more even, more smooth it could not possibly become. Along with the lawn tractor, which almost filled the speck of lawn, including the flagstone terrace, he also operated a sort of shredder, like an antitank mine, for any clumps of grass around the periphery that might have escaped; a sort of motorized water jet for annihilating any traces of weeds in the chinks between the pavers; a sort of trimmer that worked like a laser beam, only much louder, with which he pulverized the couple of blades of grass that might stick up above the rest (never did I discover through my peephole even a single blade poking up); a lawn dryer after too much rain; and all that at the same high volume, though at different pitches, from dentistlike whirring to rattling, shrieking, and thrumming, which made an ordinary banging and grating seem positively comforting.

In addition, from time to time he fired, even under a clear blue sky, a sort of weather cannon, and called in yet more machines to spear intruder leaves that blew in from neighboring yards, for burning out a mole tunnel, for smoking out an ant heap, for neutralizing the squawking of sparrows, for diverting the stronger gusts of wind.

Whenever I, sitting in my study, halfway quiet for a change, heard just beyond my yard the unmistakable squeal of the parking brake and then the crash of the garage door closing, I knew that any moment now one of these machines would start up, which one first? And while trying to take a deep breath outside the door to the study, I saw through the bushes the silhouette of my neighbor pacing off his angular course with one of his power tools, looking self-absorbed and quietly collected, while his dog, driven mad by his pitch-black garage exile, sensing my presence, let out behind the shrubbery sounds entirely different from the earthworm sucker-upper or the depth charge used for detecting a stinging-nettle root invading from next door.

Such tumult (a word which, in the decrees against disturbance of the peace, was always linked with the word "scandal" in the days when the bay was still a royal domain) I could tolerate, at least for a time, at least during the day, and much more easily during work than during mere sitting and watching. The noise receded into the work, was sonorized, so to speak, by my absorption, took on a different sound quality, a darker one. But no sooner would the beginnings of tiredness or distraction brush me than the noise would pound all the more stridently at my study door and against my skull. Then it became dangerous. My material was not yet impervious, and even now, toward the end of the year, is still not impervious. If one sentence or paragraph went, the entire thing was at risk. What was threatened was less my head, my ability to think, than the absolute necessity for me, unlike for a scientist or a chronicler, to become as one with a feeling, a heartbeat, or the rhythmic image.

And with the passage of time I then noticed that in my writing-down, as an effect of the noise, hardly any heart was involved. Without that, however, my thoughts appeared to me as mere singsong. I no longer knew what I was doing. With every attempted image immediately rubbed raw by new whanging, I ended up blindly lining up words next to each other, without any sense for transitions.

How should I call it to my neighbors' attention that I was still there—not as a writer, simply as a neighbor? In the tiny interval between the time my omni-tool neighbor got home and set the parking brake, and the moment he revved up, I would step outside the study door, for example, and try to make myself audible by blowing the shavings out of the sharpener as loudly as possible as I sharpened my pencils. No other noise occurred to me.

Should I shout my sentences into the neighborhood before I wrote them down, like Flaubert? Instead I once tossed a burning log over the hedge at man and dog, whereupon the master, invisible, retorted in a chalky-smooth Sunday voice that I was the one disturbing the peace, after which he promptly cranked up his latest acquisition, a device with which he was either drilling for oil under his seared grass or plowing it up in search of a field-mouse nest.

Thus, with the passage of time, I would jump at even the sound of birds or of water boiling in my own house, as if at the howling of a motor or raucous voices from a party on a nearby terrace.

For my first day of work out in the forest, I sat down by Lizard Way, among the trees a few steps away from it.

It was a warm, sunny May morning, and I leaned against a chestnut tree whose foliage was just beginning to bud, with mossy earth in the root hollow under me. The gentle breeze and the stillness, of which the Niagara Falls-like roar from the distant highway up on the plateau was a part, filled or inspired me with peace.

All day long people passed right by me up there on the bright path. Although I was so close to them, no one noticed me, not even their escort dogs. Around midday most of those passing were joggers from the office buildings in the corporate center of Vélizy, with the variation in this year of 1999 that almost all of them were out there without jogging suits, dressed rather in suits and overcoats, with their briefcases and even heavier ballast.

That was in between. Beforehand and afterward, however, sometimes passed by mountain bikers, figures moved across my field of vision such as I had never before seen in the woods, not even in those of the bay, which from the outset had been full of surprises. (And my head was as clear as my chest was marvelously painfully expanded; I was not having hallucinations.)

While here in the shadows of the leaves my pencils darted along evenly, over there in the sun a priest passed by, in an ankle-length soutane, accompanied by a wedding party, the bride and groom and the witnesses; then came, at a distance, relaxed yet alert, the new cast of *The Magnificent Seven*, all abreast—that was how broad the path was there; then came, after a time, hand in hand, already half lost, gazing heavenward, Hansel and Gretel; then came, hours later, an elegant couple, he in a camel-hair coat, she in high heels and an evening gown—I later recognized the man, tanned, with a blackened mustache, his arm wound around the woman, heading uphill with elastic tread along the edge of the path, through the wild broom, as Don Juan, and the lady as Marina Tsvetayeva (they spoke Russian with each other); then a horse went by, riderless, workhorselike, and with steps as slow as those of his predecessors; and common to all of them was also that they appeared to me less as human beings or as animals than as living beings.

And toward evening the stonemason turned up again, not a wanderer along the path but a person extricating himself from the thick underbrush of the forest reserve over there. He did it matter-of-factly, as if this were simply his way of crossing the countryside, and promptly sank down on the oak stump, so broad that it could have provided a resting place for a dozen hikers. He hung his doublet behind him in the bushes and sat quietly erect, without stirring. A jogger who politely circled around him called out, "Isn't it great here!" to which the stonemason did not even nod. He ate a piece of bread and an apple, which he peeled in one piece, and now gazed across from his seat, which had so often been mine, into the forest toward me.

I had long since suspended my writing. If he saw me, he did not show it; at any rate, his barely perceptible raising of one finger did not have to mean anything. And yet it seemed to me as if I was supposed to address him from among the trees. I did not do so, and he went to work on his sitting trunk with a conspicuously short-handled hammer and a chisel that I at first took for a crowbar, and finally he disappeared back into the area that had been reforested a few years earlier, where the young trees already grew so dense, with hardly a patch of sunlight on the dark ground, that only a fox could get through. He entered there into a space of his own, like a bullfighter, and in response to the pivoting of his shoulders and hips, so rapid as to be almost impossible to follow, and thus seeming all the more purposeful, the straight saplings swayed no more and no differently than in the wind.

Hadn't I imagined time and again that like a mythical beast there must also be a hermit in the bay's forests, and that the old residents knew all about him, as they knew about the beast, but they would not betray him to anyone who had moved there from somewhere else?

I finished my project for the day and then sat down outside the forest by the sandy path, already after sundown, now on the great oak stump myself. The annual rings could not be counted, since the stump was burned coal black, even down into the roots, splayed like fingers and at the same time deeply anchored, and furthermore split by fire. The dense pattern of notches around the base: did this represent the stonemason's marks, or perhaps rather the footprints of birds, the front toes as clearly delineated V's, the one back toe a mere brushmark, marks such as were already there at my feet along the path, now toward evening frequented only by birds, for dustbathing and tripping back and forth?

Across from me, right behind the bank with the lizards, which had already slipped away, and the first trees, was the empty and, to outward appearances, rather gloomy spot where I had been crouching or squatting only a little while ago, and before that the entire day. And at the thought of all the happenings during the course of a day along this woodland path, barely a few hours on foot from the Eiffel Tower, I was filled with an astonishment as powerful as that I had experienced much earlier for at most a moment when half asleep; and the question that Gregor Keuschnig had asked himself a quarter of a century earlier took on new validity: "Who can say, after all, that the world has already been discovered?"

To write I went out into nature, into the fresh air, into the day, into the wind, into the forest, and then if possible every morning, right through the summer and far into the fall. (As recently as yesterday I remained stretched out there until I could hardly make out my own handwriting, and that was also because of the evening dew, for the pencils did not mark properly on the damp paper.)

A couple of times, when the rain became too heavy, penetrating the leaf canopy and not letting up, I continued with my writing in one of the few public buildings in the bay, but hardly ever back at my house; I have been spending more time in my study only since the somewhat quieter days of early winter.

In bad weather I most often sought refuge in the bay's little post office, the "auxiliary post office"—in general the local agencies have modifiers like "branch," "annex," or *provisoire.* There was a counter there intended specifically for filling out forms, even a windowsill, a spacious, broad one for propping one's arms on and looking out, just as I had wished for from the beginning for my writing year.

Outside the window nothing was to be seen but an area marked off by a brick-red wall at the rear, resembling a grove with its few widely spaced spruces and birches, on the ground the short, thick, yet never mowed grass and the several-year layers of spruce needles and cones, among which then in the course of the summer new white-and-red mushroom caps kept erupting, harvested by me with the consent of the postmistress. This woman was alone most of the time and knitted behind the counter or talked on the telephone, as loudly as—fortunately for my concentration—incomprehensibly; she was almost deaf. The fact that I came in out of the storm, sat there, and went away again without ever leaving a letter with her did not disturb her.

When she did have customers, as a rule they were older people, with postal savings accounts. Once there was a telegram to be sent, in Spanish, and it took her an hour to transmit the few words by telephone because of having to spell out everything several times, especially the address. The little place had no telex, for there was no demand, and when a person from elsewhere blew in one day wanting to send a "chronopost" overseas, she explained to him that this was the first time she had ever been asked to do this kind of mailing, whereupon the stranger drove off with his express package, to a post office outside the bay.

Otherwise a great stillness prevailed in the auxiliary post office, without the thumping of rubber stamps or radio music; at most the postmistress's little dog sometimes shifted in his basket. Nothing but the slapping of the rain against the windowpanes; a pattern of shadow from that on the windowsill, or a flash of lightning.

The disadvantage was only that this branch closed early, and thus I sometimes finished my day of recording in the next bay over, in the back room of the restaurant run by the petty prophet of Porchefontaine, whose raging misanthropy I had almost been driven to share by my neighbors' racket; from time to time it did me good.

In his rooms, too, there by the railroad embankment, in a former station restaurant, there were windowsills, wide ones, extending out to my ribs, and even the benches that went with them, as in the ancestral house in the Jaunfeld village of Rinkolach, and all of this shaken again and again by the wonderful rumbling of the trains directly above me.

In this year the weather changed constantly, and always from one hour to the next. But whenever possible I sat outdoors with my project, out in the woods. And what then became my main sitting place was the spot that had attracted me most powerfully earlier on when I was out walking and doing nothing.

Writing beside a body of water was even more promising than writing beside a path. At first I tried it with the three ponds in the bay, one after the other. For a few days I worked halfway up the hill by a sunken road behind the Étang des Ursines, in the largest and also the oldest part of the settlement, where the prehistoric flintstone and stone ax had been found; after that at the weathered picnic table behind the pond with the crayfish, with the mental image of the war correspondent, now dead, of his shock of hair standing up, his stubble-beardedness, his paleness, his total incomprehension of a person like me; then by the one surrounded entirely by woods, without houses in view, called Hole-in-Glove Pond, under the birches there; everywhere I made good progress, except that I did not like to be seen with paper and pencil—some people did pass by, who, however, mistook what I was doing for drawing; none of them came up close—and except that some fishermen had transistor radios with them.

Nonetheless I finally set out for that body of water which, although it always struck me as the only really old one and also the most extensive one in all the forests of the Seine hills, is not marked on any map of the area, even the most detailed, nor does it have a name, even in the folklore of the bay (but who knows?), and which I privately call, after neither "bayou" (Mississippi) nor "Everglades" (Florida) stuck, the Nameless Pond.

Yet the word "pond" does not fit this puddle either, at the sight of which at least the first passersby call back their children or their dogs with exclamations of disgust and horror. In fact its surface, and not only during a longer drought, looks bubbly sometimes or glistens with an oily film, and I have hardly ever been able to see all the way to the bottom. Trees, long since dead, barkless all the way up, naked, only the whitish-gray trunks remaining, with a few broken-off forks of branches, stand there in the water, among those that have tumbled in from the banks and are still green, and aquatic vegetation with dark-haired root tangles below (masses of them in the light of low water).

A puddle, and yet extending far out? Yes, and this on the one hand by virtue of its complicated shape, going around one corner and then another, entirely different from a man-made pond, and especially by virtue of that unique shimmer of distance or enigma in its most remote spits, with a view through the vegetation and dead tree trunks, over hundreds of sawed-off trunks barely rising above the water, a glow of distance reliable in a way I have never encountered in a puddle, but also not in a full-grown lake, either in that of Gennesaret or that of Michigan or that of Neusiedl. Every time, from sitting there awhile, from the farthest tongues of the puddle, along with the water's edge, air, and shore, even when nothing was moving, a pull emanated.

And in such an environment I settled down one lovely spring day to continue my work, and that became my established place, except during torrential rains, until the first frosts.

It was in the thicket on the other side of the Nameless Pond, but I had a view of the water, through a long cut, all the way to the bays in the more accessible bank; but anyone standing over there would have had to look hard to catch sight of me, until the time of leaf drop.

At my back, after a gap to slip through, the underbrush led right up to a forest in the background, not at all dark or crowded, extending up the hill, to the south, so that the sun, filtered through the foliage, shone on my paper as it crossed the sky.

In that same place, on my very first day, I came upon what was left from the sawing up of a mammoth oak, once a cylinder, which had been burned out from the core and had fallen apart, leaving two hollowed-out half cylinders. I rolled the sounder half, with some difficulty—it was so massive—over and over along the mossy ground to a place where it bumped down a steep bank by itself to my watery corner. And there, on the soft, peat-black but not yet swampy ground, I set this shape upright, sat down on the ground, within a foot of my pond bank, leaned back into the half circle of wood, and had a wing chair, without legs, just right for my purposes.

It surrounded me literally and really like a set of wings, and moved with me on the peat soil, yielded, pushed me forward again, but would remain steadfast in the face of my most violent shoves; that was how heavy it was, also from the fire; and besides I felt protected in its curve during my work, shielded from the eyes of the joggers, one or another of whom, especially during mushroom season, would suddenly make the branches crack up there behind me.

There I sat, leaning back (and would like to continue to sit and lean back), and promptly began, with my pencils lined up, the eraser next to them, to write, as if it were child's play, without the usual fear of beginning. I imagined the sentences following the movements of the water at the tips of my shoes, the air streaming all around the trees, the open sky, not exactly right above my head, but plentifully at brow level and as a reflection from the pond, while the sun, whether on the horizons or at its zenith, followed the outline of the semicircle of my backrest.

Unlike earlier I no longer ground to a halt when I realized that something I was just writing down had already been said long ago, by me or by someone else. If I repeated myself or another person now and then, that was fine with me, and of course I did come to a halt each time, except that now I approached the repetition with additional élan, positively elated at the prospect of it.

Certain other concerns also dissolved into thin air: that in the history of the bay and of my distant friends so little was happening; that the plot was not moving; that the sentences were too long for a book nowadays. I let them get as long as the image that was inside me and motivating me required; all that mattered was having such an image inside me. And if it was long-windedness, I felt it to be in harmony with the back-and-forth ripples of the wind on the water, around all seven corners of the pond, and with all that nothing-at-all in between, a little tremble far off, the drilling motion of the red-throated downy woodpecker in the dead wood, who, when I next look up, is giving its stomach a one-second bath, swooping down, with an incomparably delicate splash. It seemed to me as though such simultaneity acted on my storytelling like a verification; as if the water above all, there in its uniqueness, was what confirmed my work—work? here more a mere synchronized breathing.

Besides, I had an infinitely easier time of it, there by that nameless pond, with my project, always in danger of becoming so tied up in knots that no air was left in it, of making paragraphs, or, instead of being forced to conjure up an appropriate transition and a compelling sequence, keeping going imperturbably. Making paragraphs in this context meant only pausing in the middle for a catching of breath, impossible for me as a rule during indoor writing, for a walking away from the page so that it, too, could have a moment's peace.

Thus I remained calm when rainfall heavy enough to force its way through the leaves interrupted me. I tucked my portfolio between my jacket and my shirt, put on my hat, actually brought along for mushrooms, and waited.

The wilder the conditions around the water, the more serene and also patient I became. Stormy winds mingled with pounding rain, sand hit me on the fingers, terminal darkness broke in, thick branches came crashing to the ground, another tree tipped headfirst from the bank into the pond, the many birds of the area, large and small, fluttered back and forth, cawing and squawking, barely missing me, and I sat there, leaning back, with my manuscript, and watched, without batting an eyelash, warm around my heart, this panic-stricken world having emerged clear and whole behind the customary, fragmentary, chimerical one, and in the panic-stricken world that mixed-up creation—not chaos—in which I had always felt at home. "Now it's right."

W hen I was busy there by the water, the surroundings looked entirely different from the way they would have looked if I had merely been sitting there idle. Without my specifically taking them in, they became part of me, in passing.

And again in my memory the animals appear first. (Yet I am not thinking here of the mosquitoes that fell upon me in droves, though not until dusk, when I was usually already finished.)

That all began with the migration of the hitherto completely invisible tribes of toads downhill through the woods to their spawning grounds. The Nameless Pond, by which I was sitting, was their chief destination, even for those toads coming from the most distant of the hills of the Seine, although all the other bodies of water offered more room.

But either they were polluted, like the most appealing of them, that pond called Hole-in-Glove, by the oily effluent from the factories up on the plateau, or they had unscalably steep banks, like the Crayfish Pond, unsuitable for amphibians, or, like the other pond, the largest pond in the bay, the Étang des Ursines, they were separated from the forest by a highway. A resident of the bay had tacked a sign to a tree, asking that people leave the crossing as free of traffic as possible during the couple of days every year when the toad migration could be predicted; the animals were threatened with extinction. But, and not only because of the note on the tree, inconspicuous even to a pedestrian, most of the locals' cars drove as they always did, and every time I walked the road in those days, on my way to my writing place, the flattened corpses were stuck to the asphalt, and the few toads that had made it to the water alive were swimming along the edge of the pond, each seemingly all by itself.

Only to the Nameless Pond, in its hollow deep in the woods, far from the beaten path, was it safe to go; from the toads' regular stamping grounds they had at most to cross footpaths, going more through underbrush, then through swamps, without firm bank lines, and the oil film sometimes floating on the water probably came only from decomposing wood; at any rate nothing flowed into there but rain and a spring, from which the water bubbled transparent. And again and again, for days, the toads hopped past me now on their copulation journey, here and there a leaping procession, some already mounted piggyback on others, and afterward only their eye bulges peeked from the wild water, which eventually looked warty with them far and wide.

Beneath the surface reigned, denser with each passing morning, a great pushing and shoving of these allegedly dying-out animals. The toads, untold thousands of them, clumped together, separated, clumped together elsewhere, chased each other. In time the clumps became quiet, and often it was not only couples but also clusters of several, a black toad on top of a yellow one, and hanging on to this one a brown-and-white-striped one, and when the entire knot drifted to one side, underneath all the rest yet another turned up, again a black one, chieftainlike.

Equally multiple intertwinings, each day more motionless, with perhaps only about a dozen puffed-up skin pouches, producing a soft, piercing fluting, could be seen on land, at my feet on the mossy bank, and when the bodies toddled apart, there turned out to be more and more of them, as with that very small automobile from which, on the basis of a bet, one after the other an entire cohort of students used to scramble. (Where the same thing happened underwater, it was reminiscent on the contrary of the head-over-heels tumbling of a group of astronauts in zero-gravity space.)

And then one day the waters were toadless again, also cleaner than ever before, and instead other unevennesses on its surface, gelatinous masses, black-dotted, with the dots over the course of several weeks growing into the circles and lines of tadpoles, round heads with tails, which soon began to jerk. And since then in all the months I have not seen another toad in my special place.

And the muskrats, too—or is it a new, unfamiliar type of animal, something between a rat and a beaver and a dormouse?—have not been there since fall, while all summer long they scurried every day back and forth between the pond and the land, at home in the hollows of the root mound formed when a swamp birch fell, right at my feet, at the tips of my toes.

It was always liveliest there at the beginning of the week, when the whole tribe of beaver rats, giants and dwarfs and infants, was on the move, around the entire branching water source, gathering food, especially pieces of bread left behind by Sunday hikers on the other, open shore, and almost every minute another animal head would pop out of one of the holes in the root mound, sniffing like a rabbit, the hairs of its beard bristling, translucent roundish cat ears.

As I watched them, I continued writing, and I often used the sight of them, of their reddish, deeply soft coat, of their paws, which looked to me more like delicate white fingers, of their dark, point-glowing eyes, to ponder a word, a connection; their faces, likewise their stocky necks, suddenly of snakelike length when they reached for a morsel, helped me achieve a particular tremulous presence of mind; and with the passing months they no longer jerked back into their hiding places at my writing movements, with which intermittently, at the beginning of a new line, I also sketched their squirrel cheeks, or the apple peels they held between their teeth like a knife—the presence of those muskrats restrained my hand, not always with success, from becoming abrupt.

I also tried simply sitting still with them—but no, only with my writing did they come out of their holes, and similarly only when I

was writing did the big turtle sit on the trunk that had fallen into the
water and stretch its head toward the sun.

A nd in the course of the year, of the summer, of the fall, it seemed
that when I sat still that way, but yet was busy, events occurred in
my field of vision that would never have come about through observation
or pure contemplation, even an entire day's worth; yes, it was as if only
my constant writing provoked the appearance of living things previously
invisible in the landscape, perhaps not even existent.

Was a certain way of glancing away from the space or the field of
vision, of looking elsewhere, all that was needed for a form of flora or
fauna unheard of even in this area, including those thought to have died
off long ago, to reveal itself, as if it had always been there? A leaf, quietly
drifting on the water, suddenly turned, stood straight up, and revealed
itself as a primeval animal.

How often in childhood I had crouched in the deepest underbrush,
by the overgrown ditches, waiting for an event. Nothing had stirred.
But now, surreptitiously, as I sat engrossed in the story of my distant
friends, so much was happening, things I could never even have dreamed
of in those days, in a more original period, in a still hardly disturbed
countryside.

On one of my first summer writing days, quiet, warm, with a high
blue sky, on the way to the woods I had had the phrase "eagle-circle
day" in my head, and sure enough, at midday, when far and wide nothing
more was moving, the embodiment of that notion, an eagle, *the* eagle,
after prolonged circling at the zenith, landed, even if only for an instant,
in the highest fork of the sturdiest, most cliff-gray of the dead trees in
the pond, with a profile such as has never been seen on any coat of arms,
and for whose return I have now been waiting for months; the entire
trunk rocked when it flew away, and part of the fork broke off into the
water.

And for several days, later in high summer, little fishes leaped up out
of the puddle, as if prodded by the blustery wind, leaped in a wide arc,
making the water spray all over, each time one swarm of fins after the
other, lengthwise over the body of water, with a whiplike crack, which

in turn scared into the deciduous forest the bunch of wild doves, which, sitting on the leafless branches above the pond, were more apt to be mistaken for vultures than elsewhere.

And likewise in this succession the water snakes returned, last seen by me a decade ago, in the summer when I moved there, and since then never again; glided from a grassy bay into the pond and made it twice as large by plowing through it, changing direction again and again, one here, one there, thin, so fragile, on their raised heads white blurry spots. Only after the Sundays when the opposite bank became bright (not black) with people and dogs, I often had to wait for the middle of the week until, during my writing, on the otherwise perhaps smooth pond surface in one spot the odd teeny-weeny waves would turn up and then for hours move back and forth on a very curvy cruise.

Each of these animals had its more or less brief heyday during the summer, so that I have a clear impression, for instance, of the week of the water strider, of the day of the hornets, of the dusk of that giant hedgehog, tapping its way, mammoth-sized, through last year's leaf layers, the hour of the seagull that fluttered into the bayou by mistake, the long, long moment of the giant dragonfly, hovering in the air directly before my eyes, face to face with me, its four-wing rotor transparent, nothing of the insect clearly outlined except the seemingly eyeless face, of an uncanny yellow, or the entire face a single universe-sized yellow eye, in whose omnipresence, after a moment's pause, I continued my sentence.

That was already in early fall, and then the dragonflies continued to come, even on warm November days, though also never again so close.

The only creatures besides the little birds in the bush that kept me company the entire time were the ordinary pond ducks and the coots. The latter, light in weight, could skim across the leaves that had fallen into the water, or, when they swam, they glided along in a straight line, their tail feathers sticking straight up in the air, beyond the densest thicket of the nameless lake, like Indian canoes, from which sometimes a warning cry sounded.

And the ducks here on the Nameless Pond had the peculiarity that they did not look all that ordinary as they rolled and pitched in the confusion of water, greenery, and decomposing wood, but rather as rare and remarkable as all the rest of the animal life; each, in its appointed time, was a mythical beast (including the few squirrels).

With the people who appeared at intervals on the opposite bank, such correspondences manifested themselves less frequently, and hardly ever on holidays, when, enhanced by the surface of the water, at times something like a human loudspeaker wall was going full blast over there. (But here it helped to remember that the place where I was, unlike a house, did not give me any particular rights.)

Nevertheless, when a dog suddenly threw itself into the water, it sometimes came across as the leaps, along with the splashdowns, of heavy fish, not yet discovered by me, or I heard the whir of the mountain bikes during the downhill swoops of the self-appointed adventurers, more properly called path destroyers, as the sound of the wild doves circling the treetops.

And in the course of the seasons altogether different forest people gained the upper hand in the clearing on the other side, people of whom I sometimes thought, when I had my eyes first on my paper, then over there on them, that they, too, had been sketched in the air or summoned to that spot only by my own activity.

One day a heavily laden group of emigrants or Sherpas trudged past over there; on another the woodsmen were cooking their lunch on a fire so big that even days later I could still warm my hands, chilly from all my sitting by the water, over the residual glow; on a third I wrote until sundown while watching a young man who during all those hours sat on one of the other banks, went into the pond, swam, washed his hair, shaved, slipped back and forth between the swamp vegetation, always almost just as noiselessly, and in whom I eventually recognized an es-caped murderer, after his picture appeared in *The Hauts-de-Seine News*. And Don Juan returned, his mustache neatly brushed as always, and with the same woman!

And the noisemakers, at least those on the weekdays, with their rest-lessness, never lingered by the Nameless Pond, and precisely the intervals were then filled with a never before experienced sort of stillness, so de-lightful that often and even more often I felt my eyes grow moist from the feeling; it was not permissible for me to remain alone with this silence; it was supposed to be shared.

And not only because of the many helicopters above me, continuing all summer to shuttle between the peace talks in Paris and the air base at my back, I hardly ever felt outside of time by the water; I was not merely intermittently a witness of world events during the year but also a participant. Sitting in that natural wing chair with my pencils on the bare earth while the waters before me coursed back and forth, I traveled with the day through the world. Who knows of, who can describe to me a lovelier round-the-world tour?

Thus during the day I stayed away from life in the bay. On my circuitous morning route to my water seat, I avoided the railway station square with its shops, the only realm where from time to time, especially on market mornings, things were lively in an ordinary sense. Only in the evening did the time come for moving about there, preferably on one of the straightforwardly loud tangential streets. After the daylong secrecy out there by the damp-black hairy cones of the willow roots arching over the pond surface, among which a crocodile mouth would have seemed almost too familiar, I felt swept by a particular wind on these arteries and highway access roads, as once on the boulevards in the middle of Paris after my dim-room work.

Of course here there were no sidewalk cafés, and hardly passersby. But it had been a long time since I had felt drawn, as when I was younger, to sit on terraces of an evening and people-watch. And the right place for such reflective relaxation was inside the bars, while standing at the counter, following the example of the majority there.

Most often in the evening I sought out those two or three bars in the bay where, because rooms were also available, in addition to the local drinkers, male and female, almost always the same ones, you could also find itinerant workers—though only for one glass; after that they sat down to supper in another room, clearly separated from the taproom: in the Hôtel des Voyageurs by a fabric-covered sliding door that opened only when the individual courses were served to those workers by the proprietress in person; in the Hôtel Rive Gauche by a curtain, carefully drawn by the workers themselves. There in their dining chambers they seemed to be carrying on the only important conversations of the moment, with barely moving lips, inaudible, and came at intervals out to the telephone corner to transmit their decisions to the world.

I did not listen in on their conversations; perhaps precisely because my thoughts were elsewhere, or nowhere, I picked up various things. These itinerant workers were very fussy about their food, and not infrequently a group would change lodgings for this reason. For their aperitif—with appropriate facial expressions, and freshly combed and shaved, they drank or sipped it—they stood in a group by themselves, and afterward sat very straight at their tables, reserved for them, painstakingly set, illuminated altogether differently from the bar, each man as collected as courteous, and all of them always equally unapproachable. Yet their evening meal did not last long; as a rule they went up to their rooms early, in summer even before dark, and sometimes I heard one of them complain the following evening about the noise outside, with a quiet assurance I would have wished to have myself. They also did not play cards or dice as the locals did.

A few of the crews remained in the bay for months; and in the course of the year I also encountered them during the day, at their work, the replacement of the gas pipeline through the woods, the building of a railroad viaduct, the renovation of the bus station. There, on my circuitous routes, it was easier for me, indeed entirely natural, to stop and take in their work (something otherwise done by only the oldest long-term inhabitants here). They pounded stones into place, now and then putting their ear to them, in a manner similar to that in which they spent their time after hours, except that they preferred to be watched at work, it seemed to me. Pride was not the same as unapproachability.

I often stood like this for an hour, for instance when another of these itinerant crews was digging out a spring in the forest, until the moment when shovelful by shovelful the trickle of water became a jet, and one of the workers, in the absence for the time being of a tile, got it to rattle into a hollow leaf. And now we greeted one another. And then we did that as well in the evenings, from a distance, without shaking hands as local bar frequenters customarily did.

Only once did one member of such a team address me in the evening, followed by the man next to him, and so on, until long after midnight. Without their relinquishing their masterful air, like that of dignitaries, it came out that in their eyes it was not they who were shutting out the population of this region, but rather the residents who were ignoring them. No one, except perhaps the proprietor of the inn—but he himself was a foreigner—ever had a word for the itinerant work crews, or even a flicker of a facial expression. And everywhere they worked it was the same, and this one small exception seemed to these itinerant workers such a joyous occasion that they surrounded me, plucked at me, and finally shoved me around like a newly discovered member of the tribe. (On subsequent evenings, however, all we exchanged was greetings.)

With the itinerant workers, the majority of them Frenchmen from the provinces who on weekends went home to their families, no matter how far it was, for the only time up to now I found myself enjoying spending time with people here, being cheerful and in good spirits; the gleaming floor tiles and the snowy glistening of the walls in the dining room formed part of this experience. I have never sat or even just stood around this way somewhere with any of the original inhabitants of the bay, although in the meantime I have come to know there is something special about them; at the very most someone—where else but in the bars or perhaps also on a wood road?—confided in me, and then it was only the deranged or those with their heads not screwed on right; but these merely stuttered incomprehensibly and in any case avoided storytelling altogether, and if a question slipped out of me: immediate clamming up, turning away, end of conversation.

That the original population of the bay, although lacking any allures, was somehow unique and perhaps also wanted to maintain that quality, was something I deduced from a fragmentary local chronicle printed in *The Hauts-de-Seine News*. The bay, it said, had been a place of asylum since the beginning of the century, first for Russians and Armenians, then for Italians under Mussolini and Spaniards under Franco. Between the two world wars as much as a quarter of the population here were newly arrived asylum seekers, unusual for a western suburb of Paris.

And that was still reflected, it seemed to me, in the comportment as well as the housing of those who were now old: they, too, had been itinerant workers, and here was their residence (for instance with names like "Our Sundays" or "Sweet Refuge"). As far as I could ascertain, they spoke with the quick tongue characteristic of French small farmers, but in their case it was not at the cost of reflectiveness; they combined the natives' rhetoric with the eyes of foreigners; but wanted, however, to keep the latter for themselves.

During this year, after the one week of escape to Salamanca, I rarely went outside the bay.

After working on my project, I was too tired to stride along briskly, and thus I took the commuter train to Paris, if I was going at all. Only once, on the return trip, did I get off one station early, in Meudon–Val Fleury, and walk home, as I had always pictured doing, through the 3,233-meter tunnel under the Seine hills, in a draft smelling slightly scorched, feeling relieved after all when the occasional "Exit" arrows no longer pointed toward my back but forward, toward the bay.

How astonishing it was each time to see the horizon-wide scattered white splendor of the capital, which during my entire time by the jungle waters would actually have beckoned to me, with all its landmarks, if the wooded hills had not stood between us, as a prolongation of my shoe tip, of the skiff almost entirely sunk in the pond, and the muskrats splashing around there.

Nevertheless, on those few Paris evenings I almost never went all the way into one of its centers. Since I had long since begun to shun the movie theaters, boulevards, and sidewalk cafés—and this year all the more—there were only two destinations left for me in Paris. One of them was those interior spaces that were shaken periodically by the Métro underneath; and it was for that, not the film, that I descended into a movie theater one time. And the other was a certain pissoir, perhaps the last of the old kind, made of iron, painted in dark enamel, with a sort of temple roof, the whole thing a miniature round temple, partitioned in two by a pissing wall, down which on both sides water ran constantly from a gutter at eye level, both halves offering standing room for a man in need, shielded from eyes on the street, except for his head and feet, by milk-glass screens, which gently reflected the sun and the city lights.

This little cottage was located by the Pont Mirabeau, actually on the edge of the city, and it still existed, they said, only because of the taxi drivers who had a stand next to there and resisted having to stick money in a slot to urinate. And meanwhile that had become the only place in Paris to which I felt drawn from time to time. Having got out at Javel station and trudged across the bridge (from which the Seine, certainly mighty at that point, each time seemed less significant to me than my wild little pond) and then being greeted by this structure, otherwise easy to mistake for an empty kiosk, but chimerically changing its form with each of my steps, I would as a rule simply post myself in one of the semicircles, stare for a while at the gutter up above, from which for an eternity the water has been rolling down, wall-wide, listen to it running, also contemplating the spotlights refracted by the milk-glass screen on the other side, and before leaving dip my fingertips into the gutter up above.

And one time during this year I did make my way into a Parisian center after all: that of St.-Germain-des-Près, to contemplate the frieze of the Last Supper above the portal of the church there, from the twelfth century, where the heads that had been knocked off, one after the other, in the revolutionary eighteenth, leaving only the outlines, one of which, that of the apostle John, who has thrown himself on the table before his master, revealed to me the entire planet, the earth.

On the few evenings between the summer and now when I again wandered around the city, I saw the woman from Catalonia every time: not her imperial self, but in the form of other women, and once that of a man.

On one of these evenings I ran into Ana in a Métro station near the periphery, let's say at the Porte d'Auteuil, as a transient. She was young, tall and broad-shouldered, with long dark hair, and of a beauty that pierced me to the quick. I was surprised that all the lady-killers in the city, in Montparnasse or on the Champs-Elysées, had not caught wind of her and formed a cavalcade behind her. But that was a year in which more and more young women were wandering around, and thus she was alone there in the half-dusk, as perhaps only such a beauty could be, with her bundle of bursting plastic bags, her fur coat in August, and her head askew.

I followed Ana out of the subway up onto the broad square from which roads led out of the city, where nocturnal plane trees rustled as they always had, and from all directions the headlights of cars crossed. She walked slowly, but without the load that hung down on both sides of her she would simply have remained in one spot; she moved crookedly, as if in a squall, following her wind-cocked head, diagonally across the square, dodging vehicles. And finally she stopped in front of a bustling sidewalk café and unexpectedly, with a simultaneous curtsy, thrust out both hands in a ballet-dancer gesture by a table, begging, without success, and had already disappeared around the corner.

Another time I came upon my wife while crossing, let's say, the Avenue de Versailles, as a woman hobbling along on crutches, except that the foot was not in a cast, it was missing. She acted as though nothing were wrong, moving gracefully, she, too, out and about alone, and with her one-legged hobbling and at the same time rapidly hastening steps, turned her head every few seconds to look over her shoulder into the void, for a contented blink, as if she were marching overland (she made me realize that an individual can "march" as well).

And as I stared after the cripple, I recalled a dream about the two of us. In it I had sawed off one of Ana's arms, and then did the same thing to myself, and only when I was through with the saw did I become aware that I, too, was now missing a hand, equally indispensable for writing and for something else. And what had the woman from Catalonia said once in response to my story of that time under the staircase in my brother's house in the village?: "That kind of under-stair person is just what you are, turned in on yourself, warmed by yourself. But again and again a hand reaches out from under your staircase and grabs the person who is passing by outside, or at any rate me, in a way no hand ever grabbed me before."

Then I once saw Ana as a man, in a restaurant one evening along the outer boulevards. It was a guest just coming in from the dark outside, neither young nor old, a sort of faceless Everyman in a hat and gray raincoat, and as I took him out of the corner of my eye for the woman from Gerona and El Paso, whom he did not resemble in the slightest, I realized that I had been expecting her, and at the same time, from my shock at seeing the angular masculine figure, that my waiting was actually full of apprehension.

And the vanished woman appeared to me one last time in the nocturnal commuter railway, in a stranger, with a very different face, eyes, hair. As I sat facing this unknown woman, I suddenly found myself contemplating my wife of many years.

I had not been able to look at the real Ana this way even once. An expectant calm emanated from her, at the same time impudence or playfulness, or the storytelling urge (as indeed she often said after a bruising quarrel that she had been dying the entire time to tell me how her day had gone). This fellow passenger did not avoid my gaze; she allowed it to have its way, then even responded with a smile, created in her expressionless face merely by my looking at it.

This was thinking in images, wordlessly. In this image the woman from Catalonia had a plane tree from the forest of Gerona as a background, from which a sparrow burst forth like a flying fish. She was a bride, would be that to the end; a needy person; a person pleading for protection. And so were other women, mothers of eleven, murderers of six, strumpets, high jumpers, Amazons.

And an almost forgotten yearning returned. And that was the night when I got out early in Meudon–Val Fleury, while the Gypsy woman continued on to St.-Quentin-en-Yvelines, and hiked home on foot through the scorched tunnel under the hills of the Seine. (And for the very last time I saw Ana in the form of a woman's lost glove in the bushes.)

It is of course not true that during this year of 1999 I had no contact with a local resident. I even acquired a good neighbor, at least one, a child.

Before the child turned out to be a neighbor, I had already seen him quite often, in the little Russian church on the edge of one of the forests here, and once also on the handball court during a game played by the local team, the pride of the region after working its way up into the First League. He was with his parents, but I actually had eyes only for him.

In the Slavic church he, for his part, once looked during the whole Sunday Mass only in my direction, though alternating between my face and my shoulder, or the empty space above it, back and forth, until I imagined he was looking for another child there. He was still almost a baby, not yet speaking, only from time to time making sounds, once a bull bellowing, then the harsh cry of a large bird, and in between he crawled around on all fours among the congregation.

It was during this spring that his father, with him in his arms, un-expectedly came crashing through the bushes and pounded on my door, his eyes so big that I took their expression for ecstasy. In actuality he had just been informed that during an operation on his wife in the Sèvres hospital her heart had stopped under anesthesia. He asked me to watch the child until he got back, in a stammer that was more Russian than French, and I went on with my writing, holding the small child on my lap, the rhythm making him soon nod off, heavy in my arm, until after some time the father returned with news of her death.

From then on I also met this neighbor away from the chapel, at his house. There, to be sure, I was usually alone with the boy, who was called Vladimir; the man, one of the drivers of the peculiar buses in the bay—of which more later—occasionally worked until almost midnight, and it had become the routine for me to stay with the child if possible.

Whenever I prepared the evening meal for us both, it came to mind how at one time the thought of having a family, my family, had not made me feel strange or beside myself, but rather positively sturdy, with both feet on the ground. To create a family: for me in those days there was, as far as everyday life was concerned, no greater fulfillment; and I wanted to do my work not merely for those entrusted to me but also in their midst, unisolated, without a solitary study. To do the housework as well, washing windows, cooking, darning stockings, was all right with me; I had not really needed the precedent of David Herbert Lawrence, another cottager's son, who had expertly scrubbed the floor for his aris-tocratic wife.

Now during evenings with Vladimir, and most powerfully during apple peeling or cutting bread, the memory of that meant it was coming alive again for me, also as something I had been missing after all throughout the time I was alone. The half orphan's ways intensified this feeling. If I, worn down by my neighbors' racket, actually felt hostile toward one child or another out there, that was unthinkable with this one here.

When he imitated me, it was never a question of mimicking; he did it in his own unique way, in whose reflection my actions in turn pleased me and made me happy. Thus it happened that in his presence I sketched out on a piece of paper what I had in mind to write the following morning, whereupon he, though only beginning to speak, every time wrote and drew something, which, although it seemed fairly similar, was an entirely different process: his writing was very vehement, yet his drawing was very deliberate. And both were done smoothly, without hesitation, and he always knew when something was finished; with the dashing final stroke and a last mighty drop of spit falling from his open mouth onto the paper came the decisive: "Done!" (But with the start of an undertaking, even selecting crayons, he was choosy, like the itinerant workers.) Compared with his, my own handwriting seemed to me ugly, also insignificant, and I wished it were as indecipherable, dense, and delicate as that of this little child.

When in the course of the year he acquired speech, it was quite an event to hear his first questions. That raising of the voice at the end of a sentence had the ring of a formulation never heard in such a way, close to song. And I experienced an even greater event when Vladimir then, in response to a question of mine, for the first time began to tell a story. That happened completely apart from his usual speaking and even singing; a long, tense silence preceded it, followed by a palpable formation of images and then a rhythm in the deepest recesses of the child's inward being, a shining forth, and then he launched into it, his introductory sound a rolling of the tongue, a clacking, a positively melodic jubilation.

Yet in his everyday speech, too, he visibly had an object before his eyes for every word, in contrast to so many French children, who before the first image had learned already the words for it, so that even for them as adults the words could never represent something actually seen.

And another special thing happened with him: when he began to stammer. It was not regression into infant babbling, but rather a sort of ecstatic state, from which the child, so fiery and imperious that no one needed a translation, took a position on the world's goings-on and proclaimed his view of the situation. These speeches always began with a sharply articulated, almost shouted "And now!" and only after that launched into inspired stammering.

If Vladimir could say of someone: "I know him," the expression was infused with pure pleasure. If he was asked what this person or that "did," he would reply: "He's there." But at intervals he would fall completely silent, and when I then glanced over at him, his eyes would be wide open, focused on me, as they had been for a long time already, almost alarmingly. And when he played, what credulous playing it was —the credulity of play.

Sometimes he merely listened for a while, and it became clear to me, from the birdsong, trains pulling in and out (which in the meantime I had otherwise long since stopped hearing), the rattling of the garbage trucks (here often in the evening), how wide the bay was becoming. With him at my side, it was as if the barking of dogs, as well as the year-round screeching of the ravens, were happening for his and our protection. And when he then slept, I sat next to his room in the kitchen as the household employee on call, and I liked that as much as the unaccustomed view from there through the trees of my own house, with lights on, as always at nightfall, in every room, and looking so mysterious from the unfamiliar kitchen.

"A child," I thought, "keeps joy going in the world, and what else is the world?" That I had already had a similar thought: all the better.

Then in the course of the summer the business with the mushrooms in the bay began, in time even interfering with my year's work, and this time the danger came from me myself.

But perhaps I am exaggerating, and mushroom hunting should be seen more as a kind of competition to sitting and recording, a fruitful one?

During that year every species of edible mushroom gradually found its way to my heart, and the main characters, yes, were the cèpes, or, as we called them in Austria, king boletes. I had never been a mushroom expert, and am still not one today. (Or any kind of "expert," God forbid.) Yet finding them had been a great pleasure way back in my childhood, even if in the Jaunfeld region I had at most had an eye for what we called egg yolk mushrooms, or chanterelles, which often had parasols or umbrellas that more than covered both palms. I recall how after an extraordinarily rich find, halfway into the mountains along the Yugoslav border, when I was out hiking with my grandfather, a night came during which in my sleep I zigzagged from one yellow patch of chanterelles to the next, scooping them up, and in the end that was one of my most enduring nightmares. And no one in the house ate these yellow ones; they were sold (I owed my first paperbacks to the proceeds) to a cooperative and transported from there by truck to the regional capital. And if memory serves me, there was not a single find of king mushrooms in my entire childhood. My grandfather turned up, rarely enough, with one, called *jurček* in Slovenian—rather disrespectfully, precisely out of admiration?—but he, who otherwise was happy to share, did not reveal his sources to me, his frequent companion, and I still picture stumbling one day upon a sealed testament in which he passes on to me the secret locations.

Not until the summer of my move here on the other side of the hills above the Seine did I suddenly see, without really looking, on a sunken road, from whose crest it was not all that far east to the next Métro, and only a hop, skip, and jump to the Eiffel Tower, king boletes standing there, amazing also in their perfection so close to the mountain-bike ruts, and as if they were there just for me. The hat in the crook of my arm was then wonderfully weighed down by the few light brown caps, whose fresh smell accompanied me through the subway and along the avenues, except that the pedestrians in the metropolis took them, along with the leaves clinging to them, for theatrical props, real live objects like the edibles in the windows of Japanese restaurants.

That summer was also the summer of the king boletes on the future Bordeaux bank, along the forest side of the bay's main road, grubbed out of the earth by children sliding down for fun. And both finds I cooked for a reconciliation meal with the woman from Catalonia, or wasn't it simply a matter of enjoying them together, without any particular purpose? And of these meals I still recall that we immediately pushed aside the other ingredients, meat as well as herbs, because all at once these tasted so insistent, even coarse, and put only the white thin mushroom slices into our mouths, one piece only after we had thoroughly savored the previous one; that with each bite the taste promptly became a feeling, not merely gratifying the palate but also the head and then the entire body; and that, if we two mushroom eaters took on the air of conspirators, certainly not ones planning anything bad.

———

Since then I have been on the lookout every year in the bay, but have hardly ever encountered the king bolete again (except in the autumn at the market on the railroad station square, though heaps of them there, at fruit and potato stands, with a little sign indicating their origin, *cèpes de Corrèze*, a region considered the most remote or interior in France).

Instead I collected the multitude of other edible varieties, and was happy with every russula, cèpe, or ringed bolete, varieties the mushroom-seeking clubs tended to leave behind. For years I also spent not a few autumn evenings studying a large-format, thick book with the title *The Mushrooms of Alaska*, simply as a stimulus to fantasizing, at the same time struck by the similarities among a number of mushrooms from the tundra up by the Bering Strait or from the volcanic Aleutian Islands and those here in the bay, for instance in their rich coloration, along with their adaptation to the soil colors, also their woodiness (especially those under birches). And I encountered variations so rare in the forests here that they were not mentioned in even one of the French mushroom guides—which claimed that the chestnut forests and acidic soil around Paris made for poor mushroom country—but turned up in a Slovenian guide, the fruit of an expedition of engineers, as researchers and authors.

The king boletes, after almost a decade in which they had not allowed me to catch a glimpse of them in this area, returned only this year, and again unexpectedly, without my having to search for them, and most abundantly right around my spot deep in the woods behind the Nameless Pond, where I settled down two seasons ago to get on with my work.

One midsummer morning when I arrived there, the first one received me, majestically, right after I had slipped through to the burned-out stump, my backrest. And to convey the sight, I shall use after all what I noted down at the time: "Reflection in the face of a beautiful thing: 'I have never seen such a thing before!' And although he had often seen it before, he was thinking the truth."

I then waited a long time to pick it, traced an arc around my find, first picked one of the much softer and more yielding ringed boletes, in which, when I held it to my ear, maggots were raging audibly. And when I finally took hold of the shaft of the thing, or being, or king— without my fingers' quite getting around it—I felt a trembling in it, and when I cut it off, with utmost care, using my pocketknife, there was a sound from the last subterranean fiber as if from a string even

lower than the lowest guitar string, and certainly not one that was snapping.

As I then took my place, with a glance at the rotund form at my
side, it was as if my daily work quota were already done for today.

From that time on, for months, until late fall, I did not once begin
my writing until I had found at least a hatful of edible mushrooms, which I first lined up on the forest floor, with all their faces
toward me.

Initially there was hardly another king bolete among them; coming
upon one remained for a goodly time a rarity. But gathering the other
kinds (and they, too, had to be searched for attentively) in the forests
around the bay, and occasionally eyeing them, in the midst of my work,
could be refreshing and cheering. I then saw myself, while I continued
writing about the year here and my distant friends, as having company,
one which with its so varied colorations and sizes accompanied me.

And this did not produce a sense of guilt like picking wildflowers:
these mushrooms, the fragile, snow-white head of the inky caps (still too
young to have ink in their lamellae), the rough-skinned boletes, called
birch scaberstalks, repeating in miniature a birch with their scarred-
looking stems (though with a reddish-brown mushroom cap in place of
the tree's crown), the bluish russulas, called indigo milkcap, at the same
time spattered with the clay of the sunken path—they had all lived for
the purpose of being found by someone, by me, for example.

Whenever such a mushroom had already been nibbled away by worms,
I had a sense of having missed something, and specifically with this one;
as if it had grown not for this brood of worms but only for being consumed by someone like me, and perhaps beforehand being gnawed at a
bit by a snail. And it was the same with the mushrooms that had simply
dried up or rotted: I felt sorry for them, sorry that at the appointed time
they had not become a taste sensation in a human mouth.

No more delicious sight than these intact little mushroom tribes on
my right, which had clearly just thrust their way before sunrise out of
the earth, and were still damp from it. If I ever had to offer an image
of what "virginal" looks like, I would point to the underside of the cap
of a baby ringed bolete (the kind that most quickly falls prey to de-

vouring worms), and from there would as carefully as possible peel off
the stem casing or dress: never has the world seen a color as pale and
bright as in the flesh that would come into view, never such purity as
that of the tiny and evenly patterned—in the quintessential hexagon—
mushroom fleshland. Come ye and see: when you have removed that
spongy underlayer, the naked ringed bolete, or butter mushroom, or
whatever name you give it, offers a cross section of a heavenly body on
which no human foot has ever stepped, void and pure, at the same time
of concentrated fruitiness. You cannot preserve both of those, except
perhaps if you consume the mushroom, if possible without delay.

But of course since that one midsummer moment, on my morning
circuitous paths to my sitting place, I was on the lookout for further
bolete majesties. Even one was a find. It alone could send a thrill through
me (even if at the beginning I would usually back away from it in
spirals); it contributed to my sense of revelation that, simultaneously
with the charm and the power at my feet, bombers were flying over the
treetops, from the highways audible in the distance ambulance sirens
wailed, or even just a team of mountain bikers, helmet after helmet,
came crashing out of the underbrush on one side.

Finding the few king boletes during that summer was something I
actually owed almost every time to the mountain bikers. They carved
such deep ruts through the several years' layers of leaves, especially in
the steep sunken roads, that as a result mushrooms were sprung from
the otherwise covered ground, like stones under heavy tires, and, if by
some lucky chance they were not beheaded or crushed, lay there on top
in the light of day, ready to pick up.

It could happen that in the tire tracks of the previous days I then
found another, one the downhill swoop had merely bumped, which had
continued growing, but instead of up toward the air, down into the
humus, head down toward the earth's interior, and harshly bent back
against its stem, in the crouching position of an embryo, which also
hides its face. For this one I had first to burrow my way in; by itself,
deformed as it was, it would never have come to light.

Only after the autumn rains did the finds begin to multiply. Nevertheless, every single one of the king boletes was still a revelation to me. When there came a day on which there were too many for me, that did not mean that I had grown tired of them, but I could not grasp all the revelations anymore: the one giant king bolete that I found that evening growing under the edible chestnut in my yard, as if it had followed me there from the woods, almost belonged in a horror tale—and the next morning I woke up longing for another just like it, under the same tree.

But most of them turned up around the spot where I sat and wrote, beyond the pond, in a space the size of a room, for weeks on end, day after day. And each time hours were spent on looking around, hunting, poking for them, before I finally got down to my project.

But my project, what was it now? A single object like this, as earthly heavy as unearthly in my hand: how could anything I might write down in the course of the day outweigh such a living thing? Even when I felt sure a place that yielded rich finds was empty, at least until the coming year, there, or a few underground flame-yellow root tangles farther along, overnight a new majesty of the forest floor had shouldered its way to the surface and had appeared on the scene or the stage, so monumentally that precisely for that reason it was easy to overlook, next to other, much more eye-catching mushrooms.

In such a moment there came from my lips, without premeditation, and not only once: "My friend." And first I would dig away the leaf mold from around it, until the oval stem was exposed down to its very base and perhaps even tipped over all by itself, freeing itself from its net of roots; then I would sniff it, taking in the essence of the forest, and only then, much later, would I harvest the king bolete, whereupon I silently displayed it to my gathered ancestors from the Jaunfeld, who had been looking over my shoulder the entire time in a way that I never felt when I was writing—except when it was my mother.

It could happen that one of these finds made when I arrived in the morning was merely child-sized, so to speak, and also correspondingly pale, and I let it grow and take on color until quitting time (though in between I went back again and again to check on it). And only later, when the mushroom seekers appeared—of them more in a moment—whom no king bolete, however infant-sized, escaped, even if I had hidden it under moss and branches, did I pick each one immediately—they were not to have it!

Yet in my desire to forestall the troops of mushroom seekers, as time went by I overdid my own seeking. In my backwoods realm, and that meant within sight of my sitting stump, my pencils, and my writing portfolio, I grubbed up every inch of layered leaves, and soon I was doing it every day, down to the rotted mold and even deeper, into the black, long since compacted, then light and sandy, original soil.

I divided my search area into a grid of parcels or claims, and on one of them, I stumbled one day, in a former grub hole, on such a tribe of king boletes, actually resembling whitish pupae, but with firm flesh, almost all of them lying horizontally, facing in one and the same direction, like mummies in the hold of those ancient Egyptian ships of the dead, buried in desert sand for their crossing to another life and immortality.

I ended up with coal-black fingers that could not be scrubbed clean, and my nails broke off from almost an entire autumn of digging for mushrooms around my writing materials, and when, from time to time, I went for the evening to the restaurant of the prophet of Porchefontaine, almost the only person with whom I had any regular contact during the current year, he waved me over to the corner table "for hunters and woodsmen."

Even though, after such king bolete expeditions, carried out in one location, I sometimes did not sit down to write until afternoon, dangerously late, it seemed to me, in fact I hardly ever experienced that as a disadvantage after all. Agitated both by the exertion of searching and by the enthusiasm of discovery, I found peace when I finally got down to writing. I recovered my breath while doing work that seemed incidental, also a part or the essence of my free time; I recovered with its help, came up for air. Weak was not the same as lacking strength.

On my autumnal walks home from the woods, for the first time in my decade here one original inhabitant of the bay or another addressed a word to me, because of the mushrooms in my hat.

At first that happened only in passing, in the shouts of fishermen, to the effect that it was "forbidden" to "transport" such things "in a hat!," or in the resounding astonishment of an old woman, who, as she said, had hunted the eyes out of her head every fall, but never yet with success.

Then one time an equally elderly loner began, at the sight of the mushrooms, to tell stories, without directing them particularly at me: that
the nameless body of water had been created by an American bomb,
which was intended for the air base of Villacoublay, in those days occupied by the Germans, but went off course like ten thousand others;
that the woods in his youth had been even more of a jungle; and the
loneliness was enormous, "rougher" than before; retired people did play
boules together, but never had anyone invited him over; at home he was
keeping a cèpe, at least as large as all of mine together there, for Sunday
dinner, "not in the refrigerator, in the cellar!" and this one, unlike my
chestnut king boletes, was from an oak tree, with just a bit of a bloom
on the cap, otherwise colorless, "that's the only kind I gather"; at the
time of the German occupation, the woods here had been full of cannon,
off-limits; and he had never yet found a good mushroom in a bomb
crater; the water did not drain out.

And whenever I came home with a particularly good find, a model,
an example, a model example, I felt a desire to invite someone, an enemy
(but did I still have one left?), to a reconciliation meal, or my noisy
neighbors. It was not right to cook and eat by oneself this manna, not
fallen from heaven but risen from the earth, unpredictable, untamable,
even in this day and age unplantable. And yet that is what I did every
time, consumed it all, my eyes closed.

What happened in the process: as I cut up the mushrooms, almost
every evening, sautéed, perhaps salted, perhaps drizzled them with olive
oil or something else, the kitchen, neglected for a long time, became a
place for me again, and thus the house was altogether inhabited anew.
Come ye and taste.

And afterward I sat in the very back of the yard and wanted to wake
all my neighbors with my Arab kitchen-radio music.

And the dreams afterward at night, no matter how unfathomable they
remained, became light in exemplary fashion for this eater.

It was after the autumn rains that in the forests of the bay the mushroom-seeking guilds appeared. The region in the hills of the Seine was
not overrun by them; there were only a couple, but they searched all the
more thoroughly. They seldom allowed themselves to be seen, and in

the beginning almost all I encountered was their tracks. These came from the burrowers; from day to day the light gray leafy ground was punctuated by more mold-dark places, where the deepest layer had been brought to the surface.

Sometimes this resulted in actual seeker-marks—circles, spirals, wavy lines, zigzags, rectangles and triangles, labyrinths, and I imagined a series of photographs, "Symbols of the Search." But mostly it was scenes of violence, as if a wild animal had suddenly pounced on its prey, except that not a hair of this particular prey was left, save a black, deep hole in the earth.

Later I encountered this or that mushroom seeker in person, or actually only the sounds of him reached me at my open-air seat by the Nameless Pond. Each time it was heavy steps coming suddenly out of the tree-stillness, behind my back on the bank, and then stillness again, followed by more pounding and crashing through the underbrush. Otherwise I never heard a sound from a mushroom seeker, no whistling, certainly no humming, not even breathing. At most a dog accompanying him would begin to bark, and would also do so at tooth-baring range, which forced me to get up and continue writing in a standing position.

It could occur that I would turn toward a master or apprentice seeker, but not once was I greeted by him or even favored with a glance; he always kept his gaze, as if cross-eyed, fixed on the ground, sideways. If I saw such a person at all, he was often standing just as a silhouette behind some bushes, motionless and soundless, in a manner otherwise familiar from exhibitionists.

Yet even those who showed themselves clearly had no face, and likewise no discernible age. I never succeeded in looking one in the eye. They camouflaged their hunting, pretended, for instance with a long pole whose tip ended in a metal point, to be gathering edible chestnuts, and when they came upon a king bolete, it was seized in a flash—the bare space afterward looking clawed up and scratched out—and on they went, as if nothing had happened. They were always strangers, people from elsewhere, at times even with hidden sonar devices and mechanical mushroom vacuums, which, operated for moments at high speed, were promptly stashed away again.

That the mushroom seekers roamed the forest in twos or threes was actually more the exception; as a rule they were loners, and from one fall day to the next pretty much the same ones. And nevertheless even the single ones had something of the air of gang members; at any rate they reminded me altogether of a band of card sharks roving the wooded hills. I perceived these seekers as sinister fellows, or shabby sniffers, or at least as crooked birds, their shoes worn down in an entirely different way from those of so-called hoboes, and with their uncanny scraping at my back, for the first time I felt relieved at the sight of the light and bright, and oh so contemporary runners in the clearing beyond the bayou.

In my imagination the gangs of mushroom seekers were after the king boletes—all other edible mushrooms were casually annihilated with a disdainful kick or scraping of the tips of their shoes—with the help of those long poles, as if made for jabbing into the hole of the mythical beast. And in between they also tossed their knives at a find, as one would a hunting knife. They tore up, like new bomb-droppers, the entire forest floor, these seeker-sharks. Since they appeared, I had taken on the habit, before I settled in my writing place, of arranging all my finds from that spot not just next to me, but rather in a circle, clearly on display, which indeed had the effect of forcing them to beat a hasty retreat. At the same time I was prepared for an attack.

But was I any different in my mushroom seeking? Hadn't I time and again lost any sense of distance as a result of my seeker's gaze? Had become seeking-blind, as one can become snow-blind? At any rate the moment arrived once a day when my seeking turned into a form of obsession, close to a mania. In the end I, too, was seeking in an ever-increasing radius, away, out of sight of my writing pages (of which one then blew into the water once). How often I had scolded myself for my seeking, wanting to shoo it away from my brow, as Horace shooed away sorrow.

With the recognition that I could not give up seeking, it became clear to me that I had to seek in a different way. When the seeking was right, I had always known I was having an adventure, whether I then found anything or not. Thus I felt a powerful urge to introduce the seeker into my story, the book, even if only the mushroom seeker. For I know how I went seeking (but not how I found).

How does one become a good seeker? For instance, by having something else in mind while seeking, but firmly. For instance, by not turning away instantly from a mistake, but observing it thoroughly. For instance, by learning to seek where there are no signs, perhaps precisely there, at the tips of your shoes, and immediately upon entering the woods, not only deep into it.

I often stood and looked at the ground until the forms there, of fallen branches, leaves, moss, each began to glow separately: only thus did I get into seeking, without specific purpose. And I went seeking where most of the others did, on the path or close to it, and only late in autumn farther into the underbrush: my most astonishing, my most wonderful finds occurred as a rule where everybody passed through. Whenever I became tired, I rested, continuing to seek more slowly, or caught my breath while focusing on an optical illusion, a piece of rind, a patch of sunlight, also a poisonous mushroom. Time and again I also went seeking with the light shining in my eyes; to concentrate then was a game. I was less successful in noisy conditions, for instance near a highway; only in silence did I feel that I was now in Findland, at least in the find direction—although in time I also knew otherwise.

It was fruitful to look up from the ground at intervals, treetop- and skyward, after which things down below on the ground took on clearer contours; likewise to seek while concentrating on the day before yesterday—almost always something heaved up from underground, even if instead of the Bordeaux mushroom it was merely a little cèpe, the sight of whose flesh flooded my heart with a joyous yellow; and likewise to seek after a moment of terror, because after that my eyes looked sharper, by themselves, without any effort on my part.

Whenever those troops of seekers or plunderers or forest pirates crossed my path, I imagined, in contrast to them, a different, new kind of seeker. He did not seek in orthodox fashion, which in the case of mushroom seeking meant at a distance, actually at a distance from at a distance. What did that mean? For instance, following in the muddy footsteps of the organized, mechanized seekers: it turned out, and not only once, that he found himself facing a king bolete too large for the keen eyes and sonar devices, which otherwise did not miss so much as a button; so huge that the entire forest appeared around it as a Baroque setting, and he stammered at the majesty reposing in glory in its midst, "My, my, where did *you* come from?"

To seek at a distance also meant: at a distance from time. For instance, my new seeker hardly believed in Sunday finds, but certainly, and without reservation, in those of Mondays. A huge sigh of relief, after the hordes passed through, had gone through the woods during the night and sunrise hours and had had its most immediate effect on the mushrooms; the Monday finds, in the renewed stillness, with cricket-harping, could be counted on to be the freshest, and turned up primarily on the main paths, which the previous evening had still been tramping and bicycle-racing zones. The Monday mushrooms could be so beautiful that the seeker would say at the sight of one: "Boy, you're so beautiful you should be real!"

But for a modern seeker like this, in addition to the temporal there was also a spatial distance from the distance of the seeker guilds, at a distance from their underbrush seeking grounds or hardly traversable plantations, for example the places behind the cemeteries here in the bay's forests, where the layers of leaves were not only considerably thicker but also mixed with rotted flowers and such, which had been thrown over the wall. Altogether, it was the delimited, overseeable spots, and not the great expanses, where one got into the right kind of seeking without even trying. The modern seeker had only to walk up and down there attentively, and at the same time selflessly.

Was being free of oneself desirable, then? Yes. And how? Something like this: "Be still now! Be still in yourself!"

And it got warm again during the search, when leaves blown from far away, from trees entirely different from those hereabouts, mingled with the local ones. Then it became a matter of getting one's head into the searching angle, especially since late fall played tricks on the seeker more and more, to mention only the slanting light, and the mushrooms, under the fallen leaves, took on camouflage colors.

That seeker figure that hovered before my eyes while I myself was seeking moved with a particular seeking step, of unprecedented elegance, in a unique search dance, from one foot to the other, at the same time the most inconspicuous of dances. And from his sort of seeking he had become athletic, and part of it was that again and again he went backward, or turned in a circle for a while (did not merely look over his shoulder), in a fashion similar to that in which long ago, on the Jaunfeld Plain, at the celebration of the summer solstice, the young men carrying torches had swung them around during the procession, according to ancient custom, to get these torches to flare up constantly—a custom which, according to the latest parish bulletin, is supposed to be revived soon.

But what did such renewed seeking lead to, except perhaps to a small meal? Aside from the fact that I have never in my life eaten as well and as nicely as in this year—the different kind of seeker, as I conjured him up in my imagination, let me tell you, noticed in passing more than before: saw in passing the transition in the Seine hills from the grayish-blue Fontainebleau sand to the white sandstone named after the Montmorency region, and in passing the hundreds-of-years-old wagon tracks in the forest, going back to the days of kings, and in passing the boulders thrown up half a century ago already, and now again from the bomb craters, and in passing the often amazingly intricate leaf-covered huts of the increasing numbers of homeless in the region.

And he succeeded, simply through his seeking, even without finding anything, in collecting himself. For what? For naught. And precisely when he made a great, marvelous find he was seized with anxiety: a small, innocuous one should be added to it, by way of confirmation, reassurance. And toward the end of autumn a longing for nothing but modest finds set in, for russulas, ringed boletes, blewits, and ordinary little moss mushrooms—no more majestic mushrooms! And from time to time the seeker actually set out with the motto "Today I shall succeed in not finding anything!" And in midstream, precisely because of his searching, he forgot this, too, and the beauty of the land, the clouds, the trees, and the paths gained the upper hand.

And an ever-new source of pleasure in seeking would be the mistakes. "What a sad day it will be when I no longer make mistakes!" My future seeker would welcome his mix-ups, would fondle them, use them to study the laws governing human error (and himself), would finally set up a room in his house just "for my mistakes"; would use his optical illusions to keep himself impressionable, as he would use the places in the woods searched until completely empty to collect himself. And thus collected, to continue seeking will appear to him as a renewal of the world. It will become bright, within him as well as in the landscape, from his collected seeking.

And what now, in wintertime, in the cold, when there is nothing more to seek for in the wooded areas? Yes, there was hoarfrost this morning on the few remaining mushrooms there, which, one way or another, like the ice-covered pond, across which my stones pinged, no longer had a name. And my three-season writing seat, tipped into the water by children playing, stuck up from among the ice floes. And the hoarfrosted cap of one of these nameless mushroom-people bore the mark, paper-thin, of the foot of a very light, very small, seemingly one-legged bird. And at home, from the window of my mistake room, I contemplated the plaster cast, a present from the priest in the village of my birth, of the Magi, out there under the garden beech, and likewise saw in all the lumpy gift packages, which they held out into the void, in the frankincense, gold, and myrrh, likewise a king bolete, lord of the mushrooms.

In the meantime my son Valentin, on his crisscross journey through Greece, had long since put the site of the ancient oracle in Dodona behind him. It had become a place that he now recalled in approximately the following terms: "That was where, in the morning, when I went on foot from Ioannina up into the mountains, along the road it was still white with April frost, where at noon, as the only guest sitting outdoors in front of the snack shack near the amphitheater, I had a bee fall into my glass, and where, on my way back over the hills toward evening, from behind and in front sheep dogs jumped up on me." From Dodona he had sent me a leaf from a chestnut oak, so hard that when it was shaken or even just held up in the wind it produced a metallic clanging sound, and I could imagine how the entire oracle's grove had once droned, rattled, spoken. (Hadn't leaves also been gilded?)

He involuntarily spent the summer in Athens, for in the great heat the leg that had almost been severed in his accident swelled up, and he lay there, hardly able to move, in a room in a pension. In the course of the month he covered the walls with paintings, motifs, festively colorful people, ditto flowers as large as people, of the sort he had taken note of in the prehistoric frescoes from Thera or Santorini, removed to the Greek National Museum.

And one day the woman stepped through his door whom he referred to in my presence only as "your woman from Catalonia," his mother, the person with the most reliable intuition (like me more in connection with bad luck), and took up quarters next to him for a while. For the first time she cared for her son, as if only now the moment had come, and was solicitous, so unobtrusively, as was her style, that he was not even alarmed, as was in turn his style. "My mother was good to me," he wrote me later.

And she was then the one who helped him get back on his feet by grabbing her overgrown son, on the August-dusty Lykabettos Hill in the middle of Athens and dragging him, half naked, through a very special patch of stinging nettles: "The nettle run healed me." After that, again as was her style, the woman from Catalonia vanished.

Not once during this year did Valentin make the crossing to one of the Greek islands. He had promised his girlfriend that he would visit them only with her, at some later date; he got as far as watching the ferries in Piraeus. In the fall, on the Peloponnesus, he received word that his text on the different winter grays, which he had illustrated with drawings and watercolors, had received a prize, was being printed and displayed in a gallery.

Never would he have thought that he could be so pleased by a success—his first. And now: how bright the foreign lights became, of Corinth, then Nemea, then Argos, then Nauplia; how it gave him, who had meanwhile been feeling the tug of home, the impetus to continue his journey, to set out on foot. There were successes that hollowed one out; not this small first one. "I would like to make something," he wrote to me on his twenty-second birthday from mountainous Tripoli in Arcadia, "that would put me in a class with the painter of the chambers of Thera."

Upon receiving notice of the prize, he had bought himself a suit, as well as shoes, which, hardly worn, he is wearing today as he waits, in mid-December, in Patras for the ferry to Brindisi to dock. He long ago learned not merely to read Greek but also to speak a few words, whether ancient or modern, such as *helios*, sun, and *cheimon*, winter, and in every place he immediately found the one roomy café, each time with a high

plaster ceiling and the most elaborate neon-light patterns, where he had
his spot, with or without drawing pad, amid the clicking of the dice
tossed by the old customers, and no matter where he was, he called it
Neos Kosmos, New World. (Didn't *kosmos* originally mean "decoration"?)

Now in wintertime the shrill chirping of the cicadas had long since
fallen silent, yet in the rocky expanse, especially that of Arcadia, one
could imagine it all the more vividly. Only a short time ago, toward the
end of his year's journey, Valentin informed me that he encountered his
father a few times, in the form of doubles, and very strange ones indeed.
This happened to him, however, almost only by hearsay, once in Delphi,
where in a tourist café there was talk of a rather scruffy fellow who had
introduced himself as "Gregor Keuschnig, writer," had let others pay for
his meal and then disappeared with the loveliest woman in the group;
and then again in a restaurant, *estiatorion*, by the Lion Gate of Mycenae,
where on the wall hung a postcard, addressed to the proprietor's lovely
daughter, with my signature forged, and above it thanks for help in time
of need and for the unforgettable hours with her (postmarked Paris).

And one time Valentin even saw me in person, by the Piraeus ferries
to the Aegean islands, where "I," barefoot, ragged, younger than in
reality, "the writer G.K. in crisis," was offering to sell to my fellow
countrymen waiting in line cartoons that I had drawn myself and carried
in a portfolio. Again and again my son in his days as a disc jockey had
played a song by the singer titled "I'll Throw My Father Off My Back":
there, at the sight of my double and counterfeiter he recognized that he
had stopped needing to do that a long time ago.

This morning in Patras, on the stone steps, in the upper town, he had
witnessed a man trying to lure his escaped parrot back into its cage from
a tree. The bird's master did this by calling up patiently to the escapee,
for hours on end, in a very tender voice, while the bird talked back to
him, and he had the cage on his head, its door open, and on the tip of
the cage, the sharp spike there, he had stuck an apple, which he turned
now and then, or also tossed away into the air, while out of the tree only
sparrows flew constantly.

In between the man put down the empty cage, withdrew, and waited
in silence. The escaped bird did not budge. More and more neighbors
approached, cautiously, and softly offered advice. And then, as the midday ferry was already blowing its whistle down in the harbor, my son

came over and gave the apple on the spike a gentle push, so that the stem, instead of sideways as previously, now pointed straight up toward the *pappagallo* in the tree. And in that moment the parrot dropped, as if in free fall, jungle-yellow.

And now Valentin is making his way slowly toward the bay here, for the reunion we are all going to celebrate.

M y friend the priest on the Jaunfeld Plain had been constantly on the move all year, but hardly outside of his parish, except for the visit, occasioned by his sermon defying the Pope, to the bishop in K., who, without a word's being spoken between them about the whole matter, agreed with him that the caption under a photograph of the two of them in the next church bulletin should read that the child of Siebenbrunn had merely come into town, as farmers often had in earlier times, "to look at the clock again."

It was chiefly on account of the dying that he could not get away, even though he did long to now and then. There were no more of them than usual this year, but the need seemed to have grown, among the old as well as among the young, for someone like him, since no one else did it anymore, to stop by, every day if possible, with his disdainful gaze, and lay on his hands. Then they wanted him to stay, even if he just gazed out at the landscape, with his back to them, or read the paper. He was in agreement with the Protestants in at least one respect, namely that faith alone was decisive, and was close to disapproving of so-called good works; these, and here he was of one mind with "his" writer, the apostle Paul, should be refrained from, "lest any man should boast."

Except for those who lay dying, all year long hardly a soul in his parish of many villages asked for him, and only very rarely did his appearing cause eyes to light up anywhere; the majority even turned away, not hostilely, only sullenly: "Oh, him again."

At the end of October he telephoned me, as promised, because on the Jaunfeld, in the village of Rinkolach, and on the house of my ancestors there, the first snow was falling, "flakes feathered like arrows," falling in town, on the contrary, horizontally, looking in the headlights of the dense stream of rush-hour traffic like towropes; besides, my brother had discovered his singing voice, the last one in the family to do so, and was singing in the church choir, with such a beautiful voice that Urban, as happened every time when he succeeded at something—and he succeeded at almost everything—broke out in lamentations at his own life-weariness.

In dark November, lacking sun also because of the mist off the dammed-up Drau in the west, the priest dreamed a repetition of the event that had preoccupied him since that night in the Lower Austrian seminary for those called late to the priesthood: again he found himself, as in reality there, lying in the bed of someone else, who was fast asleep, as he had just been, and he? How in the world had he ended up in this other bed, next to a huge strange body that left him no room? Where was his own bed? How would he be punished? Expulsion from the institution? A mark of Cain on his forehead, for life?

Then at the beginning of December came such a heavy frost that the bed of the brooks flowing through the Jaunfeld toward the Drau, from the Petzen and the Karawanken Mountains, froze over from the bottom, up over the pebbles, enlarged into ice balls, whereupon the water on top, forced upward, spilled far over the banks. And for the first time in decades the villagers became skaters again, out until late on full-moon nights, as if things had never been any different in the interval; and blocks of ice weighing tons were cut, as if for the icehouses of a different turn of the century.

Advent had long since arrived, and there were still a few refugees in the rectory, from the German civil or cousins' war, refugees from the north and west for a change, instead of from the south or east as usual, Bavarians and Hessians from larger cities, driven out by the Saxons or Frisians or Saarlanders, then seized here by a kind of paralysis, incapable of going home, although since the summer peace had returned to their areas; perhaps they also harbored thoughts of remaining forever in this rather empty land of pines and wayside shrines.

For a while these few traumatized individuals were lodged in one of the abandoned schoolhouses of the area, speechless, their eyes lowered, and just last night, before his departure today, he had said Mass for them there. While at the Kyrie eleison, the sentences from Scripture, the Hallelujah, his heart as always was suffused with warmth, and, he told himself, as he did every day, he could get along without any celebration except, for all eternity, that of the Eucharist, of thanksgiving, of Communion, with the transformation of bread and wine into the divine body and the divine blood, still he gazed at the refugees' absent or confused faces with such scorn, increasing as the moments passed—"Could you stop boring the whole world with your misery!"—that the final blessing with which he sent them forth was hardly out of his mouth when all of them burst into laughter, at first still awkwardly here and there, then unanimously relieved.

And this morning he sat by the window of his office and waited for daybreak—while yearning for the winter's night to last a good while longer (as the weeks of Advent meant more to him than Christmas itself; for its celebration this time the priest from the next parish would take his place). He, without domestic help, had ironed his shirts, rinsed out his coffee cup, had even, long before sunrise, gone skidding over the most terrible roads around the Rinkenberg to give his vehicle the patina of a forester's car, for my sake, and the day before had instructed all the dying to hold off until the new year and his return, and was now sitting, as he otherwise seldom did, quietly, in his traveling clothes, the heavy tome he had just been reading balanced on his shoulder.

Down below on the icy path, likewise as if for the first time since all the wars and events of the century, a glazier with his rack of panes on his back, which caused a glittering all around in the first rays of the sun. But his main attention was focused on the holes, the ventilation pattern in the wall of the tumbledown barn across the way, shaped like a circle of sunflowers, in the middle an opening in the shape of an acorn, like that of the ace in a deck of cards. Pavel had already been waiting a long time for something to waft into his face from these pitch-black grids, like that third calling. And what if this one revoked the two previous ones?

With my other distant friends I shared during the year here in my bay fewer such moments, perhaps because they all ended up too far away, and furthermore in places of which I hardly had an image (or too definite a one), perhaps because they were either too young or less old than my son Valentin and Father Pavel, perhaps also because I received no word of them, as was the case with my singer.

Nevertheless, even without a complete train of images, I continued to see the wandering through the world of each individual friend—I had only to point my thoughts in his direction—in a sharply delineated light: this was like looking through the telescope in my house at the moon, the full moon, which each time made me feel as if I were not only seeing the glaring white surface but were also gazing into the depths of the smallest crater, at the bottom of the basin there with its boulders and their shadows.

Thus almost the only thing I knew about the architect and carpenter was that he, more in the latter role, had been on the move until now, into the winter, from one mountain village to the next in southern Japan, and was offering to work for farmers, repairing their wooden structures. As a rule he did not even ask, but without ado worked his way in from the outer edge of the property, from a lean-to in the meadow, a turnstile, a rack for drying straw, the lattice door of a root cellar. Just the sight of these Japanese villages, huddled together with their curved, bronze-dark roofs overlapping, as if dedicated to the heavens, made tears sometimes come to his eyes. Not to jump onto the train of images like so many architects today, but to add his own to the organically developed image!

If he was not remunerated every time, he was at least tolerated, especially since he promptly went to work in a way that brooked no contradiction. He did, to be sure, stay out of the way, yet did not behave like a stranger, but as if he were at home, on the karst or in Friuli, except that now, abroad, he finished every one of his projects. And after his return he would adhere to this pattern on his own building site. "It's time to build"—this was one of the few messages I received from him.

The tools for his repair work, work which had the aura of inconspicuousness, he fabricated himself, or the Japanese farmers occasionally helped him out with tools that had long since been deposited in corners, behind the machinery: there were still carpenter's pencils around, for marking boards, no different from everywhere in Europe, the special short-handled hatchets, the long, flexible string, and to go with it the old carpenter's cans with a red liquid through which the string was drawn and then snapped against a tree trunk to mark the cutting line, a smacking sound on the wood probably heard everywhere in the world.

Occasionally he also came through large cities like Osaka, and noticed that there all the physical or "dirty" work was usually done clandestinely, by strangers like him, only with darker skin; the screens in front of new buildings under construction allowed one to see in even less than those elsewhere, and it was also as if the workers there had explicit instructions to remain out of sight: a rarity when in the midst of the construction noise a human figure could be seen in a gap in the screen, and then with his back to the street, a rear view, and promptly swinging hand over hand back into the wings.

For a few hours, during a night in a hotel by the station, somewhat like one in England, made of brick, except that it was in Tokyo, after he had looked out at the maze of tracks in the railroad yard until the last commuter trains pulled in, from which station officials with long poles with hooks on the end fished out more and more drowsy drunks, in suit and tie, with briefcases—a constant staggering back and forth over all the platforms, combined with being shoved along, push after push—the carpenter in wintry Japan went insane. In him, this patient man, it was more the eruption of an impatience he had been holding in for a lifetime, or the sudden cessation of those different experts' voices in him; it jolted him out of his sleep, whereupon he paced up and down until daybreak, repeatedly and with all his might pounding his head with both fists; the last time this had happened to him he had been a child. And he would have continued in this fashion if, with a small billowing of curtains, the Mongolian woman, the bride of Hokkaido, had not appeared to save him, putting him to bed and silently taking him between her legs.

And the following morning, alone again, Guido set out toward me in the bay, with a stopover in Alaska, where he wanted to study the characteristic wooden shelters known as *cachés*, which were built on stilts against bears and had always interested him; and on the telephone he promised to build a window seat in my study, with a writing surface above it.

Since the flight from Narita to Anchorage did not leave until late in the evening, by way of farewell on his last day in Japan the architect took for the second time the commuter train to the Eastern Sea of Kamakura, to try, weak as he still was from his night of madness, trembling in every limb, to gain new tranquillity before the house-sized Buddha there. And afterward he had time for the beach on the Pacific, where at sunset yet another (or the same?) group of girls in dark blue school uniforms yet again threw very long-stemmed roses into the waves, like lances, at intervals, into dusk, in which the colors of the flowers drifting out to sea, especially the red, became things unto themselves.

Perhaps I succeeded least in traveling along later on with my woman friend: "Because you (thus that master of explanation, my petty prophet of Porchefontaine) lost, with the disappearance of the woman from Catalonia, your wife, any image at all of a woman."

But as I now think back to those months, to Helena's moment by the sea-flooded stone sarcophagi in the Turkish bay, I see that somewhat differently. I felt as though I was there when she, weary of the eternally wine-dark sea and of the ship's helm, merely simulating a gathering of people with its jerky movements, in between turned back toward Dalmatia, heartily laughed at there by her two children, who, as always, were no longer and not yet expecting her, and in the following autumn set out again, this time to Egypt.

Instead of continuing to wander around there, she worked until now, using a skill she had once acquired, one of her many, on the restoration of an early Christian Coptic church in Cairo. She was the oldest in the group. Yet no one would have noticed that; she presented herself as an apprentice just like all the others, and during this time made herself, as only she, the beauty queen, could, invisible.

Although there, already fairly close to the edge of the city, or at least in an enclave far from the center of town, almost exclusively natives were at work, in the barely chapel-sized building young people from all over the world had come together, youth such as was perhaps to be observed only here, at this little-bitty restoration work, on the door ornamentation, the inlays, and especially the frescoes, and otherwise nowhere else on earth.

From outside one's eye at first fell on only scattered individuals, for instance the girl up in the tower, who, her upper body leaning out of an opening, yet without twisting, was scrubbing down the wall. The interior, however, was packed, up to the ceiling, with similar young people, busy scraping, injecting, stroking, brushing. Each of these hand movements required hardly any room, took place in one spot, like a dot, close to soundlessness, at the same time with an intensity that bent all parts of the body to the task. Often elbow to elbow with the next person, from one level of staging to the next, they all had a place to work in and radiated that certainty, as uncramped on their knees as on their tiptoes.

The satisfaction, so quiet, that emanated from the restorers—along with a little transistor-radio music, whether the Mississippi sound of Creedence Clearwater Revival, the Central European Tyrolienne of Haydn, or the inner-Arabian singing of Uum Kalsum, at whose sound the walls of Jericho came tumbling down in an entirely different way— was, as the work progressed steadily, one that resulted from having time; or, as if what they were doing were something like gaining time, the most precious thing, not only for them, the young people, here alone, but of general utility and general validity: no matter what troop of warriors, to whom in their killing-training camp such a restoration might be shown on film, would have their eyes opened to the fact that in the current era there were other images besides those of the evil empire in their video games.

Yet away from such activity my woman friend was caught up in a state of near oblivion, menacing as never before. Not the fact that she was constantly losing her way in Cairo afflicted her, but that her wandering each time led her into seemingly permanently ruined and garbage-strewn areas, where the dusty lump of rubble that she just barely missed stepping on was the face of a human being, very alive and not at all old, lying there amid rags and charred animal skulls, and the rusty tin can next to him was his blood-warm hand. Once, thinking herself completely alone in an expanse of smoking tatters, she had, crouching down to relieve herself, almost done it on one of these seemingly camouflaged people, asleep, or unconscious, or dying.

More and more she felt the urge to fall down beside them. Into the North African winter she did not speak another word, remained, except when at work, silent even with herself, no longer knew her name (that single name that otherwise tripped off her tongue with such gentle self-confidence). It did her good, in between and on days of rest, to turn away from the unchanging, also all equally round and naive-eyed faces of the Coptic saints, which day in, day out were as close to her as under a microscope, and look into those so differently alike faces of Egyptian antiquity, and at the bodies belonging to them, by no means so childlike, inside which, in the heart muscle, the pyramids had palpably been first of all, even before the actual building, like funeral barges ready to set sail for infinity.

Two cards Helena sent me, wordless ones: one of just such a broad-shouldered ancient Egyptian, striding along with a curved space between his trunk and the arch of his shoulders (unthinkable in Christian figures of that region), onto which she had sketched on one side the moon, on the other the sun; the second with a papyrus, as the hieroglyph for "green."

Before her departure, she took the train to Helwan, up the Nile, where the deserts were closer, and also because of the similarity of the town with her "Helena." (The river itself remained for her not only nameless; with time she had also forgotten it so completely that one day on a bridge her heart stopped at the sight of the oil-streaked water in the unsuspected depths.) In Helwan a December rain was falling, a child was making its way carefully through the wet part of a puddle, as if to wash off the citywide mud, and my woman friend sat down outside of town on a pile of rubble in the Arabian Desert, which appealed to her more because of its darker coloration, also the absence of human beings, than the left-bank section facing Libya. The sand there also had coarser grains, and the rain could be heard very clearly plashing on it, also more into the wide-open spaces, all the way to—here articulated thoughts finally resumed inside her—"the Red Sea," over the empty, rippled expanse, which appeared tinted and inscribed like the roof-tile landscape back in Maribor outside her bedroom window. And here, too, there were sparrows.

The painter lost in the course of this year just about everything that could be lost.

The Catalan state, whose reestablishment he, previously the world-famous artist of that country, had cursed—"This state is an injustice, its establishers are traitors"—confiscated his estates there. His foreign properties burned down, along with the arsenals of paintings. A new iconoclastic movement, fleeting as a dream and all the more lasting in effect, also destroyed his works in museums (his black was stamped over with Day-Glo corrosive paint). The banks once founded specifically for painter-princes went bankrupt. One of the last gallery owners announced an exhibition with my friend's few remaining paintings and then disinvited him, without explanation. His film, which premiered in the fall in Madrid, in a theater so full that the audience was also sitting on the steps, was crowded out a week later by an American film, which the theater owner had to run, lest he be prevented from ever showing another Hollywood film. The one copy disappeared, and the original cans of film, the negatives, without which no further copies could be made, were tossed out onto the rails as worthless during a train robbery, run over by the train, and, it was reported on the news, shredded beyond repair.

And still, after the time spent filmmaking, he was incapable of going back to his painting. "I don't know anything about painting, have never known anything—except perhaps what not to do." For a time there was probably a voice inside him repeating over and over that he was finished (or something of the sort). Yet the moment then came when he no longer wanted to have that said of him. To be sure, he seemed to accept it when on his trip up the Spanish *meseta*, to the sources of the Río Duero, here and there, in Tordesillas, in Burgos, in Soria, an old admirer expressed pity for him. Yet within himself he had long since achieved the Roman *amor fati*, love of fate. Yes, he was glowing with love for everything that had happened to him during the year. In the pitch-darkness within which he moved, his eyes opened wide not only with watchfulness but also with passion for knowledge. He was ready for a battle, though in his own way, instead of with clenched fists with fingers spread wide.

Later in the summer he then turned away from the water of the river, as if he did not want to see himself comforted by it anymore: it was comfort, in fact, which seemed to awaken in him that sorrow he had always resisted, out of the experience that it was almost certain to be followed by bad temper and even world-weariness. He swerved off to the south and all fall roamed back and forth across La Mancha, that almost shadowless rump and residual landscape, so easy to recapitulate with every glance, where the few watercourses had been dried out for years now, and as if forever.

He also ended up there farther away from the parts of Spain "behind the mirror," Vigo, La Coruña, Pontevedra, the fjords deep in the interior of Galicia, where he had shot his film and which, it seemed to him in retrospect, had been damaged by the picture making, the spotlighting. Although the camera had always remained at a distance, it was as if the areas had been plundered by the process. And only now, with time, and also with his, the responsible party's, distancing himself, did these areas gradually return to their senses and go back, recovered, like grass that bounces back after being trampled down, to their place behind the mirror, into the very special light there, which arrayed them as if nothing had happened.

And he, as far from the sea as also from a source, now became in barren La Mancha—the end of sorrow and of guilt, and no one left who recognized him—entirely free for his love of fate, a love that more than anything else drove him to create, but what? For the time being at any rate Francisco simply kept on reading that kindly master, Horace, who taught him that a god did not have to intervene in a situation until "the knot is worthy of such a savior."

And now, yesterday, on a winter evening in Albacete, the city of knives, seemingly only recently bombed to pieces in the civil war, after one of his daily trips to the movies—the latest Hollywood film—mothered by the movies as in his childhood, the painter stumbled upon something in a corner of the open projection booth, without a projectionist: the copy of his *As I Lay Dying* that had disappeared from Madrid, six reels, too heavy for a man, but not for him: already they were stowed in his camper, ready to be shown when all his friends were gathered here in the no-man's-bay. And last night there appeared to him Horace, son of a freedman, with a little paunch, and instructed him to go out and simply ask a young person: "What should I paint?" Upon awakening, Francisco resolved to pose this question to Valentin, Gregor Keuschnig's son. He would have an answer for him, and he would act upon it. And the following morning the few paintings by the painter that had been spared by the iconoclasts revealed changes; for instance, mine here, the only piece of art in the house, had acquired a black rocky mountain hovering in the air, a hole, or rather a place where one could see through, while the other undamaged pictures changed their coloration.

And soon after setting out for the north he drove on the high plateau past a shallow depression, apparently dug out centuries earlier, an empty square a little lower than the plowed fields already sown with winter rye, a former livestock pen, overgrown, with bristly grass, the remains of a wooden fence, also of a shed, with shreds of horse tethers, on the ground a donkey's hoof, a bird skeleton, and he thought: "This is Cervantes' world! This is Spain!" and then: "This is what my next film will begin with," and then: "How the human race needs such ridiculous, pointless, and one-sided heroes as Don Quixote from time to time!"

The reader, on his tour of Germany, long after the end of the hostilities there, sparked his own civil war—to be precise, one day in some small city he took an iron rod and hurled himself at the tribe of automobile drivers lined up at a traffic light as if at a starting line, revving their engines and honking at each other. As a result of this violent act, which was leniently punished, to be sure—as an extenuating circumstance the "nosogenous" or illness-generating glitter of the thousands of chrome auto parts was cited—he had once again become incapable of doing his reading, and to this day has not recovered, and the reading policewoman from Jade Bay was far away.

In this state of deprivation, however, he gained the ability to articulate what reading had meant to him, and would mean again. "When I could still read, I looked at the individual words until I saw them in stone or on bark—except that the words had to be the right ones. Heart of the world, writing: a secret matched only by the wheel and the eyes of children. I must read again. Reading would be a passion, a wondrous one, if it is a passionate desire for understanding; I feel compelled to read because I want to understand. Not simply to plunge into reading: you must be receptive to a particular story or book. Are you receptive?"

In compensation for having forfeited his reading for the time being, he had become capable—again as a result of loss?—of a kind of looking fundamentally different from contemplating: an accomplishment, a very rare and precious one. The object looked at, however inconspicuous, could expand into the entire world. Looking in this way, he had the paradigm of the world before his eyes—only he could no longer say it. "So I simply have to say it anew!" And in looking at an object until he had become part of the object (just as during his reading period he had looked at many a word until he became the word), he became disarming, of himself first of all, and had a contagious effect.

And for this period, for the summer, for the fall, and up to this day, in winter!, objects in his Germany, previously inexplicably abstract and downright nauseating—an old phenomenon, not merely since the last Reich—finally also became concrete, just as, from time immemorial, so many, so wonderfully many German words had been. After the civil war, a clothes hanger in a German hotel room, a lamp, a chair, a wheelbarrow up on a German railroad platform took on—an unprecedented occurrence—shape, were nothing to be ashamed of, O peace!, the sight of them no longer pierced one to the heart. During this autumn they filled out and actually acquired color, even "apples from German orchards," and then, when on the same day the first postwar snow fell, from the Kiel Canal down to the Saarland, there was a new generation of children, who, unlike the previous ones, upon seeing snowflakes when they woke up, no longer merely stared at them dully.

To get beyond individual objects: in the months following the domestic blitzkrieg, all of Germany seemed liberated from whatever had been weighing on it (for how long?), as a massif is said to have become lighter as a result of erosion and could even grow higher, or as the melting of a vast expanse of glacier freed the earth's crust underneath to heave upward. In fact, even German landscapes had taken on different features, in that, for instance, between skyscrapers vistas suddenly revealed themselves in the sky where none had been since Hölderlin, or the Spree River in Berlin, until then puddlelike and sluggish, unexpectedly began to rush, and thundered again over cataracts and waterfalls through an ancient river valley.

Understanding was so powerfully abroad in the land that for the time being the opinion molders in the newspapers of Germany remained alone behind their office windows with their brain-swelling language, and my former enemy, still active with his book interrogations and sniffing-out, no longer found gawkers for his word-spectacles and for the first time was forced to leave his ghetto, condemned to take walks out in nature, which he heartily despised, where from every flower and every bush nothing but his own mug stared back at him.

Instead, altogether different from that literary Old Nick, Johann Wolfgang von Goethe had passed by just recently, flesh and blood as only he could be, on his two hundred fiftieth birthday, coming through the side door behind which he had been sitting all the while, not like Emperor Frederick Barbarossa in Mount So-and-so, but in a picture, and had taken the new, enlarged Germany in his two hands, with the expression "dear little place," the sort of diminutive otherwise used by him only in conjunction with observation of his beloved plants.

And with him the Brothers Grimm once again set about collecting fairy tales; Novalis returned, as a sculptor, at the sight of whose sculptures people, themselves turned to stone, at the same time continued on their way lighter of foot; Eduard Mörike went out and bought an answering machine for his rectory; August Sander prepared to do photographic portraits of the German faces of the twenty-first century; and entire army groups on their newly saddled horses mobilized in underground clay pits all across the country—not to seize power but merely to send a signal. The reader's tour through Germany became a trip around the world.

On the eve of his departure for the bay here, he sat by that pond on the forest's edge where once upon a time he had seen himself and his love as one in perpetuity (and the very next day they had already come to a parting of the ways). The water was in an entirely different place from the original water, and yet was the same, down to the very reeds: the period now—or the interval?—had made every individual place in Germany interchangeable with all others; one place there contained them all.

Over his shoulder, in the last light of this December day, he had in view a field with apple trees, one of them in its leaflessness still chockfull of golden-and-white fruit, and below at its foot, in the already almost night-dark realm or little place, the silhouettes of two children, both with an apple in hand, as the last spots of brightness, in each of which he saw an open book, held out toward the other, or a palm frond. And a dream appeared to him in which he, surrounded by marksmen and dart throwers, had said, "Enough. This is my house, the reader's house. Get out!" The throwers and shooters obeyed, and one of them even said, "We have need of your steadfastness!"

As Wilhelm turned from the apple tree back to the waters of his youth, he saw himself there as a silhouette from those days, now with the first stars, whose silent reflection in the pond was crisscrossed by the shadows of bats. The grass on the bank was furrowed by tank tracks, and beyond the apple orchard stood a dark farmstead, abandoned by German emigrants.

From the singer no word had been received to this day, since his hike in the summer snow way up north on the Scottish island of Skye. In the eyes of the world, he was missing and presumed dead. At the same time he was spotted going on a bear hunt in Skopje in Macedonia; as a mercenary in Africa; dancing with a native woman in New Guinea; covered with blood as he came to the aid of a woman who had had an accident on a highway in the Tyrol; lying drunk on the steps of a Moscow subway station while hordes of passengers stepped over him—and all that on one and the same day, and at least as many similar situations on each of the following.

I myself saw him driven far off his original course, as had always happened to him on his hikes to the ends of the earth, only more willingly this time than ever. Precisely as a result he would bring back all the more from his journey. And that was of course what he had in mind: to return to us with a song such as had never been heard in the world, his "last" insofar as after it silence would reign, once and for all, also for further last songs, to be sung by others, not by him.

Thus on the move, in the meantime hardly off the beaten track and alone anymore, but in the midst of masses of humanity, he sang, as I pictured him, not a single note during the entire year, likewise gave anything explicitly designated as music a wide berth, whenever he could, which was becoming increasingly difficult toward the end of the century. In order to expand, and also to break, albeit harmoniously, his own voice, with which he never wanted to be finished or completely trained, he sought out and sampled, from continent to continent, unfamiliar voices, not those of singers, but rather of people who were merely talking, unheard of and unsung. How rare in the world was a voice *de profundis*, from the very depths, at the same time light as a bird, at the same time piercing. When he thought back over the year, from everywhere almost exclusively insulting and angry speaking voices came to mind, and the most angry ones, also the most ugly and despicable, were as a rule the authoritative or indeed the trained ones; what a relief, for instance, to hear for a change, coming from a train loudspeaker, the voices of the railroadmen themselves.

If he tended to seek out people on the margins, he did so not because the oppressed, minorities, and refugees were to be found there, but because of the voices there. If elsewhere the laughter and even the weeping of passersby seemed corrupted, in the shadows and the underground world he encountered at least occasionally a sound he could then allow to resonate in his song. And also without weeping and laughter: how beautifully many an Albanian in Kosovo spoke his Albanian, many a Georgian in Azerbaijan his Georgian (and vice versa), with what purity many a pair of lovers spoke the language of their country, many a dead-tired or angry person said whatever he said (the conventional folk music was something else again).

Thus the singer learned for his voice. The melodies and rhythms, on the other hand, just came to him as always, when everyday sounds continued to reverberate in his ear—an accordion door closing, steps running in the salty desert, branches brushing against the bus window. What he was finally still lacking for his "last song" was the lyrics, except perhaps for the snippet "soul of lovers, sound of the people" (not by him). Yet once he had the right voice inside him, quietly stored there and ready to be amplified at the right moment, in a way the world had never yet heard, why shouldn't simple humming suffice—even if for an entire hour—and it would be a revelation (with room for another)?

Yet now he still needs the concluding voice, the fade-out, the fade-away, and for that he must go to the region he comes from, here in the no-man's-bay. To be sure, yesterday, Christmas Day, he was recognized in Venice, pissing off the Rialto; in an old-age home in Dublin, playing Father Christmas; and in New Zealand, watching a charity rugby game all alone. But I knew that Emmanuel was in one of the cemeteries here in the wooded hills above the Seine, taking part, as the third mourner from the left to the rear, in the funeral of a resident of the bay, unknown to him as to me, in the course of which no word was spoken. Next to the house of the cemetery watchman, among the graves, children's clothing was hanging out to dry on the line. On not only one of the edge-of-the-highway bushes did I see scraps of a poster with the singer's face that had blown there, though for a concert of the previous year and in another city. And at the same time, or so I pictured it, he was standing

at a densely populated central intersection, among the passersby, a pad
in the crook of his arm, on which he was sketching out his song, note
by note, roughly following the sounds on the asphalt, a somewhat different kind of pollster.

Hardly any of what happened during the year in the bay became public
knowledge, except for the emergency landing of a visitor of state,
on the way from Villacoublay to Paris by helicopter, in a clearing here:
a photograph in *Parisien libéré*, though only in the suburban edition, of
the man with his entourage standing with a drink in the Bar des Voyageurs.

Even in *The Hauts-de-Seine News* there is space for items from the bay,
but the only news there remained the regular announcement of that
storytelling hour (more like a "fairy-tale hour") in a community hall,
even a detailed program, simply to fill up the column for the area. Theme
for this week: the only surviving local legend, in which a long time ago
an unregenerate noisemaker was stoned by the original inhabitants—to
be precise, at that *pointe* or spit of land.

Whereas in Clamart, Meudon, Boulogne, Sèvres, also in the much
smaller Ville d'Avray, to judge by the newspaper, week after week there
were all kinds of happenings, with concerts, exhibitions, building projects, births, weddings, deaths, if I wanted anything eventful here I had
to turn to the sports section, where in a dozen pages I might find a few
lines devoted to the local handball club, or just the score might be
reported, with the team lineup, the majority of the names Portuguese,
Italian, Arabic.

Not that there was no news in the bay worthy of publicity: there was
simply no reporter available. At the beginning of my stay here I at least
found notices of births and deaths—in the meantime, under *Naissances*,
as well as *Décès*, the only notation is always *Néant* (nothing). When this
past summer the traditional bay festival took place by one of the ponds,
the *News* repeated word for word the article from the previous year, and
that in turn, with hardly any variation, is familiar to me from my almost
eleven years here.

Instead I kept up to date, day by day, during this entire year of 1999, with the Spanish provincial town of Benavente, where I have never been. A reader who has lived there all his life sends me, day in, day out, the section of *La Opinión*, which is published in Zamora, devoted in words and pictures to his town, the simple facts from there, the page with the local news (editorial opinion, according to my Spanish reader, a member of the *guardia civil*, is to be found, in plenty, on the front page). Thus I am informed about Benavente, far off in Castile, on the Portuguese border, much better than about my place of residence here. I know all about the constant well drillings there, made necessary by the water shortage; about the processions of pilgrims in May to the Cristo de la Vega, in the meadows; about the schedule at the Avenida, the only movie theater, with a thousand seats, from which on a summer evening I sometimes heard behind me, when I was out in my garden, a member of the audience nibbling his sunflower seeds; about the tax inspector who was beaten up by the proprietor of the Viena restaurant; about the town gardener, Eustaquio B., who is supposed to have exposed himself to a nun and for whom his brother provided an alibi the following day; and even about the departure times for the buses to Madrid, the same all year long, and nevertheless scrutinized by me in each clipping so intensely that eventually I at least felt the draft of the morning bus making its loop at the Estación of Benavente.

What was transmitted of the history of the bay, even over the centuries, did not in itself yield enough for a book.

The author of the chronicle *The Locality from Ancient Times to Today*, which then appeared this year, had felt obliged, in order to give his account book length, to devote most of one main section to facts drawn from the history of all of France. What is known of this particular region could be recorded, at least from the point of view of a professional historian, on one page of the community bulletin (which does not exist here). Almost the only thing I recall from my reading is that during the French Revolution more soldiers were drafted from the forest bay than from elsewhere, since those eighteen- to forty-year-olds had neither a profession nor an official position "essential to the life of the country"; that in the mid-nineteenth century the township was the poorest in the entire *département*; and that of the new arrivals in the local refugee asylum, from the beginning of this century on, each demanded the food of his country of origin, "which was not possible."

The other main section in the chronicle of the bay was devoted to the building of its churches. Was this history, when none of the churches here even predated the older inhabitants? No matter: these building histories, or so I thought then, were something I wanted to go on reading for a long time. And they came from someone who, a chronicler, was also noticeably well disposed toward the actors and their most inconspicuous actions.

For almost a thousand years, until after the Second World War, the bay had lacked a church. For Sunday Mass the natives had gone up the hills through the woods to the plateau of Vélizy. When the church there was destroyed by bombing in 1944, the inhabitants of the bay built themselves a chapel out of wood, with their own hands, dedicated to Joseph, the carpenter. The wooden tower, standing apart, went for years without bells. Attendance in the postwar years, far above the country average, required expansion of the barracklike structure, which thus acquired a transept, and then the decision was made to erect a proper church, a basilica, of stone and concrete; the chronicler cited the precise day and even the house where the decision was reached, complete with street and number.

The bay at that point was not yet an independent parish, only an apostolic zone, provisionally. The photograph of the cornerstone laying on the edge of a cleared stretch of forest even showed a sight particularly disconcerting here, the figure of a bishop, with his crooked staff, something hardly ever seen before in the bay ("1857: Confirmation—For the First Time in Thirty Years a Bishop"), and at any rate never again since; and that great crowd, according to the caption present for the celebration: has anything like it ever gathered here again, no matter where?

For this church an architect had to be called in, and it was the same one who had designed the low-income apartment houses right next door, and since I discovered that, I have viewed both structures somewhat differently. The cross, of iron, was made by a locksmith/stove fitter. The Sunday offerings—this I gathered by way of additional information from the parish newsletter, appearing more and more irregularly—were meager and steady in the bay, the same expression used by the chronicle for the donations of churchgoers through the centuries.

There is no connection with the fact that no Pope, neither the present one nor any other, will ever kiss the ground of the no-man's-bay. And no conqueror or liberator will ever place his boot on one of the former royal border markers (the few remaining ones are, by the way, not mentioned in the chronicle; are as obvious as secret; the crown chiseled into them looks fake at first sight).

The wood crickets seemed to have finally fallen silent for the year, after unexpectedly announcing their presence time and again on the occasional warm, sunny day far into the fall, sometimes after an absence of weeks, the last time being in the middle of November, though only as a little fading chirp somewhere, to which no second voice responded.

Or was I merely imagining that? Even when I now walked the wintry paths, the summery cricket calls piped up, especially if I stood still now and then, and also in the dead of night, in my house, I heard them recently, impossible to tell whether outdoors or in my head; it woke me up, more easily and instantaneously than usual, and in the dark I allowed the sound to spin on.

During the summer, what the crickets were engaged in seemed in fact to be the creating of a web. With their voices, as it sounded to me, they were knotting the silence into a tissue. Noise-sick, as I so often was when I got to the woods, I promptly felt, once in their realm, a wonderful soothing. More gently and reliably than the rustling of the trees, they healed my noise-worm-eaten head. Although the chirping of the crickets emanated from the ground, from the earth's interior, it drew me upward. I had a visual image of the sound: a Jacob's ladder, knotted from the most delicate ropes. And thus I also had an image of the crickets themselves: thousands and thousands of them rocking in a heavenly wheat field. No other animal, no bird could call this way, so monotonously and intensely, and in even, sonorous unison; more than an image, an infinitely repeating ornament, which, to be sure, broke off at once as I approached or made my presence felt.

The crickets were most likely to be heard in the more inaccessible and

at the same time sparse parts of the forest, on the steepest crest of the
sunken roads, behind seven-kindling-bundle obstacles, and on still days.
Often there was nothing for miles around to be heard but them, whom,
however, I never actually got to see. But even among so many other
sounds theirs remained the penetrating and decisive one. I felt when I
heard it as though I were standing on tiptoe. It summoned me to listen,
as silence alone could hardly do anymore, and that then appeared to me
as the task to be completed, a sweet one. The cricket concert was moving,
and in its furtiveness spoke to my heart like no other sound in this year.
Yet I often found myself thinking only of a clock, or rather of the
winding of one, as quietly as possible, on and on, close to the limit of
audibility.

I have no reason to miss the cricket music now; but I would have
liked to play it for my friends when we celebrate our reunion. But did
it even come from crickets? Didn't it sound more gentle and at the same
time more choral, more far-flung than the shriller, as it were more constricted, Austrian chirping that I have in mind from my childhood? And
why am I also unable to imagine as its source the crickets from those
days, black as they were, roundish, robust, armored? Isn't it more likely
those particularly tiny grasshoppers or locusts of which I found one on
an already cold evening in my chimney corner, grass-root-pale and fragile, perching motionless and silent on the side of my finger? And that
is how the animal remained when I held it up to the full moon; except
that for the moment its silhouette became gigantic.

In the first months of the year there was a particular group of itinerant
workers in the bay who were cutting down and sawing up trees in the
windbreak sections of the forest. They not only worked in the forest;
they also lived there, in huts on wheels (not the same as house trailers).

During almost my entire time here I had been running into them,
and always there was at least one woman among them, often children and
dogs as well. But this year's workers had no family members along, and,
as far as I could tell, there were never more than two of them together. Laundry hardly ever hung out to dry, and since they had only
the one unit of housing, there was no circle or kraal as in previous years.
They were either at work, with their one-man chain saws, often at a

considerable distance from one another, or in the evening in the hut, by kerosene light behind the always drawn curtain over the doorway, smoke eddying from the pipe in the roof (or not, as the case might be), a teakettle, slim as a minaret, with two spouts!, on a camp stove outside, and incessantly piping Arab music, audible far off at the edge of the forest, yet not turned up loud at all.

They had hammered together a table of birch logs outside, the seats consisting of oil canisters, the Islamic half-moon on their sides indicating their origin. Yet I never found them there, and only once outside the forest, at night down in the settlement, or only one of them, the older one, when he joined us in a bar. The woodsman said something, in sounds that were incomprehensible not because they were in Arabic or Berber, but unlike any language ever heard; and without even raising his voice in the racket of the bar. All that was certain was that he was not placing an order, or begging, also not asking a question, but rather making a request, a large, plaintive one, in which the only clear thing was the movements of his mouth and his eyes, at the same time half in shadow, because of the distance between those standing at the counter and him, which he made no move to reduce. He addressed everyone that way, from a distance, except me, probably the only one he recognized, from our daily exchange of greetings up there in the woods. I was dying to have him finally turn to me, as if I alone could have been of service to him, and on the other hand I acted as though I did not know him, and as if in his eyes I was supposed to behave this way. The old man left; the others had long since focused their attention elsewhere. He also hardly gave me time, and I missed the moment. And out on the streets, whose darkness was so different from that of the woods, where I subsequently ran into him as he continued his roaming around on that one evening, it was too late. He did not need anything now, or did not show it, or could not show it anymore.

A little while ago, almost a year since that evening, when I again passed the two woodsmen's campsite, not the slightest trace remained, neither the birch table nor even a spot of oil. Nothing but a feeling, as broad as the cleared ground, was there, for which I sought the fitting image for writing about it, but in vain.

———

And what happened later with the birds' sleeping tree, that one plane tree on the square in front of the railroad station?

The sparrows spent the night there all through the summer, merely becoming invisible in the dense foliage. They could be heard, however, in early evening, from far away on the side streets, through the sound of the trains and the noise of the cars, jockeying for position or conducting other negotiations. When the square underwent repairs in August, they at first stayed away because of the jackhammers, also at night, but toward Assumption Day they returned and when the asphalt was put down, they were the first (not, as is usually the case, dogs) to leave their tracks in the still-soft material, in the form of large loops and suggestions of meanders, made not by hopping but by running.

Late at night it happened sometimes, and without one's clapping one's hands down below, that they, or a couple of them, would fly up out of their foliage, which would suddenly crash apart, and like a swarm of flying fish would plunge into one of the neighboring tree crowns, though every time soon returning, each separately, to the original tree; likewise none of the new plantings on the square became a second sleeping place; though the new bamboo stalks served during the day as swings.

In late fall, in the bare time of year, the best place to observe the sparrows perched in their limb forks was indoors behind the high glass façade of the Bar des Voyageurs, from its counter. Several steps led up to it, and thus I had the birds, at least those in the lowest story of the plane tree, at eye level, without making myself conspicuous by craning my neck, as I would have out on the sidewalk. On one side they were sharply illuminated by the café's neon sign (and brightly daubed by its three-coloredness), and on the other side lit by the strong yellow lighting on the railway platform behind them on the embankment, which projected their shadows, close enough to touch, onto the glass door, very distinctly and larger than life, with blackbird or even raven beaks.

With this view of the more or less sleeping birds, I received indoors from the bar, and also from outside, more stimuli than I had probably ever received from any observations of whatever kind. I participated in the video games—in whose variations I then saw nothing much different from the sparrows' jerking of their heads—as well as in the hurrying home of those who arrived by train, which occurred in batches, with their classic light brown baguettes, across the dusky square. On Sunday evenings the silhouettes of large, heavy suitcases crisscrossed each other there, almost always carried by single passersby, unaccompanied, and the duffel bags of young soldiers called up for duty, who often set out on foot through the forest to the fighter-pilot base on the plateau.

The inhabitants of the bay, with the exception of those standing at the bar, almost always the same people, also showed nothing but their silhouettes. It was something else again with those without a permanent residence here, who, until the first cold weather, often even after dark, even in the rain, perched together on a bench next to the station entrance, they, too, very visible in the lighting of the square. The majority of them looked to me pretty much like those everywhere, although in the course of the year at least one had joined them, who, still young, was different.

I first ran into him in the woods, always alone, either as a mushroom seeker, rushing along, his head constantly twisted to one side, or as a tree-stump anchorite, sitting there as still as if he were studying entrails in the sand at his feet all day long. He had thick, curly hair, a narrow, stern face, wore a windbreaker, and he made me think of an anthroposophic teacher or an apprentice, who, to complete his course of study, had to spend some time voluntarily in this remote spot.

Once, when I wished him good day in a clearing, he even answered me, with a hardly noticeable but all the more noteworthy nod, while his eyes, unchanging in their sternness, showed me his pure, undimmed color of sorrow. Then, still in summertime, I saw him for the first time sitting with the suburban vagrants by the station, much larger than they, erect, with the most balanced face, but in his hand a beer bottle like the rest. Yet it was not completely natural to him; among the others he seemed rigid and wooden, without their melodramatic gestures and voices, and his head constantly jerking to one side, where no one was sitting.

In the months there on the bench, a transformation then began to take place in him. At the same time it seemed to me as abrupt as those in an animated cartoon. In the twinkling of an eye his smooth skin erupted in grayish-bluish swellings, his lips elongated into a trunk, his ears grew into his skull, his forehead was flattened, his hair stuck to his head, and finally he joined the chorus, reverberating over the entire square, of bleating laughter typical of *clochards*; not even the jerking of his head, away from the group into the void, is there anymore.

But from time to time he also unexpectedly came striding out of the darkness past the glass bar, with an elegant, slow stride, in his clean blue windbreaker, his face unmarred as before, the handsomest person in the bay here since the disappearance of the woman from Catalonia, a figure of light, and threw me such an impudent or amused look that I wondered, as I had initially, whether he wasn't actually engaging in a masquerade, for instance with the intention of writing a book about the region, among whose characters one, and a fairly odd one at that, would be me.

And then again, one or another of his drinking buddies, just a moment ago one big urine spot from his belt to his shoes, and a billow of stench, would stroll one morning across the square as a gentleman in a camel-hair coat, his hair combed back, Clark Gable engaged in casual conversation with Miss No-Man's-Bay on his arm, or with his very own son, not in the slightest ashamed of his father.

And then again: the only one in the group of seated boozers who had ever directed a word at me, except to panhandle, was, as he said, there "because of the secret of this place." Did this mean that only the mentally disturbed knew that this region was a place? But: they, or the one of them there, were not to be interrogated on this subject! First of all, no answer would be forthcoming, and then, in my life, every time I tried to interrogate someone, I always lost my substance, or any substance at all.

And meanwhile, on this cold December night, the sparrows puffed themselves up in their sleeping tree almost to the size of pigeons or vultures, and suddenly shrank to their natural tinyness upon waking and tiptoeing away. For a time during the fall some of them did try out the neighboring plane trees for sleeping, but now they are all together again in their original tree, even if there seem to me to be far fewer of them than in the previous winter.

Last night there was a constant splashing from the branches down onto the square: not their droppings, and not they themselves, but the melting snow. The day before yesterday, however, in the pre-snow frost, two of them were sleeping as I had never seen sparrows sleep, side by side on their limb like Siamese twins. Not even in their giant shadow on the dusty bar window could I discover any movement. And the last tattered leaf fluttered all the more violently back and forth above them in the night wind. And in the background of the square, along the retaining wall below the railroad yard, passed the bay's one painter, who paints landscapes here in the open, by the ponds, in the forest, although on his easel I always saw a region entirely different from the one he had before his eyes. And at my back a brainsick man with a deep scar on his temple, whom his mother was bringing back to the nursing home after his Sunday outing, was drinking beer with coffee; he was spilling most of it; the old woman was dabbing it up, again and again.

I must also tell of an attraction here in the bay, indeed the only one. And that is the hanging gardens on either side of the commuter-railway cut, from the end of the mile-long mountain tunnel under the hills of the Seine to the spot where the cut meets the station embankment.

They always struck me as something special, and when I was riding the train they always gave me, according to my direction, the most powerful impression of leave-taking or homecoming. Yet it was only in the course of this year of 1999 that I looked at them more closely, up above from the highway overpass and then down below from their midst, on that strangest of paths that ran along the beds and toolsheds.

As I descended into the cut at the one spot that was accessible—because of a house under construction by the bridge—I was doing something forbidden; but there was no one there to stop me; the gardens had no connection with the bay houses behind them, were separated from them by gateless fences or walls. At worst I could be tooted at by the train engineers, as I have experienced time and again while walking along the tracks. They were the property owners, so to speak; the gardens, as I deduced from the padlocks on the sheds, belonged to the national railroad company. Not once did I encounter on my sneaky excursions—

no, I was not sneaking—one of these gentlemen on his home ground, though sometimes from the train I saw them on their plots, as a rule all by themselves, probably already retired older men, otherwise unfamiliar to me in the region.

The gardens, between the tunnel mouth and the railroad station curve, took up an entire stretch, and were staggered on more and more terraces in the direction of the eastern hills, one above the other, finally even as many as four. They were not fenced off from each other, and you could pass along an uninterrupted, several-kilometer-long field of beds, planted with all sorts of things. That footpath was actually the course of the irrigation channel, its water drawn higher up from the forest-edge pond, and overlaid at precise footstep intervals with stone pavers; in between, in the even gaps, the water could be seen flowing under the walker, so that, from one step to the next, stone and sky reflection alternated.

The attraction seemed to me to consist even more of the beds and sheds, with their surroundings. At each of my illegal crossings of the much-terraced railroad-garden territory, undertaken in an ever more up-right posture, I always encountered, among dozens and later hundreds of types of fruit, at least one kind previously undiscovered by me, even if merely a cultivar.

In the smallest space there was often so much crowded in together that one noticed the fine distinctions only when crouching down, and then again a single bed could expand into an acre, a little espaliered tree could be the beginning of an orchard, in which ladders as tall as houses leaned; a forest of dill gave way to a raspberry patch, this to a border of lavender and thyme, that in turn to a row of cherry trees, with trunks thicker than I had ever seen, these finally to a sorrel meadow, into whose middle a peach tree broke, at its feet a bed of artichokes or the most ordinary carrots, turnips—purple and yellow—or cabbages in every imaginable color, almost identical with the Japanese ornamental brassi-cas, or with nothing at all, spiked with several years' fallen leaves.

The sheds as a rule were made of corrugated metal, without windows, but often with wooden doors, which came from somewhere else entirely, and wooden additions of the same kind, roofed like porches: there, or in front under the cherry trees, a table and chairs (never more than two), here and there wreathed with grapevines that dangled from forks in the branches.

The hanging gardens first revealed themselves as an attraction, indeed as a sort of cultural monument, in their totality, in their delicate and yet rich and spacious being-in-themselves, next to which all the surroundings, the apartment houses, the wooded hills, receded into mere background, except for the bundles of tracks running through them and the tunnel opening, from which, with every train pulling into the bay, a scorched iron smell puffed over the slopes and their fruits and vegetables, but in harmony with them.

And thus even the individual phenomenon there became worth seeing, and along with the rollers, the wheeled storage chests, and the railroad retirees' special *boules* court, merited a detour, as did the rose trellises on a metal shed or an old French door serving as a ladder. And even the former entrance gate to the gardens, standing alone in hip-high fringed grass on the embankment, with the seemingly same-aged willow bent over it, its head touching the earth, forming a round-arched portal from which, on top, thousands of yellow-reddish shoots thrust up toward the heavens, seemed worth a trip to me—what do you Spaniards, Swiss, Americans, Swedes down there in the train want with the palace of Versailles? This is where it is!

And another thing in the bay's hanging gardens acquired value for me in this particular year: a square, carefully edged in blocks of sandstone, an entirely empty, pebble-strewn square next to the wall of a bower, raised above the beds, at the same time much smaller than these, drip-irrigated as artfully as pointlessly, in years of lying fallow, by a roof gutter, at which I always thought: "This a railwayman built in memory of his wife."

The only gatherings in the bay in which I participated all year long were the Sunday Masses (other gatherings—were there any at all here?).

I did not go to the French Catholic church for them—I was there almost always only in passing—but to that Russian one, likewise on the edge of the forest, diagonally across the way, which was log-cabin-small, and where the Mass was in part read or sung in Slavic. I had already visited it earlier from time to time, with Ana, whom I was once able to embrace there as hardly anywhere else, with Valentin, my son, whom I once, when I turned to look at the adolescent, saw crying, and who never wanted to go to church again after that.

But in this year of 1999 I made it a rule not to miss a single celebration of the Mass, if possible; it took place in any case only twice a month; the priest also had responsibility for another congregation in the Seine hills. On the Sunday morning in question I became impatient to get there, was afraid of being too late for the Kyrie eleison!, went all the way there at a jog trot.

From outside—no sound ever issued from the building—the chapel with the blue onion dome on top, the only instantly distinct color in the region, seemed, even when one was standing right in front, always locked up, yes, as if abandoned, closed down—unlike the church vis-à-vis, its bells never rang—and on the way I never encountered another churchgoer. And only once past the outer door, in the porch, could one see from the shopping bags deposited there, with baguettes and bunches of vegetables for Sunday dinner, that the building was occupied, and inside was waiting, each time a surprise, a whole crowd, even if it was perhaps only two dozen, one head next to the other. And at the same time, when one entered, it was unexpectedly as spacious as in a dream, perhaps also because of the candles and their reflection on the wall of icons, likewise because of the priest's chamber beyond the arched opening, which led back as if into the depths.

In the cold months the church was always overheated, and that such heating be safeguarded seemed to be the first condition for the continued existence of the congregation: would the priest otherwise have reported on the Sunday before last with such joy on the yield from the collection, taken up for this winter's heating?

As for me, the so-and-so from the Slovenian village of Rinkolach on the Jaunfeld Plain, going to Mass was something that had to be done! To hear Slavic spoken, here in the cosmopolitan bay, every second Sunday, in the company of a few others, was not the main thing. But it opened me up first of all; no, ripped me open. No matter how high the notes became, the sound seemed very deep to me. It did not bring back childhood, but with it I became the person I am, often tremulous, yet not defenseless. Without my ever singing along, my lungs expanded. I found myself blending in with the rest, yet I did not once have to open my mouth.

That I was hearing my ancestors' Slavic at the same time as a Mass was an essential part of the experience. Only in this form did my participatory feeling become as monosyllabic and as emphatic as it was supposed to. There was a joyousness in me, which, however, could find its way out only through the company of others, this company, for instance. And the gradual unfolding of the Mass made me patient. Furthermore, even if I merely stood quietly in the back for an hour or so, it was a form of physical exercise more refreshing than any kind of gymnastics I could name: free of my aches and pains, I went on my way sound as a bell, and with both feet on the ground. And above all, from the ceremony Gregor Keuschnig saw the things he did only for himself as grounded and illuminated, at least for a short stretch of his way back home to continue his work. And all too soon he felt the urge again to go back to the church to find peace.

Right inside the entrance, on a chair at the foot of a staircase, for the first few months there was still an old man sitting, who usually nodded off during the reading from Scripture (the spot has been empty for some time). Now and then during the year, when the priest called upon us to think of the victims of the world's civil wars, he left out the names of the countries involved—there were so many of them—and merely said, in the singular and inclusively, "in the civil war." Whenever a member of the congregation had read in singsong Russian from an epistle, almost always one of St. Paul's, the priest would respond, "Peace be with you, reader!" When he disappeared behind the wall of icons, he hoisted his Bible onto his shoulder. And of all the readings, the one that has remained most forcefully in my mind is that sentence addressed to the people of Ephesus that says more or less that as the entourage of the Crucified they are now no longer passersby but have a house.

How bored and annoyed I sometimes was by the heathens, of whom I quickly became one myself once outside. Although I listened to the Slavic words of the Lord's Prayer so much more attentively than to the French, that was still, along with the Credo, the only part of the liturgy where I felt excluded. I also missed, from my familiar Catholic Masses, that moment when the priest cried, "*Sursum corda!* Lift up your hearts!" (Or have I merely failed to hear it until now?) And it struck me as odd that the priest of the Eastern Church, to have the bread and wine become flesh and blood, had to make a point of speaking the appropriate formula,

whereas in the Catholic ritual all that was necessary for the transubstantiation was the simple narrative: "On the evening before Jesus was crucified, he took the bread . . ." This transubstantiation brought about
simply by narrative was closer to my heart.

Whenever the singers drifted out of the melody, someone, usually
on the sidelines, would join in and bring them back together with his
strong voice. And after Communion the wings of the icon angel were
kissed. And the eagle, the emblem of John the Evangelist, with its damp-
looking robe of feathers, seemed to me as if it had just escaped from
deep waters, into which it had been drawn by a monster fish; yet it
flirted with its eyes, with no one in particular. And at another Sunday
Mass I again saw in the picture of the Evangelist that eagle swooping down on its prey, and, instead of striking it first, conferring shape
on it.

M y father died during the year, far off in the house on Jade Bay,
found only after his death (in the otherwise spotlessly clean bathroom, snippets of whiskers on the razor blade); which of us two was
David, and which Absalom?

And that kindhearted salesclerk in the shopping center on the plateau
of Vélizy, of whom I had thought for a moment that all that stood
between us, not only him and me, and a new, eternal brotherhood was
one blink of the eye, has not been seen since spring. And the footprint
of my son, at that time still small, in the asphalt of the sidewalk, beyond
the hills, in the first place we lived in, the place where from time to
time I went for my oracle, was tarred over during the summer. And that
ball of clay, the only impractical thing on my writing table, cracked to
bits on the day I hit myself too hard on the forehead with it. And the
eyrie of the mythical beast in my garden, created when I cut off the top
of the spruce tree, has remained empty to this day (although on the most
windless day in August a giant shadow floated over me there, and once,
when a wailing sound suddenly broke out behind the house, followed
by cries of pursuit, for a moment I saw something with gray stripes
diving down under the cherry tree, flying low, almost brushing the grass,
a falcon, as it swooped off through the underbrush, half turned onto its

back, its claws stretched out sideways, and one morning in the eyrie a wide-open beak moved, which then turned out to be the ears of a nest-robbing cat).

At the beginning of the year a hare showed itself to me in the woods, far off in the sun, and since then no other. The shots in late fall, however, were aimed more at wild doves, of whom then entire rows, shot down from the sky, cloud-gray-blue, lay displayed on the butcher's marble counter. On the other hand, the foxes have multiplied, and, as I gathered from a remark made in a bar by one of the old-timers, who usually pointedly keep silent on the subject, are larger than ever before. At the beginning of winter, I myself encountered, on another midnight walk home through the wooded heights, as many as I normally encountered only as eyes peering out of the darkness, now standing boldly along the road. And from the long since depopulated foxholes along the banks of the sunken roads, the poles stuck in by children playing have disappeared, which gives the impression that they are occupied once more.

The minibus, the bay's public transportation, which circles all day long and appears at the same places approximately every half hour, has been given a colorful high-gloss coating instead of its subdued white, and also dark-tinted windows. Nevertheless the heads of the passengers can still be made out, cut off at the bottom because of the low seats, as children's usually are, and the landscape thus visible on the other side through the rather slow-moving bus—the forest-edge trees, the ponds, the railway embankment—appears, as before the reconditioning, as part of the vehicle, grown together with it. And even now it can give me a jolt whenever I catch sight of the few people waiting at one of the poles marking a bus stop that is probably obvious only to the natives; they are leaning against a lamppost, for a bumpy ride that will take them two side streets farther, and I get on with them, just like that.

The reconditioned bus is missing that display space on the back intended for the community's barely leaflet-sized posters announcing events, perhaps because films are no longer shown anywhere here, not even slides of the Amazon or other places. Even though the display frame passed me empty for a long time, I still see there the weekly classics announced in the bay's movie theater: *Vera Cruz*—a man sentenced to death flees, *Rio Grande*. Perhaps I shall become a moviegoer again soon.

If I ask myself what happened all year on the long, hilly, yet perfectly straight street that for me constitutes the main street here, this is what comes to mind: the many moving vans, some with Cyrillic writing, others with Greek lettering on them; the flight attendant waiting, long before midday in the otherwise empty landscape, in front of the sandstone school, for the children to be let out; the young women in a hurry, coming from where?, in the morning, with the infants, who, taken in hand by older children at the door, likewise disappeared as quickly into the houses as the mothers into their cars; and of the few pedestrians, the one ordinary original resident, recognizable from the window of my study, no matter how far away he was, through the spyhole I had cut in the hedge, by the white of his cigarette, always at an angle, flaring up for a moment in front of a dark garage door, and along with it his barking cough, each time linked with the sight of his wife in their cottage around the corner by the edge of the forest, scrubbing wash outdoors behind the house, on a board with a drainage hole, though only her husband's handkerchiefs, because his smoker's-cough mucus would otherwise stain all the other things in the washing machine. And one time on that long, straight, hummocky stretch an old woman was walking alone with a shopping bag over her bent arm, and the next time I looked she had dissolved into the water-gray asphalt.

The market, set up as an experiment, with barely three or four stands, once a week, along the main street by the athletic fields, from which balls were constantly crashing against the wire fence, right behind the meat, fruit, and cheese, was given up again in the course of the year; the one on the station square was sufficient for the bay?

And what kind of main street is it, almost without stores, with only a single café, the street's middle section bordered by a forest, with king boletes right there on the bank every year, and, at its end, going uphill into a sunken road roofed over by bushes?—I saw it as such, again and again.

One of my noise neighbors, the most indefatigable of all, had an accident later in the year when one of his mini-machines slipped (achieving all the more racket production and power output), and he bored his way home with it. Or was he torn apart by his noise-sensitive German shepherd? Only subsequently did I hear that he was a philosopher and teacher, much in demand, author of a story with the title "The Legend of the Holy Noisemaker," of a book called *Zen and the Art of Loudness*, and of the brochure "How Can I Kill My Garden?"; a man like me; a colleague.

A couple of his neighbors in turn moved, or pitched their tents somewhere else. In their place came, from the civil-war-torn regions, refugees, the kind of people for whom the bay had always been more than a mere reception camp.

They settled in, here and there around my house, as if forever. They have been very quiet, at least until today, and I have already caught myself asking in the morning at my table, "Where has all the noise gone?" as though I needed it now for getting to work.

These immigrants resembled the original inhabitants, now long since in the minority, except that they were much younger, and even shyer or more timid. They clearly did not wish to be seen, and I sometimes used the child Vladimir, as I walked along side streets holding his hand, to get a good look, so to speak, at the new arrivals. Because it was natural for the child to keep stopping, they could not become suspicious when I imitated him and then perhaps simply followed his gaze.

It was even easier with their possessions, in front gardens and courtyards, or the changes, never major ones, and additions they allowed themselves with their houses. Astonishing that they decorated the exteriors far more with this or that from their new place of residence, the bay, than with things brought along and mementos from their own countries. More than one created a pattern of low miniature beds on the bit of ground between the street and his tiny house, surrounded with wooden posts cut from branches in the local forests, filled up with soil also from there, and planted at regular intervals with local tree seedlings, with plants that no one else, not even I any longer, would have noticed, and which in this region were generally considered weeds.

All this seemed remarkable to the refugees, and feathery mountain ash seedlings as well as the mullein, fox grapes as well as cattails, were given stakes, and tied, often with proper sailor's knots.

It made me realize that my own ways of doing things are still determined by my once having been a refugee, and not only during those few weeks in my childhood right after the Second World War when my mother and I, leaving my father in Wilhelmshaven, made our way back and forth across the forbidden zones in Germany to equally forbidden Austria, our only papers consisting of a letter from my grandfather: in his house, with both of his sons killed in action, a downstairs room was available, and there was work in plenty. Even years after our arrival in Rinkolach, although the local people who had survived the war showed me almost nothing but kindness, it was still as though I had no right to be in the country, and a large part of that feeling had to do with the fact that on all my report cards, from elementary school to graduation, the space designated for "citizenship" was filled in in different hands with "stateless."

And in observing my new neighbors I also recognized that my own occasional skittishness (quite unlike my mother, who soon after her return home was pretty cocky again) does not stem from the way I was later transferred so abruptly from my village to the boarding school, but rather from the twisted sense of being a refugee and illegal that had grown into me. And a difference between me and these new arrivals also became clear, in the form of a play on words, and why not, for a change?: they, the immigrants, and I, the emigrant.

And sometimes I simply stood there in the sun in front of the property of these newcomers, holding the child Vladimir by the hand, my mind blank; imitated the child's quiet, wonderful waiting and watching in the sun or just in the daylight; lost myself happily in the music of his various expressions, or in the sight of his hands held behind him as if to take a running start, as if to fly.

My year in the no-man's-bay was almost at an end when a new or previous publisher invited me to a discussion of the manuscript, wherever I pleased, in Venice, Granada, Andorra, Potsdam, in any case in "a beautiful place."

I invited him to meet me at a pub by the Pont Mirabeau in Paris, from which I could see the little square with that delicate iron and milk-glass pissoir. I brought him a couple of pages, photocopied at the only bookstore in the bay, also a toy store, having selected the pages chiefly for the names of beautiful places that occurred on them.

As far as the title was concerned, the publisher asked me to consider that the word "no-man," like "threshold" or "flight," on a book jacket had a negative and off-putting effect, and that it was old-fashioned to situate the main plot—he had seen through me—in a remote suburb; a contemporary story had to take place in an urban center; yet the book might find readers in spite of that—because it was me. And then he unexpectedly put on a scholarly air, noting that my text's way of turning verbs into nouns—instead of "I stood," "my standing," instead of "the sky turns blue," "the blueing of the sky"—corresponded precisely to what had happened to Latin after the fall of the Roman Empire, during the Middle Ages.

Once, after glancing at a couple of lines, he did say—and I noticed for the first time that this man sitting across from me had beautiful eyes now —that despite my declaration in writing, I was still not finished with myself. And afterward on the bridge he offered this to me in parting, to take back to the forest bay: "Both of us know what to think of each other." What did he mean by that? I brooded, alone in the nocturnal commuter train. And later I thought he probably had the decisive qualification for a book, intuition; but since his life was elsewhere, he despised this.

Something to which I also paid particular attention during this year here was the time thresholds—less the accustomed sequence of plum, cherry, and other blossoms than those that had previously gone unnoticed. Thus it occurred to me once in passing: "Now is the time for the hazelnuts' neck ruffs to have grown over their heads," or "It is already summer, but still too early even for the early apples," or "These are the autumn days when the acorns in the forest are no longer falling singly, but en masse, constantly, and it is advisable to stay away from the forest with children," or "Yesterday was a pre-winter day, since the ash in the yard dropped all its leaves in the course of an hour."

It was also such a time threshold when on the main street a skylight that had always been wide open during the day, long after summer, with a giant mirror on the back wall in which nothing but the sky was reflected, was now, in the November rain, more and more often closed, and one morning remained closed entirely, as if sealed up, and that to this day; or the late-fall period at my sitting place by the Nameless Pond, when, under the edible chestnut tree, I had to hold my writing portfolio over my head to protect myself from the periodic pounding, as if of stones, of the tree's fruits raining down on me, announced in advance by the sound of the husks splitting, while my other hand continued to hold my pencil, and my ears picked out the difference between the drumming on the cardboard and the melodic plunging of the chestnuts, like the plucking of a musical string, deep into the water at my feet, whereupon days followed on which nothing more happened there than the clouding over of the surface and the rising of cold from the bottom of the pond, more and more aggressively. And likewise All Souls' Day sticks in my memory as such a threshold, when until evening it remained unprecedentedly quiet around the house, and I imagined that even the most incorrigible noisemakers were now visiting their dead in the cemeteries.

By contrast, eternal sameness was embodied for me in the bay by the seasonless palm trees (although they bloomed like other trees, were trimmed, and carried their array of fruit, their dates), perhaps also because they were so sparse, and furthermore usually hidden.

To the palms I always went to find the present anew, nothing but the present. And then it seemed to me as if these took on, from the fundamental material of light, even that of night, material or physical form, through their many-fingered fronds, layered over each other, and became rhythmic, not only from an air current but simply with the constant double image on my retina and the layering of the fronds, from which the entire tree, even in the absence of wind, flickered frenetically: "Jazz tree," I thought one time.

And only now, in winter, thanks to the child Vladimir, who suddenly opened his eyes wide, did I discover a previously overlooked palm tree, now the eighth in the bay, in a gap allowing a glimpse into a backyard, and yet an object as obvious as any other; since which moment that part of town has borne for me the name "behind the temple," even if the site of the nonexistent temple occupies the place of the cottager-like Street of the Emigrants, with the uneven wooden electrical poles and tangles of wires dangling high and low in confusion, depending on the uneven heights of the houses here.

I worked less in the yard than in previous years, in recognition of the fact that, contrary to the view that gardening was relaxing, it actually induced in me that very state of agitation I wanted to avoid for my main task.

Of the cherries, I harvested only those that fell past the blackbirds' and ravens' beaks, and on the pear tree, which throughout its time threshold had displayed a single white blossom, without a leaf in sight, there was then, without a frost, only heavy rain lasting for days, not one fruit.

I was more apt to continue cutting, raking, hauling in my lane, because of the few original inhabitants passing by there, to whom my activity, like my walking elsewhere with the child Vladimir, was intended to demonstrate my harmlessness. And we actually fell into conversation, always thus: "Good day." — "Good day." — "Hard work." — "But enjoyable." — "Good day."

So many pencils have I used up in this one year that the drawer is already having trouble closing from all the stubs stuffed into it, and from each I have taken leave, on another sheet of paper, in writing: "Thank you, Spanish pencil! Thank you, Yugoslavian pencil! Thank you, white pencil from the honeymoon hotel in Nara, Japan! Thank you, twenty-second black Cumberland pencil! Thank you, pencil from Freilassing in Germany, even if that is perhaps not a beautiful place! Thank you, pencil from the bookstore in the bay, even if your lead kept breaking during sharpening!"

The path deep within the forest, with the thick white sand and the lizards along the bank, where the stonemason from the turn of the era sat on a tree trunk, was graveled and tamped down in the course of the year, and the story of the stonemason, although I wanted to trace it like those of my friends, I left lying somewhere.

Of the boat, no, the skiff, in the middle of the Nameless Pond, already in spring half sunk, but still clear in outline, there now sticks out, like the remains of a pile dwelling, only a piece of the once-lacquered hull, without the earlier blue of Istria or Wyoming.

From the one hundred-year-old façade in the bay, the four deck-of-cards emblems in the corners of the half-timbering, the painted diamond, spade, heart, and club, have fallen away along with the mortar.

The vegetable bed, in the middle of one of the bay's cemeteries, by the warden's house, bursting in summertime with tomatoes, pole beans, squash, arugula, and separated from the bare field of headstones by a row of arborvitae, seems to have been leveled, and not merely for the fallow months; yesterday a lone bean pod, blackened, still hung by its stem, scimitarlike.

Although now almost an entire year has passed, I still do not see this as "a time," and simultaneously something within me resists saying *I* to the person who was sitting at this table here in January.

I, that was back then, like today, the one who time and again lay in his bed at night lost to the world, and who, having gone too long without friends, was overcome by fear of death. Walking, looking, reading, writing were not enough for me; I needed talking, for reinforcement.

A sparrow is running just now right along a gable across the main street, up, down, back: now he knows, as well as our Pythagoras ever did, what a triangle is.

I still get lost here; and I find that all right for this region of mine.

3

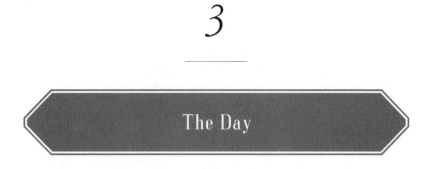

The Day

The day on which my friends were supposed to arrive in the bay fell between Christmas and the new year. That was considered the darkest time. But as far as I was concerned, since childhood I had had during that time the dreams of which I was convinced that they did not apply to me personally but were owed by me to the world.

The night before, I went to bed earlier than usual, and then during the night saw on a wall in medieval Siena a picture, about which disagreement existed as to whether it was by Giotto or not. It portrayed a procession of people, shot through by the rays of a sun, which, the dream said, was the "essence of sun." Finally the disagreement was resolved as follows: the picture had indeed been painted by Giotto, though not in the town of Siena but outside in a suburb.

I dreamt this during the night before the day before yesterday, and today I am still convinced that the painting is hanging hidden somewhere in Tuscany or elsewhere, and that the circumstances are as they were communicated in the dream.

I got up while it was still pitch dark, and absolutely silent: it was new moon, with, far from the sky over the metropolis, stars shining all the more brightly, soon covered by clouds, so that finally the only light shining into the house came from the transmitter high on the eastern range of hills, the one installation in the bay that was constantly in operation and to which I once said involuntarily, while walking home on a summer night, "Our tower!" as if it belonged solely to the population here, and I in turn to this.

There were days when I completely forgot about the sky: this was supposed not to be such a day. I immediately set out for the forest, to which, after the lane, it was only a short side street. No one else was out and about; still a good while until the first commuter train. It was below freezing. But the nocturnal darkness, both that between the houses and the even denser, more substantial darkness under the trees, warmed me, as it had long ago during the early mornings of Advent on the way to the worship service called *Rorate* ("thaw out!") in our village church —one of the few periods in the year when even in boarding school I did not mind going to church. But what then fell from the sky was, instead of dew, a fine rain that hardly wet me.

With my entry into the forest, the forest gave my head its measure. I climbed up to the top of the Seine hills on the familiar Absence Road, which I called this because its fill consists of construction debris, rubble from foundations, brick walls, bathroom tiles, thresholds, doorframes, a discarded street sign, even a piece of a ceramic house number and a crushed milk can, as if from a farm, sticking up from the bed of the path wherever one looked, forming humps, curbs, and inclined planes, a sunken ship, as it were, along whose keel, facing up, I had often picked my way in the course of the year, zigzagging and leaping, in order to keep myself impressionable, to quote old Goethe.

The morning of the day before yesterday I let this path become nameless again, and after that likewise the High Path up on the edge of the plateau, which in sweeping curves followed its spine, and on which one can circle the entire forest bay, as if on cliff paths close to a precipice; free of names, from below ground for the moment the creation rose up.

I made a little detour from the forest to the office complexes of Haut-Vélizy, one mirrored in the next, as glaringly lit up as empty, except for the night watchmen, whole divisions of them spread over the entire plateau, each by himself with his dog in his booth in front at the barred entrance. My Sunday evening walks during the year had been primarily for their benefit, and thus at least one, when he turned his head away from his tiny television monitor to look at me, his thermos bottle in his hand, raised a finger in greeting. And there was also something new: on the terrace of an abandoned office building, the company having gone bankrupt, weeds had sprung up.

Back in the forest, heading downhill on the Green Path (because of its grassy surface), instantly restored to namelessness, I smelled smoke, and then deep in the woods came, in an almost inaccessible preserve, through which I had fought and shimmied my way on many a morning (if ever a path for learning impressionability, then such a one), upon a fire, lighting up only the area around a hut, in whose middle it was, in a loose circle of fireproof poles, which led up, cylinder-shaped, to the smoke hole in the thatched roof; on one side the casbah was open, protected by the dense thicket; a layer of leaves on the ground; no human being.

But I met one, as it was gradually getting light, down in the clearing with the hollow occupied by the Nameless Pond (even it did not have its name anymore), by the spring behind it. Sometime after the lava flow from Mont St.-Valérien, this spring had become warm, which I did not notice until I was walking past one night, slipped, and ended up with my hand in its rather meager flow. It was far warmer than from even the warmest rain, and it smelled, in nose proximity, of sulfur. Later, right at its source, recognizable by a clear-clear pulsing, I dug myself a sort of tub and sometimes gargled there, or soaked my bruised, more than sore, numb feet: relief.

Early on the day before yesterday, however, I found my spring spot in the swamp beyond the bomb-crater body of water occupied by the person in whom, back in the spring of the year, on Lizard Way (this designation also canceled), I had seen the stonemason from the twelfth century. He was sitting there, up to his knees in the sulfurous water, and greeted me—here in the bay it had always, up until now, been I who greeted first—what a nodding of the head!, and shifted to one side. There was room enough for two; he had built an earthen bench, lined with stones, around the spring, in the suggestion of a half-moon. The stonemason seemed more like a gardener, in the bareness of winter.

When I untied my shoes, I noticed that they came from different pairs: my mistake in the still-nocturnal house. With my feet warmed, I took off my hat in spite of the rain, and thought, gazing over the muddy surface to the edge of the pond, that it was no distance at all from the mud long ago behind my grandfather's farm in the village of Rinkolach to this mud here now. And then, picturing my almost three seasons of writing by the root hill of the tipped-over birch, at the same time a hiding place for muskrats, I swore to myself that for me no path would lead away from this place into a so-called public arena. And at the same time I was seized with pain at the thought that I would never again sit there by the water to write, where, with my work in hand, I had been able to be with the daily world as never before. And then I saw that my year's seat, the burned-out half tree trunk, last hauled out of the ice by me, had once more been rolled into the pond, certainly not by children playing. And then in the distance ravens flapped low over the forest floor, like black horses galloping soundlessly through the trunks of the trees.

The bomb-crater pond trembled, and trembled, and trembled, the different winter-morning gray grayed, and grayed, and grayed, the stonemason kept silent, and kept silent, and kept silent, and then he said: "I wanted to go south, and I ended up here. I am not the only one scattered to the winds. When I was young, we worked as a brotherhood, under the direction of my father, whose mark in granite was also that of our group. First we were stone breakers, then stonemasons, or both at once. For splitting we had hardly more tools than a hammer. First look, then strike! What counted at the beginning were eyes and ears. With the latter we listened to see whether the stone sounded as it should—even a small off-note inside, and it was no good; with the former we saw in what direction the stone was to be cut, whether lengthwise or crosswise, or, as a third possibility, and just as important for building, in the direction of the interstices, to obtain the keystones, as support; as anchor; as resting place; and as a bridgehead for additions. In the meantime we wander alone from project to project, or have disappeared in war, and at any rate we stonemasons no longer chisel our signs anywhere, and where does the scar on your shin come from?" — "I burned myself there as a child," I replied, and invited the runner to join me for dinner with my friends in Porchefontaine.

W hen I then stepped out of the forest, already in daylight, I noticed that it was still silent as night in the bay, even down below on the bypass, and then came upon glare ice, even before I saw it, stretching far into the distance, a rigid gleam, so different from that of rain, covering and raising the asphalt, and even the pebbles in the lane, as I slithered home. Was it this way throughout the country? Would my friends be delayed by it? Then the bugles of the railway linemen, short and no-nonsense, but still lingering in the air for a long time afterward.

As I circled the house a few times in the yard, where even in the grass the ice crackled, I made two discoveries: on the one tree that I had believed all year to be without fruit, unexpectedly a pear, dwarf-sized, to be sure, and wizened, but unfrozen, and the one bite—that was all it yielded—of a sweetness that stayed with me all day; and about the other, the ash, its foot concealed by a hedge, the fact that it, which I had always thought grew on a neighbor's property, grew on mine; belonged to me! It had followed me from the former cow pasture at home in Rinkolach (where I wanted to go right after the book, to sniff the air of my birthplace).

And I promptly propped a ladder against the particularly straight, smooth ash trunk, glassy from transparent ice all around, trimmed the branches so that they resembled the heavy rip cords of a parachute, and declared the tree a monument to that unknown American soldier who, after an emergency jump, got tangled in a thicket on the Jaunfeld Plain and was beaten to death by the crowd that gathered—perhaps also one of my relatives among them?—using all those tools that today are to be seen almost exclusively in local history museums, where they exude venerability.

And in the process I made yet a third discovery: on the evergreen shrubs all around the ash there were garlands of leaves, as if from crystal chandeliers, made of ice, frozen solid after the rain landed on the leaves, which had broken off as a result, so that only their ice forms hung in the air, attached to the woody branches by ice stems, true-to-nature copies, just like the lanceolate forms pointing away from them, in whose delicate glassy bodies the snapped-off leaves were precisely copied, the midrib and all the side ribs, but in reverse, and thus all the way up the bush, green and glassy leafage in one, except that in the latter the sky shone through at the top. "That can't be!" I thought at the sight, which again meant that it seemed to me as real as anything could possibly ever be. "This empathic spelling-out means more to me than anything else." And: "For us today how much more there was to tell about our days than about our years. And all the more difficult to find clear lines to follow."

A nd what else happened the day before yesterday? The postman, who, probably like other postmen in the world, during this year of more war than peace, had stopped whistling while delivering the mail, gave me a letter from the woman from Catalonia, postmarked Girona, rather than the Spanish alternative, Gerona, the residence of her father, meanwhile become the first president of the new state of Catalunya. She wrote: "As you always wanted of me, after all: I have had enough of your reluctance, like that of an unmarried man, and curse it. To experience fragmentarily and dream comprehensively will not work with me. Why can I find no support in you? And why do I still believe, in spite of everything, that no better support can be found than in a vacillating, yearning person? As for the rest, I am finally free of parents, and besides I have now slept here so long in my girlhood bed that I am a young girl again, though differently than before." Ah, those Catalan curses, those Catalan oracles, those Catalan fairy tales.

And the day's news from the Castilian town of Benavente in the province of Zamora: on the flat steppe outside the town gates lay a corpse, smashed by a fall as if from a great height, presumably an illegal immigrant, fallen out of an airplane before its landing in Santiago de Compostela, having previously already frozen to death in his hiding place. And above the church of Cristo de la Vega, in the meadows, in an otherwise bright blue sky, a cloud had hung all day, motionless, the meadows in its rigid shadow, while round about the entire *meseta* lay in winter sunlight.

A fter that I was in a mood to stay outside in the yard for a while. I raked the almost leafless grass, merely to see it green up and to see the earth beneath it blacken—what a color—accompanied by a robin, not for my sake, but for that of the earthworms writhing under the

fractured ice; observed next to the house foundation the "bay *en minia-*
ture" that I had constructed from a piece of moss, with the moss representing the forests, the crushed rock protruding into it representing the
houses in the settlement; swept the steps to the house and the paved
part of the yard with a broom made of those wonderfully flexible tamarisk twigs, found in or borrowed from the railwaymen's hanging gardens
(what needed to be swept there?); loosened the crushed rock path, in the
process of which a button from the uniform of the general or gendarme,
one of my predecessors in the house, found its way into my hand and I
smelled the hundred-thousand-year-old oyster bed from the underground
of the bay; washed a cellar window, out of which probably no one had
ever looked, as well as the brick threshold the painter had once fired for
me with the inscription from the Gospel according to John: "The son
shall remain in the house for eternity," and thought once more how only
physical labor really got my blood to circulate, and in addition made
my hair soft and smoothed my skin, and how nevertheless of all my
activities it was only through my writing that I had ever been able to
feel something like a connection with the world.

In the meantime a repairman came to fix the oil burner in the cellar,
and I watched as he took its innermost core, a valve as small as a cherry,
between his child's fingertips and then finally blew it clean with Neptune
cheeks. In parting at the garden gate, he pointed out a hitherto overlooked, still empty blackbird nest in the cypress, made, along with grass,
moss, and inner bark, of narrow tape from thrown-away music cassettes,
and prophesied snow and a change of heart for mankind in the third
millennium.

Before I then went back into the house, I stepped back a few paces
and saw it, also with the heaps of leaves that had blown into the old
shoes outside, standing in pioneer territory, for instance near Fairbanks,
Alaska. Why was I not there? But I was there. It occurred to me that
anyone who can have a yard and does not have one is a wrongdoer, by
omission. But what good did a yard do? Wanting to go out into the
yard, again and again. And without the yard, my hummocky world, I
did not want that.

Indoors the same dark, clear light prevailed as outside, and I wished
that this initial light might remain always, similar to the sun the commanding officer orders not to set until the battle is decided. Emptying

out was lightening. The few objects, made from the salt-bleached wood of the saltworks, did not fill the house; a grayish-silvery stool caused all the living spaces to float.

And what happened then? I rubbed the long dining table with sandpaper, and rubbed and sanded and washed it, with my nose almost touching it until I was inside the smell of the wet planks, the most Sunday-like of smells, and then watched the drying, until this tabletop stood for the entire house.

B ut after that, additional air could come only from language, and so, after I had showered, with a powerful cold jet hitting my heart chamber and my armpits, and had already dressed for the evening, I sat down in the study to write.

And there was peace for a while there on the day before the day before yesterday, a tremulous one. Next to the door, which led straight outside, leaned the wrinkled, already long-standing backpack, and when I got up at intervals and sniffed inside, the smell of all Yugoslavia wafted out. And in between I read in the book of Samuel the story of David and his rebellious son Absalom: how he had suffered as a very young boy, once not being allowed to see his father's face for years.

A quiver ran through the now ice-free grass blades outside. The reproduction of the Kings of Orient from back home, in the backyard, by the beech tree, had suffered from the year's weather; the faces of Caspar, Melchior, and Balthazar seemed twisted, like those of the homeless on the square outside the commuter station, and what they were holding could also, along with gold, frankincense, myrrh, or king boletes, be a beer bottle each, and what they had on their heads had probably been from the beginning, instead of crowns, the caps of bakers and masons.

Through the spyhole to the main street white had flashed for the twinkling of an eye from a cigarette, and then again upon the return of the Eternal Smoker, and in the house across the way the woman was shouting as never before at the child entrusted to her for the day, which was screaming, likewise as never before; and then from over there silence; and I resolved to write my first letter to the editor, to *The Hauts-de-Seine News*, on the subject of such day-care mothers (what was the word in French?).

The depression in the wooded hill, at one time called the Poussin Meadow, revealed itself by the trees' there being, not brown and gray, but inky, and at the same time each tree seemed transparent for the next, and so on, and each a planetarium unto itself, such that despite the old saying I saw the forest for the trees for a change, "in its essential sun," while in the foreground almost all the chimneys were smoking, in the shape of tails, like the cedar branches even closer to my windows, only bright, so that I thought the expression in a chronicle, centuries ago, for the properties in the area, *feux*, fireplaces, was still appropriate today, and furthermore: "The chronicle does not capture the world," and furthermore, as once almost every day: "I have failed, all is lost!" and furthermore: "Today I shall find something I thought to have lost forever! There are such days," and furthermore: "My table here is too small for an epic," and furthermore: "No, too large!"

And what happened then? I wished I could put my head down on my writing table, with my arms stretched away from me, and once again I could not do it. And then I did it after all, and fell asleep, while a raven, right by the window, watched me, amiable and curious, waddling on the sill like a duck (from now on I shall see ravens differently). As sleep goes, it was at most a wink—the expression my North German father used—and having shaken it off, I woke up in an unexplored part of the world that had just descended with the dew, dew drops even in the tops of the trees, one of which was of bronze or amber.

And after that it was time to set out, around the bay and through the hill forest on into the neighboring bay of Porchefontaine. It was not raining anymore. It was clear and dark. The wind was blowing off the Atlantic, not cold, not warm. I bent down to the blowing through the grass. Along the lane, with his wares on his shoulder, an elderly rug dealer was walking, and asked, "Are you the owner?" and I said, "Yes!" From between the rows of cypresses a heavy, soft lilac bush tickled my forehead—but no, it was winter now. Lovely, strange transition from the almost roofed-over quiet lane right into the roar of a highway. And in the attic room across the way, suddenly, in the middle of winter, the skylights were open again, in the giant mirror in the background the morning sky, although it was long since not morning anymore. And in front of the mirror stood my sister—but no, she was dead, after all. The thought of my origins: it still cleansed me, stood me on my feet, and showed me the way.

In the front garden of the Russian child Vladimir lay a fork, its tines facing up, and I turned it over. To hear him as I passed roaring like an ox and a lion from deep inside the house spurred me on. It was full of playfulness, as the entire child was full of playfulness, contagious.

In the street of the immigrants or refugees, the longest, narrowest, and straightest side street in the bay, against the background of the railroad embankment, an entire procession of people was moving along, as had become almost common in this year, one behind the other, with shopping carts, suitcases on wheels, also handcarts. But for the first time, one of the cottage doors there was open, as wide as possible, uninhibitedly, and allowed one to see all the way inside: there are supposed to have been very few years, perhaps only two, in the Roman Empire when in its capital city the doors to the temple of war could be closed—and today instead the open door of peace here. In some places the walled-up gaps between the buildings had been reopened, and one was a rabbit hutch, another a baking oven area, the third simply a new vista, or seemed, if it remained dark, full of treasures, treasure-dark; the whole place was actually blooming with in-between spaces, or the brightness of bird feathers prevailed. On the carts, the immigrants had long since ceased to haul their possessions or produce. There was a glint of time- and space-eating machines.

By the railway embankment I joined those waiting by the kiosk for the bay bus and watched the commuter trains up above, where the passengers, who for a good part of the terrible year of 1999 had almost all sat motionless behind the panes, had begun here and there to wipe off the steam again. From the nearby station the loudspeaker became audible, which for foreigners on their way to Versailles called out the name of the station for a change: Hakubutsukandubutsuen! (But wasn't that a stop in Tokyo?) Let those people on the train see me: I was proud to be standing here, precisely in this place, and obviously also to live here.

Those of us who got onto the small bus, with my neighbor as driver, to whom I said, *"Dober dan!,"* greeted those who were already sitting there. It was a day when the children were out of school, yet because the seats were so low we all looked somewhat like schoolchildren, and also perched there, squeezed together like children in school buses. The newly tinted windows darkened the view from inside much less than the other way around. From the most remote tip of the bay, the camel herd with rocking humps again headed for the Turkish Mediterranean, and the large, snow-white bird that calmly strutted across the street ahead of the bus, right at the crosswalk, and then rose into the air on the other side, was no seagull but an albino raven ("There is no such thing!"). Two boys sat across from me, with Serbian-Balkan faces, of whom one then leaned toward me as if to hit me and picked a white hair off my collar, with the comment "Old!"

We got a good shaking from the vehicle, and I wished it were even more. As we passed the Etang des Ursines, you could tell by the water there that it had been frozen over not long ago, the ripples in the pond were so fresh and the water seemed to be flowing. We were thus circling the bay by a northern sea. The sky spread far beyond the densely stacked little houses, the drooping electrical and telephone wires like those above a fleet of boats drawn up on land for the winter, and I thought that only after all my years here in the suburbs had I seen for the first time, upon returning to Rinkolach, a sky over the Austrian village. Then a bus in the other direction crossed our path, with the autistic children clumped together in the back of the bus, who were sometimes hauled through the bay all day long, in the hope of relieving their isolatedness within themselves.

I got off by the tunnel and the railwaymen's hanging gardens and observed there from the overpass the Seine hills all around, mountainlike almost everywhere, here as a riegel, there as a saddle, though every individual spot was a saddle, and where was the "yoke"?

And having climbed over the bolted gate, under the wreathed arbor formed by the willow branches, in the silence of the wintry garden rows, on the edge of the track cut, I laid the tamarisk broom back in its place, took in return an unharvested turnip from a bed, peeled and ate it, which made me, so shortly before the end of the year, feel October more intensely than ever in reality, stumbled, next to one of the corrugated-metal huts, upon a previously overlooked fig tree, full of fruit, though withered, and thought, with nothing in my ear but the path-narrow, fast-flowing canal under my soles, covered from step to step by flagstones, that this was the place now for snowing.

Its moment, a single one, I then missed, for the first time in my life; a railroad retiree, stepping unexpectedly out of his shed, pointed his finger at me and then brushed something from my collar, which was a snowflake: *"Neige!"* — *"Ja, Schnee!"* I said, involuntarily in German.

Once out of the cut, I knocked the snow or mud off my shoes and continued on my pilgrimage, keeping to the edge of the forest, past the Russian church, where I greeted the dark blue of the onion dome and the light blue of the porch door, on to the old-fashioned remains of the bay, the length of castle-high stone wall with the well-preserved gate opening, until the day before the day before yesterday still called the Lion Gate of Mycenae, because of the two boulders sticking out on top, a door with access not to the Castle of Mycenae but to the hill forests above the Seine.

And there in the arch, in which the tree trunks, their image sharpened, shimmered, a trinity of suburban vagrants were stumbling and weaving homeward into the underbrush, among them the year's new addition, with the same plastic bags as his confreres, the same scratches on his nose from blows and falls, and even his head-wobbling, just a short while ago still maintaining a counterrhythm, already showed agreement, with puppetlike self-confidence.

And thus he also laughed at me over his shoulder, framed by the Lion Gate, with a huge toothless mouth, yet with his original wealth of curls, and said, "I don't need to be rescued." And the day before he had been sitting on the sidewalk outside the supermarket, next to him one of the bay's idiots, who was preaching to him, at which the handsome young drinker merely kept grimacing.

———

And what happened then? Having set out on my loop back to the railroad station, I had the encounter with the other fool or idiot of the bay, who stopped me on the sidewalk, with barely room for two, and said straight to my face that right there in the underpass, at the thought of Christ's sufferings, tears had come to his eyes. Sometimes God caused him pain (a fist blow to the chest), grabbed him, shook him, did not leave him in peace. It was too bright inside him, and this light was his fear—whereupon he jerked the pencil out of my hand and with glowing eyes sack-hopped away, as if nothing had happened. And I stopped at the nearby gas station, where the attendant lent me his ball-point pen for a note.

Then I went into the Bar des Voyageurs and was recognized just from my profile by the proprietor, whose head was bent: he put the usual down before me on the counter. I was so engrossed in thoughts of my book that I again said my thanks in German; and the proprietor answered me in his Arabic.

The weekly *Hauts-de-Seine News* was lying there, and I leafed through, looking for the column devoted to the bay: nothing, except the announcement of the fairy-tale hour: "The story is that of a poor woman who lives with her three daughters in a little village at the foot of a mountain. One fine day she discovers at the market a picture that will change her life." And then another fairy tale: "A princess is seeking a husband. But the suitors are all too loud for her." And I added in my thoughts: "Have I in my life as a writer ever got beyond such prehistories? I always felt a great story within me, and by the time I had finally told the prehistory, the book was already over. And hasn't it been exactly the same this time?"

I read the news from beginning to end; it was a special kind of pleasure to be a contemporary. In the man at my side I then recognized, for the first time in a bar in the bay, a neighbor, the one who on Sunday afternoons, with a face as confused as the one with which he was drinking his beer here, had the habit of burping into a battery of megaphones—to test them, as he now explained, for the fair. I treated him to a glass, as he did me. Then we remained silent, and whenever the proprietor in his taproom let one of the refrigerator compartments snap shut, my neighbor jumped, and I read from his lips, *"Quel bruit!"* (What a noise!)

In the course of the year in the Bar des Voyageurs, some of the video games had been replaced by the original pinball machines, which banged ceaselessly with free turns, and likewise a table soccer game, at which a few young people stared as if this were something that had vanished forever and they were its rediscoverers.

The battle-ready characters in the come-on images of the remaining video games kept pumping themselves up, their movements more like those of a sleeping flock of sheep, and when no one set them in motion against each other, the notion occurred to me that of all people the players at these machines would someday become the new readers of books, soon. And were the heads of the table-soccer figures all that different, after all, from the broad-lipped, full-cheeked roundheads of the early Middle Ages, to whom, as for instance to the kings in my garden, I went to be able to draw deeper breaths? And what did I see before me as I drew my deepest breath? Writing, or readiness for the written word.

The proprietor, with always the same presence of mind, had something of the air of a hostel father, and sometimes it was one of his customers who bought the bread for the itinerant workers' supper, placed the tables on the chairs, swept up the debris from the bar, and the day before the day before yesterday one of the usual steady customers unexpectedly turned up as the help, well-mannered and with authority. How old had the *patron* become in this year? And how about me? I contemplated the pattern of spots on the back of my hand; they had the form of the Big Dipper.

Behind the glass façade the day was unchangingly dark and clear, and I stayed until the first couple of sparrows appeared in the sleeping tree; they were gathering there, however, long before they were ready to go to sleep. Their wings, constantly whirring up and down the tree, provided brightness on this dark day. The smooth trunk of the plane tree, in its dew-dampness, still looked iced. And behind it the heads of the commuters in the trains up on the railway embankment repeated those of the sparrows: "If you knew how beautiful you look as silhouettes," my thoughts continued, "you would never want to be anything else again. Stay that way! If I were a painter, I would never paint anything but silhouettes, fragmentarily illuminated, in buses, trains, métros, in planes above the clouds, and these pictures would be the new Georges de La Tours." And in the plane trees on the plaza there were still multicolored lights from Christmas Eve, among which the sparrows were the other Christmas illumination, or simply a more living component.

Outside there was a smell of fish from the morning market; shreds of jute with Chinese and splinters of crates with Spanish lettering swirling into the air, and sparrow footprints on the asphalt, already slightly blurred, had the formation of the fighter wing that at the same time actually thundered over the plaza, dark as a storm cloud, heading home to the base on the plateau. But it was still the case that I gained deeper insights from the birds' traces down below on the earth than from anything in the heavens.

And I thought further: "But isn't believing in human silhouettes, at a certain remove, which must be preserved, my fundamental mistake? Wouldn't it have been essential for me to get closer, but how? To cross the threshold between silhouettes and—well, what? The figures just now in the bar: if a television interviewer had been there, how they would have spilled their most intimate life stories, from their first fear of death to their first murder and their mother's letters to them during the war. I have not asked, not once in this entire year."

Having set out for Porchefontaine, I first took the footpath between the railway line and the suburban houses, heading west. A woman was running along in a zigzag, shouting again and again, "Where's my paper? Who's seen my *Parisien libéré*? What'll I do? I have nothing to read. What'll I do?"—followed by two police officers, a rare sight in the bay, who asked whether anyone had perhaps seen an old man, "in pajamas, without glasses," while at the same time they peered farther down into the railway cut; also followed by a woman in a fur coat who said as loudly as calmly, "I've lost my husband"; and finally followed by an unknown person who took aim at me—did he shoot?—at any rate he made the noise with his mouth, and I continued on.

The palm at the crest of the path represented the bay's western cape. I paused in front of it, and at first only the kinked fronds of the palm moved, slightly, calmly, as if tuning up, and then suddenly all the fronds swung into motion, skyward, earthward, one-hundred-handed, pounded the keys of the present-day air, and following their example, I spread my fingers, let the intervals blow through me, and thought, nonetheless: "In my appreciation for music I have never got beyond the blues."

From the cape I turned to look back, with my entire body, at the no-man's-bay once more (meanwhile renamed thus), while on a side street another person also turned to look back, but while walking, once and then once again, and more in sorrow than in high spirits. The route through the broad hollow to the hill horizons on the other side led as if through one vast runway, while the veil of mist hovering over it made it seem as if something were being hatched there; as if, without factories, office buildings, research institutes, something were going at constant, silent full blast there. I saw, on this different sort of world map, finely drawn, the first, the New World. Or: the forest bay as a book, open before my eyes, clear, voluminous, colorful, airy. And this was not, as I had once thought, to be achieved through slowness, but through carefulness, or deliberateness, whether slow or fast.

But what to do with it then? Had I done anything with it? In the backyards of the bay, the clotheslines were hung with nothing but the usual tiny dust rag—of a widow? of a widower?—and the lit-up bus there in the background, at full speed, was a gym, in apparent motion from the children running along its horizontal bars, and as always I felt sad when after the last yard no other came. To leave the place seemed to me each time like a leaving-in-the-lurch. In magnificent Paris nothing required my observation anymore; here, however, in the suburb-bay, almost everything did.

It has been a long time since I went out to Porchefontaine. Our year's-end celebration there had been discussed on the telephone by the proprietor of the Auberge aux Echelles (The Ladders) and me. How long ago it is that I saw the man over there beyond the foothills and myself as those two cottage dwellers on the Japanese scroll in the Kyoto Museum, each of them on his own side, to the left and right at the foot of a knoll, in an infinite, otherwise unpopulated mountainous landscape with heavy snow falling silently, as they sit at their work

behind the windows of their hermits' huts, with the most serene expressions, in the knowledge that what they are both doing fits together,
and that they will shortly visit each other again.

Farther up the path, the picture became more lively, without any need
for snow. I was developing an appetite, not only for my friends, but just
as much for my petty prophet. And that almost painful appetite in my
breast was called longing.

And I also had in mind what one of the guests in the Bar des Voyageurs had just remarked: "There are no borders." As special as my
region was, the one through which I was now passing differed from it
in no respect, at least during this hour's journey. All day, dark and clear,
as it remained, the houses in the next suburbs stood just as well anchored
on their hill foundations, or growing out of them, and the overlapping
regions exuded a strength unlike that of any skyscraper metropolis; and
when I considered it now, I had never been anywhere, with the exception
of the boarding school, where I had not eventually been happy to be.

By the boarded-up arcade of the long-distance railroad embankment,
the walled-up former weapons depot used by the Germans, a young
couple was lingering, distraught with desire, and on the decorative dice
mounted on edge on top of a garden wall the dots had been repainted,
as had been the billiard queue along with the black and white balls on
the flank of a drinking trough. Not only the gaps between the houses,
but also the spaces under the steps leading up to the houses, which in
many places were as if barricaded, had been cleared out in the course of
the year, and many a house, with its outbuildings and crushed-rock
paths, the courtyards expanded into plazas, formed an entire village.

And then cats leaped from windowsills, the whistles of express trains
echoed from the hills, people stood in telephone booths with their backs
to the sidewalk, driving-school cars went by, on a *terrain vague* a circle
of pale grass served as a reminder of the recently departed little circus
(to which children now, to paraphrase Rilke, went to smell the lion), in
a pediment above a sundial stood in Greek letters the inscription "God
is forever measuring the world." And a procession of workers came toward me, with flags, on the last day of their protest march to the president's palace in Paris, to prevent the closing of their Land Rover factory
far off in Brittany.

And then? The one moment of sunlight that day: like another epistle. And then the forest again. It occurred to me that it was Monday, the quietest day, on which things in nature, mistreated during the weekend, revived. Branches and sections of trunks lay across the path, snapped off by the morning's ice. Here was the range of hills between the two inhabited spits, and the wind was growing stormy. I plunged off to the side through stalks of wild currants, a single one of whose tiny fruit balls in summer had the taste of an essence, and thus came upon, put on its track by a raven with something round and yellow in its beak, the tree, long since sensed, with the wild apples (but edible only in dried form, like dehydrated pears).

Striking how often in the course of the year I have got my hat and hair tangled in the thicket of the forests, almost hung up on a branch, and I thought again of Absalom, enemy of a father who stayed out of sight, and in his war against this father inescapably caught by the hair by the forest and then beaten to death by his pursuers.

Up above on the crest was a large clearing. I was dizzy and sat down there on an oak trunk. The day remained dark and clear, and whenever I closed my eyes, there was a flaring of retained images, as only in winter.

From the forests all around came a mighty roaring, to which I surrendered myself. Just as there was the expression "ravages of war," now for the stirring gray-on-gray all around there was the expression "ravages of peace." From the ground up, all colors contributed to it, and the garlands of clematis, with their appearance of gray roses, looked brighter than the white of the birches and darker than the black of the alders. "My son," I thought, "or someone else, will one day recite the epic of this thirty-times-thirty-fold winter gray, how it has overlapped and will continue to have its accumulated effect, backward and forward into the cosmos."

And I thought further there in the clearing, in my style of jumbled thinking: "I still have much walking to do. Going on foot, precisely in this automobile-dependent civilization, is more adventurous nowadays than ever. Walking, easy knowing. Too close to the human race, I feel horror. I have love of the world. It is within me. Except that I cannot keep love of the world at the heart of the story. For that I had to go to the margins. The silhouettes: I feel the weakness in them, the lack of presence. And yet a fieriness emanates from all of you, scattered as you are. The world is full of dark colors from commonalities among people unknown to one another. Perhaps the outsider is in fact best equipped to see you as all together. Long ago, during my time in court: justice came not so much from the presiding judge as from the associate judge. And since I have been here in the suburbs, I have come to see myself as such an associate judge. As a reader. To read a book of a new-blown world. Once more I should like to feel the gray wind of Yugoslavia rounding the bend. Where do I belong? At home at the edge of the field. And here I am closest to that. And yet here I walk past walls different from those in my homeland. The time has come for different words. But which ones? When something has disappeared, it means that something different is now to be found. My friends and I, we are not in any sense victors, but also not doomed to extinction. But perhaps I am lost to nature. And a terror has taken root in me, deep and ineradicable. And Ana and I: such a waste. The two of us together time and again became the black planet. And yet in my life I wanted to bring something home every day. Bring home where? To those entrusted to me. What have I given up in the course of time? The legal profession. And rightly so. My homeland. And rightly so. But not right that I gave up my family. When alone I appear to myself again and again as a villain. How often I wish I could shoo myself out of my own head, as a mother might shoo her dozen children out of the noisy house. And then again, at the thought of being alone, upon contemplating in the evening a rustling plane tree along a highway exit, I should like to spend my whole life this way. How unburdened all those men in bars used to seem to me, long since without housemates. And how does that song of the singer's go? *Who knows, who knows.* And how did I wake up this morning? With a hair in my mouth that was not mine. Dream and work!—that was on those factory workers' banners I just saw. Do not exhaust the possibilities of the day; put it all into the book; that is where it belongs. And where are the readers? Mysterious brood! Passersby, hieroglyphic mankind. No new time? Did I write that? This year? Oh, man of little faith. Those who have not undergone metamorphosis have done themselves in. New World: like walking on a street in new-fallen snow, where no one has been but a little bird."

At my feet piles of dark droppings shaped like olive pits: did that indicate there were still rabbits here in the woods? Two heavy fists pressed down on my shoulders, which were then the hoofs of a horse that whispered something into my ear.

Everything splendid I have experienced since my birth awakened in me, and I wrote my ancestors the following postcard: "Come. Get yourselves here!" "And my friends," I thought further, "in just a little while they will tell me their stories from this year, altogether differently from my versions, and also entirely different stories. Away! Out of the forest!"

Porchefontaine belongs to Versailles, yet the palace is far away. I have never felt really drawn to it, as though there, unlike in no matter what churches, final extinction reigned. The kings would never return? And a royal city without a river, even without a brook? Who knows.

Porchefontaine, more a suburb than a part of the town, has at any rate become dear to me. And at the same time the Echelles proprietor, with his establishment there, and I argue incessantly about whether his region has more to offer than mine. If I cite our transmitter, he counters with his "more essential and also more graceful" water tower (which, however, is not located within the township); if I praise our railwaymen's hanging gardens, he rates the couple of flower beds at the Porchefontaine station above them, because the (sole) shed there is made not of corrugated metal but of solid railway ties (yet the majority of the beds have gone to pot, and no trace of terracing); and even if he concedes that there are hardly any palms in his region, he still considers the only two there, which, standing side by side, constitute a pair, more interesting than our eight or nine, in that they are "like an entire forest," whereas ours are isolated, in my Goethe's expression, merely "huge stalks." The only things for which he envies us are our very own buses—those of Porchefontaine, long accordion vehicles, wide, space-devouring, belong to Versailles, the capital, which has priority. Yet we are in agreement on the fact that the houses in our two bays, with forests round about, are in all respects ideally sisterly, and therefore would not need sister cities anywhere in Europe (except that in his bay there have been rumors of the construction of an underground highway, straight through the foot of the mountain).

The day before the day before the day before yesterday, on the way there, going downhill, I pushed leaves with my foot over the traces of the wintertime mushroom seekers, if possible more violent than their predecessors, the earth churned up by them as if in a hasty burglary; or weren't these perhaps the traces of birds going after worms? And at the campsite of the foreign-seeming windbreak workers, this time I found debris, an empty pack of not at all common cigarillos and likewise a bottle with the label of a fine Bordeaux. And a desperate dog went panting through the woods after his master.

It was stormy. An express train, visible halfway up on the Porchefontaine embankment, let out an Indian war whoop, while many passengers nibbled on shish kebab as if on a train through Greece. A temple bell rang, a muezzin called out over the sea, the settlement spread far inland along a fjord, by the sunken road at my back Scottish dunes overlapped, before me lay a giant's glove, I brashly stuck my hands into the winter stinging nettles; didn't they sting? Oh my, yes!

And what happened then? Evening could come now. The light down below at the edge of the woods was rocking in time to the wind in the branches, between flaring and fizzling. From the already dark thicket a stone flew past me, no, a bottle. A child playing? The transformer, long before the first house, was clothed in marble, as one might expect of the palace town of Versailles, and was called *sirène*. Then in the first house a woman was sitting in the lamplight, snipping stitches out of a piece of fabric, while two cats sat in front of the house like a pair of shoes, and an adolescent asked me the time (my answer, as I saw later, was wrong), and a few steps farther on the first driver asked me for directions (my information, as I realized too late, was completely wrong), and the next one asked me for a light (I had none, and he drove on, cursing).

I went, as the proprietor and cook had instructed me, to buy bread, watched, in the evening line at the bakery, as the inhabitants of Porchefontaine, at least the older ones, fished for coins in purses as shabby as those in my bay—which made me think they had at home not so much piggy banks as piglet banks—and carried my sheaflike load, which my arms could barely encompass, to our place of celebration, hearing halfway there, from a sprawling orphanage, otherwise silent as the grave, the voice of my son echoing.

The restaurant gave the impression, as always, that it was just being renovated, because of the ladders leaning on all sides against the isolated building, all the way up to the eaves, so close together that from afar it looked as though they barred all access; and high above it all another ladder swayed, fastened by ropes to the ridgepole, of rubber, inflated with helium, covered with electric bulbs, which now at night were on.

The restaurant, looking from the outside otherwise like a house no different from the others in the area, stood, with a garden in between, at the foot of the embankment where commuter and express trains traveled at different levels, both above the roofline. The proprietor had secretly, immediately after moving in, uncovered the source of the Marivel brook, located there, as he had discovered from the original maps of the area, and long since integrated into the sewer system, all the way to where it flowed into the Seine at Sèvres; he had lined the trickle according to the model of the Fontaine Ste.-Marie in front of his earlier tavern. For the first time after almost a hundred years under ground the Marivel has thus become visible again, at least up to the end of his property, and also sounds decidedly different from the way it sounds through the manhole cover down the street (whose course even today, as long ago, faithfully follows the windings of the vanished brook).

On this evening our tavern had a garlanded entrance, not very conspicuous, because so soon after Christmas other doors in the village were also decorated, only differently.

———

Inside, in a space unexpectedly as large as a barn, the master of the house was standing alone by the fireplace, and it seemed to me I had already come upon him decades ago in his stirring up of the fire, in the same black custom-made suit, standing erect, with a very long poker that allowed him to do what he had to without kneeling. And as always he was showing his Egyptian profile.

But in his face, usually so unapproachable, which he surprisingly turned toward me, there now seemed to be realized what he had once so fervently invoked: "I should like to see a picture of myself as a child, and I mean a picture of me shouting, crying, lost!" There it was. And at the same time he led me, his hand on my shoulder, quietly and amiably as never before into the kitchen, where he even allowed me to help him continue to prepare the food.

I put down the just-found last mushroom of the year, from one of the bomb craters, where my searching had previously been in vain, a so-called blewit, of all edible things the one with the most delicate smell, adding it to the king boletes on the table reserved just for them. Although still deep-frozen, these also seemed freshly picked, firm, heavy, as rosy as Snow White in some illustrations, before she opens her eyes to life again: thanks to the chef, who before freezing them had extracted some of the water (the person who collected them had been someone else, however).

The swinging door to the kitchen was propped open with a chair, and there was thus an unobstructed view of both the entire curtainless restaurant as well as the bar area, separated from it by a screen.

Indoors as well the house was trellised with the proprietor's ladder collection. By now there was not a corner without rungs, and yet I did not have the same feeling as in that other restaurant in the hills of the Seine, now long closed, where every spot, ledge, niche, windowsill was occupied by a rooster in porcelain, plaster, clay, fabric, in all colors and sizes, neck after neck stretched for crowing, which made my head reel on every visit; the ladders, often set up in pairs, like husband and wife, the latter with the broader end up, had with time become an unobtrusive pattern that at the same time allowed the background happenings to enter their very own clearer, well-rounded sphere.

Such structuring was accomplished even by those fairly numerous pieces which, in conformity to a preference of the collector's, had unequal spaces between their rungs or were missing some altogether, and even by the few chicken-house ladders from five continents, simply nailed with cross-slats, boards almost without gaps.

But the eye was drawn farthest by the natural ladders, where nothing had been added, at most something taken away, like the numerous tree trunks leaning against the walls, hardly ever more than arm-thick, often left in their bark, merely capped, and the branches on the sides trimmed to just about sole-worthy rungs. And among these, my chief attention was drawn to one that, instead of segments of branch as footholds, had rock-hard tree fungi, alternating, now left, now right, actually grown out of the trunk at rung intervals, and that all the way to the top, firmer to the step than the branch stumps otherwise, a spirited formation, and furthermore in its white-on-white a handsome contrast to the blackish wood of the inn: but the person who had discovered this natural wonder in his meadow, cut it down, hauled it through the woods and over the hills, and added it to the other ladders in the restaurant, that was once again not the ladder fanatic himself.

Otherwise the dining room in the Auberge aux Echelles in Porchefontaine, as I noticed that evening, had gained a column in the middle, which, from the base up, represented a tall, shrouded figure.

And behind it, between the rung patterns, two suburban streets crossed, one leading from the railroad station in the direction of the forest, the other the local main street, with the bus line in the direction of the center and the royal palace. And here, too, outside a wide-open window, there was a birds' sleeping tree—as I was entering I had promptly received my share of their largesse on my good suit— in the prophet's view more densely occupied this year than "yours over there," also more variously, for the sparrows let in other birds as well. Just now it was the moment in the tree for competing for perches and making a racket, along with the whirring of wings like splitting pieces

of bark, as indeed the rest of the evening traffic out there was also more
lively.

By contrast every one of the chef's actions indoors took place
almost imperceptibly. When pouring seasonings he seemed to
reach into midair with both hands. And I did as he did. And likewise
I drank tap water while working ("no comparison with the water in your
bay").

And then the familiar signal for another of the petty prophet's devastating tirades: the humming, without any particularly intentional
derision, of Beethoven's "Ode to Joy"! And, this breaking off abruptly, there came, as if out of the blue: "What is left to narrate at
your eye level? No one deserves a story anymore." Or: "Where is
the person who has not gambled away his potential story during
these decades? The number of animal species is declining more and
more, and the human species are increasing steadily. And to be interested in these people you would have to be a botanist. But worms,
which do not undergo metamorphosis, still belong, according to your
Goethe, to the plants. Storytelling survives at most as a disease or
as phantom pain. The heavens have disappeared, like a book turning
in on itself, the book has disappeared like the heavens turning in
on themselves. Life still exists only in the spandrel realm between
railroad tracks, runway, and highway. Perhaps for each individual the
book of his life continues to exist. But what is in it? A person without
ideas is even more dangerous than one without feelings. Ideas: those
would be arms, durable—but I see only stumps. Metamorphosis was
demanded of you. But haven't you just continued to swindle? What has
fallen away from you but a rotten toenail? You could not be deeper,
warmer, more alert in the world than in your book. Are you still in that
book? As a storyteller you are no longer needed, and as a chronicler you
are being chased away. A ladder, quick, a ladder! were Gogol's last words.
Rainbow light, yes, but no rainbow appears. All of my chillun are
weary."

He fell silent sooner than usual, and I said, "Marina Tsvetayeva
wrote of a friend: 'As a farewell he made a fire in the stove for me'!"

Whereupon he replied, "She used to come often to my place at the Fontaine Ste.-Marie in Meudon, and in the middle of the woods she complained that there were no woods there. I wonder whether she is still so upset. On the other hand: if a poet is not upset, she will die."

"On the other hand": such an expression I had never heard from him before.

For the moment the prophet had nothing more to proclaim. Previously he would have favored the pedestrians moving past outside as if on wheels with the remark "Scurrying do-nothings!" On this evening, for the moment when they came out of the darkness and took on first form, I saw them as an infinitely repeating ornament, lacking only—but how!—linkage. This linkage, however, seemed achieved with the behind-the-ladder painting, the only one on the restaurant wall, which portrayed the great meteor of Mecca, surrounded by a huge, solid mass of people (a linkage that did not suit me, a deceptive one). And at the same time, outside, very much by himself, a black street sweeper went by, on his head, to protect him while he was vacuuming leaves, ear-muffs—but no, it was not yet autumn.

How instructive, how full of visual impressions, such waiting could be; "willing waiter"—that could have been another name for me at one time. On the railroad embankment above our heads trains were passing, for a while almost without interruption, the express trains so fast that one saw only streaks of light flashing by (accompanied by a shuddering in the restaurant from the ground up), while in the commuter trains they were passing, windows and heads remained distinct; altogether a racket that, after my time in the noise oven, spoke to my heart. At the same time, the owl's hooting from up in the woods, which could be heard intermittently, traced the outlines of all the bays in the world. And on the kitchen radio Arab music was playing, a man and a woman in turn, each snatching the last note from the other's mouth, as it were.

———

Then we paused to watch the news on television.

In a war zone, hanging gardens that covered an entire slope, nothing but purple wisteria, in the form of a frozen waterfall, were blown up—what a splintering.

Altogether, there were strange wars going on now: those of the hikers against the bikers; those of the smokers against the drinkers ("the good drinker is proverbial," the proprietor and prophet remarked, "but good smoker?"); those of letter writers against telephone callers. In another part of the world, in a muddy arena in front of a hundred thousand spectators, a larger-than-life pig and an equally enormous so-called pig fighter were rushing at each other in a life-and-death struggle, with monstrous squealing, trumpeting, snorting, and gasping, in which one could not distinguish what belonged to which. An old priest, from the looks of him the abdicated Pope, climbed into a pulpit for his last sermon, and spoke: "I shall say nothing, so that all may be made new!" whereupon his young successor called out from below, "I am afraid!" A war criminal who had slit the throats of innumerable people had to, while he factually reported this, repeatedly swallow hard. And finally, on the foreign television news program, there was a picture in which nothing was happening but a slow, steady snowing in the Pyrenees or the Alps.

And then the waiters summoned to help out for the evening arrived and were dressed by the proprietor; among them, being held by the hand by his little son, the Russian bus driver and widower, who, looking at the mushrooms on the table, announced that they were nothing compared to those in Russia.

Night came on. As usual here in the suburbs, the bustle outside, just a moment ago that of part of a metropolis, instantly subsided and even seemed almost completely at a halt. At approximately the same time all the bars went dark, and of the shops only the North African grocery store remained open, the illuminated standing scale out on the sidewalk the indication of its being open. A wind from the steppes was blowing. Between trains there were suddenly large intervals, and the buses even became as infrequent as overland buses on their way to a remoteness very far away yet similar to the one here. Up on the railroad embankment, now just a sort of stop, half in darkness, a young man was burning a letter. The couple of pedestrians, seen through the window-panes, then also turned out to have been pretty much the last. The sparrows, along with the one dove, in the local sleeping tree were rocking silently in the forks of the branches, or rather being rocked by the night wind.

And what happened then? I waited at the ladder bar, at my feet the child Vladimir, who was rolling a spool of thread back and forth across the room. "The children were running beneath the wind"? No: where the children were running was a different wind. In the upper section of the window, above the line of the wooded hills, the huntsman Orion appeared, the blinking of his shoulder and belt stars seeming all the more menacing through the wisps of clouds that hid it for moments at a time. Beyond the horizon a mighty ringing of bells sounded, which was then a squadron of night fighters booming forth from there.

Little by little my friends came through the door, one at a time, at short intervals, from all directions of the compass, and none, so far as I could see and hear, first got out of a vehicle.

They came along so quietly, also inconspicuously, that the child hardly took notice of them, and at any rate was not frightened by them; and I was reminded of my grandfather's comrades and how they, likewise seem-ingly on tiptoe, one knee in the air, a finger to their mouth, freshly bathed, in their best clothes, with playful expressions, had stepped over our threshold in Rinkolach for their regular Sunday afternoon card game. At the same time my friends' step was firm. Only Valentin, my son, came running, for the first time in a very long while, toward me.

And I? Felt at the sight of each of them as if I were being butted from below, at the knees, as if by a goat, from sheer joy. And all of them, I saw, had hangnails on their fingers from fumbling around in their pockets in foreign lands. And each had spent at least one night during the year lying in a mortal sweat. And each had celebrated his birthday alone in the course of the year. And now we celebrated the birthdays together.

The standard word of greeting among us: "And?"

But the singer was still missing. And perhaps I was a drowning man, without knowing it? All of us? Yet it remained true: a catastrophe, when it set in, first made me stiff with fear, then avid for adventure.

What we ate I have already partly given away, and of the rest I shall give away only this: it went with and enhanced it.

And then true: when the moment for storytelling arrived, the friends told of their year things entirely different from what I have told here. Common to them was that in one way or the other I had the notion that all these stories bore some resemblance to turning hay or turning and relayering, again and again, apples in a farm cellar. Each of them, even the stonemason in his festive doublet—his year is written on another page—mentioned his own situation merely in passing, and yet in this intimation the listeners found the world.

The only one who then delved all the way in was the Russian refugee child Vladimir, wide awake as no adult could be. He bellowed like a primeval forest, said his, "And now!" and then, sitting on the floor Indian-style, he shouted, shrieked, joyously hurled his version of the story of the year into the faces of those assembled, amid pounding and a spray of saliva, not comprehensible word for word, but the only one with meter, from a time even before hexameter, a chanting that rose through the air, whereupon, after his concluding shout at just the right moment and his immediately falling asleep, we sat there not only amused but also in slight uneasiness, and his father, by now seated with us at the table, remarked that at home Vladimir sounded altogether different!

To the accompaniment of all the stories, there stood outside in the ladder hinterland, by the opposite sidewalk, in the illuminated circle of the streetlights, in Porchefontaine (a section of Versailles), more luxuriously and generously than in my bay, a delivery truck in front of the mason's house that belonged to it, with shovel and broom in a pile of sand still in the back, as the emblem of the trade.

As the last daytime object, the fruitery's scale disappeared from the street; an almost painful moment when, both trays swaying, the pointer trembling, it was carried back into the shop, a bright menhir. In the single remaining lighted window, barely above street level, someone was sitting, older than all of us, with the curtains drawn back at an angle, like a tent opening, and writing and writing. Almost empty and then empty down to their poles—pole-emptiness—the buses to the royal palace drove by. A nocturnal jogger sped by with such strength in her shoulders that in the middle of the street she left a path of her own. At the one set table in the garden, next to a leafless tree, the white cloth billowed, whorled like a pyramid, in the wake of the express trains up above (if any, only these were still running).

On the embankment there the Mongols of Ulan Bator were walking. Among the strollers on the Stradun in Dubrovnik, this evening every one had the same turning point. From their lairs among the birch roots poked the sniffing snouts of the muskrats of the Nameless Pond, by which a lone fisherwoman was sitting, waiting for the magic catch. And in the house beyond the eastern foothills, all sorts of beds were set up, peacefully floodlit, and was it snowing now? no, these were flakes from the chimneys. And each of these scenes was as close as the branches of the December cherry blossoms in the vases before us, to be touched through the rungs of the ladders.

"My dream entered into the fairy tale and became land." Who said that? I thought it, and in the same breath it was spoken by the chef and petty prophet, long since at the table with the rest of us.

He was then the last to come out with his story, and not merely that of this one year of nineteen hundred ninety-eight.

I have noticed several times already that precisely the cursers, complainers, and cynics, as soon as they forget themselves and fall to telling stories, are the most profound, warm, and all-inclusive storytellers; I have never felt more tranquil inside than when I have been listening to such a Thersites, metamorphosed into an epic narrator.

The proprietor of the Auberge aux Echelles of Porchefontaine (formerly Fontaine Ste.-Marie, formerly the Upper Nile) began by laughing, and he was laughing at someone, himself in fact, with that wild anger he usually directed against others. As if energized, he then fell into his humming, but this time instead of the "Ode to Joy" it was the saddest melody I know, called on my Jaunfeld "World-Weary," a waltz more for dragging around than for dancing, or a dance of the dying, of a woeful, indeed deathly boring slowness. While humming, he yawned in accompaniment, according to all the rules of the dramatic art, and reminded me of that dying man who almost to his last gasp had not left off yawning. It was as if he needed the singer for help in striking up his own song, as indeed the prophets of old, they say, needed a musician before they could open their mouths—only then was the hand of Yahweh held over them.

The prologue to his story went as follows: "With God's summons to me, my eternal summer came to an end. Why did I not remain with my sheep in the desert of the steppe? Why did I listen to the voice from the burning bush? Or: why did I not simply continue to listen to the voice in the bush and do nothing but continue to repeat it? But as it was, I heard a command in that voice: *Take action!* and followed it, and set out into history, never-ending, and all of my kind were thus: false prophets. As the lover of history I was the eternalizer of hell. But how to deny history? Does it not matter in what country you raise your head to the heavens? Yes, in my despondency I clung to everything, even to my fatherland. And that merely pushed me deeper still into despondency. In my history time I was the crooked flame, not the straight. And yet all the time I had a photograph of myself in my memory, as a newborn, full of bright joy. But in the actual photo, when I saw it, the person with joy was the one who held me swaddled in her arms: my mother. Why did I not remain where I was from my earliest days, in the desert? The larger the desert around me, the richer the wellsprings of fairy tales within me. When I had the desert sparrows in focus, I was at my peak. The burning bush, that was them."

Here began the merging of the petty prophet into his storytelling, the first word today, more than a week later, in the new year, still echoing within me: "Afterward"; followed then, hours later—in the meantime the last passerby had long since disappeared from the wind-tattered main street, a three-legged dog, wandering home—by these essentially unconnected sentences: "If you are once driven from your promised land, you will return there only by insistently remaining elsewhere. One who is not in the world is impatient. Odysseus was patient. Gilgamesh knew distant parts. I have ceased to spit fish into the desert.

Enough of the prophet. I encounter such people now only in certain suicides. And yet I have seen it: during this century another has passed, is still with us, will continue to make itself felt, for instance in the airy dustiness of the suburbs, here and elsewhere. To move things into their place will also be the New World. At the moment numbers are the last refuge. And thus I see the circle of the world renewing itself in counting. From the two histories at odds, a third will emerge. And how will it go? For instance: When I was still slow. Or: When empty shoe-polish containers were still a treasure. Or: In this year I have not swum in a single river. Or: Once at midday a bird was hopping in the tree like a garment hung on it. Worms capable of metamorphosis represent a huge step in nature, and only then do things get lighter and have more air. Thus it is like a fairy tale when one watches the creatures. And fairy tale means: to have penetrated most deeply into the world. He who fetches the blue from the sky makes it richer up in the sky. I have dreamt: The creator went unnoticed, and the creation took heart. I have dreamt: A savior of mankind would be the great forgetter. I have dreamt: I was a handball player looking for fellow players. I have dreamt: By the way in which someone ate he created a work. I under-stand all the doers, amok-runners, warriors. But the only vision I know is reconciliation. Why is there no peace? Why is there no peace? The great are those who make peace exciting, not war. Homer today would sing the epic of the souvlaki eaters on the train from Corinth to Athens. And this morning I thought: Incomprehensible that one is not im-mortal. And on another morning: How certain I am, even in the world's worst times, that everything is different. And on yet another morning: Even if human history should come to an end soon, even in terror, something will have taken place in that history, from the beginning, and will have continued steadily, so glorious, so childlike, so gripping, so interconnected that it could happen only once; as human history in the universe could not possibly be better and more beautiful. God does not see me because I do not let myself be seen by him. Hair-root wind, from-the-ground wind, Habakkuk wind: it is still there, it still exists. The omega, the last letter of the ancient alphabet, has the form of a jump rope."

Meanwhile in the night sky floated a cloud in the form of an octopus carapace, as seen long ago in the American Appalachians, with whom? (When a memory comes back to me this way, each time it seems to me someone was with me.) And I thought: To be one with the singer, without having to sing: my ideal. How falling was in me constantly, day after day. And now peace, the great eye. And at the same time: Oh. Goodness. My, oh my! How long had I now been on the road with the book? And the footprints outside in the pale winter grass of the inn garden were mine. I was the mythical beast? Amazement. Eternally amazed, we sat together, each on a ladder rung. The adventure of life showed itself in the form of a single rolling wave in the otherwise tranquil sea.

The last word in that night of Porchefontaine came from the woman from Gerona in Catalonia, Ana, my wife. (I have not yet said that she, meanwhile having climbed down from her pedestal in the middle of the restaurant, was among our company—my first thought: What is to come of this now?"—as was the sweetheart of Valentin, my son, from Baden near Vienna; the wife of Guido, the carpenter, from Hokkaido, Japan; the woman companion of Wilhelm, the reader, that policewoman and reader from Wilhelmshaven on Jade Bay; the Dalmatian husband— or Turkish or Egyptian lover?—of my woman friend Helena; and in addition Filip Kobal, the writer from the shadowy village of Rinkenberg behind my sunny village of Rinkolach, not at all unwelcome to me, for I was happy to have one of my own kind there with me, at least for today and tomorrow—and this time it was I who seized him around the hips and hoisted him from the ground.)

While in the sidewalk window across the way, long after midnight, the old Georges Simenon continued typing away at his *Apothecary of Erdberg*, and then another automobile driver, obviously lost in search of the palace of Versailles or some other palace, rolled past outside, in his highly polished vehicle, as if not of the present—we later invited him to join us—the woman from Catalonia spoke the sentence with which she had always sealed our breakups, only this time without the usual meaning and undertone, not out of the blue and more to herself, but as if she were taking the word from the mouth of the one who had spoken before her, and were guiding it onward, as gently as possible, as factually: "This is the end."

Still missing was only my vanished friend, the singer Emmanuel, with his voice, the essential piece.

Was he missing?

"Was he missing?" With that began his new, his *Last Song*.

—January–December 1993